THE LIGHT OF LÚNASA

THE LIGHT OF LÚNASA BOOK 1

LAURA FOLEY

ALEX PARKER PUBLISHING

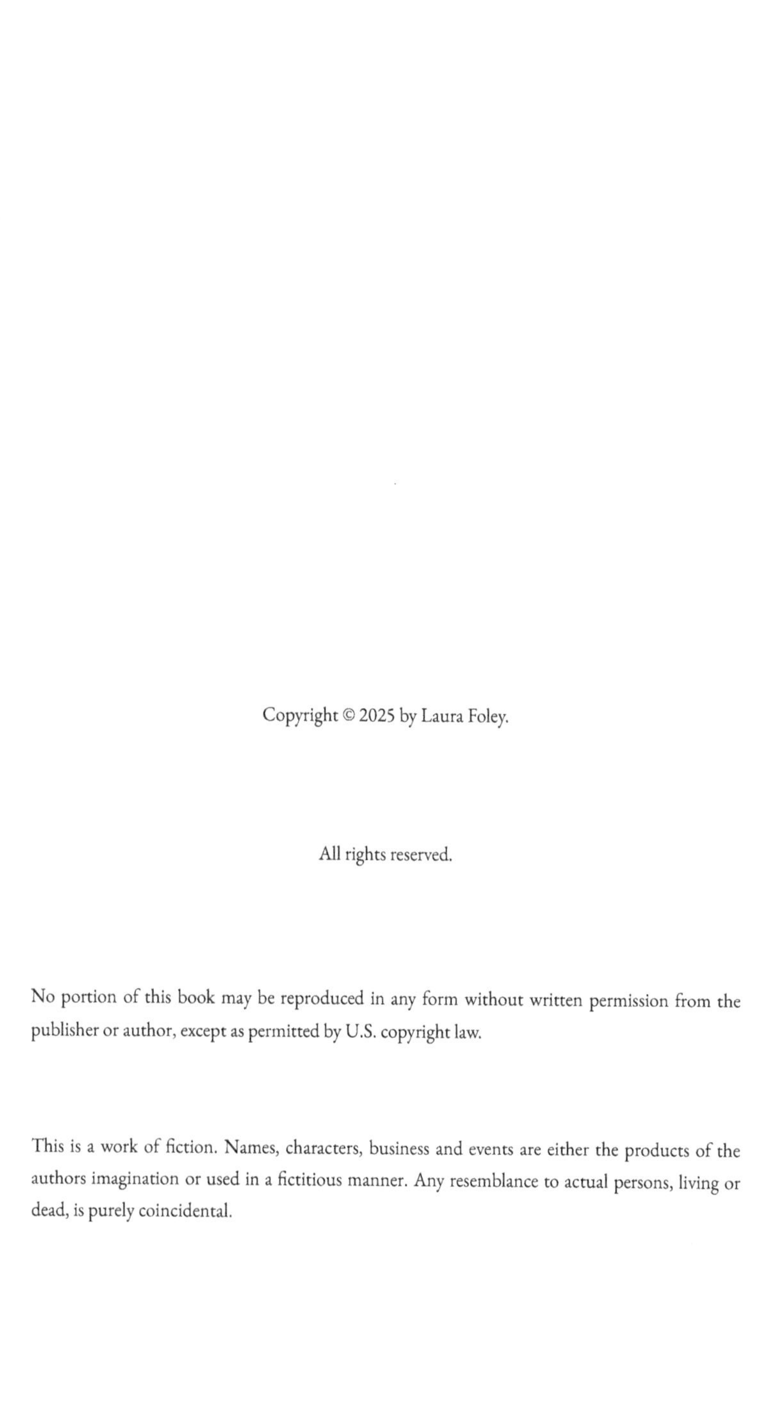

CONTENTS

ABOUT THE BOOK

The book contains explicit content that may be triggering for some.

For a full list of warnings, please turn to the end of this book.

NOTE

Pronunciation/Translation Guide and Glossary is provided in the back of the book.

***

For Lee

***

***

For the girls who want it all—I am but a humble author, and therefore can't give you that.

So, would you settle for hot Irish brothers instead?

***

PART I
GUILT

ALEX PARKER PUBLISHING

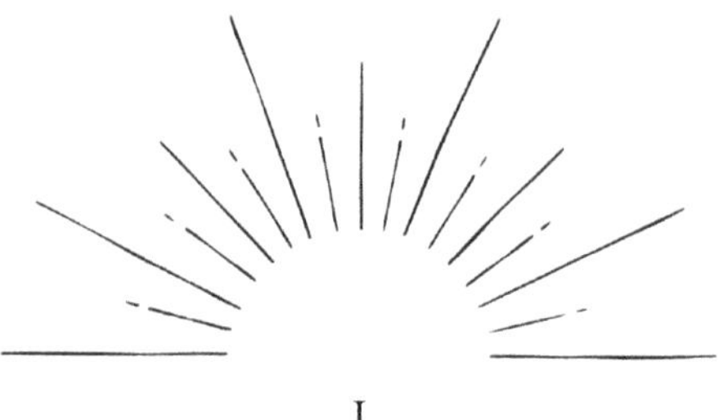

I

GOING BACKWARDS AND FALLING

East Coast of Ireland

An unnerving current of power rested beneath my fingers, prints smearing against pine as I ran my hand down the bannister. It was louder than usual today. Headache inducing, even. Mornings with Dr. Hannas usually placated the feeling, but our session today had gone against me, really.

I stalled to sit on the step with a blustering exhale, staring at my hands, wishing I could recall the exact moment this...this fucking *thing* came to me. So I could lick it and stamp it as a fact. But in a way, the curse had always been there, poorly concealed, waiting to escape when I least expected it.

And it wasn't for lack of trying that I couldn't be free of it. I'd done many things.

Exorcisms.

Bartering.

Cutting some of my baby finger off with a circle saw—by that point, I'd already lost two other tips on the hand anyway.

I also notoriously offered my hypothetical firstborn and a literal goat to several gods. Mam—or Mollie as I liked to affectionately call her—temporarily kicked me out, but the blood-stained grass in the aftermath tainted the front garden view for weeks.

I edged back onto my elbows to let the laughter of my old delusions dig them further in. The unfamiliar noise filled the echoey hallway like a ghost of happier days.

Oddly enough, the most nonsensical part wasn't the self-mutilation or the radicalised offerings, but the religious bit. Because the only thing that rose from the dead in our house was my pet hamster. All that remained of Rita's grave was the hole from her great 'post-hibernation' escape.

I'd been in a hole once, too. Only difference, there was zero chance of escape from St. Brigid's.

The locals had a different name for it: They'd say things at the pub like, "*Did ya' hear Bernard McDonald was stark naked on the quay last week? He threw six prize sheep off it before they hauled him away to Briggie's Bin.*"

Poor guy.

I found the worst part of *my* time there was the suffering—which took me by surprise because I almost liked torment. Thought I deserved it. Enjoyed how it seared my skin. How it lasted after the moment of infliction. But the suffering offered in its place had come in the form of quiet fury. So quiet, I had tiny cuts on the inside of my cheeks from chewing in silent frustration.

I tilted my head to the cobwebbed ceiling. Let my elbows scratch the carpet fibres.

God, to be a normal Irish citizen—to have religion—would have made things easier. With religion came confession, and with that, forgiveness. A way to find redemption.

I had certainly sinned. Sinned universally, and in the absolute worst way. I guess that's why it came as no surprise it was only now, five years on, that I'd started to gnaw the binds I'd put myself in for it.

My phone beeped.

I'LL SCHEDULE YOU ONCE A WEEK AS PROMISED. ALSO, I RECOMMEND TOUCHING ON SOME OF THE MEMORIES OF FIONN WE SPOKE ABOUT. INTERPRET THAT HOW YOU LIKE. HAPPY WEEKEND. DR H

Dr. Hannas' message gave me a literal 'lightbulb in my head' idea.

I stood. Stalled. Swayed a little when considering where I needed to go. Then I found resolve and grabbed a pink hoodie from the coat hook graveyard. The cute pug calendar next to it had *Grand Opening of Wexford Quay* written on June 2nd—today. Beneath it: *Mam Home from Dublin*.

I grimaced, part of me knowing she'd arrive home expecting the old Clío. It wouldn't be the first time. Instead, she'd be greeted by the Clío who perpetually lived seconds from midnight on her personal Doomsday Clock—and that bitch was hard work.

Taking the back garden entrance straight into the forest, I broke out of the heavy thicket and onto the track in less than a minute. My arms were already covered in tiny scratches from newly blossomed brambles, and the forest air was fresh. Static, even. As if the day's heat hadn't yet infested its pores. I honestly felt kind of rude for interrupting it. That was until the old treehouse came into view, and I felt worse things. Coiling, barbed things in my belly.

People claim there's comfort in familiarity. Well, not when it comes to my guilt.

My gut painfully tightened at the mere thought of heeding its direction, but Dr. Hannas was indirectly right; I might find one of the books from our childhood—or at least that's the idea it gave me. If I could revisit the stories instead of the direct memories of Fionn, it might not hurt as bad. It might not trigger the curse the way these things usually did when it all got overwhelming.

My head swivelled to the grounded treehouse beyond the first row of trees, and all my calculated breaths diminished into frantic frets. I couldn't tear my eyes from the sinister, overgrown version of what was once a haven. It was deathly. Crushing my muscles and will.

A root embedded in the soil snagged my foot.

"Oh shit—"

My legs buckled.

Jagged rock crunched into my forehead. Red and black spots danced among the moss where I lay for a defeated moment, hoping the roots might take me under. Swallow me.

When the blotches faded, like so many times before, I clenched my eyes and pressed myself up, palms barely taking the weight of my wobbling form.

And with that, I managed to find the silver lining: at least no one saw.

To anyone local, the choice to be dramatic, to seek attention even by accident, would have been deemed worse than the impossible madness of someone being cursed. People were so quick to explain away the impossible. A catch in the light. A drink too many. A miracle under the guise of luck. The contradiction to sanity was not a place many dared to enter.

I remembered Bernard McDonald and his sheep then, and how when Briggie's Bin finally let him out, he drove them and himself off the quay to the death of all but one: Claire, the sheep. Then for some reason in the months after, his mother would go round the pubs with a bell on Claire's neck, and people would give her money and attention because her only son was dead.

Indoctrinated myself, I thought that was epitome of attention seeking.

Blotting the last of the blood on my sleeve, I drew my eyes back to the treehouse.

It was waiting. A cruel entity, feeding on the dregs of my will to feel less miserable.

So, I faced it. What else could I do? The alternative—for my fragile tendency to relapse into madness—would only lead to St. Brigid's having the kettle on for my homecoming.

A rapid headshake.

Forward was the only way.

I swung the stiff door to let it fan my face—which didn't help much for the smell, but it did allow me to pause. To admire what we'd built.

In the treehouse centre stood a grand Sitka spruce, insulated with brown moss, etched jagged with our names. Faded snack wrappers scattered the lino floor. A wooden sofa occupied the right warped wall. An empty can of Guinness from my seventeenth birthday was displayed like a youthful trophy on the half-pallet dubbed "The Shelf."

A fleeting laugh escaped me.

Jesus, we were messers.

Nah, that's just you, Clío. I'm as good as gold.

I ran my fingers over its bumpy exhibition of Fionn's Dinky cars. Next, was a small collection of explicit *Maxim* magazines and—I gasped—the book.

Grabbing it, I naturally turned to visit my usual spot on the sofa, feet kicking through leaves of orange and brown that had wandered in over time as if warmth and refuge appeased them. Nostalgia lived in every aspect of the room. It was as though I'd never left.

Then the hook dug in, curling under my rib. I hunched and cradled my midsection. It was guilt, and it was spreading. It was shrapnel, moving further and further into my aching chest. With Fionn gone, the treehouse would never be revived. All it represented now was a place filled with moments I was sure if I truly tapped into it, I'd have to rip out what was left of my disgusting heart just to avoid the brutal anguish.

Falling back into the sofa, I clutched the hood to extend it over my face, tightening the frayed strings and locking myself inside.

Deep breath in.

A pause...

Deep exhale out.

Stale warmth drew into my nostrils over and over, suffocating me within the hood for so long, I began to toe the line of consciousness. But giving in to this pain never did me any fucking good, did it? It never freed me of my prison.

I sighed and loosened the hood strings to shove it down. My pulsing breaths seeped out for the forest to feast on.

I came with purpose, I reminded myself. It literally lay in my hands for the taking. My fingers ran through the book's delicate pages, searching for something that called to me. To Fionn, and to our good memories—albeit not the memories directly.

The Fianna, Tír na nÓg, The Children of Lír. Title after title of Irish-knotted artistry flashed passed my eyes. I loved these tales, so rich in the lore of times and lives that were gut-wrenchingly sad yet always enchanting.

My thumb excitedly dug further into the page titled, *Queen Medb and the Brown Bull of Cooley*. I pretended to be her most often—the warrior Queen of Connacht. Belligerent to men, and a red-headed threat to anyone who stood in her way. For our similar appearance and attitude, she was surely the source of my overconfidence. Of my promise to women that I'd never submit to the patriarchy.

Medb was so fierce, they buried her upright to face her enemies. I used to think about her being tired from standing all day in her coffin. Used to wake Mollie in the middle of the night crying about it. It was a piece of cheese that killed her, so Mollie claimed, which oddly had me give less time to thinking about her being dead and more time to the mechanics of how it happened in the first place.

I sat straighter as the flying pages came to a stop on the Mythological Cycle—Fionn's favourite stories. The Tuatha Dé Danann were central to this, the oldest of Irish lore. Even now, I could recite Fionn's view of them to the letter. He'd loved them. They could be heroes. Ancestors. His religious ideology.

I skimmed the room again, unwillingly finding all the memories of us as I painfully struggled to resist recalling the day Fionn tried to convince me our folklore lived parallel to us—in the Otherworld.

He's leaning against The Shelf, blocking my view of the Guinness can we shared last week on my birthday.

The wood groans.

Both our eyes widen for the threat of its break until it holds out, and we relax with exhales of condensation.

His fluffy-hooded coat is zipped to his chin; mine isn't zipped at all. The Christmas multicoloured lights we set up in a spiral around the tree are in full glow, powered by just two triple-A batteries. It's kind of magical—maybe that's why I don't feel cold.

"Think about our folklore and how our ancestors spoke of the Otherworld," Fionn says as he rolls a sliotar between his hands and passionately rambles on. "Look at Óisin in Tir na nÓg. He followed his love Niamh there, never to see his family again. These stories. No, these possibilities," he adds with a wink, "were only put aside because Christianity became *trendy* in the fifth bloody century. Now they're just a tick box on the curriculum that most never think about again after turning eight."

"So, what you're really saying is you hate nine-year-olds, right?" I tease. "Because only people under that age will listen to your bullshit." I grab a hard-boiled sweet from the jar on the armrest where I'm sitting comfortably.

His brow cocks high, knowing I despise liquorice. "You have the worst jokes! Even Mam says that."

I launch the sweet at the ball to knock it from his hand.

With athletic speed, he dodges it, and another, all while wearing his endearingly clown-like smile. Heath Ledger, the girls at school called him. "C'mon, Clío," he groans, his hands shaking with needless enthusiasm. "Don't be a silent sceptic! There's proof everywhere. Look at Newgrange and the Dolmens. Look at Lia Fáil, a Treasure of the Tuatha Dé Danann, standing in Meath to this day. There's your proof, you big naysayer!"

"Naysayer?" I'm getting riled up now. Just how he wants, but I eat the bait. "Oh, and the earth is flat, too, I suppose, Fionn?"

He tousles his dark curls with his free hand as he contemplates a comeback. It's good his hands aren't free altogether, so I don't have to bear witness to the wild gesticulation that accompanies anything he feels remotely passionate about. He always says a story told sitting down is a bad one. Whatever the hell that means.

"How would you know the universe is even real?" he quizzes me. "You've barely left the county."

My scoff deepens into a wild laugh. "I shouldn't have to prove the blatant existence of the universe if you've nothing but a few Yank tourist sites to claim a whole world lives alongside us. And you obviously didn't need to careen yourself upside down and kiss the Blarney-fucking-stone to talk this much in the space of five minutes."

He chuckles more with his shoulders as he turns to place the ball on The Shelf.

I fold my arms and satisfyingly snuggle into them. I do have good jokes. It's just that nobody ever wants to admit it.

"A half-decent point," he pipes up. "Although we did actually visit the Blarney stone years ago. Do you not remember throwing up your bowl of cornflakes all over the car when we drove through Youghal?"

"Um, no? You made that up."

"Maybe I did. You'll never know. I'll tell you what is real though, and I have eyewitnesses for this one." His back is still turned, shoulders arched.

It's not his style to shy away. I daresay it's rarer than an eclipse.

"Dolly kissed me the other night down in Dicey's pub," he says, and I can hear the smile in his words. "Couldn't believe my luck."

A pang of jealousy hollows out my cheeks. It feels strange to be jealous, but I know it's just another sign we're on the cusp of life without each other. For Irish twins, the age gap seems closer to two years; he's in the pub talking about heading off to college in September and kissing girls while I'm stuck at home under Mollie's watch.

Fionn turns, lighting a cigarette between his lips, his head tilted to avoid the breeze through the palleted walls. A cloud of smoke puffs around him like he's appeared by magic. He fills the cloud further with his exhale. "What do you think of her anyway?" He looks at me doe-eyed and hopeful, perhaps in search of my approval. He's fancied Dolly for years, passing her pink sticky notes in school and whatnot.

"She's a grand girl—nice personality." I pause to let the devious smirk find my lips. "Great arse, too."

"Hey, hands off." He jokes with a double finger gun pointed my way. "Don't think I forgot the parish disco when I was laying the groundwork for Alanna Morris. There *you* were an hour later kissing her in a dark corner when the DJ was butchering '500 Miles' for the second time that night."

I smile to myself when Fionn passes over his cigarette for the last few drags, like he always does. Our arms stretch for the overextended pass over.

"Will you be bringing her here?" I croak through the first, dizzying inhale.

A cloud of smoke is fogging the entire room now, stinging my waterline, but I feel edgy.

Fionn shuffles from one foot to the other while chewing his lip into bits. "Would ya' mind?"

I suck another drag allowing the rim to sting my lips. To give me time to answer. "I guess not. It's more your place than mine."

He grins, possessed by his true form. "Hey, let's not forget that nail you hammered in when we were building her."

I launch another sweet at him, bouncing it off his forehead before he gets a chance to dodge it. "Cheeky bastard! I dragged every pallet out here." I stub the cigarette with my foot and stretch back on the sofa, locked fingers pillowing my head. "Look, if you want to bring Dolly here, I don't mind." I mean it, if this is what makes him happy. The world needs more of that.

Not giving me the thanks I expect, he digs into his tracksuit, fingers rattling amongst coins until he pulls out the box of cigarettes.

I squint at him. He's up to something.

Fionn walks to the tree to tug on a narrow metal bar protruding from the bark between two rows of Christmas lights, dislodging a square section of the trunk.

With mouth agape like a cow chewing the cud, I perch my bottom on the chair's edge as my head cranes to get a better view of his secret compartment. How did I miss that?

He shoves the box into the gap, then glances at me before replacing the bark as if nothing has happened.

"Don't forget, Clío. You're the one I tell my secrets to." He smooths his fingers down the metal bar. "And I suppose—when you're not being a pain—which is often—you're my best friend."

I sat in the treehouse alone, returned to the bleak present. The room tinted a darker shade than the memory. My lips parted, but only a long-winded strain came out. This pain... it was immovable. All the memories were lovely and sad, pulling me both ways so much I almost felt nothing at all. That was until I felt *everything*.

Something rose in me then. Unlike the guilt, it felt weightless, summoned from the heat of my chest. A newborn star thrusting into the void of space. A beginning meeting its end. I stood. The book fell as I clutched my stomach for the fright. There was really no need when this humming sensation coursing through my veins wasn't new at all.

It was old.

Very old.

And yet so familiar, it was as if the missing piece of myself had returned. Slotted into place, making me feel whole.

Clawing for release, the power, a current of thickening blood, spread right up through my chest and out to reach my weary palms—humming there just on top; a golden, glittering forcefield sprouting in flecks as the breeze took some of it away.

Panicked, I clenched my hands hoping to quell the building vibration, and what it was about to do. What I was *always about to do* when things boiled over. The power dominated, unfurling them. All the sadness remained, spurring on the vibration until I couldn't contain it.

It clawed at me, demanding to be released as if I'd been possessed. Internally seduced. The hum grew more insistent until it became pins and needles and knives and swords, growing and growing until I couldn't resist.

A gurgling scream shot from my lungs.

A ripple of golden energy erupted to strike The Shelf head-on.

Its rotted wood splintered, cracking right through its middle as Dinkys clanged from the tin, scattering away with little roller noises.

My eyes shook as I took in the damage. Another broken memory. I'd hurt and lied and cheated, but somehow this made me just as sad and repulsed by myself.

On the precipice of heaving, I pleaded with my mind to switch off the pain.

There was safety in denial.

"I need a smoke."

Dizzyingly, I spun in search of the tree's metal handle hoping something was left in the five years since I'd last been here. I pulled, and the layer of bark glued to the handle thudded onto the floor. My hand dug into the narrow hole, disturbing woodlouse that scurried their little feet over my fingers. The cigarette box film brushed the tips. Snatching it out, I unfolded the lid.

Empty.

I launched the box across the room.

It bounced off the wall to its final resting place. A *clang* drew my attention, barely steadying my raging breaths. My head curiously tilted. Something metallic lay by the discarded box. It must have been wedged into the bottom all along.

I approached, still pathetically sniffling. I crouched to inspect it, fingers trembling as I picked up a medallion and let the bronze chain dangle. How strange to find such an object in a cigarette box, and yet this hidden thing felt familiar. The Tree of Life slightly protruded from the medallion, decorated with Celtic-knotted roots and a twisted trunk.

"Where did he get you?" I whispered to it. And more importantly, why were you hidden away all these years?

The breeze grazed my neck, stirring the delicate hairs to stand on end. With a gasp, I instinctively peered over my shoulder to the open door as I protectively drew the medallion to my chest. Because wherever it came from, I knew with absolute certainty it belonged to Fionn. That it was vitally important to him.

And the singular person he trusted to know of its existence was...*me.*

The person who killed him.

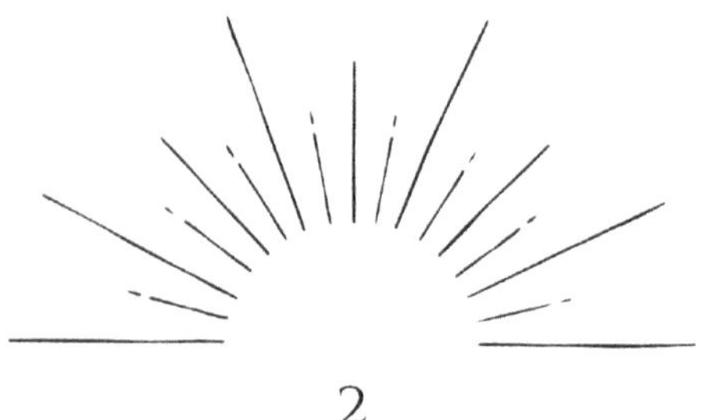

2

CARTWHEEL IN THE FAMINE MEMORIAL FOUNTAIN

Breathless from sprinting home, I slid onto my childhood bedroom floor, frantically in search of the metal spoon that lived under my bed (for ice cream). It inconveniently lay dead centre beneath the slats, only coming to me after incessant reaches and profanity-infused threats.

Shit-fork and *soup's bitch* were my best attempts at profanity in this case.

I stole a glance to the closed door, then to the shifty-eyed cat clock above it that seemed to tick faster. Mollie would be home from her trip any second, and she could *not* find out about the medallion, or else she'd lock it away with everything else Fionn had owned. Trophies. Jerseys. Keepsakes.

She had said it was her way of moving on, but I wholeheartedly didn't agree. *Didn't agree* was a diluted term for *fist fight*. Sometimes after we'd done just that, the two of us would watch a film, complete with budding black eyes and popcorn. And I swear, that was the closest I felt to happiness these last few years.

Using the spoon, I dug into the side of the blemished floorboard until it groaned the idea of jutting out.

"Come up!" My nose scrunched with malice as I pressed on the spoon's bending neck.

The floorboard popped and the patio door banged—the noise jerking my shoulders.

"I'm home, pet. The roads weren't too busy," Mollie called from the kitchen. "Hey, don't forget we're going to the opening of the new quay tonight. Mayor Gallagher will be there, and I want to ask him if I can try on his livery collar. You know, the fancy necklace they wear. Jesus, I'm starving." I counted three entirely different conversations she was having with just herself.

My attention reverted back to the medallion. This thing that teased the possibility of learning something new about Fionn. Suddenly entranced by that, all my urgency faded, steadying my beats. I dangled it over my sternum, fantasising about wearing it. How the weight of it would feel on my neck. How it might remind me endlessly of Fionn without the damn memories.

My eyes unexpectedly welled as I stood to stare at my sad reflection in the mirror, lips puffier than usual, soft freckles across my nose, cheeks magnified by the two sudden sliding tears. To have a physical piece of him so close to my heart didn't hurt as much as the memories did, but there were too many questions to own it in peace.

Did someone give it to him?

Did he steal it?

Not a chance.

Mollie taught us better. And yeah, she mightn't have known about it at all, but I wasn't willing to risk it. We just didn't grieve the same way.

I ran my finger along the overlapped knot bordering it to soothe myself. It was Celtic. That was clear. A replica of some mystical object he'd read about, perhaps. It certainly looked old and mystical.

"Clío, answer me or I'll redden the arse off you with a wooden spoon," Mollie shouted from the foot of the stairs to steal me from my thoughts.

I placed the medallion under the floorboard between a bottle of Jameson and a pink fluffy diary. Although, the diary was more angst than fluff by the time I'd finished with it.

"Clío? Do ya' hear me?" she called in Irish. There was something universally sterner in the tone of the mother tongue.

The floorboard jammed just above the hole.

Fuck.

I forced heaving exhales with each push, but the damn. Thing. Wouldn't. Click. In. "I'm—busy—Mam!"

"I'm thinking of cooking a lovely stew."

I ignored her—again.

Footsteps pounded the stairs.

This woman!

Shimmying the grubby hoodie over my head, I threw it on the gap before awkwardly diving onto my bed with flailing arms.

The door swung open.

"Did you not hear me calling?" Mollie asked out of breath with a cigarette hanging loosely between her fingers. She had untucked the front of her blouse out of her pencil skirt.

I tapped the stubs of my fingers to conceal my nerves. "I did hear you calling, yeah. I answered you back. You must be hard of hearing in your old age."

Her deep blue eyes rolled. She would often say they were her most striking feature, only barely outshone by her dark, wavy hair. The Rose of Ireland, some called her. I'd resemble her more if I hadn't gotten the ginger gene. If my bum didn't expand a gentle inch every year since turning eighteen. Of late, Mollie took great joy in people mistaking us as sisters. And to be honest, I never took offence, which seemed to disappoint people. I also never understood why girls *did* take offence to looking like their mother. *What is it that's bothering you?* I'd say, vexed. *They're literally half your DNA. Who do you want to look like?*

In hindsight, I was far too angry about it all. Incidentally, the other half of my DNA *was* unknown. He was from Cork and Mollie sometimes called him '*nothin' but a big bastard,*' when tipsy. So, in the sense of worthwhile knowledge, he was a stranger.

This bothered me less when I became an adult.

It bothered me more as I continued to be an adult.

"Oh, Lord above, what've ya' done to your beautiful head?" Mollie affectionately tutted over me, her arms and eyebrows all folded as if I was inconveniencing her by conjuring out her natural response to care.

I touched the lump on my forehead too hard, forcing it to angrily throb back. "Oh, I just...I...I fell out in the forest. It's fine, really. Doesn't even hurt." With a toothy smile, I commanded my eyes to focus on her instead of darting to the floor. I hated when that happened. Like the whole 'don't think of your parents naked' rigmarole and *boom!* Parents naked.

Again, not that I knew what my father looked like.

"You didn't...you know." She flicked her attention to the floor.

I ducked my head to catch her gaze. "Didn't what, Mam?"

She fixed her stare on the hoodie, brewing an anxious strain in my chest. I was done for. The one good thing that had come into my life for ages was about to be taken right back out again.

"Jesus, didn't *what*, Mollie?" I repeated louder to grab her focus.

Her grim eyes flickered up to me. "Do it on purpose."

Oh.

My heart morosely sank all the way down to my stomach and digested. I fought the slump of my limbs into the duvet, propping myself onto my knees. "On purpose? No...I'd never. The fact you would even suggest it." All the words sounded dragged like I was lying, like my desperation to tell the truth had invoked the opposite effect.

"Alright. Alright!" She surrendered her arms and took a pull from the butt of her cigarette. "I was just checking, love. Because...well, I read an article about keeping a close eye on that for people who've been...away." She rubbed her lips together, probably mulling over something less awkward to ask. "We'll be leaving at eight sharp tonight for the big opening. Someone on the radio mentioned fireworks for it. You're coming, yeah?"

"Yeah. I'll come," I said just to get her out of the room.

Then Mollie did her forced smile: the one where she bit her stretched lips and nodded, until she retreated to, I presume, get on that *lovely* stew she'd been raving about.

Finally alone again, all my pent-up worry released through a loud exhale. Still, I felt no better. The fact that Mollie had jumped to self-harm made me feel awful—tarnished. But I had to remember how fragile everyone saw me: the mad girl from Borín Lane who once did a drunken cartwheel right into the famine memorial fountain outside the bike shop.

The mad girl who'd confessed to killing her brother, but never *how*.

How could I tell them he never stood a chance against me? How this disgusting curse wouldn't listen. That the power didn't care who I loved. It just took and took and took. Only leaving behind one thing.

The constant question of who was next.

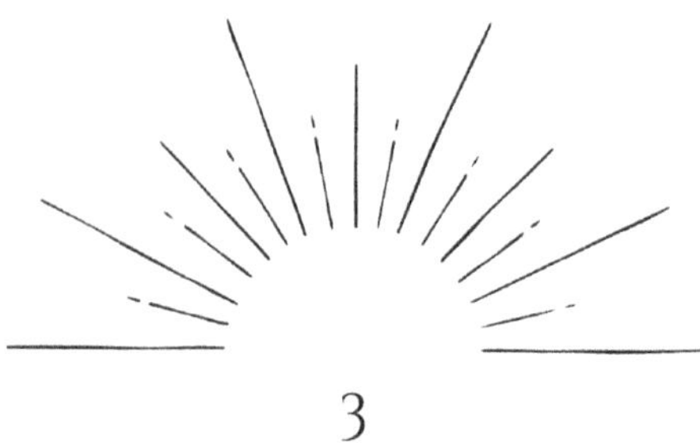

3

MR. T SINGS 'SWEET CAROLINE'

The sun had been eaten by clouds, and the chill of its absence crept onto the curve of my ears as Mollie and I walked along the busy footpath. We were headed toward the pop-up stage on the new quay front. It had been freshly laid with concrete, replacing the rotted woodworks which made it resemble everything else in the town when it was kind of rustic pretty before.

Almost poetic.

At least the stench of fish from the trawlers lingered. It was an uncomfortable smell, but I'd take its nostalgic, rank presence any day.

I inhaled and clenched the old storybook tighter. I'd brought it along in the hopes of reading it, maybe finding something about Fionn's medallion in it.

Just then, an elderly couple cut us off on the footpath, canes on either side. Their fingers were intertwined like it was their first date.

I tutted and inched my chin to the pinking sky. I didn't enjoy thinking about love anymore—the possibility of it. And I especially didn't like to mention it out loud. All it ever did was create a challenge for people. The ego of thinking they'd be the one to crack me open. Like I was a cursed princess or…a hard-boiled egg.

Those same men couldn't even induce an orgasm, let alone revive a mouldy heart. One thousand pussy licks and I'd be cured, they might have thought. Now, women on the other hand…at least they tried, even if I always held back, afraid if I let go entirely, I might hurt them. Kill them.

But being *in* love—ahh—that was something that surely had to feel different than anything I'd experienced. Something that would suspend me into a state of bliss, and fear of losing that bliss, all at once.

I shook that idea away, bringing my old windbreaker, all purple and white shapes, closer to my chin. High emotions meant high fallouts. No matter whether it was good or bad, cursed things were never too far behind. And so being in love was never an option. I was destined to live alone forever. And maybe that's what I deserved, but I wished it wasn't such a constant feeling. That the gap in my heart for such companionship wasn't so vacant and lonely. I swore it had started to smell and fill with pus, reminding me near constantly of how the body begins to shut down when its needs aren't met.

But that was the reality of my situation: I couldn't have love. And people couldn't love me without risking their life.

The couple veered right, freeing me of the torture of their cuteness.

I slid on the aviators stuffed in my pocket to take an inconspicuous peek inside the book.

A girl I'd gone to school with, Jessica Maloney, walked past with her ring finger weighed down by a sparkling rock.

Her eyes shot to my hand, the mangled one.

Not only was I a twenty-two-year-old spinster in her eyes, but I was also missing half the finger where the ring would go to get me off the shelf.

Christ, it wasn't like I'd chopped *all* the fingers off myself and earned the crazy title.

I met Jessica's stare with the biggest smile I could muster—wisdom teeth and all. But when she continued to gawk, determination to flaunt my brutish, metaphorical ball sack fuelled me, and so I gave her the finger, too—with the other hand that could actually erect a whole middle finger.

Red-faced, she shifted her disgruntled gaze elsewhere.

"Yeah, that's it, keep walking."

Didn't she know?

I am my mother's savage daughter.

I grinned in that savagery, but the smile quickly began to fade, feeling foreign like wearing someone else's clothes.

Mollie, with her head in the clouds as usual, hadn't said a word since the earlier bedroom edition of, 'how to parent your messed-up adult child.' Instead, she had been repositioning all her forces to edge us towards the barriers just past the train tracks, surely hoping for a good view of the mayor, the commotion, and the fireworks.

Surveying the grounds, I became acutely aware that I needed to be careful tonight with so many people around. Or rather *they* needed to be careful because something was brewing. The current resting underneath my skin was closer to the surface since visiting the treehouse. I had to keep my head low. Keep my mouth shut. Keep my shit together.

"Will we sit here for a few minutes?" Mollie gestured to the dewy bench as the crowd piled into the area.

Reading my hesitation, she flamboyantly flung her hands and sat. "Mother of God. I want to talk to you is all."

I joined her with a dramatic *plonk*. "Talk about what?"

"Anything you want, darling. I've been away for a few days and it's nice to be out together tonight. We used to be so close before everything went...sideways." Mollie cracked a smile to disguise her quivering lip.

Oh no, not the tears. The fights I could handle, but the tears. The wretched cries over the toilet bowl—

"Look what I found." I waved the book to distract from her brimming sadness. "It's like the ones you used to read to us. Remember? Before we built the extension on the back of the house, when Fionn and I had to share a bedroom, half pink, half blue."

She knuckled her eye to catch a tear as a false smile spread across her face: the one where her mouth pushed her lips out and her few wrinkles set into the cracks they made for themselves. "Those stories are child's play." Mollie nodded to the book and crossed her arms like she had all the secrets of the universe up her sleeve. "Now the stories passed on by grandmothers and the like. The ones told by flames. Told at dawn when the creatures turned in. Told and never written. They're the true tales of our ancestors."

"Spooky," I whispered, already enthralled. "Go on, tell me a real one. One not for children." I missed these moments with her. The ones all wrapped up in shiny nostalgia, transporting me back to the time of happiness.

She tapped her finger against her lips, ruminating. "Well, there was a story your Granny Murphy told, God rest her soul. It's called *Banríon*." Mollie placed her arm on the bench's back, and I snuggled into her with a sheepish nod to continue, my sudden, childish yearning for a cuddle loud.

"They name her Mórrígan. She is of the five *pure* Tuatha Dé Danann, a direct root from her mother, Danu. I believe she was truly the daughter of Balor—God of Evil. Granny Murphy would say, '*Destruction carried out on the face of happiness is the truest form of malevolence.*'"

"Sounds like a right sour bitch. What did she do?"

Mollie and I bent our knees sideways for a cart with light-up toys and popcorn to pass. "Mórrígan was a woman possessed by the darkest shade of jealousy, surged from her desire to rule all. She was to lose this power when the prophecy, foretold by the greatest of red-robed Druids, declared a baby born on the eve of the new moon would overthrow her reign. In a black-eyed rage, she ordered any baby born this eve to be slaughtered in their cribs."

Choking on my own spit, I leapt from Mollie's comfort, spluttering a cough into my elbow crease. "Fucking babies?"

Heads were turning now. I was used to it—some were compelled to look; others, conditioned to turn away. They didn't want to get caught in the backdraft of whatever I did next. The static of the microphone coming into play instantly led the stragglers to more interesting things on stage.

"Oh, Christ, I should have known this would happen!" Mollie flustered and hid her bulging eyes into her hitching shoulder. "Don't look now."

I blatantly looked everywhere, my head swivelling loose. "Look at what? Who is it now?"

"It's the postman. I'm talking about the postman."

"The postman?" I strained far too loud.

"Shh! Yes. He asked me if I wanted to go for a drink after this. After Mayor Gallagher's speech."

"Milkman didn't work out then?" I said, squeezing the edges of my eyes just to stop them rolling.

"No, he had too much of a subconscious predilection for my boobs." She wiped nothing off her knee and crossed her legs. "And I'd rather a stamp discount over a milk one anyway. The price of them is outrageous these days. Oh, and before I forget"—she whipped out the car keys now swinging like a pendulum from her finger—"you can drive yourself home if you want."

I sighed. This was her plan all along. "I'm not legally allowed to drive for another twelve weeks, which you know."

She laughed. "So, you're saying I should have seduced the policeman instead of the post one, is it?"

"If I get caught—"

"Shush, now. You won't!" She slid the keys into my hand and folded it over. "All the Garda are working here for crowd control anyway. Nobody will be manning the roads tonight. You have to get back on the horse at some point." Her tone was getting gentle now—convincing.

"Yeah," I said, resigned, my head tilting to the sky. "You're right." I only half believed it.

She gave me a curt nod, reaffirming her mothering had worked. That she'd done the right thing when she hadn't so many times before.

A postman with shorts welded to his rugby build was waving from across the full crowd.

Mollie pointed to her chest and mouthed, "Me?"

"Obviously you!" I snapped.

"I must have gotten a letter delivered to the wrong house," she said in jest before fixing her boobs with a two-way rocking system and quick shove up. "I'll be back in a minute."

I waved her off. "Take your time. Mayor Gallagher is about to start anyway."

She gracefully made her way to him, effortlessly parting the crowd with her charm, while I slipped into the bustling crowd near the front. I glanced at either side of me. This was kind of nice. Just blending into normality for a moment. *Feeling* normal.

I leaned into the barrier with my knees between the gaps just as the round man in a tuxedo swanned across the stage while fixing his giant chain.

Ahh. The famous Mayor Gallagher.

Someone behind with a thick townie accent heckled some nondescript Mr. T joke.

I smiled a little into my windbreaker. Because honestly, he really did look like the result of an affair between a darts player and a magpie with a penchant for shiny things.

More static interference rang out of the microphone, spurring everyone around me to dramatically block their ears. I pressed my thumb to the little chip on my canine. That whiny noise reminded me of the time I thought the karaoke microphone in Dicey's Pub was an ice cream cone and took a bite out of it.

"Is this thing on?" Mayor Gallagher tapped the microphone and brought it to his ear, stirring the crowd to laugh again. He grew redder by the minute, likely from the thick suit, as he waved and revelled in the attention. "Welcome all to the grand opening of Wexford's new quay. I'm delighted to have you all here for this long-awaited moment. There's many on the list I want to thank today for rallying together. For getting this proposal brought to fruition..."

He rambled on this way for some time before finally someone wound their finger up at him. "Four years and seventeen million pounds later, the moment has finally come." During the commotion of clapping and the train loudly arriving at the station down the road, the mayor nodded to a staff member holding a giant pair of scissors on the sidelines. The fuzzy-haired woman jolted like she'd forgotten her role in all this, then walked onto the stage with an embarrassed wave before passing it to him, only to immediately scurry off again.

"Ladies and gentlemen, boys and girls, the new quay," he announced, then snipped the red ribbon behind him as a flurry of cameras secured blinding shots of his grinning face. His smile spread wider and wider to an increasingly clapping crowd where the smell of well-fermented beer thickened. I joined the commotion, feeling a fleeting second of belonging. That new beginnings were possible. God, was this all it took? A bit of comradery?

"Now, I've been asked to sing you all out," he said with fake vexation. "Shirley, I'm talking about you. I know you're out in the audience somewhere holding me to my word." A finger pointed to some hidden sound technician. "So away we go! And a one, and a two, and—"

"He'd do anything to sing for an audience, that man. And hardly a note in his head," someone whispered to the guy next to me with a sticky-faced kid on his shoulders.

Backing music—a gentle percussion of trombones—began to rise, growing louder. The mayor was wisping his fingers jokingly as though he was leading an orchestra. The tune carried a sense of familiarity that had me shaking my head ever so slightly.

Not a sway to the music.

A tic.

The space of the movement grew smaller and faster.

"Oh, I love Neil Diamond," a woman said.

"Neil Diamond?" I whispered to myself. My eyebrows suddenly sat heavier as I searched through the new cemented ground for nothing. My throat thickened, a sensation as if something had nested there, like the muscles painfully and unwillingly were malleating to adjust the space.

Oh no.

The song stirred an achy sense of dread in me as if the melody was needling an omen into my chest.

The mayor, in deep, off-key baritones, belted out the first line of "Sweet Caroline," triggering the sensation of falling into an endless pit. Triggering the worst memory of all.

The day of Fionn's death.

I cleared my throat again. My head twitched, over and over.

No. Not this one. *Anyone* but this one.

My knees dug further into the gaps of the railing, bruising a cruel pain into them as a black tide surged, dragging me into its undercurrent. Into the one forsaken memory I thought I'd banished from my mind for good.

The sun's light is casting warmth on my freckled arm as it lies on the car's door frame. Fresh-cut grass wafts through the window, so potent I swear the blades themselves are invading my nose. I sneeze and sneeze again, cursing whatever deities come to mind.

"You're supposed to say *bless you*," I sass.

"Bless you," Fionn mutters.

He's been quiet all day. Nothing but tonsillitis could keep his mouth shut for this long.

I clear my throat, loudly, so he knows I intend to *make* him talk. "Have you been searching for accommodation near the DCU campus?"

We drive past the local sports pitch busy with matches as we head home with a boot full of groceries. He waits an entire minute before answering, making sure not to look my way. "Ahh, sure, I might as well wait until the college offers come out."

That doesn't make sense. Accommodation in Dublin will be gone in no time, and he's a cert for getting accepted into his course. "Were you swaying towards your second choice? Or did you get the sports scholarship you applied for?"

He laughs through his nose, though it doesn't meet his mouth or his deep brown eyes—so unlike my blue. This is worse than I thought. "No. I didn't. There's too many better players out there."

"It's all your gallivanting with Dolly that got in the way of going to the football county trials. You'd have been good enough if you focused," I tease, hoping humour will snap him out of it. Maybe it *is* his love life that's bothering him. "What's Dolly planning on studying?"

"I wouldn't know," he says rather quickly, his elongated arm stiffening on the wheel.

I bite my lip then pry anyway. "What, did ye' break up?"

"No. I just don't think what Dolly is doing coincides with my decisions for life after school. I've seen plenty of friends put their girlfriends' first choice down on the form instead of their own."

It isn't like Fionn to be snippy, but my concern turns to frustration. "My God, the drama. Will you stop being vague and tell me what's bothering you?"

He pulls out left at the T-junction, forgetting to signal, and an aggrieved driver honks behind us.

We both simultaneously give him the finger even though we're in the wrong.

"Maybe I don't want to go to college, alright?" he says, still snappy. "There are more important things than sitting in a classroom for another four years."

"Jesus Christ, DCU is what *you* wanted," I shout. "Mam wouldn't care if you were shovelling shite as long as you were happy." His nostrils flare. And I know. I know I'm making this worse, but I can't help but bicker for the sake of it at this point.

"If you knew the truth, you wouldn't care about college, either," he says. "Or the Debs or graduation or any other unimportant bollox."

I smack the dashboard for his insolence. "Woah. Unimportant bollox? Fionn, you can't be serious." Seeing Fionn angry is rarer than hen's teeth. I hate it. I hate how constricted and tense it makes me. How the mood of a room has to change to revolve around him. "And I suppose you'll be giving up Gaelic football, too?" That'll catch him out. He'll never quit his first love in life.

He's staring at the road, a blotchy heat crawling up his neck, nostrils flaring wider by the second. He turns up the radio to drown me out; the chorus of "Sweet Caroline" rings out of the speakers.

"Will you answer me, Fionn? Please! I'm starting to get genuinely worried now," I beg over the music.

When I try to twist the volume down, he smacks my hand away. I slide my tongue over my teeth and reach to turn it down again. I'll do this all day if I have to.

Following through, he reaches over to clench my arm, squeezing the skin until it bulges under his grip. The callus touch is the most foreign thing

I've ever endured from him. So much so, I'm at a loss to describe the core of what emotion I'm actually feeling. Fear? Shock? Anger?

"Fionn...Fionn, stop." There's a tenderness in my plea. Even now I want to put his concern over my own. By order of birth.

"You haven't a clue, Clío. You're a fool."

Pulling away from him with hefty recoils is no use; he's too strong. Too full of venom. Too consumed by whatever aches him.

My body swelters as if my blood is bubbling and popping beneath the surface. "Let go of me, Fionn." I yank my arm back but fail to make any ground. "You're hurting me."

He leans into me with a wild glare I swear turns his eyes black. Not muddy or coal, but an abyss, calling on me. "It's all irrelevant for us. There's no truth or purpose to any of this. Open your eyes! You're a naive child and nothing more!"

The anger and fear mesh inside me, encapsulating all my will into a single, sinister form. I swing my free arm into his elbow to break his grip. My palms radiate heat. My fingers pulsate beyond the thrum of pins and needles. I can't catch my breath, and Fionn's hollow stare doesn't falter.

I can't hold onto the pulse in my hands. I can't. I can't breathe. I can't fight this feeling. I don't *want* to fight it.

So, I free it.

This silence is ephemeral, a momentary whisper in the symphony of the unending noise.

A light expels, drinking in every inch of the car.

The wheels lift from tarmac, sticking my body to the seat, levitating my cheeks. My arms float like I'm underwater as we spin, poetically, like a ballerina in freefall. But I can't breathe, and I can't think. Or I don't want to because all my mind is screaming is *I'm about to die*.

There are no flashes of my life or pleading to God. Just weightless spinning into the inevitable.

Fencing penetrates the backseat. Glass shatters. Cows flee to a far corner of the field we somehow ended up in when we were just on a road living a normal life.

Our bodies thrust to a standstill as the car lands upside down.

Blurred versions of mint ice cream and potatoes scatter along the busy road where cars are screeching and swerving.

I blink out of consciousness only to rejoin it seconds later by the call of his voice. "Your hand! Don't move," Fionn says to me through an echo. "I lost control. Clío, I'm sorry. I never meant to hurt you."

There's blood from his nose dripping onto his forehead, and his face blots red from the pressure of being hung from his seatbelt.

"What—" I drift off trying to figure out which one of him is the real one in my double vision. Everything moves in slow motion. As if each moment is caught in a languid drifting, lagging behind its own existence.

"Don't look, Clío. You hear me, don't look at your hand. Just keeping looking at me."

He coughs and blood splatters over what's left of the smashed, beaded windscreen.

He doesn't see it yet.

He's so focused on me he doesn't realise that I couldn't possibly look anywhere but at him. Everything that was so slow just moments ago is moving too fast now. Too fast to stop it.

"Fionn."

"I can already hear the sirens. Can't you?"

"Fionn," I say, my voice rising in panic as my brain tries to find a solution it's never going to get.

"Just focus on me and in a couple of minutes we'll be out of this mess. You hear the sirens too, yeah?"

"Fionn," I scream hysterically.

He follows my tear-filled stare to his stomach. Then back to me. Then back to his stomach again.

The post of the fence is lodged through his gut, barbed wire still attached. The wound is cavernous, consuming the entire left side.

His breathing turns to hyperventilating. To hysteria as the inevitable plays out before us and the timer to his death runs out faster than the blood spilling onto the ceiling carpet.

"Look at me," he says, unexpectedly smiling. I know it's for my sake, but I can't stop staring at the mangled mess of his body. "Clío, look at my face. Nothing else," he shouts firmer when realising the smiling won't work.

I rip my tortured eyes from the wound, staring right into his eyes where a greyness has taken hold of their true brightness.

"Don't worry about me. I'm...I'll be okay. I'm always okay." But he isn't. "The sirens are close now."

"Fionn, please. Please don't die. Please don't leave me alone." I sob. "Please don't..."

Just as fast as I say the words I see it now; I'm already alone.

I hang next to him, knowing he's dead. He might have been dead before he even spoke.

The song. I'd almost forgotten it. I pushed that day away. It wasn't to be revisited. He wasn't to be remembered that way—fragmented. By my hands. I figured that out quickly—my curse. That was the first time it ever sparked. The anger I'd felt in my youthful, hormonal mind exacerbated everything. It had been so consuming that I'd flipped an entire car—and then, my world.

Power ignited in me, a searing force that gnawed at my fingers and stubs, at my heart and fraying sanity. I shouldn't have come. Too many people were around. Too many children. As my curse breached the surface, heaving for release and calling to my primal side, my body staggered into the huffing, heckling crowd.

"Watch it," someone hissed, shoving me back.

How could you kill him when he was the one driving?

How could you possibly think that you did it?

You're probably saying it for attention. So people feel sorry for you.

You're pathetic.

You're nothing.

You should have been the one who died.

"NO!" I screamed, clutching my head at both sides as all the fear and pain and anger shot out in smooth golden flecks.

Fireworks popped and exploded across the sky in yellows and reds, greens and golds. The crowd *oohed* and *ahhed*.

Pain consumed me. In bursts of golden shimmers and slender spurts, the curse curled around the giant scissors lying on the stage.

My grip on it grew tighter. The seduction of power ran over the inlay of my lips, chattering them. Its darkness felt so much better than the sadness.

I twisted my hand upright; the scissors rattled before finding a steady balance midair. A voice, distant in my mind, called on me, begging me to stop. To show restraint. But the curse was louder. I *needed* to expel it before it ingested me.

With a mere flick of my wrist, the scissors shot into the mayor's stomach.

Squish.

Another explosion of squeals and lights.

Satisfaction and air seeped out of me like a quiet puncture. My shoulders relaxed.

But as blinding power receded, all I could see was the horrific fallout in front of me—centre stage.

Oh no. No, no, no.

I slid my hands down my face, still humming as the gentle wind wrapped strands of hair over my eyes. Any strength to finger them away was gone. Taken by the stiffness in my arms and loud ringing in my ears.

With a steady stream of blood gushing from his open mouth, Mayor Gallagher looked down on me.

I edged back, repelling the accusation. *It wasn't me*, I wanted to say. *It's not my fault.* But that was a lie.

His eyes glossed over; he collapsed to buckled knees, tilting further forward against the scissors which had gruesomely pushed through to poke out his back.

For a second, the world felt occupied by just us. The giver and the taker. Him giving me a moment of respite from the swell of power, and me taking his life.

The ringing dulled, pulling me back to the chaos and screams as the world caught up to the fallout.

Staff and family flocked to him, near shrouding his body as I stood there, the spotlight reverted to me from those who saw, who finally believed. Who dared to enter the place where impossible things happened.

Me.

Yes. It was me.

I looked down at my shaking hands where the final wisps of power floated away. My stare shifted back to the body.

I killed Mayor Gallagher.

I think I might have even *wanted* to kill him.

And now, no one could deny me as the murderer I always claimed to be.

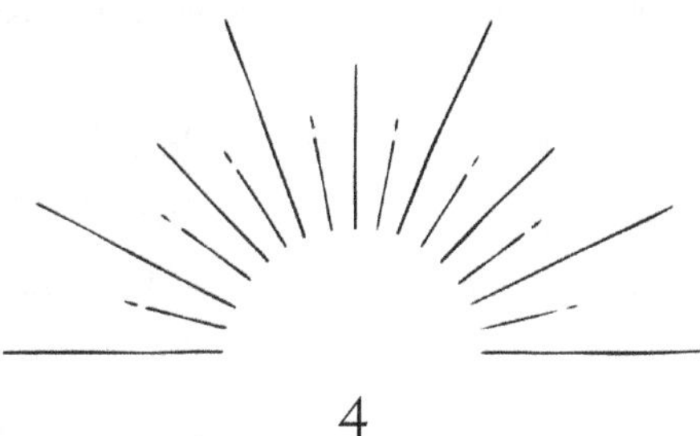

4
RUN, RUN, AS FAST AS YOU CAN

I ran, immersed in the frantic crowd, the heat of panic sweltering through my pores. All of us fled and scattered in directionless mayhem from the danger, most oblivious to the fact it was me who threatened them. It was *always* going to be me.

My hands violently shook as I stabbed the car with my key, scratching red paint over and over until it finally lodged into the keyhole.

I focused more on the rearview mirror than the windscreen until the darkening, winding roads eventually brought me home to Borín Lane by instinct. Because where else could I go? I didn't have friends. Or family outside of poor Mollie. Nothing. Just Dr. Hannas. And even he couldn't justify this—although maybe he'd finally understand. Maybe some journalist or security camera had eternalised the proof that I wasn't like everyone else. That Briggie's Bin had never been the place for me.

I abandoned the still running car, kicked off my shoes, and bounded up the stairs for refuge. The light was off in my room, but I recalled my hiding spot by instinct.

It was the bottle of Jameson beneath the floorboard I sought out. I twisted the cap and chugged, tilting my head so far back, it felt like my neck might bend out of place. Swallowing in masochistic gulps, the burning numbed me. It let warmth reach my chest until pleasurable tears hung in the corners of my eyes. Until the edge was taken off and I could see this for what it was.

If not tonight, the accusation of bystanders was inevitably coming my way. And what would happen in the confinement of an interrogation room now the curse had taken new life?

Nothing fucking good—that's what.

I was an outsider. The witch to be persecuted and burned. Although I actually wasn't innocent in this case. The stake might even be justified.

If only they listened when I screamed that I wasn't crazy until the whites of my eyes turned red. But it was impossible to prove the existence of my curse when the witness would get caught in the blast the moment I triggered it.

I fixed the cap and hugged the bottle close. The day Fionn died had been buried for good reason. It was the only leash I had on my sanity. Keeping it locked away was the only medium I had to survive. I bent to take his medallion from the gap in the floor.

"What is it, Fionn? Why was it hidden?"

A dull noise in the distance began to grow louder, piercing the night. I stuffed the medallion into my pocket and ran to the front window, separating the curtains I'd never bothered to pull in the first place. Faint lights of electric blue poked into the trees and low hanging clouds in the distance. The noise became clear.

Sirens.

Frenzied, I searched all around the room, like maybe I could hide, like I could contort myself into the hole in the floor. Discounting the irrational thought, I fled downstairs and out the back door toward the forest.

A wind stirred as I bounded barefoot along the trail. My breath haunted me worse than the ghosts who endlessly roamed by night. And each time I swallowed, I regurgitated my pulsing heart over and over, reminding me of how futile this situation was.

I instinctively pulled right towards the treehouse, scratching my toes against the mesh of terrain beneath.

Once inside, my fumbling fingers slid the lock closed behind me. Was I locking myself in to keep them safe? Or me?

Hopelessness gripped me from all angles. I screamed incessantly, beating my head and clutching at roots. My instincts begged for an escape—a freedom I felt unworthy of.

The drifting sounds of howls and barks grew closer.

I jerked my head up, my hand slamming against the wooden wall to steady myself. They'd find me in minutes. Everything had caught up with me so much sooner than I'd anticipated.

I contemplated the idea of being imprisoned forever. How would it be explained in court? Would the government experiment on me between free pints in their parliament bar?

I'd never get my redemption now, but maybe—finally—Fionn's justice would come.

Huddling myself into the corner of the sofa, I found myself clenching his medallion inside my pocket. My thumb caressed its minuscule knobbles representing leaves. It was almost soothing to touch, keeping me sedentary for a moment.

Fionn wanted me to find this. I knew that much. This was our last secret, just for us.

I took it from my pocket to swirl my thumb clockwise on the knots as I began to make peace with what was incoming.

At my touch, the medallion retracted from its centre, like it was made of hundreds of tiny needles that got scared and hid away in the circles' crevices.

I shot up. "Holy shit!"

Beneath the needles was a sub-layer where deep purple liquid filled a circular sunken glass.

I instinctively pressed my thumb against the surface. Maybe it might change to red, gauging my fear how a mood ring might. A spike released from its twelve o'clock point, jabbing my thumb right into the gap between my nail and skin.

"Ouch!" I seethed. Blood bubbled from the tiny puncture, and a strange stench of sour berries filled my nose.

The barking was close now. It snapped at my ears, jolted my shoulders.

"Clíona Murphy?" called voices from outside. "Clío, we know you're in there. It's best for all of us if you come out with your arms raised with no intent to harm."

The worst weapon they probably had was a taser or baton. I wanted to go willingly—I really did—but the curse had begun to rise at the idea of their threats.

The door rattled violently, so hard the hinges were coming loose, but I couldn't tell if it was their hands or mine causing the commotion.

"I don't want to hurt you either!" I shouted, knowing there was no guarantee.

The curse was calling. I was a wild animal backed into a corner.

Stumbling into the chair's wooden edge, an unbalance overcame me, as if I'd stood too fast. The inside of my mouth felt numb. Too pliable. I rolled my tongue against the soft flesh. Something wasn't right. The release of the curse never felt this way before. Unless...the whiskey? "Please," I mumbled, staggering. I squeezed the chair's arm to steady myself, both hands encapsulated by golden light.

The door swung open as uniformed guards swarmed the room.

The edges of the world blurred, meshing wood and bark and memories until every inch of my strength plummeted from my core and reality slipped from my grasp.

With outstretched arms, I followed the impetuous beckon of unconscious calm—the one place I ever found respite from guilt.

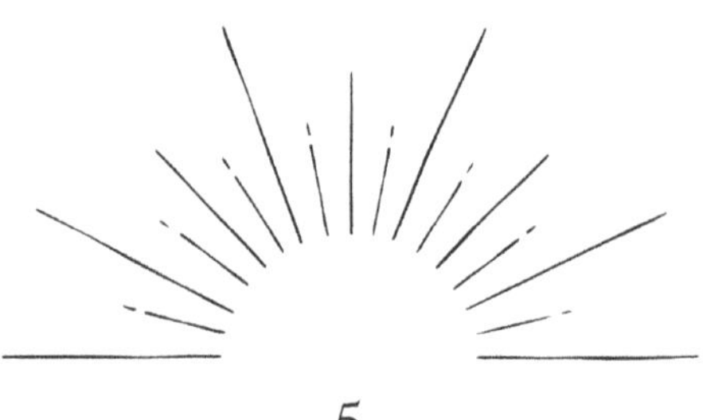

5
THE MOST WANTED PERSON IN THE COUNTRY

Noise.

Thunderous noise so loud it was as if I lived within the roaring sound. As if I'd taken residency and paid my rent religiously. My eyelids were heavy. Pressing, whispering to me to stay closed. I opened them anyway, fighting their exhausting ache.

How dare the thing that's meant to replenish make me worse off.

I stretched my fingers through blades of damp grass instead of sheets. Morning's disarray refused to dull, dreams still meshing through reality. I managed to stand despite the feeling, though wobbling in utter confusion; mere feet away hung a towering waterfall. My gawking gaze followed its cascade right into the calming river running next to me.

I stepped backwards—slowly. In that one explanation of what the noise was, came *far* more questions. Whatever this was, it wasn't good.

I spun around, my gasps lagging as I found myself in a field of blooming poppies. Spanning far and wide.

The trees swaying at the field's edges only worsened my dizziness and churning stomach.

"Where the hell—" My throat, suddenly hot and full, I twisted to the river, piercing the water with blobs of carrots as my belly strained like a wet cloth. At least the ungodly retching coming out of me would scare off any wildlife thinking I looked delicious.

After a relentless minute, the heaves ended with my poor sleeve suffering the swipe of my tacky mouth. I shrunk into the sodden grass. Thinking anything linear was difficult. Everything felt so disjointed, like I was giving out oxygen instead of breathing it in, but I could only guess...I'd died?

I noted the beauty of my surroundings. The way the light caught on the red of the poppies to make them glow. Almost ethereal. This sure didn't look like hell. Unless the Irish countryside had been secretly colonised by the devil, too.

I ran my rattling fingers through my hair, yanking its knots as panic took me by the throat like it was sentient and I was its whore. I patted my windbreaker for my phone.

Empty.

"Fuck. This isn't good. This is very, very not good!"

It seemed my one, tiny, remaining ounce of rationale had a clear frontrunner: if I wasn't already dead, I was about to be soon. Because you don't kill a mayor without a nationwide manhunt. I pulled my hair so tight the roots *screamed* for release. I had no direction. Nowhere to go. Nowhere to hide and no idea where I was or how I got here.

One second, I'm in the treehouse with the entire county police force ready to take me out and next...

I shrunk lower. It made no sense. I knew crazy, and this wasn't it. Something was off. Like the pH in the air was slightly less acidic. Like there was no true north. Like the constants of the universe were a little too far to the left.

The shine of Fionn's medallion on the flattened patch I woke from caught my attention. I grasped it with a raw-throated groan, letting its sun-warmed coating sting my fingers. I looped it around my neck, furthering that sting as I tucked inside my top for safekeeping. Then, leaning on the comfort it brought me like a taped-together crutch, I decided I was no sitting duck and left the crimson field with hefty, barefoot strides.

The forest, soothed by spots of shade, had offered so many dirt tracks I marched blindly, with no bearing of which one was right—or safe. Thankfully, my singular saving grace—albeit a minor one—was the trees: sessile oak, native to Ireland, towering and intertwining at every turn. Back in my school days, Mrs. Noonan, the biology teacher with the lazy eye, had said the acorns hung instead of clustering around the leaves. Of course, I only remembered the lesson because Donal McDonald proceeded to ask the boys in class if their balls were clustered or hanging. No matter. I was grateful for his antics because it clarified I *was* in Ireland and hadn't managed to get on the local ferry to Wales. Not that I would, but every possibility was fair game at this point.

Opting to take the next left path, a conversation I once had with Dr. Hannas about hitting rock bottom came to mind. How do you know the moment you've touched the bottom? How do you clarify it? So many times, I thought I couldn't fall any deeper, but here I was, a murderer at large and probably the most wanted person in the country. God, this day was inevitable, really. I was stupid to walk into that crowd; I was no better than a ticking time bomb without control over the detonator.

Rustling came from the bushes, perking my head up like I was a startled bird sensing the shadow of a predator.

"Halt," a voice called in Gaeilge.

I stopped short, startled by the sound of another person, and even more so because the voice had spoken Irish. It meant I could have wandered as far as the west coast to a Gaeltacht region.

"Who's there?" I shouted in the native tongue. It always made my mouth feel rounder on the inside, as if something had inflated it, and now whenever I switched to Irish, it stretched easier from use. Made me feel more myself.

My jittering toes stubbed a rock.

I grabbed it knowing damn well it wouldn't help me.

A young man emerged from behind bramble bushes, his hair dark and ear-length, with a thick furrowed brow that led into his sharp nose. Held in his fist was a large bow.

"Release the rock," he commanded, furrowing further.

It rolled from my fingers.

His lean, muscular arms stretched the bow taut; the arrow poised to shoot. "On your knees."

"Wait—" I harshly fell to them.

A brief glimpse of his clothes confused me: a tired tunic beneath a muddy-green tartan cloak. In a whiplash of emotions I asked, "What the hell are you wearing?" I could feel all my face muscles crease at him. I could feel myself adopting the power of slight seniority despite being too far in danger to be sassing. "Are you doing one of those re-enactments for the Yank tourists, or are you...I don't know, a pagan?"

Did Gaeltacht regions even do that?

He stood tall, puffing his chest. Deciding something I wasn't sure I wanted the answer to. The beads of sweat collecting on his forehead were making me nervous, sending my eyes haywire. Whatever he struggled with was pushing through. There was familiarity in that.

"Will you lower that bow and tell me where we are?" I hoped being stern might help him see sense. I raised my hands, still rattling. "Please."

"Your fingers." He nodded to the contradiction of his words. To what was left of them.

I swiped them a peripheral glance like maybe they'd somehow grown back all of a sudden. They hadn't. But the disappointment of that discovery never came. They were gone, and that was that.

"Yeah, bad accident. Can still play a mean guitar solo." No. Deflection and humour were not the right playing cards for this situation. "And again, where are we?"

"We dwell in Ériu."

"Ériu?" My chin tucked inward of its own accord. The dialect was unusually strong; the tone clear-cut with no singsong in his vowels or slang between words like most accents. Was it part of his play to sound more olden?

Nothing made sense. It was as if someone had taken an eraser to the last few hours of my life, and I was using the lingering smudges of chalk to piece this all together.

He growled with impatience when lowering the bow to unlatch rope hanging from his leather belt. Considering all the sharp things dangling from it, this was almost positive.

Almost.

"We will journey to the village. Rathnor must be addressed," he said, making for me with the rope.

"Woah. Woah. Wait!" I stood, staggering away from him, my wrists regressing so far back, I thought they might snap and fall off all together. I sniffled; it was getting stronger. This feeling of something off in the air. Something impossible to describe or put your finger on. "Just answer me one thing. Just one, and I'll let you play your game." A lie. "Who is Rathnor?"

The young man's deep breath stopped short, and I wondered if he could taste that something was off too, until I realised he was hesitating. "He is the man who will slaughter you. Make no doubt of that. This is the day you die, wildling."

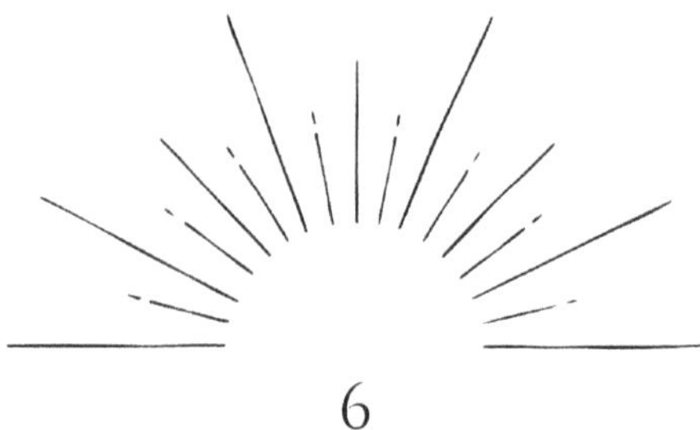

6

THE EARTH IS FOR OUR DEAD TO LAY

This was my death march.

This was complacency in the wake of having no idea what the fuck I should do.

We followed the forest's pathway—each step closer to my threatened end.

And yet, I'd obeyed.

I swiped my conjoined thumbs across my brow to scant relief. Sweat had taken residence in my every crevice making me curse the sun that so rarely shone, even in summer. Still, it was my rigid spine that stole most of my attention, aching and too afraid to twist towards the threat.

My capturer, tall and dirty, trailed behind, surely with his arrow poised to shoot. This wasn't a re-enactment for tourists, I knew that much now. No, this was something worse. A weird, sick game. One I wanted no part in.

Time had pressed on my legs, making them throb as we continued past never-ending trees and foliage of sloe bushes, teasing my grumbling stomach with their blue, sweet scent. I sought anywhere to escape a hundred times already, but not even a hill to recklessly dive down came forth. My God, I would've gladly dived—broken limbs and all—to be free. Because what was the alternative? Offering the service of being his eternal concubine in exchange for living? I mean, there were worse people to look at for the rest of my life. People who didn't look like they were sculpted from marble and genetic fortune, but no, a concubine I was not.

I craned my stiff neck back. The sun was nearing its zenith to mark midday. Poor Mollie. What was she thinking? Feeling? What was the word for a mother who lost all her children? We—kids—got to use the term *orphan* for the loss of our parents. But if I didn't make it out of this, what would she be?

I used to think disappointment was a feeling dedicated to children. That parents would stop feeling letdown when you grew up, or you would stop doing things to cause reproach. This wasn't the case at all—for me, at least. I disappointed Mollie all the time. Not through unviable expectations and standards, but just through poor living, and insane decisions with no origin of rationale to fall back on.

All I ever saw was my own pain for so long, nothing else mattered. At times, it still didn't.

So yeah, if I didn't get out of this, I'd be making my mother face her greatest disappointment: I'd be the person who killed all of her children. And that wouldn't do.

Persisting over fear, shoulder to cheek, I glimpsed the assailant. "Can you tell me your name, love?" That's what Mollie would say. She'd try and affectionately butter them up so much she'd slip through their greasy fingers with the false gain of trust.

Silence.

"Are you local?" I tried for the last time. A third without a reply might be pushing it.

"I am Rían."

I nodded slowly, feeling a hint of accomplishment. First name basis. Great. The hard part was over—if I disregarded the threat of being killed.

"What a nice name. Really rolls off the tongue." My words came out too enthusiastic and rhythmic, and I found myself morbidly grateful he couldn't see my face and all the fear I was failing to keep behind jittering lips.

"Rían, I think we both know I'd never overpower you with that big bow. So, there's really no need for these." I jangled my bound hands over my head for him to see, letting the chaff dig deeper and spoil the light smile I was trying to channel. "I won't hurt you."

I could never guarantee those words.

He scoffed as if I said something ridiculous. "I walk through these woodlands in the light of the sun or stars. I see more than any person living. Trust, it is not you who worries me."

I perked a little. I was getting somewhere inside his twisted words. Even the slightest piece of information might steer me and my palpitating heart out of this mess.

"What is it you're worried about? That Rathnor guy? Is he making you do this?"

He growled, revving the frustration out of his throat. "You question too much." Heavy palms met my back's damp arch. The force sent me fumbling onto the balls of my feet where softer soil balmed my aching toes.

I scurried ahead, keenly aware his hands were free of the bow. No, not aware—*afraid*. Afraid of the responsibility I felt to seize this opportunity to escape.

Always getting yourself into pickles, Fionn's voice said with teasing tuts.

Something told me this was a *pickle* I'd have to get myself out of—preferably without accidentally murdering this guy. And what was to come of him if I didn't kill him? Did he know his future was worth more than whoever put the bow in his hand? I wished someone had thought the same for me; one day I was a 'confused' teenage girl worth the pity of strangers, then, not long after my eighteenth birthday, I became the adult who deserved my pain because I was old enough to have my shit together. I shivered. Something still haunted me about crossing that threshold.

Continuing to heed his brash directions (*straight...left...keep moving...move faster*), we eventually descended into low grass where, through a tall line of saplings, was an adjacent oat field. It was nearly at peak harvest, all of the grain swaying as one in the soft breeze. Maybe...maybe it could provide coverage—if I could get there. It was risky, but it provoked my devious side to kick in, leading me astray if only just to rebel. I guess it was urges like this that landed me into pickles in the first place.

I gnawed at my lips for all of five seconds.

Fuck it.

Edging in the oat field's direction more diagonally, I hoped it was subtle enough to go unnoticed.

He marched ten feet behind, his bow looped across his chest, and his sight sufficiently distracted by circling crows to catch my spying.

Now was my chance.

One...two...

I sprinted, faster than I expected my tired legs to ever take me, heart booming and pulsating in my head with a desire to have faith or hope suddenly centre stage. My hands were still bound, but I scrambled anyway, leveraging my way up the little bank border, nails filling with soil so deeply my eyes watered.

An arrow whizzed past, sending a sharp gust into my ear canal before lodging itself into the sapling ahead. As I stood to tumble down the other side of the bank, searing, red heat radiated from the flesh of my shoulder. Agony. A crippling scream tore from my throat, locking me in its grasp, each breath steeped in torment. My blind, curious fingers reached behind to feel the slender wood still wobbling from reaching its target.

I'd been hit.

I froze, not even swallowing the acidic bile clawing at my throat.

"The next will not miss," Rían shouted, his breath loud from the chase. "I can impale your skull with ease."

"Wait!" Despite the sharp pain it would bring, I faced him to stretch my bound hands as wide as possible to signal surrender.

He approached, disgruntled, bending his hand over his shoulder to nock a second fletched arrow. Even locking it into place, his stretched arm pulsed with firm muscle. I swapped my gaze to meet his green one, angled now, coated with the darkest lashes and intention. He was no stranger to this bow.

"Approach. Slowly," he warned.

Hunched and struggling to keep my balance, I hobbled down to the flat plain, the wind knocking out of me worse for each step. But it wasn't from effort; it was the rising of a current inside of me.

The quickening pulse of power surfaced at my core, teasing the idea of spilling out and ripping him to pieces. "Please. Please, Rían. Let me go!"

I shouted in tattered cries. In my one display of control over the curse, I sourced it to my hands unsure if, by protecting myself, *he* would become my next vict—

Rían pounced, stalling an inch from my face. "Lower your voice, nut! Unless you seek to be slaughtered." He inhaled through his nose, stirring me to mimic him. "Be calm."

The fuel of fear immediately emptied. The curse fell into depths I could never find on my own. When I needed it. This man, boy, or whatever he was, had given me something I wasn't all that familiar with. "Are...are you helping me?" I whispered.

He twisted my torso, harsh fingers digging into the hollow of my collarbones with a merciless grip. "I will not hold your blood on my hands. Now"—he gripped the arrow— "deep breath."

My eyes widened with horror as a scream tore from my throat. Hot pain grew deeper into my body with each excruciating tug against the arrow, fighting extraction. "I have caught—a whiny—one," he muttered to himself. Then, with a gasp of relief, the pressure released.

"It will heal." He wiped my blood nonchalantly on his pants before restocking the arrow into his quiver. "*Now*, seal your mouth and follow my guide, wildling."

I did as I was told, letting him march me toward the smoke, a firm hand remaining on my shoulder just shy of his attack.

Whoever gave him his orders must've terrified him. Unless I was wrong about everything because nothing made sense.

Either way, with a snail's caution and a heavily rising chest, we marched on, my great escape the shortest one in history.

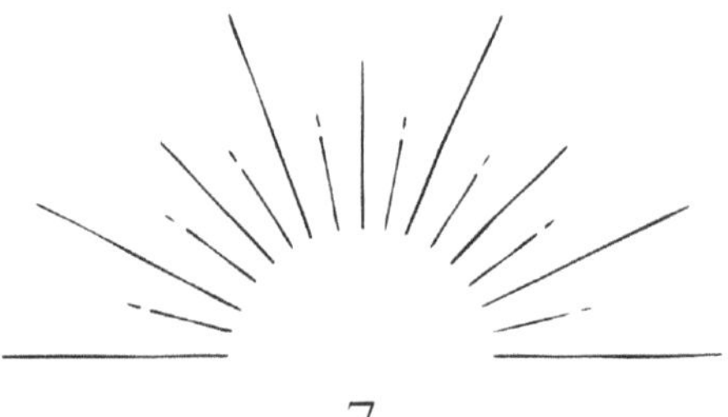

7

LOVE AT FIRST FIGHT

Since my epic failure to escape, we had slogged through more barren fields and forest for miles—or at least what felt like miles—when the nearly flat plain suddenly rose into a steep hill.

"Best not to use the front entrance this morn. The soldiers will be suspect," he said like I gave a shit. "We must climb from its flank."

"This somehow feels familiar. I just—*woah*—" My foot slipped on loose stone. "I just can't place where..." Maybe I had a concussion from falling in the forest yesterday. Nothing was stringing together right. Or the strings were soggy and too limp to make the synaptic connection.

Climbing the hill's flank—and failing—Rían helped me sneak through the small terrain of thistles and rocks that scraped and scratched me. His approach was harsh and rather heavy-handed but always a millimetre from anywhere considered inappropriate. A push on the back of my thigh. A support on the edge of my upper—

As if reading my thoughts, his hand broke that line, grazing my left breast. He quickly moved it elsewhere, and I swore a soft blush creeped into his cheeks.

I smirked, defying the outrage simmering beneath, happy to have the upper hand in at least one thing.

When finally reaching the top, we approached a gap in an unfinished wall of stone and moss. I failed twice to climb over it with bound hands before he sighed and scooped me up like it was our wedding day, not a threshold to the end of my life.

"The old ways are dying in the place of a new age," he said, swinging one calculated leg over the wall, then the other. "They say we build it to defend ourselves, though from whom I do not see. To me, it is a cage. A small green cliff to throw the weak from when we are no longer of any use."

Vacuumed by his words of old ways and cliffs I didn't think he'd intended for my ears, I'd hardly noticed how close his mouth was to mine. Now I couldn't notice anything else if I wanted to. His breath was controlled beneath my weight, but his mouth parted as he appeared to battle the pull of his eyes towards mine.

Was he afraid I'd bewitch him?

He wouldn't be the first.

"Does it hurt?"

I blinked. "What?"

He finally took to looking at me. "The wound."

Oh.

"Yes," I said through gritted teeth.

"Good." He roughly withdrew his hand from beneath my legs, dropping me to stand. "Let it be your reminder not to escape me again."

I swayed on weak legs.

Rían's hands reached out to steady me. "Here—"

Pushing back, I said, "I'm not going to thank you when this was your doing. And don't think I didn't notice your fingers getting happy on my tit just there when you were meant to be 'helping' me."

"You ungrateful little wild—" He bit off the end of his sentence, snapping his mouth closed only to let his anger spew out more slowly. "I will impale you with another arrow if you do not keep that wicked little mouth of yours closed!" He shook his head as he closed his eyes and took a heavy breath. "We have arrived."

I turned. Beyond the wall, past a lining of trees, came a bark pathway, either side engulfed by houses, thatched, with muddy or circular stone exteriors as far as I could see. Roundhouses.

But that would make this—what had he said again? *We build it to defend ourselves. A small green cliff.*

"A hillfort," I murmured.

I was standing on top of a hillfort. Which was impossible. They were half-buried, half-forgotten historical sites, not in commission villages.

I spun, blinking the homes away to no result. The part of my brain that produced logic was clearly out of service. All the strength from my limbs, all the words from my jittering mouth, had been sucked into the void of crippling fear.

This. Wasn't. The West.

Or real.

Or possible.

Forts were archaeological. None were in use. *None.* And this one was huge—acres. With its own forest lining most of the perimeter, stretching as far as I could see.

Where was the village he said he'd bring me to? The white-marked road? Pub on the corner or local post office? Where were the mams out for brisk walks pushing prams? The fish n' chip shop?

What the hell was happening to me?

This wasn't the time for worst-case scenarios, but with no escape route, no plausible explanation for anything, and the anticipation of Rían's help falling through sooner rather than later, it was apparent now—I was absolutely fucked.

I tipped a little sideways.

"Come." Rían grabbed my arm to lead. "We need to keep on foot. We must move quickly before whispers travel. All paths have danger."

My frozen frame staggered against his sudden yank. My arms numbed. I fell onto all fours, succumbing to the dirt, heaving.

A ringing blocked out everything, but at least no guilt resided there.

"There is no time," he growled more to himself as he ran a hand through the few loosening braids of his hair. Then he stomped towards me, fingers clenching my cheeks, puffing out my lips. "What do I name you?" The voice was distant, beyond the ringing. Rían shouted louder to overcome my delirium, "What do I name you, love?"

"Name me...Clíona," I managed. Using my full Irish name sounded pleasant in the native tongue. It sounded like I didn't need to be Clío anymore—something I'd craved for years.

"Stand, Clíona," he ordered. "Our earth is for the dead to lie."

He was right. If I wanted to be dead, I'd have done it years ago. That much was always true no matter the temptation.

Fixing a snarl, I stumbled upright with his help focused on my midsection. My consciousness was clearing. My legs were sturdier again, and I needed to *use* them, because whatever this village was, moving forward was the only route to safety. If safety was a thing of this place.

Dusting my knees, I shot him a deep scowl. "Don't call me love."

He smirked, unleashing a side of him I didn't think could exist. "It is what you named me when asking *my* name, wildling."

I bit back the urge to punch his arm; it probably wouldn't hurt him anyway. "Are you really going to help me or was that just a lie to make this easier for you?"

He mirrored my stern stare. "Would you trust me either way?"

I squared to him, foolishly. "No."

"Then be wise and take the path of least danger."

"What path is that?"

His mouth edged closer to me. "The one I travel."

My insides turned stiff. Why, I couldn't say. But if there was any wondering about whether this person who stood before me was a boy or man, it was gone now. His youthful face had confident, quiet eyes. He was a hunter. Dominant. There was something in him that made me think it wasn't Rathnor who controlled him. It was something else. *Something*. I searched his eyes again, gripping them until I saw it: darkness. A force I recognized.

I swallowed and gave him a curt nod, coaxing myself to believe he was trying to keep me safe in some inadvertent way. That he fought away the shadows just as much as I did.

He continued to lead, his touch barely gentler as we entered the heart of the village where scattered stalls of food and weaponry, and clothes and instruments lined the busy tracks. We passed a young boy trying to barter a dead mouse for an apple. The fruit stall's stout owner humoured the unfair swap. Commotion bustled in every direction: men hammering iron and bronze armour as a chorus of repetitive *tings* echoed and sent sparks dancing high above the stalls. A warm aroma of fresh bread filled the air as women with woven baskets tucked under their arms walked by, chattering amongst themselves with hushed gossip.

Villagers' eyes gradually began to follow us, hooking into me. I foolishly stared back, too confrontational for my own good. Perhaps still in shock, and unable to process all of this. There was an eerie authenticity to it all; the older women donned long dresses of tartan tweed. The colours were dull in gradient forms, while the younger wore knee-length variations with silk looped on their waists to enhance curves. Many men dressed in similar attire to Rían, wearing belts full of weapons or tools.

Beyond the stalls covered in tattered canopies, past the village's border trees, a tall stone temple slightly jutted into view. It resembled a flat-top pyramid, each layer of stone in the centre of the semicircle a step onto another. I'd never seen anything like it—not in Ireland. Not anywhere, really. The people who worked throughout it hammered or placed calculated blocks, disappearing into the thick of the base consumed by tree line.

"Rían. Where. Am. I?" I asked slow and firm, unable to tear my stare from the temple. My frame was becoming unbalanced again. "This...I know something is wrong." My voice was shaking, pushing me to the precipice of pointless tears. "I feel like I'm dreaming. Like I'm stuck in some hellish nightmare where everyone else is in on the joke except me."

Rían's emerald eyes jumped from one gawking villager to the next, his focus barely registering me. I didn't belong in this commune—or whatever it was—and they all knew. Some clenched their children tighter while men stood forward, their hands suddenly on unhooked weapons.

There was no place in this world where I wasn't an outcast. But the hostility had never scared me like this. The villagers' stares evolved into a chorus of angry chatter.

Then the chatter grew quiet. The sparks sizzled out. Even the breeze suddenly softened.

I edged back only to thump into Rían's impossibly hard chest.

He twisted me in one swoop to dip and meet my gaze. "Come, Clíona, to the Carraig." He pointed to the temple. "Too many eyes follow our intentions. I did not foresee this outcome, for the previous visit of an outsider differed greatly. Come. Come now!"

I thought the retro windbreaker and bound wrists would've given it away, but this wasn't the time for sassy retorts.

"Run," he ordered, fighting my lack of urgency. "Run at once!" He pushed me forwards as the atmosphere—unanimously hostile—had him set off sprinting, forcing my pace to quicken to counter his harsh pull of the rope.

"Slow down, Rían!"

Through the bustle, a brigade of iron-armoured soldiers fell in from all angles. Their hair and swords coordinated to the man next to them—the former in long, plaited ponytails, the latter a hip scabbard.

We skidded to a stop on the edge of the village where the coverage of trees was a leap away. The people's business was suddenly back to their own. The shallow puddle I found myself in sloshed as I spun in frantic circles within their hunt. The soldiers were everywhere now.

This was no longer a pickle. This was terrifying. My heart banged and throbbed against my ribs so hard they felt splintered. Rían sidestepped around the small circle, his chest rising no matter how hard he tried to stifle it with heavy breaths. And, suddenly, trust came easily; he had truly planned to help me. This situation was not one he ever wanted to be in. "They are the Great Goddess's private soldiers," he spoke quickly. "The Fir na Solas. Too well-trained for the likes of you, wildling. Forgive me, it is my fault in seeking the shortest route. Trust, I did try. Any other would have left you for the forest boars. To the hands of thieves or worse."

He unsheathed a knife to free my wrists. If he needed me to fight for our lives, I would.

Time paced itself a little slower then. As he slotted his weapon back into the hilt. The act twisted my gut into a permanent, bony coil.

"Wait," I said, clenching his wrist, "why are you freeing me?" His eyes were glued to my touch, avoiding mine. My mouth downturned. "Oh." I guess I didn't need the answer.

Rían backed away, gently unfurling my fingers to raise his hands either side of his head. "It is a final chance," he murmured. Then he whispered to a soldier who stood aside to offer his freedom immediately. It made no sense. Were these the men of Rathnor? The one who wanted me dead despite never having met me?

They edged closer in stomping formation, closing the gap.

"No. Please, Rían. Don't let them take me! Christ, please! Please..." I trailed off, clasping my hands together to beg with my body instead, ready to offer more than just words—ready to give anything, even my firstborn, if it meant securing my freedom.

With an apologetic nod, he slid between the soldiers and disappeared. The formation gap instantly closed.

"You filthy rotten rat. I will haunt you. I promise you that!" I spat and heckled loud enough for him to hear, but the short-lived anger reverted to fear. Because I was not brave in the face of imminent pain. I was utterly human. Utterly fragile and ready to be snuffed out at any second. My hard exterior was built for words, not swords.

The mud sucked me further into the puddle as I raised my shaking hands. Perhaps they might take pity on my fingerless disability.

Threats echoed the circle.

"Eyes wide for her Bua," said one.

"Ardagh scum," another said through teeth that dripped with plaque.

"Please," I cried, confused by their jargon. "I'm not going to hurt anyone. I put spiders outside—the big ones and all." They ignored my pleas. My lies that already tingled the tips of my fingers with power.

My lips quaked, each breath teetering on the edge of hyperventilation.

One leaped at me, then several more, their weight bearing down as they grappled me to the ground. No swords were drawn; no power was unleashed.

"Please!" I thrashed, splashing water and gargling the dead flies and grime that slid down my throat. I leaned my upper weight on my quaking hands. The anger and fear I expected to ignite in my chest and coarse my veins with power wouldn't come. Because all my body handed me was an urge to surrender...to be free from pain, and the fastest way to do that was simply to let them kill me quickly.

A woman with Celtic knots across her breastplate ordered, "Take her to the Carraig. Rathnor will determine her fate."

"Help," I shrieked, over and over.

A heavy kick to my spine smacked me into the puddle for good. I had nothing left to give. No reason to fight. Summoning my last ounce of strength, I twisted sideways for a final, ragged breath of air. Before it ever reached my lungs, something hard whacked the back of my head. Dulling my shrieks.

Then wet warmth began to pool through my hair until consciousness faded to nothing, leaving me in the haze of silent oblivion.

8

CADAVEROUS HIPPY

The stillness of a hard surface woke me, so frigid it bit my cheek. I pressed my freed, icy hands against foreign ground to sit. Each breath burned my lungs and seized my back right down into my deep tissue that felt two-ply at this point.

"Ugh."

I flexed my mangled hand until the tendons called their limit. The stumps got achy and sensitive when cold from all the nerve damage. But if I tried to caress any warmth into them, even now, muscle memory tried to touch the tips. It made me nauseous, like my brain couldn't figure out fast enough why they weren't there anymore, which was just as bad as the residual pain. Still, pain had been my only long-term friend, and I didn't want that to leave, either.

Slivers of orange light crept through bars from a bleak hallway. I scurried backwards, my fretting echoes in tow. I met a wall with a *thump* as I squinted in the poor light to scan the room: a wall, another wall, a chamber pot.

Nothing else. No way out. No hope.

My pulsating head shook against the grainy wall. Either I'd lost my mind, or the community who'd taken me had—both situations I'd once again landed *myself* in.

This can't be happening. Nope. Mm-hmm. Not happening.

I clawed my chest. As though irrationally trying to mend my rapidly beating heart with my literal hands would ease the discomfort.

I'd felt this exact way once before: when I was six, I went to a mega car boot sale with Mollie. It was a hot day, and the vendors were charging double for water bottles for profit. Mollie was bartering for a ceramic mug a little too bold in her approach; her fingers tugging at a round man's coat tassels while I was tugging at her leg, insisting, "*Come look at the bubble machine. Please, Mammy.*" Never one for patience, I stomped away in my cute cord dungarees. When I returned to the mug stand, she was gone. Fear and panic *blinded* me. My vision was just black spots. Then came the wailing. The isolation. The genuine belief I'd never be found. And it was as if that belief had somehow imprinted on my sense of self—even as an adult.

A distant dripping brought me back to the room. The difference was my mother wasn't going to find me this time.

Breathing in the cell's sickly taste, I snapped my jaw shut.

Don't do it. Don't swallow. Breathe through your nose.

The reflex kicked in anyway. Instant regret. The burn of the awful air filled my throat. "No fucking way..." I gagged, tongue reeling over my lips. "...am I staying in here." I peeled off my bloodstained windbreaker, wincing as I dumped it in the corner. My loose white top beneath was grimy and stretched, but it would have to do. Besides, it wasn't as if I was known for upholding any sense of decorum.

I touched my way to the bars with outstretched hands and barefooted steps on grit. "Hello," I called to the echoing hallway. "Is anybody there?"

Silence answered; the panicked isolation pressed tears into my eyes. I jutted my jaw harder in retaliation. Surrendering to fear wouldn't get me out. Because I was many things—many awful things—but *weak* was never one of them.

"Hello," I called again, my tone stronger. Reinforced with determination. "I need help. And well...the smell in here is shocking."

"*Shh*," called a voice.

I pressed against the bars so hard my few curves slugged through the gaps. "Yes! Can you help me?" I whispered urgently into the darkness.

A faint light sparked from the close cell opposite, held by a kneeling figure: a gaunt, grey-bearded man. The strange light illuminated my cell a bright green as he stood to hang a hexagonal crystal on a rusted hook.

I reached for his thick, ragged, red robe with both hands to pull him in close, but he was just out of reach, the frays of fabric tickling the tips of my fingers. "You have to help me," I pleaded. Or was I shouting? "I don't know where I am. I literally don't understand what the hell is happening to me."

His hands batted in gentle waves. "Do not fear. I am Finegas. I will guide you, youngling," he whispered in Gaeilge, just as Rían had.

Finegas' words, the quiet, soothing tone of them, the unalarming way he carried himself, rested a weighted calm over me. He glanced down the hallway, sweat collecting in his forehead wrinkles, although his herbaceous aroma masked any form of body odour. The poor man. Even within his large robes, his frame was little more than bone.

I followed his gaze to the darkness but saw nothing.

"Why are you in here?" My echo bounced through the passageway like a ghost's lament.

"Disobedience. I believe it is my twentieth year of imprisonment."

I swore he shrugged as if the sentence were a mere inconvenience. Then he brought his hands to lines for lips, words lingering on them. "Three secrets await you, youngling."

"What does that mean?"

"Divination."

I scoffed, half-muttering the word under a breath. A parlour trick is what he meant to say. I needed a straight-thinking person to help me, not a...a cadaverous hippy.

Right on the precipice of giving up on this lunatic, his mellow expression morphed to one of weary concern. He unhooked his odd crystal to stagger closer to me. It swung in his shaking hand. Drawing his gaunt face in and out of the light as he warned, "Worlds collide. The rune shall bring you a journey of anguish."

I followed his gaze to Fionn's medallion before meeting his bulging stare.

Divination again. Such bullshit.

"It's just keeping me on the absolutely miserable track I've been on, then. What gave it away, I wonder?" I performatively tapped my chin. "Is it the lack of fingers? No, that's too obvious. So—aha! It's because I've the body of a healthy woman, but the tormented eyes of a fucking frontline trench dweller." My tone was so dry it parched my throat, and yet I felt warmly satisfied by my fluid conviction.

He grinned.

Finally, someone thinks I'm funny. *Finally*.

Then I recalled he probably hadn't spoken to someone in my lifetime and felt my face revert to its default expression of scrunched up and scornful.

A percussion of footsteps approached, startling Finegas so fiercely his robed shoulders convulsed. Stilling, he caught my gaze. His lips trembled with all the answers I feared I'd never get now. "This is not the first, nor will it be the last of us," he rushed. The green light faded.

"Wait." My arms stretched out. "What do you mean by a rune? Have you seen this medallion before?"

Silence. He was gone.

Though where I couldn't say.

A rumble of frustration leached from my throat as I clenched my hair and spun. I wanted to kick myself for not asking more questions. Or at least for not asking *useful* ones.

Three figures surfaced from the depths of darkness. The leading soldier illuminated them with his long fire torch.

"Ugh, it stinks," cried the woman scurrying alongside him. And was that—

"Rían?" His return bubbled anger in me so hot I swore my heart had come to a boil. This bastard had thrown me to the wolves, and I'd get my revenge one way or another.

He reached the cell first, fingers stretching through the damp bars to tilt my aching jaw. "They harmed you worse than I imagined."

I slapped his touch away. "It wasn't like you gave two shits when those soldiers had us surrounded." My bite could've taken a lump out of him. A trophy. To remind me never to rely on a man so easily again. Though on immediate reflection, maybe I shouldn't have snapped. I chewed my lip to keep the anger at bay. I needed to be smarter when *I* was the prisoner.

Heat rose up his neck, stirring the older woman to chuckle so heartily, the beaded plaits either side of her ears swayed.

I outwardly cocked my head at the woman. She bore Rían no resemblance though she caressed his shoulder the way Mollie often did for me since my release from St. Brigid's and life had somewhat improved...until it didn't. Until I killed the damn *mayor* and somehow woke up a poppy field.

Taking encouragement from the woman, Rían cleared his throat. "We are of little time to speak."

"Then speak," I urged him, winding my hands to speed him up.

He frowned at the rapid gesture as he leaned into the woman. "I told you she was cracked, Bébhinn," he said so loud he needn't have leaned at all.

Deep breaths.

My frown evened—almost.

"What are you doing here?" I asked, genuinely curious. "Or better yet, can you please—I'll get on my knees in this piss-puddled cell to beg if I have to—please...tell me where I am."

The woman, Bébhinn, grabbed my hand through the bars—the one with only half fingers, and it struck me as such an uncommon occurrence in my jagged memories, that I found myself instinctively pulling away, my eyes prickling with, perhaps, an afterthought of gratitude.

"We come to help free you," Bébhinn said, assertively. Not a half-baked plan, but fact.

Rían tightened himself straight next to her, both hands gripping his belt. "You should not have been condemned to imprisonment. It was the cowardly choice to abandon you. Once seeking help in Bébhinn, she led us to this path, for she also wishes to free you of your fate."

I nodded gratuitously—yes, *that* was the feeling—more gratitude. Maybe that was foolish, but Bébhinn's smile also reminded me of Mollie's:

hazel eyes squinting when she worried. I had to trust this woman was kind, whoever she was.

Rían spat at the floor, souring the moment. "The gods believe they can do as they please and we will lie on our bellies to take it as cowards."

Gods? Maybe this *was* a radical commune after all, though I struggled to convince myself of even that. I was seconds from spinning out. I felt as though my brain was running on a collapsed hamster wheel. Having structure was one of the few things that kept me out of the depths of depression. And, more importantly, kept people safe from me.

But there was something here, happening right under the surface of my understanding, telling me the only way to undercover it was to move forward.

To live.

Bébhinn shushed us as she peeked down the passageway, but neither of them must have been truly scared considering the guard, garbed like those who'd attacked me, stood placidly on their peripheral to keep their conversation lit by flames.

I absolutely wasn't going to be the one to question that.

Bébhinn quivered in her inhale, spurred by the sudden horn droning from outside.

At that, Rían tapped the soldier's plated arm. There was a silent command within it I couldn't decipher. The soldier stood to attention with a stomp, promptly followed by the unhooking of his keys.

Whatever that horn signalled made me think Finegas' twenty years of imprisonment might pale in comparison to what the future had in store for me.

The cell door whined open. Bébhinn beckoned me out.

I didn't budge.

"Our path is closing," Rían warned Bébhinn. Warned me.

"I have you, wild one." Bébhinn rested her arm over my mangled frame, dipping to do so, but with all the comfort I needed to move my chaffed feet. Onwards then through the bleak, dripping tunnels, Rían stormed ahead with the soldier. I was still no closer to figuring out that dynamic, no matter how much I scrutinised their few interactions.

"I see your mind, but the boy has a kind heart. It is simply that he shares his own worries of safety," Bébhinn said, pulling me from my itching thoughts. "Perhaps your last encounter marked him cruel. I assure you, freeing you in the forest would have solely sacrificed you to wilder threats. Threats only suffered by the young."

Maybe I *was* lucky to have stumbled upon Rían, which seemed bizarre, all things considered. I patted Bébhinn's back to deflect from the fear creeping up my arm hairs. "I might only have enough boobs to fill two teacups, but I assure you I'm not a child," I watched Rían again. Not scrutinising this time. Just watching. "And neither is he."

Her fingers tenderly clenched my face in a way that slotted her thumb into my lone left dimple. "These rounded cheeks tell me otherwise."

Sunlight gradually peeked into the hallway, drawing a sharp line of brightness over Bébhinn's face. Seeing it, all the hold I had over my fear collapsed, beckoning on my body to follow suit, to melt into a puddle of entrails and guilt. It instantly made my legs heavier, and all my dormant aches rose to the surface, turning patches of my skin purple under the sun's growing light.

"What's out there, Bébhinn? Don't lie to me. It's better I know. Better I have a chance."

"Hush, now," Bébhinn hummed to no effect on my worried soul. "The Fir na Solas await to escort you to Rathnor. We do not foresee the fate he intends for you. All we can do is make you desirable and attempt to intervene in the hope it is enough to spare you. Beauty, torture, and power are all that entice him."

I gulped down the worry trying to infect my facial features and settled for a still-faced nod. It was all I could manage anyway.

So, this wasn't a rescue mission.

Bébhinn licked the cloth she'd taken from her apron pocket and began to scrub at the muck and cuts on my face. Despite the sting of each swipe, I allowed her to continue, drawing sharp breaths to keep me centred.

"It will do her no good. Even an eyeless man could tell she is a wildling," Rían rasped, surveying the area.

She shot him a quick glare before dabbing my lips with the juice of a red berry sprung from a nearby bush. "Ignore him. We will help when the moment presents itself. I make no guarantee, but trust, we will try. Now—" She pinched my cheeks to get the blood flowing, completing the look. "Rían says the word 'Tearminn' is the signal."

Signal for what?

I wanted to ask what her part was, what the word meant, or an actual answer to where the fuck I was, but after whispering into the soldier's ear, Rían and Bébhinn immediately scurried out of sight, leaving me alone.

"What...what happens now?" I asked the stocky soldier, a hesitancy blatant on my jittering lips.

He removed a black cloth from beneath his tunic as his mouth contorted into an unexpected snarl. His eyes had lost the gloss that had gleaned them just moments ago. Only in the absence of it did I think it shouldn't have been there at all.

Confused, I edged away from his newfound anger. But not far enough—

He pounced, forcing the musty cloth over my head, submerging me back into darkness. Then new hands on either side of my body dragged me by my armpits through the heat. Their grips were rough against my weakening thrash. Abrasive.

My bruises roared.

My toenails scratched against stone.

My struggle to maintain their stomping pace grew weaker with each breathless jerk.

Still, on what I was sure was a path to insurmountable pain—purgatory to inevitable death—I was, at the very least, thankful for the departing stench of piss.

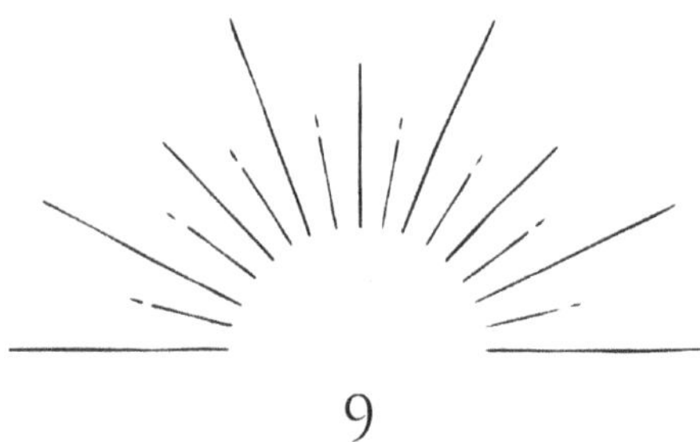

9
SWEET IRONIC GOAT SLAUGHTER

Dark, blind solitude brought no ease to my clapping heart; I swore I'd hear it pounding if it wasn't for the bustle of an ever-growing crowd below. Although exactly where below, I couldn't deduce, too distracted by primal fear and aching arms, bound above my weary frame with no slack for comfort.

The bustle silenced—worryingly so.

I inhaled the boiling, musty cloth over and over, leaving no time to catch a breath between the panic.

I'm sorry, Mollie. I've somehow ruined everything for the worse.

"Witness me, the one who will determine her fate," a well-spoken voice announced.

Thick fingers that smelled no better than my cell fumbled to release my head from the bag. I thrashed at their heavy touch. "Get—off—of—me."

"On with it, Fir, or I will string you up with her," the authoritative voice threatened.

With a harsh tug on my nape, the bag freed. I flung my face skywards to gulp and swallow fresh air. Anyone else might have thought I was praying, which, even in a time like this, would've been unlikely.

How much simpler things would be if I believed some eternal, ethereal being was out there watching over me. Then again, to be cursed was one thing, but to *know* your creator chose to bestow such a cruel thing onto your soul...no. My dissident mindset was for the best.

I strained my eyes against the sun's glaring light to offset its sting. Accustomed to darkness, it was a slow adjustment as I began to discern the hundreds if not thousands of villagers gathered in the open plain below the Carraig. Yes, that's what Rían had called it—the Carraig. And I had been sentenced to its crypts.

The villagers' weary faces tilted upwards, staring at me as I stood on what seemed to be the temple's top tier. Glancing down from the sheer height of the wide steps leading to the crowd made my head spin.

Was I their goat awaiting its sweet sacrifice to the gods?

Right this damn instant was the time to screech for mercy I never deserved. But knowing Rían was waiting on the sidelines kept me remotely calm. Or at least it portrayed my exterior as such. My insides were somersaulting. Pulsing, despite the fact that for some insane reason, I was choosing to trust him against my better judgement all over again. Still, I latched onto that like a hungry newborn for lack of other options.

That latch slightly wavered along with my chin when a lean man approached with unnecessary suave. His feline grin nearly touched his dark curls; the ink of Celtic knots spun across the neck he stroked. Completing his look was bronze armour and a sapphire tartan cloak. I deduced—much easier than I had my bearings—that this was likely a cruel man.

I'd met enough of those over the years to smell the narcissism a mile away. I often thought they smelled it themselves and enjoyed forcing people to suffer its stench for their own sadistic pleasure.

"It pleases me you could join us." The man spoke loud enough for all to hear. And though he didn't wear enough wrinkles to show experience, I was sure this was their leader—Rathnor.

"Tell me, person of Ardagh, why do you invade our lands?" He inched toward me, awaiting a response I didn't have.

I looked out to the crowd feeling as though I had only been let in on half the plan. Where was Rían?

Rathnor jumped to my step, his cloak following.

Unwillingingly sucked into his personal space, I pressed back into the pole. His taunting, muddy stare gripped me, not swaying to soldiers lining the steps or the growing crowd he clearly revelled in. Instead, it pinned me, pressing a weight so strong onto my body I could hardly find my breath. "It seems seeking penance is beyond you."

He pressed my lips with his coarse thumb, quenching the retaliation lurching on the tip of my tongue.

It was for the best. The words in my mental reserve were harsh enough to sear skin. I slid my tongue along the back of my teeth. I had to remember this wasn't some local scumbag I wanted to squabble with for skipping the post office queue. This was someone who played rigged games.

He unsheathed a knife, coming closer again. Its edge pressed to my lip. "I am not one to be ignored." He jabbed, and the skin punctured like a ripe berry, draining warm juice—a beacon of my internal anguish.

The sting watered my eyes, accelerated my heart, but I *refused* to clench.

"Please, pretty one, if you wish to cry..." The scent of mint leaves on his tongue trickled into my mouth like a kiss without consent. "I will not judge." He smirked, salivating over the torment I desperately tried to contain. It was slipping. Slipping. *Slipping.*

Fighting my bounds, fighting the opaque layer of tears blurring my vision, I leaned closer to him, unblinking, defiant and lathered in sweat. Then I pressed my lips to worsen the bleed. Let it dribble down my chin.

"Here," he said, breaking his fleeting moment of marvel to snatch my hair. "Let me help assist with this mess." He tilted my head back to lick the blood, his sloppy tongue curving into the groove of my chin right up to the wound itself. The tears I'd been holding erupted. My stomach heaved. Tensed all my hidden abs.

My very nature to speak up overshadowed any route to safety. "Put. That. Tongue. Back in your mouth. Or first chance I get, I'll cut it off," I warned—slowly. His face stiffened, fuelling my venom. "I won't care about your gurgling screams. I've heard worse—I really have. And when you die from choking on your own blood, I'll shove your tongue up your hole. So that you'll know in your last fucking breath, people will laugh at your corpse. All your accolades will be overshadowed in history by your branding as the man who died with his own tongue up his arse," I threatened with full delusional intent.

Taken aback, his grasp on the knife slightly faltered, though he quickly recovered, turning to address the crowd with a blazing smile. "She speaks."

The crowd heckled nothings, no sooner dying down as he held a fist to silence them.

"That's right, I speak," I announced.

And I know I rattled you, you bastard.

I spat the blood that had been pooling on the inlay of my lips.

He smirked. "I ask a final time: why are you here, Ardagh scum?"

Saying I'd never heard of Ardagh felt...unfavourable.

"Answer me!" He squeezed my cheeks to pry open my mouth, his wormy fingers pinching at my tongue. "Or I'll take yours first!"

My eyes achingly widened.

I battled the abrasive binds on my wrists. Wet warmth trickled down my forearms until it dripped from my elbows into dotted pools of red. "Rían," I called out urgently, clenched cheeks muffling the word. The moment for intervening had *long* passed.

"Ahh!" True delight lit up Rathnor's eyes. "Beautiful *and* clever." He released his hold to direct soldiers who lined the bottom steps. "Fir na Solas," he barked. Their spears banged the ground twice. "Bring him."

A timid gap sliced into the crowd, more out of fear than adoration. Rían walked from its rear but a mouse, as Fir na Solas marched his flank to the Carraig's base.

He bowed his rigid head merely an inch to protest fealty.

"This Ardagh creature befriends you?" Rathnor asked of him.

"No."

"No?" Rathnor shrieked, bowing his body to hold a higher tone. "Yet, she calls for you alone?"

Had I ruined Rían's plan by calling him? There goes my one chance out of here.

Rían shrugged himself from the soldier's barrier, ascending the first step. "It was I who found her travelling the forest. She is of no harm. Perhaps..."

"On with it, boy!"

"She could be a youngling of Ardagh's Tearminn," Rían proposed quickly. "I am told it is where people of maimed minds are shunned when families no longer care for them."

Rathnor cocked his sharp brow at me. "Does he speak your truth? Are you from this Tearminn?"

That was my cue. "Yes. I escaped that evil place." I forced my eyes so wide and crazed my temples throbbed from the strain. "I can't remember how long it's been."

Rathnor studied me, his expression calm and smile lines smooth as he decided, perhaps, if I was lying. Or deserved to live. No sooner, a fake, solemn pout overcame him as he pressed the knife to my neck's pulse, giving me my answer. "If this is your truth, we cannot let you live."

There was a finality to his tone I was tempted to embrace, like I'd been living on borrowed time for so long, I should just feel grateful for managing to get this far. But guilt—living with guilt, that is—was not always linear. The invitation to be punished for it wasn't constant. Deserved and accepted were not to be conflated.

No sooner than I had invited it in, Rían drew me away, lunging to the next step and another before two hefty soldiers blocked him. He squared to them, drawing his shoulders back as he went nose to nose with one. So cool and collected in the face of these men. Still the hunter. Still dominant despite his circumstances. And yet, I couldn't understand why I was worth the gesture.

"The innocent cannot be punished, Rathnor," he said through gritted teeth.

"She is of danger, not solely to herself but to Saoirse," Rathnor barked, fighting back. "My command is final. Know your place. You have no say here."

A rumble of fear surged in me as safety spiralled further out of reach. My last line of defence was failing. The veil between life and death was closing, and what? I was *choosing* to be idle to that prospect?

Fear sparked my pulsing power to life, always starting low, tingling, floating in my core until rising like the beat of a fervent drum. It flowed through me, quickening and thickening my veins all the way to the tips of my bound fingers and stumps. Yet, even in restraint, Rathnor's knife began to rattle against my neck, battling against the force of power, guided more by instinct than my command. Just this once, I needed the curse to listen!

Rathnor caught my gaze. There was a sharpness to it I couldn't explain as he shifted between me and the blade he was losing control of.

Breath couldn't find me as the growing pins and needles stomped on my palms so hard they ached. It was coming—

His arm bent, and the knife released from his fighting grasp, skimming over the temple's drop behind us. He stared at the ledge for a long moment before drifting back to me, to my trembling lips that had no answer for whatever played in his mind.

I audibly gulped. If I was screwed before, this would be the final nail in my shoddy coffin.

Rathnor abandoned his firm stare, eyes lighting up excitedly as I sought any stream of words to come from my gaping mouth. I couldn't say it was the curse. That it was getting worse since I'd left my actual Tearminn.

He grinned and rolled his shoulders, cracked his neck before bringing his lips to the cusp of my ear. "You *are* a rarity," he swooned in a hush.

I recoiled, setting my jaw upright. But however much I despised this man, we shared something now. He was the single living person in the world to know my secret.

"I call on you, Rathnor," came a voice from the crowd, tearing us from our seclusion.

Rathnor's curious attention strayed to the woman who'd stepped forward.

Bébhinn.

His tattooed neck recoiled. "Who are you to address me?"

"No, Bébhinn," Rían called. "You are not—"

"I will take the girl into my home." Bébhinn tapped her chest as she called up, "Teach her to understand our way of life. Past events prove this can be achieved."

Her selflessness filled me with recurring, warm gratitude like a mother's knitted blanket.

Rathnor's slow, curling smile overshadowed the gesture. "What if she slaughters your youngling? She is a blackened fruit!" he seethed, emphasising each word.

Bébhinn pushed her shoulders back, brave and fierce in her stance. Her sleeves were rolled now in the heat, displaying her own Celtic knots of blue ink twisting around her forearms. She reminded me of Queen Medb. "This is Saoirse, the land of freedom. A place where compassion should trump power. Let me not remind you of who truly rules these lands. The pure Tuatha Dé Danann. The five and beyond. You are but the underruler, here to carry out their commands since the departure."

As if catching her threat in the wind, Rathnor's mouth hung agape. No longer ready to spew more hatred-laced taunts.

The Tuatha Dé Dannan were the ancient gods of Ireland. The gods Fionn had adored in his bizarre and wonderful way. The immortal clan I'd read about not two days ago. What did this mean? There wasn't time to dwell. Rathnor descended the steps, heavy-handedly drawing a longsword. The glint of his weapon against sunlight momentarily blinded me.

Bébhinn staggered onto her bottom only to be met with a wall of cowering arms and torsos. "Rathnor, I have committed no crime." Face dipped into her shoulder, her tremor-filled eyes remained steadfastly locked on him, unable to be torn away.

With his back facing me, I could still easily picture his maniacal smile as he took pleasure in provoking fear.

I wrenched my wrists harder against the binds, worsening the chafe I feared had stripped layers of skin and tissue.

"Who said you committed a crime, Bébhinn?" He flailed both his free hand and sword in the air. "Not I." Laughing to the timid crowd, it quickly morphed to that of eerie indifference. He pointed his sword at her heaving chest.

"Please, Rathnor," she begged. "I will not question your ruling."

"Indeed. The dead do not question," he taunted in a cruel breath.

He raised his glinting weapon, ready to puncture her core.

Bébhinn's rattling hands blocked her face.

My own, still echoing with power, broke free from the rope just in time to have me collapse to my aching knees, sadistically unable to tear my eyes from the inevitable massacre.

"Halt!" A man galloped through the parting crowd on a white-spotted horse, a trail of dust clouding his wake. His off-white shirt was filled with muscular shoulders—muscular everything. The markings of black warrior paint clawed his face but not even that could mask his apparent anger. He effortlessly jumped from the slowing horse, bending his knees as he met the soil so hard I swore the ground rumbled—or at the very least it caused my thighs to.

Rathnor tutted, threw his eyes to the sky at the interruption in such a moment of personal glory. "Welcome home, Caolann. Or should I name thee '*Man of the People*'?"

"What treacherous antics have you committed in my absence?" The warrior squared to him; his jaw tensed in what looked like self-restraint.

Although I wasn't familiar with the emotional trait. Act-now, regret-later was more my thing.

"Heel, boy!" Rathnor ordered. "Know your place."

The warrior clenched both sides of Rathnor's face, wildly bashing their foreheads and dissipating my theory of restraint. Rathnor staggered back from the blow and spray of blood. Absent of mercy, Caolann doubled down and swung for his eye whole-fisted and primitively grunting.

Rathnor fell into the Carraig's bottom steps, bloodied on the ledge of his brow. Even heaped and displaced, he'd managed to cling to his sword amidst the rubble of the step that had somehow crumbled around him.

"Impossible," I gasped.

Pushing past the line of Fir na Solas restraining him, Rían joined the warrior, gripping his arm in tight solidarity. "Brother, he wishes to slaughter Bébhinn. Save her. Save them both."

"Rían. Take—Bébhinn." The warrior's breath was steaming as his gaze firmly fixed on Rathnor.

He had called him brother—a fact I couldn't unsee now. Apart from size, the resemblance was uncanny.

Rían helped Bébhinn to her feet to retreat as Rathnor found his own; he raised his sword to parry.

"She has never committed a crime in these lands," the warrior spat. "Without her this village would surely starve. You *cannot* invade Saoirse and slaughter whomever you wish. This village will be barren by your hands if you continue. And in the name of the Tuatha Dé Danann, who then do you rule?"

Rathnor spat blood into the dirt, grinning with red-stained teeth. "It is I who holds the authority here, Caolann," he boasted as if he hadn't just taken a beating.

The warrior stopped mere inches from Rathnor's haughty smile. "And I know the law!" he shouted, spit flying from his mouth. "These people deserve protection, not a man who boasts his cruelty."

Rathnor sheathed his sword and performatively dusted the edge of his cloak, pretending he was tired of this game. Like it was a fair fight despite getting his arse kicked. "Oh, Caolann, they may adore you, but you are given command by *her* just as I am, and we both know our morals are as brittle as the branches of an Elder tree."

"Bébhinn lives," Caolann demanded.

Rathnor drew his attention to me, licking his bloody lips. "I will take just the girl, then. It would be a shame to slaughter such a wild and powerful beauty."

The way he called me a girl and not a woman made me feel prune-like, sucked of all autonomy. How dare he infantilize me into the narrative of whatever sick future plans he had.

I reverted my stare to Caolann. Would he save me from Rathnor, too? Did he have his brother's guts? He took me in his regard, but the distance was too far to form even the slightest connection or manipulation. A flutter of the eyes would simply look like a blink. And as skilled as I was at seduction, a flutter might not cut it when trying to save myself from eventual death.

Rían stepped to his brother again, fingers locked onto the side of his neck. "He will do no good with her. His pile of women's bodies runs higher than this temple."

"Yield, brother," Caolann said through clenched teeth.

Rían stood firm though nowhere near his height. "She is of *Ardagh* blood." Their heated exchange was too far to hear the rest as firm stares and heavy pushes went on for what felt like a lifetime. But it *was* enough time to know this was my last chance. Everything hinged on the virtue of two brothers who couldn't agree on the value of my life.

Finally settling with no clear conclusion of who had won, Caolann addressed Rathnor, "The innocent cannot be punished. Rían tells me no crime has been committed. Release the wildling to Bébhinn."

Sparse members of the crowd rallied to echo him. "The innocent cannot be punished."

A heavy sigh of relief bellowed from me so hard, I thought my lungs might become displaced and saggy.

Thank you, Rían.

Rathnor mockingly curtsied to Caolann. I was sure both their egos were bruised if not feeling a little delicate. "Be it then, if you wish so desperately for this woman to live, may it now be the burden of you and your brother to keep her from trouble. On your heads will the punishment come."

Oh no.

"And make no mistake," he said, his voice rising for the crowd, "the punishments of this land come in gluttonous portions. If she takes so much as a grain of salt without an equal offering, I will take your brother's head, Caolann."

Big fucking *oh no.*

"I will feast from his skull with my bare hands and make it so that the gods ensure his name vanishes from the minds of all common folk until his pitiful life is utterly forgotten." Rathnor spun to me, running a finger over his lips as he called up in a false act of adoration. "So, I suggest you keep an eye on this one. At least she is not a sight for sore eyes."

"The gods forsake me!" Caolann's body heaved with fury as the regret hardened his expression. And yet, I couldn't blame him when staying out of trouble was not my forte.

"I count the moons until we cross paths once more, maimed one," Rathnor said, that disgusting grin of his twisting his feline mouth. He bowed, and a gust of wind enshrouded my face with damp hair. In the settle of dust, he was gone, vanished from existence on the wind's back, leaving nothing but a browning patch of grass where he stood.

I wheezed a shallow gasp and staggered onto my bottom.

This...this place wasn't possible. What Rathnor did wasn't possible. I knew impossible. I'd lived with it for five years.

I hooked those brothers in my gaze once more before looking out beyond a horizon I didn't recognize.

Yes. I knew my gut and intuition more than I knew sanity. I led with it, and all signals were directing me to the same conclusion: this place wasn't home. It didn't even *smell* like home. It was...something else. Something I wanted to chastise myself for thinking. But now that it did come to me, it was an impractical question to ignore.

Were Fionn's theories of the Otherworld true? And places like Tír na nÓg were real after all?

Told you so, you big naysayer.

10

CRACKED NUT

My legs were moving, but I couldn't quite recall the moment I'd chosen to do that amongst the madness of my discovery that I was no longer in my own world.

Bébhinn had diverted us from the village onto a path lined with roundhouses, different in size but alike in brown tones and circular build. Counting and colour-coding eased my anxiety—a trick from Dr. Hannas, whom I fondly missed now the idea of never seeing him again felt very real.

But having Bébhinn by my side also daubed me with an unexpected layer of ease, which was helpful, all things considered. And by all things, I meant divinations, almost dying, and still struggling to comprehend how I ended up here—the Otherworld.

Just the fact I didn't die of a heart attack when figuring it out told me I was stronger than I thought. Having an impossible curse might do that to a person. Having to live with the murder of your brother without going entirely insane felt in a similar category, too.

At least it was Bébhinn who helped now and not the warrior, Caolann. Or Rían, who'd disappeared at the hands of his brother once the commotion ended. Literally. Caolann dragged him away by the scruff like he weighed nothing. I guessed I didn't need to be babysat after all.

A relief, really.

I could have come around to the idea of being forced to spend time with Rían after what he'd done for me in the end. I could have endured. But the older one…my mouth twisted.

A neighbour, hooded in scraggly, grey hair, rested in a pile of straw outside his home, squirting tobacco through a gap missing a canine. He saluted Bébhinn, spitting more into a browning patch of straw as we passed.

Fewer took notice of me now, though the ones who did quickly took interest in other things. Their laundry, their nails, their neighbour's business.

"They aren't staring as much," I said, as if that could be considered a positive.

Bébhinn continued to wave and mumble to her neighbours, unaware of her blatant popularity. "If Rathnor declares your freedom, it is not for Saoirsians to question, for that is the god's ruling. I can assure you, eyes will follow when yours are distracted."

"Great." Little was worse than knowing eyes were on me. It made me do paranoid things like tripping over air, or becoming annoyingly aware of how much I blinked in a conversation. That was introverted anxiety, because I was also known to not give a shit when manic. I once flashed my old principal at the St. Patrick's Day parade without any embarrassment. If anything, it was him who still went red-faced and crossed the street if he were ever to see me out and about.

I watched Bébhinn out of the corner of my swollen eye, feeling embarrassed about the maturing question on my lips. "Since you came to my cell,

I've been thinkin'—and I don't mean to question your decisions—but I just can't think of one reason why you would risk your life for me."

Maybe she couldn't yet see the kind of person I was. Couldn't see that I didn't actually deserve to be saved. And yet, that's what I always seemed to let people do.

Bébhinn swallowed hard but bore a reminiscent smile. "I had a youngling. Would have been your age about now—Bláthnid. I could not save her from the sickness that ravaged our land some Samhain gone. But you, I *could* save with just my words. No matter how small my place in these lands is, my voice still has power." Though she managed to part her lips wider, the pain in her ageing eyes was apparent now. Were my eyes like that, too? Somehow hollow. Unreachable.

Outside the last house in the row, a girl no older than ten with an uncanny resemblance to Bébhinn waved to us. The reed-roofed structure was shielded by the tree border's shade—and as a veteran ginger, some would say that was my natural habitat.

The girl shied away from me into her dress, though her doe blue eyes peered at Bébhinn.

Yeah. You see the monster in me. Smart kid.

"Mother, I feared you would not return."

Bébhinn caressed her rosy cheek. "Do not be foolish."

The girl welcomed her mother's embrace, her eyes clenched while she toyed with the red cloth bow binding her ponytail.

I drew my gaze into the clouds to deter me from watching such an intimate family reunion. Mollie probably thought I'd done away with myself to avoid arrest. And who could blame her for thinking as much?

I shook my head loosely. There had to be a way home. Because if I got here, I could leave. I scrutinised the sky more. How *did* I get here?

Thinking back to those final moments in the treehouse, the slow gears of recall churned through my mind. There was panic. Barking. The chill of the treehouse. The Garda, seconds from arresting me...

"Oh my God." I staggered, clutching the medallion—the rune. I understood now. *Worlds collide. The rune shall bring you a journey of anguish.* That's what Finegas had said. This. This was what he meant—Fionn's rune had brought me here. There was no other explanation. Turning from Bébhinn and her little one, I hunched into myself to quickly open its centre. The same ritual as that night.

I pressed my fingers against the gauge—waiting. The spike didn't come. Nothing. Even the purple liquid had been reduced to remnants barely clinging to the glass inlay.

The second it stabbed my thumb at the treehouse, that smell of sour berries had filled my nose and made me dizzy. My curse never made me feel that.

"Clíona," came a gentle call. I ignored it, trapped in the possibilities and unknowns of this rune and world. I'd need to go back to visit Finegas. He was the only one who might have answers.

But for what? What was there to go home to?

Mollie. Nothing else. There was nothing there for me anymore. Not that I wanted to stay here, but what other choice did I have?

Pressure built behind the bridge of my nose, swelling as if a sneeze was gathering force.

I was spiralling again.

Fucking plummeting, more like it.

Bébhinn looped her arm around the girl's waist and mine. "Shall we go in?" Her touch, like in the Carraig, was a comfort, and enough to draw me away from worrying, if only for the moment.

The smoky house appeared larger inside, but it was cramped all the same: three knee-high beds curved along its mudded wall, and a table stood next to the crackling fire.

A fire hazard.

"I really am in debt to you, Bébhinn." I snuffled and smiled to ease my stiff tone. "I *will* repay you for helping me. Make me your damn slave if you have to."

"Here." She passed me a small glass bottle of green balm from a shelf of a hundred other concoctions. "A salve for your wounds." I popped the cork lid to give it a sniff. Oof. The scent licked the back of my throat with pungent waves of rosemary and seaweed.

"Thank you," I said, scooping a cool portion onto my sceptical fingers to lather it on every hint of injury. The bruises. The cut on my lips. The hole in my shoulder from Rían's arrow. How quickly I'd forgotten that when he'd vouched for me. No, that didn't make him better, it just made me feel more foolish.

"Thank me at eve, for the fields await my labour." She hesitated, holding worried words on her tongue. "Rathnor will double our crop quota."

I froze mid massage of the cuts on my wrist. Christ, had I caused a quota increase? I bunched my fists, squeezing until my knuckles throbbed and the tendons rolled over them. A modern plague would do less damage.

"Róisín, watch over her." Bébhinn caressed her face. "And recall—"

"I know, Mother," the girl interrupted with monotonous angst. "I must not walk the forest alone."

Bébhinn kissed Róisín's forehead. "Yes, mo ghrá, but also fetch me fish from the river and carrots from the market for the Fulacht Fiadh. All families must provide. Clíona's company will keep you on the safe path." Masking her black-eyed tiredness with a grin, Bébhinn slung a bag over her shoulder and left. Watching the door she'd just passed through, I found myself envying the ease with which she wore that false smile.

I twisted the cap on the salve and forced myself to get over the vanity of my internal hatred for at least one fucking minute to put this poor girl at ease. Scraping my nail on the table where someone else had already taken up the habit, I chose dry humour for my opening. "So, I'm Clíona. The one who was nearly slaughtered today." Kids were never my strong point of communication. "I'm sure you're angry with me—"

"Angry?" the girl croaked in forced dismay, a newfound confidence in her form. "Why in the land of Saoirse would there be cause for anger?"

"Your mother...he wanted to hurt her." My lips receded into my gums. That right there was the problem. Always saying the wrong thing. I didn't want to scare the child. This was literally me trying to put her at ease. Although she must've been somewhat street smart and sharp-witted for her age if she was babysitting the crazy girl.

It was the same job that Caolann and Rían had been tasked with and had abandoned as soon as Rathnor was out of sight. Even they didn't want me, and I couldn't blame them.

Róisín stepped closer, enough for me to smell her fitting rose scent. "Unexpected and dangerous happenings often occur in these lands."

My cheeks flushed. "Like me showing up."

"You don't scare me, wild one." Her words felt like a challenge to do exactly that. "Though truth be told, you are the first outsider to come live in our fort since four Lúnasa past," she continued. "Visitors and dwellers lived among us for centuries. Now, the sole exception is competitors from the outer clans of Saoirse, and even they stay only briefly. Those of human kind—from Ardagh, as are you—were the last to come live with us permanently."

My head tilted. The mention of humans sounded odd: a word used for distinction. What else lay beyond the forest? Or within it? Asking might bring unwanted suspicion. It might also have brought me a mental breakdown—a real one this time.

I rubbed my hands down my blustering face, still aching and overwhelmed now the immediate danger had eased.

"Perhaps enough of this talk for one day." Róisín smiled, inching me away from the idle knife on the table.

Smart kid.

"Where exactly are we?" I asked anyway, the heel on my palm taking the weight of my forehead. I was desperate for confirmation at this point.

Róisín's squint widened, and her sparse brows arched. "Oh, you truly do hold a maimed mind." She laughed, more in her belly this time. "This is Ériu, in the Tuatha Dé Danann's reign. We dwell in the southern lands of Saoirse."

I caressed Fionn's rune.

Did he really know of this world? It would certainly explain his obsession with the Tuatha, and how at times it felt like he really did believe this very place existed. Which led me to the logical, albeit frightening, question: had he been here first?

Róisín tugged at my hand, and in turn, something in my heart. "Let us fetch the fish and carrots for nightfall's feast, wild one."

Though I almost like how her little tug made me feel something that wasn't guilt or fear—something just above neutral—I resisted. Wary of what other trouble I could fall into. At least in the house, only mild smoke inhalation threatened my life.

She sighed, no doubt growing tired of her duties already. "I will lend you a basin to wash and a dress stitched by Mother."

"Aw, kid, I dunno..."

"Would I lay my new friend's life in the hands of danger?"

Without that answer, I followed the pull of her little hand.

Our journey was a sauntering one. That was until we passed toiling men upon the Carraig, stirring us both to quicken our pace, to come free of the stench of caustic sweat.

Róisín ventured us into the northern forest, where faint whispers of water gradually swelled, until my ears felt submerged within the luscious sound of flowing water. Until a river materialised. Its bank was mounted by a gathering of women who scrubbed linen as they chatted, interrupting themselves to warn their children to stay close. The ones not strapped to their backs, that is. Others, men and their sons, sat placidly in boats, the lead netting swaying by their sterns.

"It's stunning here," I admitted, surprising myself.

"If you think it is beautiful here, wait until you are free to cast your eyes on the forest by night." Róisín smiled. "The sloes are delicious when coated with a thin layer of moon frost."

I mirrored her without any force or ulterior motive because I was already starting to enjoy her company. Being with the kid felt easier, maybe because she was younger and innocent. Or maybe it was because she didn't know what I had done.

Guilt, sharp and calloused, struck the smile off my face. I flinched from its very real touch. Not even innocence could deter it. It was like an entity attacking me from the inside out. Until all I had left was autopilot, mechanically pulling me through the motions of surviving.

With a basket of a mere three brown trout from the fisherman's haul in exchange for vials of herbs, we journeyed through the forest for the village. It was a silent affair, and I wondered if she sensed that I needed time to claw my way out of the shadows.

Finding a crack in the door when you cannot see or feel it—when the whispers are urging you to stay—was a struggle. Fighting that temptation always brought me a breath away from surrendering to the future the darkness wanted for me.

After several more passing moments, I eventually saw the light I always expected to finally give up on me.

I hurried to catch up to Róisín, my mind a whirlwind of thoughts too chaotic to encapsulate in a singular sentence. "So, what's the problem with being alone out here? Why can't kids travel alone? Surely if an animal wants to eat you, it'll want your friend, too. Unless travelling in groups makes your odds better," I rambled. People hated when I did that.

As it goes, so did I.

Róisín switched her basket from one arm to the other, walking ahead with nothing of interest to lure her. "I wish for it to be an animal."

"Then what is it?"

She spoke over her shoulder, her plush face sombre. "A creature takes our young."

"Takes them where?" I asked with genuine alarm.

Her shoulders tensed as she half-turned to me. "To their graves."

The words, flowing like a spooky ghost story under torchlight, illuminated an image of decomposing children among feeding worms. A shudder forced itself down my spine.

The glaze in Róisín's eyes faltered. "It is not safe in Saoirse for younglings. We began to perish in the forest last Samhain. Villagers question the claws of wild animals or the Giants of Blasket. Oldlings vow it is the souls of Fomorians. They have closed their minds to true possibilities."

I'd heard many stories of the Fomorians—the Celtic Titans. If they had somehow found a way to revive themselves, a few lost children would be the least of this world's worries.

No, this was something quieter. Something that *chose* to pray on easy flesh.

"Hmm. You've got your own ideas?"

She stared at her feet, brows furrowed. "Yes."

Very smart kid.

"Twelve younglings are lost to the forest—most of our village. It takes those who travel alone, and Saoirsians believe an extinct enemy is behind it." Róisín plonked her bottom onto a crooked tree stump, arms folded. "Nor have the Giants of Blasket travelled through our lands for moons. Caolann led search clans over fallen leaf and frost far beyond the lands of Saoirse. Alas, with hope dwindling, he now searches alone."

"It's not as if they vanished into thin air." Invested in this travesty already, I found for every second spent here, the less I could deny its existence. The less I *wanted* to.

She chewed her lips between words, engrossed in her passion. "Younglings are being taken, and Saoirsians are rocking in their garden chairs, spittin' bark."

I beckoned Róisín from the tree stump into my arms to hug her tiny frame. My chin rested against her head. It was warmed from the day's heat. No child deserved this kind of stress. Their companions were meant to be dolls or dogs—not fucking death. "I can help search for them," I offered, my mouth bobbing against her hair, a pointless gesture that might placate her. "I once tracked down a stolen painting for an artsy friend of mine. Although that might not be the same because I found it in my own bedroom..."

Róisín huffed to herself. "No unkindness to you, wild one, but if Caolann cannot find them, no Tearminn girl will." Breaking from the embrace she stomped off to pluck purple bundles of morning glory. But it was no longer her woes that concerned me; in her absence, the tree stump's rings had sunken into themselves where she had sat. Rotted and outlined in black circles.

I brought my fingers to my lips so as not to reach out and touch it. Had Róisín changed it? I wouldn't ask. Not when I was barely holding onto my sanity.

Strange things were happening in this world.

And yet something louder than a whisper or inkling told me I was only standing on the precipice of more than I dared to find out.

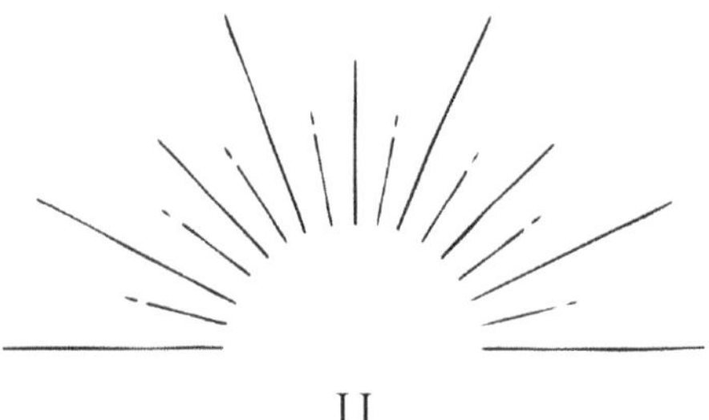

II

MAJESTIC

Róisín and I stopped to rest against a well to hydrate. I had chosen to ignore whatever I'd seen in the forest, instead focusing on drinking glutinous mouthfuls of the freshest water I'd ever tasted from a loose ladle. Róisín sat on the well's stone ledge, running her toes through the grass. The tickling of it seemed to bring her peace I wished I wasn't so envious of. "This marks the village's centre. Danu, the Goddess of Life and Water is the core of our existence. This honours her."

I couldn't tell her a well wouldn't make a believer out of me. That I was eternally sceptical and needed visual proof to believe anything. I looked down at the raw cuts encircling my wrists, considering how much worse it could have been. That was something I did believe in: without Rían—the hunter—I'd be dead.

"Could you point me in the right direction to find Rían?" I asked Róisín, squinting against the edge of daylight to feign nonchalance. Sure, he had risked his life for me, but more than giving thanks for that, I needed to know *why*—the real explanation. I wanted to stick my literal fingers into his mind and root for the true reason when I'd seen too much of humanity to believe altruism actually existed.

That the longer I spent away from him, the more it felt less like relief and more like an absence of his protection. At least with him, I didn't feel so helpless.

Róisín leaned over my grasped shoulder to wave at someone. "*He* will tell us."

My mouth spun cotton. The brother—Caolann.

Oh, here we fucking go. Just when I thought all the danger had mellowed.

Caolann's towering, broad body and tense stare were enough to intimidate an entire army. And it might have been his clear distaste for me or the fact that every part, every muscle and segment of his body, looked carved for the purpose of twisting and cracking limbs, that simply being in his company made my insides stiff and my outsides wobbly. Or maybe it was the other way around...

"Dia dhuit, Róisín. I have missed your kind face."

"Be truthful. You missed my mother's stew."

He kneaded the back of his neck. "That, too."

He didn't acknowledge me during his approach, but I could tell it was intentional. Could see the distaste hugging his betraying eyes. Pulling them tighter into sparse crow's feet. And though I wanted to ask him if I'd turned invisible, for once, I kept my mouth shut.

"We search for Rían. Clíona wishes to speak with him," Róisín said, innocently.

Caolann's tired eyes swept over me, his fingers lightly grazing the hilt of his weapon before reverting to Róisín. "Does she intend to have him nearly slaughtered twice this day?"

I clamped on my tongue to stifle the torrent of fucks bursting to stream out of my mouth.

Fuck you. Fuck your majestic hair. Fuck your mother. The fuck you looking at?

He bent to my eyeline, definitely not avoiding me now.

"Do you hear me, you cracked nut?" he bellowed, each word enunciated.

Róisín stood on the well to match his height. "She did not ask for Rían's help."

I suppressed a laugh. She was incredibly brave and diplomatic for a kid. It was comforting to have someone in my corner. Even if she was half my age.

Fionn was the one who had my back so many times I'd lost count.

But I'm not here anymore, so have your own.

Steeling myself, I locked eyes with Caolann, scrutinising his features. He appeared more youthful than before, sporting Rían's emerald eye intensity. His dark hair was shaved at the sides and loosely plaited on top to loop into a single knot at the back. He could have been considered handsome if it wasn't for the dirt and stubble and Celtic knot tattooed above his eyebrow.

I mustered my courage one step further. "Listen, Action Man." Oh God, what a shameful comeback. Bury me now. "All I want to do is say how *grateful* I am for him saving me. Fortunately, I bumped into the *right* brother in the forest. Who knows where I'd be if not."

Róisín gasped and grabbed my arm. She should've grabbed him—the damn instigator.

I smirked at him. C'mon take the bait. Take a bite.

Caolann spat at the ground. It was so loud my skin crawled at its wetness. "Witness her. How could one of her stature travel the desert or sea from Ardagh and remain unscathed? She has been well fed."

All of a sudden, my love handles sang their residency on my hips.

I shrugged Róisín's hand from my arm and stood—an act that, in hindsight, made no sense when I barely reached his chest. "Wanting to thank your brother doesn't mean you get to be rude or hurt me. You've clenched your fist a dozen times since walking over here. Grazed your fingers over your weapon along with it." His nostrils flared. Oh yeah, I saw that. "I see who you are, too. You'll get no thanks from me for barely showing restraint. And my wide hips are fucking fabulous, I'll have you know."

"Hurt you?" He recoiled as if I'd swung for him. Like I'd tried to clock his jaw but barely missed. Of all the things I just spewed, that's what bothered him? His offence quickly morphed into calm composure. To something less angry. "Róisín, leave us to speak. Travel to your friend Shayla's home. Rían will bring game at nightfall. And recall—"

"Do not walk the forest alone." She pecked his cheek, then mine. "He is kinder beneath the anger," she whispered before scurrying amongst the bustle.

I didn't believe that for one second.

My legs wanted to run, but I stood firm so he couldn't see their threat of wobbling. He didn't have Rathnor's malice, but who was I to know what he would do? This man clearly had some authority here.

"With me. To the forest. At once." He marched ahead.

I folded my arms. "Absolutely not. I can look after myself."

Stalling in his next step, his shoulders clinched before he turned and paced back towards me so quickly, I worried he might mow me down. I stiffened.

"Our situation would be much easier if I believed that." He stopped a mere inch from my face. "Recall, you are bound to me, Clíona. Leaving you at the Carraig was not me abandoning my post. I had to ensure my brother's safety before taking on this burden. If the agreement fell his way, it would be him in my place now. He can be foolish. Headstrong. But this is not the safest path for him."

So, I was to be babysat for eternity after all. He was simply getting his affairs in order first. I scoped my surroundings. There had to be a way out of this. I brushed my finger over my brow, still thick and swollen. Bébinn's salve was good, but the healing was slow. I wouldn't get very far before he caught me. Maybe I could annoy him enough to drive him away instead.

"So, you *do know* my name," I sassed. "It's a relief, really, when I was beginning to worry there was nothing in your noggin' but air. You know, like someone just pumped you up with muscle and gave you the simple vocabulary of smash and kill. And"—I raised my finger—"just so there's no mistake of what else you know, if I am forced to be 'bound' I'd pick *him*."

"Who?"

"Your brother. The one who doesn't look like he wants to rip my throat out...mostly."

"You are not to visit Rían. You are bound to me and me alone. Now"—he gripped the back of my neck to push me forward—"move."

"Hey!" I resisted, but would staying put provoke another outburst? Would that be the line to break his composure and have him draw his weapon on me? My feet started to stumble forward as I realised if he didn't want me as his burden, what was to say he wouldn't take my life?

My chest tightened until my breath became short and scattered. I needed to take a leaf out of Róisín's book; I needed to be smarter.

I inclined my gaze up to him, intentionally softening it. "Look, I am grateful for what you did, Caolann, especially for Bébhinn."

"Not here." His eyes skimmed the village. To the stalls and people about their business. Then his warm grip fell, leaving my little neck hairs static. "It is not safe."

12
THE WHOLE SUN

Caolann led, anticipating every tree we curved around and each bush we scraped past. I kept my distance five steps behind for good measure. This man knew where he intended to take me. Or perhaps a more fitting word was *lure*—luring me towards something beyond the rapidly setting sun that kissed the forest canopy. Its glow created a silver lining, eliciting warmth in me, something I'd found to be a recurring sensation since falling into this world. This place...somehow it made the baggage of my past feel lighter, made my shoulders feel hollow, and the lessening of that weight to carry was—*nice*—all things considered.

Caolann was accounting for most of those 'things' right now.

My legs ached with each step now. "How much longer?"

"Two days."

"TWO DAYS?"

His shoulders bobbed as he continued ahead. I settled in myself, rolling my eyes at how easily I'd fallen for it. But that's all this man could have of me—a fleeting moment of naivety I wouldn't make the mistaking of allowing him to indulge in twice.

Ten seconds away from complaining about my legs being tired, we came upon a cabin which, admittedly, was low on my list of expected destinations. It reminded me of the treehouse but with better foundations independent of a tree and overgrown with ivy vines. A passerby might not even notice it. Which, I supposed, was exactly the point.

Caolann wedged his blade into the door's narrow gap, shifting it from the frame. Then he oscillated the black, serrated knife between me and the open door, gesturing to me to enter.

I stood my ground.

The cabin might as well have had a neon sign that read *The Place Where You Will Die*.

The knife secured on his hilt flashed an image of Rathnor into my mind. Of his blade pressed to my neck. Of the one I'd taken from him. It was happening more these past few days: my curse, stirring inside me, rising to the edge of a cliff I wasn't quite ready to jump from. A cliff I feared someone was secretly preparing to push me off. But the curse *had* helped me on the Carraig; it had almost *listened*. This thing had usurped my childhood, and still I found myself only grateful for being saved on top of that temple.

Fuck. I was in a relationship with my abuser.

"Inside," Caolann ordered, snapping me out of the internal worry. He'd clocked my eyes on his weapon. Of course he did. "If I wished to slaughter you, worms would feast upon your flesh."

"Who pissed on you in your sleep?" I huffed.

"Inside."

I set my jaw. "I'll pass."

"In—" He struck the wall open-handed, a mere inch from my head "—side."

"No!"

Don't push him.

Growling, he seized my wrists, spinning me. My chest slammed against the wall with a forceful thud that stole my breath. I spoke despite it. "Is this the part where you pull my pants down?"

He stilled, gripping my unhealed wrists firmer. I swallowed back the pain as his weight pressed against me tighter and *tighter* until I broke, a soft shriek escaping my lips.

He kicked the inlay of my ankles, forcing my stance to widen as he whispered into my ear, "Do you desire to find out if you are right in that presumption, wildling?"

My throat thickened, blocking any response.

I loathed the satisfaction he'd undoubtedly derive from my silence. How he'd look for more. But his hands remained locked over mine, resisting their undoubted urge to roam my body.

Was he deciding? Feeding into the temptation of that fantasy?

Fionn was right; I needed to stop provoking people who were probably more than happy to do awful things to me.

I pushed back, reclaiming precious inches before he banged me against the wall so violently, my cheek and lips puckered against the scratching wood.

A shudder of pain ripped through me.

But I wouldn't surrender without a fight.

Closing my eyes, I harshly exhaled, deflating my body, relaxing my shoulders until it gave me enough space to leverage back again.

To my surprise, Caolann didn't fight this time, instead he twisted me to face him. "Be—" His knife was to my neck in a heartbeat, his stare firm and narrow. "—have." The cold, sharp touch kissed my skin. An icy tingle rushed down my spine.

"How can I when I don't trust you?" I said, perhaps too honestly. "I've been stuck between a rock and a man trying to kill me since I set foot in this place, and something tells me you're no different."

His gaze drifted between my eyes. Processing. Gathering. Assessing. "Your gut is wiser than most." He sheathed his weapon. "Now, move."

With my stare set on him, I resentfully stepped inside the musty room. Cobwebs dangled from the ceiling, intertwining like ripped, cotton wool, while the walls infested with mould turned the rounded planks a dirty green.

It was a dump.

Caolann, confident his message was clear, overtook me to dust the spindly chair standing alone in the room's centre. Its back faced an overgrown fireplace that might have been beautiful at one point.

His shift to chivalry surprised me.

"Sit," he commanded, his tone contradicting my last thought. "I ache. I am tired. I am in no mood for childish conversations with some wildling who has little understanding of this land or when to keep her mouth sealed."

I did as he asked, sitting with a thud so harsh my hair crawled over my face. I didn't even know why I obeyed. Maybe because if things went smoother, I might not fly off the handle. Maybe I was protecting him from the destruction I could cause if he pushed me to it.

Or maybe I was just scared shitless.

Caolann slouched against the crooked table, unhooking his belt of weapons and haphazardly dropping it next to what I worried was a straw bed with an old coat of fur. It wasn't fit for a pig. Although, as it stood, I didn't hold him in much higher regard. Next to it was a bronze tub he mustn't have been fond of considering how filthy he was.

"Where are we?" I asked, swallowing the unexpected shake in my voice.

Taking to loosening the twine looping the front of his tartan tunic, he spoke more to his task than me. "A safe place for us to speak. Death is solely the secondary option." His voice rang softer now, brassy but still with too much conviction in each word. It was a tone I used myself when I wanted things to go my way.

I stilled. "Wait, why are you undressing?"

He shimmied the fabric behind shoulders, down his back and onto the floor. His brown pants hugged above his hips almost cutting through his belly button.

"I must bathe."

"Excuse me?" The words stretched from my mouth like warm taffy.

Taking his attention from the twine of his leather bottoms a tailor must have made for how perfect they hugged his wide legs, he nodded behind me to the cramped tub. "I built this cabin over a hot spring."

My entire body swivelled on the chair to look at it. Then back to him. "You brought me here to watch you clean yourself?" The audacity. The sick freak. If I didn't despise him, I did now. The modern man didn't play this game. They played PlayStation, or with the skin above your clit.

I had to keep my cool to stay on top.

Forcing all the muscles on my face to relax, he immediately smirked, perhaps not buying it. "Does my body frighten you?" He sprawled his hands across his muscular chest speckled with hair, running them down over the bumps of his abs, half taunting, half flaunting. "It is often men who cry these fears, not the women I cross paths with."

Moving past me across the room, he unlatched the gushing tap and shoved his pants down.

And I didn't look away.

Until he caught me.

I sharply inhaled and averted my gaze, waiting until I could hear the splash of his body submerging into the tub. When managing to look back, he was enveloped in hot steam, almost lost to it. His arm hung loose on the side displaying the only item left on him: a golden armlet. It twisted around his bicep, easily kept in place by a width of muscle.

He was important to this village, but I still couldn't put my finger on why.

"You're staring," he teased.

I blinked. "You wish." I wasn't staring, I was pushing the fear aside, staying strong. I was...assessing. And my results had just been faxed through; this was the best time to get my answers. When he was occupied.

"Alright. Let's cut the shit," I started, folding one leg over the other while dusting nothing off my knee. "You don't like me. I *certainly* don't like you, or your fancy knife. But if you didn't bring me here to fawn over your naked body or kill me, then you have something you need to get off your chest. Something that apparently *had* to be said in complete privacy." I rolled my vexed eyes. "So out with it, and I'll get out of your hair." The long-winded statement left me so out of breath I inhaled through my nose to hide it. The attack yesterday must have bruised my lungs.

He frowned, the deep blue ink of his Celtic tattoo bleeding into the edge of his eyebrow. "The way you speak is not of any natives I have crossed paths with. If others held better ears, you would be slaughtered."

"Oh, fine. No problem, I'll change my voice," I said dryly. I stood and grabbed a fistful of my bottom. "Or what about my arse? Will I just magically change the size of that too because apparently, I'm 'too big' to make it across a fucking desert?"

He swallowed, but his fixed glower never broke contact with mine, never looked at my dramatic arse grab—which was not how it usually played out. I stared back relentlessly until he sighed his surrender and I, the clench of my bottom.

A gentle mist had taken over the room, curling the ends of my hair—and his.

"You *are* bound to me, Clíona. You must make peace with that. Rathnor made his command, and as much as I crave to plummet my fist into his chest and out the other side, his ruling is that of the gods will."

"You make it sound like you own me."

He frowned. "Own? No. There is no value in this for me. You are a burden."

I sat back with a heavy *plonk*, letting his words sink in. My glorified babysitter was an otherworldly warrior who preferred me dead. Great. "I won't be controlled. You won't have your way with me."

Using sex as a currency only worked when it was on my terms.

He tilted his head back against the tub's edge. "The only way I must have you is out of trouble."

"Then you need to trust me," I said, exasperated. "We can't be glued at the hip forever. You made that clear when you immediately left me with Bébhinn."

"I left you to bring my brother to safety!"

I pouted. "Aw, is he a touchy subject for you?"

The water sloshed as he gripped both sides of the tub. "You do not—" He cut himself off with his tensing jaw.

A snicker escaped my nose.

His eye twitched as he bit his silence and eased himself back into the water.

I loved this game. Thrived on it. I shouldn't have, considering the isolation and how easy it would be for him to take me out. Pin me against the wall again. But slicing skin to get under it and sear the wound behind me so my words lived within them—it was delicious. Cocooning.

"You truly do hold a maimed mind." He tilted his head more to the roof, still-faced. Calmer.

I slumped, fully aware I was getting overly comfortable when I was supposed to be just channelling 'not scared.' But what could he do when sitting in a tub, and all his weapons on the opposite side of the room? If I was actually smarter, I'd leave now.

Too curious for my own good, I abandoned that idea and said, "If you weren't afraid of a villager hearing you apologise, what am I doing here?"

Shaking his head charmed a leaf from his hair. He untied the loose knot and submerged himself whole. About thirty seconds in and half-convinced he'd drowned himself, I stood to creep over to the table. Placing the belt of weapons onto it with a quiet thud, I unsheathed his hunting knife. The blade was almost the length of my forearm. I twisted my wrist, letting the sheen glistening in the final shine of sunlight through a crack in the wall. How often had it been used? Had it hurt good men or bad?

"The towel."

My heart lodged in my throat as I spun, the knife still in my hand. "Huh?"

He pointed to the towel hooked on the back of the front door.

"And if I don't," I protested, wagging his weapon.

"I do this as a courtesy to you. Perhaps it is women you prefer to take to bed. I do not judge."

"Stop goading me. It won't work." God, if he wanted me to believe he was a good guy, he was frighteningly convincing, even when there were so many red flags. When there was no kindness to him. Yet all his words carried a sense of sureness and deliberate provocation, wrapped in the ridiculous insinuation that he was helping me.

I needed to leave when at an advantage. When I had the weapon—and clothes on.

"The towel," he repeated, nodding to it.

My hand squeaked against its grip on the leather handle. The right path wasn't clear. If there was a chance to make him an ally, surely, I had to take it. He wasn't assigned to protect me, but to keep me out of trouble. Those things were not mutually exclusive. Sighing, I dropped the knife—I needed him on my side.

I fetched the towel, holding it square in front of his body with my head turned away.

"I do like women, by the way," I said more to the wall than him. "They're usually looking for pleasure, not power."

He stepped out of the water, towering so high over me the towel barely covered a third of his body.

Shooting glimpses at his marred, tattooed figure, I toyed with the idea of where each one came from. A scar on his navel that held a deep red shade. The three raised white knots in a row on his forearm.

"In truth, I, too, am of Ardagh blood," he said casually as he took the towel to dry himself.

I blinked excessively like I hadn't heard him right, and suddenly the fact he was naked didn't matter as much anymore. My bones suddenly felt brittle and stiff all over again. My fake background story surely wouldn't outlast the rest of our conversation. My overconfidence instantly slid away from my skin, melting onto the floor with half my ego in tow.

This is bad. *He* is dangerous.

"You see now. We are paired by blood, too." His emerald eyes were solemn, unmatching his form as he went about his business of plaiting parts of his hair right to the scalp and unlatching the wooden trunk at the tub's end to fetch fresh clothes near identical to the ones just worn. Leather pants and a twined linen tunic that appeared too snug for the width of him. "Desperation led us here, forcing us to travel through Glas—the desert."

I was no stranger to Irish lore. The Otherworld was a replica of the modern map, a blanket of impossible things lying beneath it. But this world was so vast with its impossible deserts and rotting tree stumps, that even eating a stray berry was perhaps a daring act.

I mindlessly followed him, more questions pressing on the soft, inside part of my lips. "Yeah, but are you really the only ones?" I asked. "This island is small. Small enough for people to migrate to other towns and villages on foot."

"Yes," he stated, disappearing for a moment beneath his overgarment, muddy green and embroidered with perfect Celtic knots along its hemline. "This hillfort is a black spot to uninvited clans. We are the sole to take up residence for moons—apart from you." It seemed so obvious now. His bow lips curled into a smile as if to congratulate me for also surviving the treacherous journey. It seemed he was starting to believe my lie. But the shared connection was false. This felt different to the lies I told Rathnor—more personal. This man had clearly suffered. The scars were enough for me to know that much.

I wanted to ask if he deserved them. If he'd given worse ones in return. Instead, I let the mildewed wall suffer my grimace as he knotted up his pants with his chin tucked into chest.

"Tell me about it," I urged. "What was your life there?" Learning as much as possible about Ardagh to fake residency, if even to survive another day, was my only plan. My only chance of making this work.

"No. I buried it." He stilled. Just for a moment. A fraction of a moment, before lifting his mask back up.

Had he worried he'd look weak?

"I promise I won't tell a soul," I said softly, turning for a moment to sweep my eyes up and down his body. Finally playing the game of seduction. Besides, that word always got people talking. As if a promise was some binding spell when it actually meant nothing. Promises were just potential commitments until someone pissed you off enough.

He nodded to himself, still about his business. "Perhaps you share the burden. Understand we are touched with darkness."

The word *darkness* had me shuffling my feet with unease. So many times, that's exactly how I described myself. "I don't remember much of Ardagh," I lied.

"I wish I could say similar. Ardagh born are forged survivalists. Dagda ensured that."

Caolann really was a man of few words. One sentence and it was my turn again, but I couldn't yet say whose favour that leaned toward.

"Why would he hurt his own people?" I asked, a fragility in my words. What if that was something I was supposed to know? "I mean, I...I never understood that."

He paced back to the table to tidy his weapons. Maybe he really did just need to wash himself. Maybe exposure was the culture here and this was no play of seduction.

"What runs those to madness, Clíona?" he asked, sheathing the knife I'd pointlessly taken out. "The root of all wickedness creates the tree of power. And often that tree is planted by man."

"And when it's a woman who plants the tree?" I challenged lightly.

He blew a large exhale and massaged his brow like the answer was something close to home. "For women, it is destruction on the face of *pleasure.*"

I worried for him if he were ever to see the atrocities of my world. A new millennia and bombs were still going off like celebratory fireworks all around the world, lighting up the sky with limbs and blood and cheers.

"I sacrificed all to come here. To save my brother. Which is why you are to leave him in peace. Saoirse is the better of sliced evil, and I am grateful for their hospitality, but he must stay out of harm's way." Caolann shook his head again, annoyed by himself. "We hold greater words to speak of. Suspicions rise among the villagers. Whispers. Yet it could spread as wildfire would."

Planting my hand softly on his hilt to caress it, I looked up at him, my head titled. "Suspicions of what?"

He smacked my hand away and I smirked that the failed flirting at the very least annoyed him.

"That you are a spy, sent by Dagda," he explained. "You hold a role of innocent Tearminn girl."

I forced a laugh at his ridiculous idea of me. Innocence was for the young. For those who weren't murderers. "Do you honestly think that?"

He smiled for all of a second, like his brother, with creases in their cheeks. "You are wiser than you show yourself to others. Yet—" The hint of his cockiness faded. "This land is protected. It is not ventured to by southern clans, or even northern. I believe you are a cracked nut. The way you speak. The way you were dressed upon your arrival. I cannot place your truth yet. It will come, rest assured, but you are no fool."

Not drawn by the intent of teasing this time, I spiralled my finger on the engraving etched into his hilt, a triskele, branching out in three circles: life, rebirth, death. "So, you're saying I should keep up this maimed role?"

I peered at him as he watched me trace it. *Letting* me, now.

I really was no threat to him.

Just an inconvenience.

"If you wish to live," he said. "Villagers who believe your mind is not maimed will conclude a sole reason brings you to Saoirse."

"Which is..."

"An Ardagh spy."

"Why are you so sure I'm not a spy?" I challenged him, firmer this time, my hand slipping to my side as my body grew poised and feline like.

He huffed an unamused laugh. "I trained Ardagh spies, moulding them from frightened younglings to strangers of their former selves. Trust in me, you are not carved from the warrior's line."

Who was this man? How deep did his power run? I skimmed him over, gathering nothing but a tightness in my throat. It still wasn't the time to ask those questions. I inched closer. "And to summarize, what *the fuck* do you want me to do about local gossip?"

He nodded to the door. "Travel with Bébhinn to the fields until the whispers fade. Saoirsians who work there are praised and rarely seen in preparation for Lúnasa. I will visit you daily to ensure no trouble comes your way or the way of those you work with."

I was no man's puppet. Mollie had conditioned me to rebel against the authority of man so instinctively, I feared it might just be the thing to end me this time. I pushed further. "They trust you, don't they?" My voice rose against my will. "You want me to believe they let you in with open arms, but *I'm* a spy? A spy would have snuck past the walls inside a cart of straw. Hunny, I basically tumbled into the village square with bells on!"

He growled deep in the back of his throat, surely fed up that I had the audacity to do anything other than thank him for keeping me alive. "Saoirsians did not trust us for moons. Nor were we welcomed. Words of you being a spy could lead to us."

I scoffed, flinching from nothing. Berating myself more than him. I should have known. Should have been wiser. "Oh, I see it now. You're asking me to exile myself to protect you and Rían."

"By the True Gods, listen to me!" His fist's edge banged the wall. A crack rippled through the rotted grain. I staggered back, my thighs tensing to hold off the threat of them wobbling again. He ran his finger along the crack, branched like an autumn tree. There was a tenderness to it I didn't expect.

Laughter from outside roused the forest.

Caolann raised his finger to silence my opened mouth, but curiosity led me to the crack in the rotted wall. Orange light shone through the gap, illuminating the room in a soft glow.

"Down," Caolann whispered. He shielded me under his protective weight, his hand heavy on my hunched back as we peeked through the opening one atop the other.

Two men passed, their path lit by a single torch as they spoke too loud for the peace of a sleeping forest. "I bet all fish I catch this cycle of the moon Lindy will claim victory," the taller man challenged.

"It is Con's final Lúnasa to compete," the companion replied. "And the gods punish mortals who bet on slaughter."

"If gods truly punished, my limbs would have been taken the night I fucked the steel master's youngest daughter."

They burst into putrid laughter I swore I could smell.

As their light grew smaller, Caolann's close presence became apparent, his earthy smell stronger and strangely pleasant.

He'd cut your throat in a heartbeat.

"They are gone," he confirmed on the cusp of my ear long after the traveller's light had faded.

I leaned into the shiver it stirred in me before twitching my head away. "Great, now can you please get off me? I kind of need to breathe."

His stare settled on my mouth, his own mere inches away while he lingered. Sometimes I liked silence. It said more than an entire conversation. But more often than not, it just gave space for the guilt. I waited, but...it didn't come.

His tongue touched the outskirts of his teeth before he snapped them shut. "A precaution," he said firmly upon standing. "You draw attention."

"Precaution. Is that what you call it?" I laughed with my belly. "You've pretty much implied you bring all the girls here. Bet you fuck them on that weird straw bed over there like ye're animals."

He gripped his belt. "Who I fuck is of no business to you. And that chair you sat on is my usual preference."

I opened my mouth to counter his jibe—

"It *is* best we sleep here, though," he said. "If caught by more wanderers, we will only give rise to worse suspicions. That we are colluding. That this was the plan from the moment I stepped foot on these lands."

"You bring women here, and then you don't let them leave," I said more to myself, berating again, because I'd usually come to this realisation much faster.

I headed for the door before he had a chance to show his true colours. Or, well, his greyer ones. There was a time I would have felt bad for thinking the worst of him. A silent accusation was often louder than the direct words. But feeling bad for men stopped happening when I realised just being polite was often the invitation.

Not me, they'd say with gruff offence and their hand still on your leg.

Caolann sidestepped to block the exit, his arms folded. "You *will* leave for the fields come morn," he cautioned. "There is no other option."

"The other option is what happens when I tell you again, the answer is no."

"Why can you not submit?" he asked with quiet frustration. Then he inhaled—sharp—quickly skirting a look to his weapons out of reach.

And there it was: the choice to take my life and save himself the burden was that simple.

"I'm going back to the village," I tried again with full expectation this would be a fight. I could feel it in the bend of my fingers. In the clench of my thighs. Fear and anger were relentlessly taking it in turns buoying to the surface of my thoughts.

"Do not force me to be your villain, Clíona," he warned.

"Force?" I scoffed. "I force nothing! And whilst we're on the topic, if you're looking to lob your dick into something dry and uninterested, go carve a hole in one of the trees outside. And if you're looking to kill me, know I won't go down easy. You wonder how I, a feeble woman, got to these lands unharmed?" I moved a daring step closer. "I promise you, someone of your size means nothing to me if pushed to it. I'm the villain in my story, darling, not you." I swerved from his empty grasp.

"I cannot allow you to leave." His eyes skimmed to his weapons belt again. "You are—"

"Bound to you. Yeah, I heard you the first time."

It was clear now; he was always going to use force if I didn't play along.

I should have run when he got in the tub.

I'm a fool.

Searching the room for something, anything close enough to grab, I clenched my fist when nothing came to mind. Goddammit. I guess my fist would have to do.

Winding it back, thumb out, knuckles inclined, just how one of my exes had shown me, I closed my eyes, thrusted all my weight and struck him full force, managing to collide with his cheek.

He barely flinched as I drew my arm to my side, ignoring its wild throbbing. His head had tilted away from me ever-so-slightly, a smirk dancing on his lips, as if my audacity had merely amused him.

Bastard.

My heart pounded chaotically as he went to boot up his shoes, reading my intentions to run. His lack of urgency told me I stood no chance, that my ego wouldn't help this time despite how much I crutched on it; still, I squared my shoulders, tossed my hair, and left with a heavy slam of the door.

"I know this forest all too well. Outrunning me is a pointless affair," he called with a strained shout. I never should have considered him safe. This man who was prepared to throw me into the hands of Rathnor not a few hours ago.

Searching the forest filled with cool night air, I contemplated whether to run or hide. To fight or beg.

A grizzly voice startled me, frozen. "I thought we heard somethin' out here." A torch illuminated the man's sinister grin as his companion flanked him, pretending to be preoccupied by the dagger he toyed with. They must have looped back.

My eyes curved left into the abyss of darkness. The contemplation of outrunning them was blemished by exhaustion. Or just the continuous feeling over the last forty-eight hours that maybe my comeuppance was due, and it was time to accept fate.

A sensation of swarming flies infested my stomach.

Caolann was going to come up on my back at any second, and they were on my front. I was surrounded.

I tensed my legs to keep myself afoot, heaving in the cool air through clenched teeth.

"Guess it is our blessed moon," the smaller companion sang. "The Ardagh spy. Many would praise us for slaughtering her." In sync, they edged closer. "Do it with haste!"

My bones clawed at me to run.

The tall man passed his torch to his creepy friend and began to rub his hands together as if the chill of night had found him. From his palms, a light sparked—bright and yellow. Somehow, he held the sun in his hands, no matter how many times I tried to blink it away.

I stumbled back into the door, unsure if shock or weakness had brought me there. "You...you have power, too." I would have named it beautiful if not for him drawing his hand back to shoot the bulbous light straight at me.

The door opened. Caolann stood out, his wide arms flexed, more stone than flesh.

The primal urge of retaliation surged a power through me, not steered by my hands' guide or by volition, but by gripping fear. The curse currented through all my fibres, beating louder until the blood in my ears throbbed. A golden burst of power propelled outwards to meet the source of the attack, the clash momentarily illuminating the forest in a blinding flash. The ball of light shifted to turn on its master.

I stumbled from the clashing force that determined the lives of one of us within its light. Then I tipped sideways as if the gods of this land had rolled the Earth slightly off its axis. I landed on my knees seeing two of the all the stars. Hazy screams permeated the clearing. It took me a disorientating moment to realise they weren't my own.

"What is that light?" I asked Caolann over the fading noise, desperate to know the answer from anyone willing. But Caolann—both of him—had their attention solely on the attackers, reformed to the wild warrior I'd met at the Carraig. His body raised and deflated with steaming breaths, hand rested on hilt. Though he didn't draw the weapon. His presence alone was enough to strike fear—he knew that. Everyone seemed to know that.

"What is that light?" I shouted.

The volume of my question managed to snap him from whatever fury lured his darker side. But it was me he was contemplating now. With a deep sigh he gripped me by my armpits to drag me inside and onto the chair.

I barely had the strength to weakly thrash. "Please, I'll go. I'll go to the fields," I begged in shallow breaths.

He paced barely the distance of the chair. "What am I to do with you?"

My forehead was layered with sweat. "What...what happened?"

His step stopped short. He appeared confused as he dipped his hand to my face. "Your nose bleeds," he said inspecting the drops on his finger. Then coming back to himself, he gripped my cheeks to see his words: "Do you not understand? You slaughtered those men."

No.

Again. I'd killed again.

"I swear," I managed between tiny gasps of air. "I'm not a spy!"

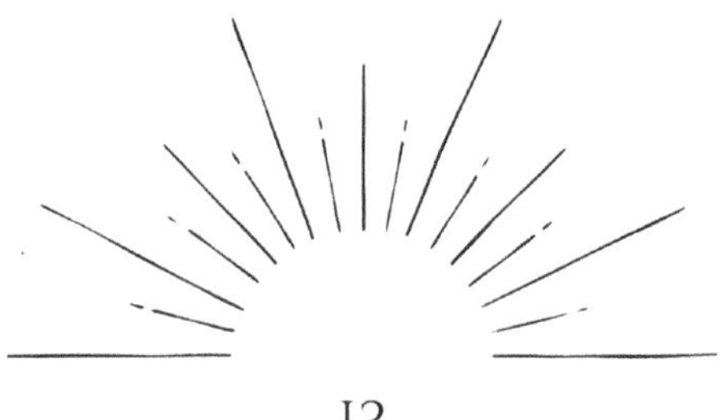

13

CAN YOU SCARE A CROW?

A breeze, wafting fresh oak, fluttered my lashes and south of that, my heart. The sight of cobwebs spun across the ceiling—I was still in the cabin.

Laying in a bed of straw.

I turned my head in anticipation.

Alone.

A heavy sigh.

"Caolann," I called hoarsely, my shout catching in my throat as I stood.

No reply.

A sinking sensation gripped my chest as the events of last night came back to me—the light. The curdling screams.

Taking a life no matter how malicious the owner was—it wasn't mine to decide. My mouth twisted. Damn those bastards for forcing my hand. For giving me another taste of murder when I knew the temptation of simply adopting that way of life was the easier choice.

I scanned the empty room again. The absence of Caolann—the fact I was still breathing—brought me no ease. It just meant my fight to survive bled into this day, too.

Exhausted simply thinking about what lay ahead, I leveraged my weight behind my thighs to push the stiff door open. It creaked loudly—painfully so—as I tumbled into the warming forest where the humidity rested heavy on my arms as I took stock of the area. There was no trace of the men. Nothing. Not even a speck of dried blood on the ground.

I spun in dizzying circles.

"How?"

For every question answered in this world another one stepped up to replace it. But where was I to go for answers this time? Back to Bébhinn? I exhaled in a rush, lips flapping. Caolann may have already beaten me to it. Told her what I'd done. I'd be walking into my own trap going back there.

I'd need to skip town and hope the next ruler wasn't as cruel. I paused, scanning the ground for any sign of blood again. Last night, I'd barely made it out alive. But as Caolann had warned, "*Saoirse is the better of sliced evil.*" Which meant I wouldn't be safer in any other region of Ériu. Running wouldn't help—I needed to do damage control, not flee like a coward.

It all came full circle; I needed answers. That vile man in the forest, he had power in him, too. Impossible things were contagious here. And a contagion often had a cure. There was a chance *I* could be cured of my curse.

I flexed my hands I swore still hummed with the aftermath of last night. The darkness in my power would have called on me to lick my fingers and savour it.

Flinching at that thought, I harboured a guess as to the right direction of the village.

I walked for miles and hours, marking the trees with smears of tiny, ripened elderberries that had infested the forest. Their tone was dark purple, but bright enough to signal if I crossed the same tracks. This was probably the only smart decision I'd made since arriving and it was just smearing fucking trees.

Another mile. And another.

My mouth had become so tacky and dry it was becoming difficult to swallow. Difficult to think straight. All the trees were beginning to look somewhat tilted. I needed to get into open land. Fast.

Finally breaking free of the forest, my achy steps slackened to a creep. I came upon a maize field. Like the one I'd tried to flee to when Rían captured me. That moment seemed distant though barely a few days had passed. The more I recalled it, the more I understood the gravity of what Rían had done. He had vouched for me, and now he was forced to do that forever. No wonder Caolann didn't want me anywhere near him. Me—the ticking time bomb. If I messed up, it was on Rían's head—literally. I wouldn't have that. Not when I saw a flicker of light in him—light beneath the dark that wasn't mine to snuff out with bad decisions.

My stomach squelched like a slurry pit.

Failing to ignore the feeling, I rested my hands on my knees, willing myself to go the rest the way. I scanned the field to get some bearings. To maybe see smoke in the clearing.

Oh.

I drew myself painfully straight.

A scarecrow at the field's far edge was carrying out its placid duties while birds chewed at its arms. It was hoisted high above the grain like a drunkard getting carried home from the pub.

A second flock of crows suddenly descended onto its arms.

My brow furrowed. I was beginning to think I didn't know how scarecrows work.

Taking off in the *opposite* direction of the creepy scarecrow, I caught sight of smoke billowing above the distant treetops.

The relief of seeing the village dissipated. I bristled. A whisper of quiet caution rippled through me, calling on me to raise my guard. Telling me I wasn't alone. I held my breath to somehow harbour the courage trying to leak out. I twisted just my head to find the source of what disturbed my senses. My entire body wasn't long following. The grain was unnaturally susurrating, gaining ground with each of my retreating steps. I tripped and tripped again, unable to tear my eyes from the dividing maize. Whatever was coming for me, was coming fast.

Come on, Clío. Get your arse in gear.

I gritted my teeth and bolted into the vast spread of grain, blind to everything else. The rustling of the secret assailant shifted suddenly to my flank—and again. Constantly moving.

My jolting head ached from following the hissing oats. The sound grew louder and closer until I froze in anticipation, my heart lodged in my stretched throat. I raised my hands, hoping this wasn't another person forcing the curse to rear its ugly head. Or getting ready to shoot another arrow at me.

Human palms gently spread the grain—the curtains for his show. A dramatic reveal of those bouncing curls, and a feline grin that flashed against the citrine sunlight.

"Rathnor," I breathed.

Without his sapphire cloak, his intimidation had lessened, until the isolation immediately cancelled that feeling.

Oh, this was premeditated.

"Clíona." He bowed, overextending his arch. "How I have taken great pleasure in watching you. And you were so kind as to leave a trail of markings for me to follow along the trees."

My lips flattened. The fucking berries.

So, I was back to zero on my tally of good decisions.

He stroked his chin, loose fingers skimming the edges of his smirk. "I am told women enjoy touching themselves in privacy, among the tall grass, and yet you have granted me no pleasure to witness such things this morn."

Nausea ensnared my mouth for the mere sight of his white-rimmed tongue. He was utterly repulsive. Who in their right mind chases someone through a field to mess with them? Nobody. Which meant on top of being repulsive, I was also dealing with a lunatic. "How did you—"

He threw me a sheath of water from his belt.

I grasped it, not caring of poison when the thirst screamed at me. Gulping it down he answered my half question.

"I have many eyes," he sang. "Yet you slipped into the forest with our precious Caolann when darkness touched our land. To my pleasure, this morn I found you alone." Stroking the tattoos of his upturned neck, his mouth widened into a monstrous grin. He relished the control he'd so deftly snatched from me. The taunts. The amusement. The stalking. It was all a tormenting power play.

"What do you want from me?" I asked with a callous tone any sane person would've suppressed.

His forehead creased in surprise—or maybe something more sinister. "I witnessed your harvest of my blade upon the Carraig."

"What do you think you saw?" I challenged, throwing the sheath of water back.

He caught it easily, not tearing his wicked, muddy gaze from me. "I saw power. I saw strength from a line I do not entirely recognise."

Every time he opened his mouth the words came out in twisted riddles. Harvests and lines. These words meant nothing to me. Did he mean my curse? Was he saying I *wasn't* cursed?

"Perhaps with the guidance of one like myself"—he placed his hand on heart—"in all your forms, you could become mighty."

I laughed one long, bleating *ha*, filling the clearing with so much noise, I swore the grain rattled. I couldn't help it, even in confusion and danger. "Not sure what forms you're talking about, but I get the gist." I patted my own heart. "And I'm afraid the answer is no."

"Ah. Well." His head dipped to the beat of both syllables. "It is a pity." He sucked his lip inside his mouth as he stretched his arms like the hoisted scarecrow. "If you do not wish to join me, let us play a departing game." He drew the dagger from his waist, stained with dried blood: a warning in itself.

I edged back, stumbling, but he matched each quaking step. Why couldn't I keep my stupid mouth closed?

"Oh, do not fear. I bring you a choice! I will rescind the crop quota in exchange for a simple token."

My body constricted into every crevice. That word—token—had too many eerie connotations to be regarded as simple.

"Would you rather I take, or you give?" he asked, his finger drifting between the options. "Take. Give. Take. Give."

For all the awful things racing through my thoughts, I couldn't determine which option was better. My mouth opened and closed, but only loud breaths came from it.

Impatiently growling, Rathnor pounced and fisted the hair at the nape of my neck, pulling so that all I could see were birds above encircling us.

My roots screamed and the tip of my spine throbbed. "Get your dirty rotten hands off me!" I grabbed his arm, power filtering into my hands as the pulsing came with brute speed from within. Then I recalled the two men from last night. I'd killed them so frighteningly easy. I needed composure now—not another death on my hands. The curse built anyway.

"Hold steady, nut!" The dagger swiped a chunk of hair.

I staggered away from his grip breathless, my curse fading and my stance wide in anticipation for another attack.

He sheathed his blade, dangling a lock of amber hair between his fingers to taunt its new ownership. "A fair trade, no? Let this be a reminder, I can take any part of you, and you cannot challenge me. Power does not exceed rule in these lands."

His eyes fell to my chest. I peered down.

Fionn's rune had fallen free in the commotion. I quickly tucked it back inside.

"Interesting," he said before immediately reverting to disinterest. "Now be free, wild beauty, for now." As he shooed me off, a windy hiss filled the field. Then, in an instant, he was gone, leaving behind a blackened patch that now smelled of burnt porridge, the maize reduced to ashes.

While Rathnor's absence allowed me to breathe, I struggled to catch my next inhale. I was helpless while he no doubt had allies in high places. And

I couldn't get rid of him; I was left to wait in worry until he came for me again—which seemed likely given his final words. Living another day was the only way I could win his game.

I grasped the rune through my dress. Rathnor had recognised it, but so had another—Finegas. I needed to find him. He was the only one who might have answers. But first, I needed to find Bébhinn and plead my case.

Shaken by Rathnor's violation, I ran to the village acutely aware there was less of me leaving the field than had entered.

Perhaps when the day arrived to finally leave this world, there would be nothing of me left.

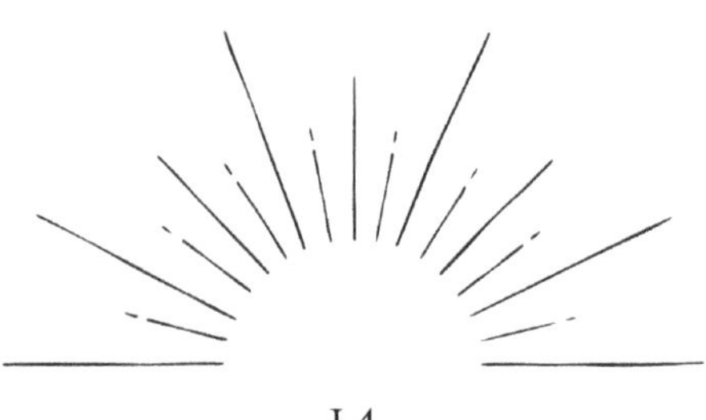

14

RELIGIOUS RELFEXES

My legs dragged heavy with worry when approaching Bébhinn's home. Her curvaceous silhouette shone through hanging linen as she added a final sheet to the dipped line.

The fallout of what happened last night engulfed me.

I took a deep breath—an act I'd done a lot these past few days. Mollie would say I was being mindful and calming my state, but I never felt better for it. More so, I was just a woman with lots of unnecessary air in her lungs.

"Bébhinn?" My voice was hoarse, like sharp foil had been shoved inside my throat.

She pushed the linen aside.

I took an uneasy step back before she reached with—

The air gushed out of me.

A warm embrace. The nurturing sentiment I melted into was stomped out by the memory of minty, ice breath. That target on my back would be a constant, very real sensation now.

"Thank the gods!" she said. "I fretted your entire absence. I saved you from the Carraig for little if you choose to wander these lands without protection." I swore there was a lightness to her tone, as if she were teasing now she knew that I was okay.

Maybe she didn't know. I pulled back. "Did Caolann—"

"Come. Let us speak inside."

She placed a teapot above the dim fire as we sat nearby. Mollie once told me, "A teapot is a necessary component of any serious conversation in Ireland."

It was also necessary to gauge Bébhinn's thoughts.

"Whatever you've heard. I'm not a spy. I—"

Her fingers pressed my lips, immediately drowning out my rant. "I do not hold anger," Bébhinn reassured me, her brow rising with an open-eyed sternness as her fingers slipped away. "And what's more, I do not believe you are a spy. Nor does Caolann." She removed the whistling pot. "Tea?"

A stream poured into my clay mug. I took it into my hands, relishing its warmth melting through layers of my skin. "Caolann came to visit me this morn, before sunlight broke. He appeared unlike himself." The more engrossed she became in her words, the more her beads swayed. "He trusts few in these lands, and I hardly blame him, but know, he *did* tell me of what happened. Of what you did to those men, Clíona."

I drew my eyes to the wooden floor.

"He left you to rest while he hid the men. Hid their *bodies*. I do not know of why you slaughtered them, yet Caolann stressed their burial was in an unmarked grave."

I shot my gaze back to her, my brow raised. An unmarked grave.

"Why?"

"He wished them no safe travel in their voyage to damnation. And so, your actions, I believe, were ones of justice. I walk these lands alone, wild one. Trust, any woman who wishes to take the life of a man with no bearing of regret, does so with reason." She paused, holding my palm still warm from the tea out flat to run her fingers over its delicate surface. "Clíona, you hold power..." Her eyes flicked to me, gripping me in place. "Perhaps it is time to use it."

Power. Just like Rathnor had said. Said it in such an accepting way it made me wonder if I wasn't the only cursed person to walk among these people. What if everyone here was like the man—*men*—I'd killed last night?

It didn't feel like reaching to consider. Whatever truth encompassed these lands—this world—a man with the sun in his hands felt like the surface of it all.

"I understand what happened to me sounds strange but—"

Her brow arched again, sterner than before, if possible. I snapped my mouth shut. "You were told many untrue words in the Tearminn if such happenings worry you, for it is of nature's doing."

I was getting somewhere, but still, I needed to be careful about how close to the line of prying I could come. Being classified as crazy could only cover so many lies before I had to make smarter moves toward the answers. "Has this got to do with the same thing that lets Rathnor disappear?"

She placed my mug on the table to hold both my hands. "No. Saoirsians cannot do as he can. Nor you. Nor I."

"Nor you?" I asked, pulling back despite the hold she refused to break. "But Rathnor at the Carraig..." And in the field not an hour ago.

I searched her eyes so fast my pupils lost focus, barely catching glimpses of her soft, feminine features.

"What Rathnor did at the Carraig is a gift from Mórrígan."

Snatching away, I pressed my body into the chair's back. "*Mórrígan?*" The name felt so familiar, my mouth curved with ease to pronounce it. Was the evil woman Mollie spoke of more than a story? Rathnor was child's play in comparison to the stories of the baby killer.

"Indeed. Mórrígan, ruler of these lands, granted him the ability to divinely move when he earned comradery with the Tuatha Dé Danann."

"M—Mórrígan rules this land?" My stomach suddenly wanted to fall out of my arse and immigrate. "Where is she?" I whipped my chin over my shoulder as if she might appear behind.

"A long way west from here on the island of Magh Mell." Bébhinn momentarily clenched her hazel eyes. "It is not visible to the mortal eye." Her movement reminded me of those who'd blessed themselves passing a graveyard or an ambulance. Religious reflexes, I called them. "It is said to have endless fields of gold and green. Its water has healing powers by the hands of Dian Cecht—Mórrígan's brother. Some villagers say its grand hall's pillars stretch so high they kiss the clouds!"

Mollie's story that last day at home... "*Destruction carried out on the face of happiness is the truest form of malevolence,*" she had said to me. Caolann had echoed it almost word for word last night, "*destruction on the face of pleasure.*" It was Mórrígan. My breath rattled as the connection ripened. God, he was speaking of Mórrígan.

"Bébhinn!" The shout pierced the air. No sooner, the owner peeled the sheepskin door back with blood-soaked fingers.

Caolann.

Bébhinn stood, her chair knocking onto the wooden floor.

His breath was raised, lips parted for air, increasing in rhythm when he caught sight of me.

I matched his beats, checking where he was injured. Wondering how anyone could get close to him to even inflict a wound so bloody.

But there was nothing. No entry point. No wounds. Just...blood.

"Your hands," Bébhinn trembled.

He wiped the fresh blood on his pants, his head shaking before he managed to get the words out. "Fintan of Fire is gone. Walked to Réimse Mór alone."

Did he mean *gone* like those other lost children? Oh. That was a child's blood. I clenched the table's edge to aid the unexpected catch in my breath. Seeing this firsthand didn't make it sound like a spooky story anymore. This was real. Barbaric.

"He must have fought," Bébhinn said. "There has never been a trace, and now, blood."

I looked at Caolann—not the blood—*him*. I had thought he might try to capture or kill me the moment he got sight of me. It seemed there were more pressing things to this man than wanting me dead. I wasn't important enough. Not that I was complaining.

Without hesitation, Bébhinn grabbed the work bag from her bed and bunned her beaded hair. "I must find Róisín. She told me she would visit her friend Shayla, but the child lies. Meet me at Réimse Mór when the sun licks its peak."

She dipped past Caolann who remained stiffer than stone.

This man had buried the bodies of my victims while I slept in his bed. He'd chosen not to condemn me when all signs pointed to me being the monster I undoubtedly was. Which meant he was up to something. And I needed to find out what it was.

"Are you...alright?" I asked, trying a softer approach. One of empathy, I only half meant. I stepped to hug him, arms abreast to lure him in his moment of vulnerability. The nurses in St. Brigid's used to say it helped release a build-up of emotions, then they'd jab you in the neck with a sedative.

His chin recoiled at my offer. "This is no moment for such things! The blood of a child rests on my hands." He shook them at me, dotting the floor in red specks. "This was all I found of him on the trail. And make no mistake, I am yet undecided if your blood will lay there next."

Heat inflamed me as my arms hung limp and awkward. And so, I opted for an offence strategy to mask it. "Well, fucking excuse me, I was trying to...comfort you. I'm not good at this." I spun on my heel to dodge past him. "I'll go."

He wasn't so easy to influence. And I wasn't so blind that I didn't immediately see how conniving and cruel I was being.

"Wait," Caolann called through a deep sigh.

I ran but a few feet, nearly tripping over a trough with half my shin when he called to me again. "You seek my help, Clíona."

I couldn't bear to face him, or my reflection in the trough's water. The guilt was always so quick to return, worming its way in through the suffering of others. "Help with what?" I called over my shoulder.

"You hold questions of your attacker's harvest."

I turned to him, scrunching my face with an expression most suitors would grimace at the sight of. He was cleaning his bloody hands on Bébhinn's linen. Disgusted by his piggery, I forced myself to stay on point. "Harvest? Why do people keep saying that, like it has nothing to do with working in a field?"

He outstretched his hands, inviting me to disarm. "Travel with me to Réimse Mór, and I will show you. I have secrets on my lips even you would wish to touch." Tossing the bloodstained cloth into the piled basket, he smirked and started for the field out past Bébhinn's home.

Oh, that smirk. My eyes narrowed. I hated it. How it slipped out right at the moment he knew he had me. How it tugged at just one side of his mouth and brought a bright joy to his eyes that made them sheen over and crease. Just. For. A. Moment.

"And if I don't?" I heckled, stubbornly staying put.

He called over his shoulder, "Then the bind is severed, and I have no choice but to slit your delicate neck."

I growled—a noise I'd never managed to surface in my entire miserable life. Then I lifted myself onto tiptoes to keep him in sight, resisting the urge to follow. Did he expect me to run after him like a loyal sheepdog to its farmer? But it was no different than our situation yesterday; at best, he could be an ally, and at worst, I could be dead.

"Wait," I shouted, stomping after him with sharp, swinging arms. "My legs are half your bloody size!"

Caolann led us out past the village onto a track just wide enough to fit the passing carts. This hillfort really was enormous.

Our journey was a silent one, and silence tended to let memories seep in, so I focused on my surroundings to keep myself grounded. The trail led us past fenced fields, both sides penned with livestock. In the nearest of them dwelled calves suckling their brown-coated mothers. Beyond them again, embracing the shade of trees, were sheep, goats and horses who harmoniously ate the pasture.

As a child, I'd imagined this world, the Otherworld, to be filled with dragons and bean sí, enchanted lakes and people who never grew hungry or old. All I saw so far was a place much more in tune with my own world. It wasn't mystical in the vein of my youthful thoughts, but a myriad of shitstorms I kept getting pulled into against my will. Then again, I'd barely left the village.

Taking a hard right at the end of the beaten path, we found ourselves on the cusp of an apple orchard enclosed by yellow broom bushes and a crumbling stone wall.

Caolann stepped over it with one swift glide.

I stayed put on the *right* side of the wall.

His shoulders lifted as he huffed what might have been a laugh. Although I still wasn't sure he was capable of such a feat.

"Come, Clíona." Grabbing two abandoned sacks from beneath a tree, he laid one on the wall for me with a lingering, emerald stare. It pinned me to where I stood. Ensnared me. Grabbed me by the throat. He could kill me so easily here. Bury me beneath the trees and consider it just when my body mulched and became fertiliser to nourish the land. "If your words are true, you have braved worse than a day in my company." A strand of his hair loosened as he reached into curling branches, plucking two apples at a time.

I gnawed on my bottom lip. He was like an Irish Adonis, chiselled and strong, and yet for each way that went in his favour visually, I knew his insides were cold and callused. But then why—*why* did his eyes glow with an unyielding warmth?

My lip unfurled from my teeth. It didn't matter why.

I was a thing for him to toy with, to pass the time he was forced to spend with me.

One second, he wanted me to abide by all the rules to keep his brother safe, and now…I brought the edge of my nail to my mouth, now he wanted me to break a pointless one like trespassing. It took all of five minutes until the rebellious tic in me itched my fingers, the mangled ones more so.

Screw it.

I grabbed the other sack while he wasn't looking and attempted to shimmy over the wall. The endeavour was ungraceful, ending with my underwear briefly on display.

Filling my bag, I nodded at the tattoo above his brow to make light conversation. The alternative was bringing up last night. "When did you get that *statement* piece?"

His fingers pressed the ink as though he'd forgotten it. "In my twentieth year. Not long after my arrival here. A mark of loyalty."

That made him twenty-four, if even. Fionn would've been coming up to that soon.

I plucked another apple, too engrossed in my sadness that Fionn would never celebrate another birthday. He didn't get birthday cakes or presents anymore. I took that from him. The wedding he wouldn't have. The child. Career. Retirement. They passed by behind my eyes on a conveyor: things, places, moments. By the time Caolann's bag was full, I'd barely gotten halfway. That happened sometimes when grief struck hard and unexpectedly; even lifting an arm required great effort because all I wanted was to lay down and never get back up.

"Let us take our leave for Réimse Mór." He bit into an apple, being sure to wipe the excess juice from his chin.

To no one's surprise more than my own, I laughed, a soft little noise. There was a homely comfort in the act. He smiled back close-lipped as if even that was a strain against his hostile nature. But I had laughed, and it was nice.

Carrying that feeling and a surprisingly heavy apple sack over my shoulder, we travelled the forest. My attention drifted from Caolann's mouth, the deepest pink and bow-shaped, to the loose piece of hair still hanging by his ear. It bothered me, calling for my prickling fingers to tuck it into place.

His eyes met mine. No. *Caught* them.

"You don't want to kill me anymore then," I blurted.

"It is undecided."

"You buried those men for me."

"I buried those men. That is all."

"Not for me?"

He shifted the weight of the sack despite it appearing to cause him no strain. "All I do is to protect my brother. I do not know you, Clíona. You slaughter men by my cabin, and I am left to clean up the mess."

"Keeping me alive doesn't make any sense. You were ready to chase me into the forest when I refused your plan to send me to work the fields. Now that doesn't seem to be the case at all."

He scanned the forest. Always on alert. "I am no executioner. I follow command, but I would find no pleasure in taking your life from you."

"Even though I'm a murderer and probably deserve it," I pressed, seeking even one person to hold me accountable.

"The moment you slaughtered those men, we—*I*—took a new path. You need to learn our ways before all else. I see that now. Hiding you among fields would only sear a cut already rife with infection."

I scoffed, giving way for the forest heat to press on my tongue. "I'm an infection?"

He watched me on his periphery, and the pinning feeling in my chest and feet returned all at once. "The whispers of you being a spy are the infection. We must dwell in the here and now, rather be swayed by prophecies and the inevitable. When Rathnor spoke of keeping you, I should have helped without my brother's plea. Forgive me. Being away from humans, hunting the forest for the younglings...I moved in the mind of an animal too long."

Every part of me had anticipated another layer of argument, or another insult, or even a dagger to the throat because he finally realised I wasn't worth keeping alive. But an apology? Never.

And for that, my tense shoulders suddenly ached without use. "Well, I guess I can forgive you for sentencing me to suffer Rathnor's plans, *and* shouting at me for getting Rían involved when it was out of my control." He'd come to regret choosing a kinder approach when I was known for taking the mile when given the inch. I was also known for regretting taking the mile, but old habits and that.

I nonchalantly inspected my fingers where the nail buds used to be. Still, I was conflicted, unable to total up this ambivalent feeling I had around him. Because why did he so easily choose silence as his response to just about everything?

Riling myself up, I blurted out another thing I shouldn't have. "Rathnor visited me after I woke, out in the fields on my way back to the village." I nodded somewhere that probably wasn't the fields—or the village. "He ended the crop quota in exchange for some of my hair." Saying the words aloud sounded bizarre and drenched my mouth with an aftertaste of mint.

Caolann fixed his eyes straight, his sharp jaw tense on newly shaven skin. "It will not end with a token of such little value," he warned. Which was better than no response again. "Next time, you must fight back."

I ran my fingers over the hidden, blunt patch and shuddered. It would be wiser not to tell him about me moving the knife and why that seemed to be the reason for Rathnor's fascination. How my rebellious side ignited a challenge in him I think he wasn't used to anymore.

"It feels like he's evil for the sake of it. He really enjoyed it."

Caolann held a branch aside for me. I quickly passed it, eyes down, before he returned to match my pace. "Stories say his father had him sleep outside as a hound when a youngling. No matter the length of his cries into nightfall, his father's treachery would persist."

"Where was his mother?"

"Captured by bored soldiers not long after his birth," he remarked with a dismissive sigh. "I am told she was one of great beauty, and yet in her end, she was but beauty abandoned beneath soil, where such virtues hold no value."

"That's awful." And it was, but understanding why a person does bad things doesn't justify or erase them. "Maybe his games now are making up for all the ones he was deprived of as a child."

Caolann huffed another presumed laugh, then placed his hand on the small of my back to quicken my pace. "Come, wildling, the truth of the harvest awaits you."

Though I was surprised at the tenderness of it when all I'd known of him was brute-forced, I didn't protest the warm touch. Nor did I deny the gratifying tingle it sent up my spine.

15
BUA

We were surrounded—soldiering trees ran along the edge of a large, open field. The grass, even and short, was dotted by children from young to those on the cusp of facial hair. Some shot straw archery targets while others joked in huddles as if the threat of being taken was but hearsay. Of course, children often thought they were invincible, until they weren't.

Bébhinn waited for us alongside a disgruntled Róisín who pulled from her mother's grasp to join a train of girls plaiting hair.

"*This* is Réimse Mór?" I asked Caolann, my mouth gawping. I don't know what I was expecting, but it wasn't whatever the hell this was.

He nodded and dropped his bag by a rack of blunt swords, uncaring of the escaping apples. I followed suit, rolling my shoulders to paltry relief.

Bébhinn scooped an apple, her nostrils flaring as she chomped to its core. "I bring Róisín here to protect her from the fate of those taken. I wish she would see the danger for herself instead of fretting those already lost." Her thoughts shifted, spurring her to frown at Caolann. "You believe Clíona holds the strength to hear all of our lands?"

He bowed his head to her. "I entrust Róisín to show her. It will be a lesson at both ends."

I curved around Bébhinn, half-tempted to remind them of my existence—the person they were openly discussing. The adults were talking, and I apparently wasn't part of that circle. That happened a lot in St. Brigid's. Naturally, I vocalised my annoyance on several occasions, but the nuns were always quick to offer archaic punishments like a rap on the knuckles. In retaliation, I'd hold my hands up for more and tell them it didn't hurt despite the gloss coating my eyes.

"Take your leave, Bébhinn. Workers await you," Caolann told her. "Paths have changed. Clíona is to remain by my side. Working the fields is no longer her path." He'd started to test the weapons from the wooden rack, swiping quick swings through the *whooshing* air. "I will watch the young."

Bébhinn kissed my forehead, holding my gaze as she squeezed my cheeks. "Learn our way of life, and perhaps the happiness I see you crave will return to your soul." Then she hurried away to her duties like she wasn't spitting out a Plath poem every time she spoke.

Watching her go, I folded my arms wishing it were that simple to be happy.

"Fall in," Caolann bellowed across the clearing.

Children's backs turned rigid, mine included. The seated sprung from the grass as if the earth beneath had clay hands to push them up. Two words had controlled them all in an instant. He wasn't just a warrior; he was a commander. That innate ability to lead was just in him.

If he wasn't such an arse, I might have even considered it sexy.

Under Caolann's orders, Róisín brought me away from the hoard who continued to beeline for him and his sack of apples. I craned my gaze over my shoulder to keep him and the commotion in sight a moment longer.

She laughed. This kid and her laughs, making me soft. "It is not Caolann's words you wish to hear this day." With an abrupt stop at the forest's edge, she plonked onto the ground, cross-legged. I touched the grass for damp before joining her.

She stroked the soft blades like they were of an animal she was fond of. Maybe her god—Danu—was on her mind again. "I wonder the kindest way to share the Bua without startling you."

"It's hardly that daunting a word." In truth, I couldn't even translate the word to make sense of it.

Her plump hand rubbed my arm to offer comfort how perhaps she saw her mother do. Only in receiving it did I realise how much I needed any human touch. How warm it made me feel. Maybe that's what I was feeling when Caolann touched my back—the appreciation of simply being touched. It was the only confirmation I was more than a sad apparition readying itself to wisp away in the slightest wind.

"Róisín, please tell me what it is and let me deal with the fallout," I said, barely veiling my impatience with a smile.

"Forgive me, for I have not told another." Her round eyes wandered into the grass, seeing through me as though I were the very thing I was just fearing. "Aha!" She stretched her short frame to pluck a buttery flower. "Have you ever believed you held an ability to do an impossible act? Saw or felt it happen?"

My heart quickened, consideration absent as the words tumbled out. "All the time. Sometimes I make things happen. Sometimes I think it's all in my mind until it happens again. But every time the outcome is…bad. Stained by my hands—or what's left of them."

She sweetly laughed, brushing her palm along mine starting from my scabbed-over wrists right down to those missing tips. "You *can* speak of it. You are safe in these lands. When mother told me of your light—"

"Wait, what's with the flower?"

Holding the brown stem between pinched fingers, she twirled it under my nose.

Appeasing her, I inhaled its soft wild scent, grinning.

She mirrored me before proudly declaring, "I created this."

"You planted a weed?" I laughed, unimpressed by her opening line.

She tutted and threw me a glare that I was sure she'd also learnt from her mother. "No. I truly created this. It is my Bua."

Handing me the flower, she rummaged into her dress pocket—an act that, for some reason, loosened her tongue. A seed rolled to the centre of her palm between two lines Mollie would've tried to tell her fortune with. Róisín enclosed it with cupped hands for a concentrated moment before exhaling, hands separated.

My lashes fluttered, and my mind filled with too many profanities for a child to hear.

But *what-in-the-ever-loving fuck* was the gist of it.

A bell-shaped flower lay in the crack of her tiny hands. It had come from nowhere, arriving as if by the will of the universe itself, delivered into the palms of a little girl who was just as important as anything else the entirety of the cosmos could create.

"How did you do that?" I shrieked, snatching the purple flower so harshly, its petals tinted navy. This was beyond comprehension. It wasn't possible.

I looked around at this world, swaying, letting it run waves over me, just as I'd done a hundred times since waking up at that waterfall. Too many times now I'd seen inconceivable things with my own eyes. So maybe I needed to give myself a good wobble and adjust the parameters of possibility.

"You will learn to harvest yours—whatever it may be—and summon and command it as you please. If you wish, you can come train with us in Réimse Mór every morn."

I inhaled a breeze flowing past my barely parted lips to hold onto my sense of calm. "Saoirsians have power. They have abilities." The words were a realisation, not a confirmation.

Róisín swirled the petal in her palm until it rolled to bleeding mush. Then she inflated it back to life again with no light or visual influence—just willpower. "*Bua*, not ability." She peered at me, squinting against the sun with one eye and a snarled lip. "Sourced often from our hands, but not always. For some, it is a single thought of the mind. For others, a spoken word, a coloured shimmer. All Saoirsians inherited them from our ancestors—the Tuatha Dé Danann. You must learn to harvest yours."

"This is too much," I breathed with stark understanding. My head spun with thoughts I couldn't distinguish or align. I melted back onto the grass to combat the overwhelming disarray, staying there so long, the cirrus clouds came and went in feathery illusions.

Was I a descendant of the Tuatha Dé Danann? Not cursed but *gifted* through lineage. Did something through the ancient line of my ancestors latch onto my genome or blood?

That meant the issue lay with me, for *my* inability to maintain control, not with the power itself. Of course, I was the fucking problem. Why did that keep coming as a surprise when I was the common denominator?

"I wish someone would've told me sooner," I eventually piped up. "I'm big enough and bold enough to have handled it." I was neither.

"Forget not, you are a cracked nut, and it seems you do not 'handle' this well." Róisín poked my ribs with tickles. "We must deliver these words gently."

I swatted her, laughing away my unwarranted annoyance. "Okay. Okay! I'm a pain in the arse and handling this terribly." I groaned as I hitched myself up onto elbows stained with grass. She was trying to help me. This child who carried far more poise than I ever could. "Thank you for having patience with me, kid. Thank you for making this as pleasant as a flower."

Róisín returned my thanks with a smile, her button nose wrinkling. I'd never thought about having—never mind *wanting*—a sister, but she'd have been a great one.

Rolling another seed between her fingers, she lobbed it in her mouth to gnaw. "Mother harvests her Bua from soil. That is why she oversees the fields. I am stronger, for I can grow at will."

"Show me what you can do," I encouraged, gesturing her to stand. "Flower power and all that."

She dashed her eyes to Caolann. He assisted pairs of sparring girls, one blocking the others hefty punches with crossed forearms. Arguments and bickering broke out among them for the smallest of faults. Their youth made them frustrated, but their effort was palpable. Not wanting to be the next child taken was a cruel motivator.

"Don't worry about them," I reassured, reading the hesitation weighing on her frame. Still unconvinced, I leaned closer to whisper some of my confidence into her. "I know you can do more than make one flower."

Her deep inhale and smile were simultaneous. She leapt up into a graceful spin. "One flower." The words had youthful malice, preparing me to be proved wrong.

Róisín scattered a reserved handful of seed across the field as if to feed flocking hens. In a still moment, her head eclipsed the sun's heat on me. With the elegance of a swan, she cupped her hands to the sky like an offering.

"Danu," she whispered graciously, then she separated her hands into curves resembling the bird's elongated neck. When her fingertips wavered as though pressing the keys of a piano, tiny sprouts broke the soil's surface in every direction, springing faster and faster until Réimse Mór resembled an adorned garden. The newborn plants became blossoming flowers in beautiful shades of purple and pink before I even had a chance to stand. I spun, slowly, drinking in her creation. She'd done in seconds what takes nature weeks. She was amazing. My heart wanted to burst for her. Pop with confetti for once instead of piping hot pain.

When finished her demonstration, children clapped, encouraging her to take a deserved bow. Her grin, her joy. The innocence. It was magnificent.

My bliss receded.

How long would this world let her have it?

Caolann offered her an amiable nod, but like every moment I'd seen before, rigidity overcame him. Made him stiff and unlike the man who soaked in a tub last night, revelling in the delight of tormenting me. He turned to address the children. "Block harder. Fight stronger. Fall out to harvest your Bua and prove your strength. You will take your leave in clans when the sun descends. No harm shall find you this nightfall."

The chattering children split into groups, some tackling archery or knife throwing while others engaged in a lesson about building snares.

I hoped to get in another question before the opportunity passed. I had to be sure I was gifted. "Can your Bua be anything?"

Róisín beckoned a group of boys to join us before they'd been tasked elsewhere. "Our power derives from the Tuatha," she said, watching them come. "There must be a connection, often from the pure five—Danu's children. My family is connected to Nuada's line. Some are great warriors and windmovers, or even readers of the mind. Caolann says what is of most importance is to know a Bua need not reach its full potential to be of use." She playfully ran two fingers along my arm. "I enjoy running, it is of use to me, but I do not desire the fastest legs in Saoirse. Simply harvesting is the gift." She smiled. "I see this is hard for you."

At her words, I became instantly aware of my perplexed state. But my constantly gaping mouth wouldn't help anyone apart from flies looking for a new home.

I snapped it shut.

"You will learn in time," she said. "Once a Bua is controlled, content will follow. Unless you harvest for Lúnasa."

"Lúnasa?"

The group of boys stopped in front of us as a pack of dogs might, panting and excitable.

"Róisín," they chanted.

"Dia dhaoibh," she welcomed them.

"Who is your friend?" asked the older one with fair patches of stubble. Even that couldn't hide his youthful face.

"The nut," someone called.

"She is too rich in beauty to be cracked," the shortest of them, a grey-eyed chap, said.

Their excitement and unfiltered innocence complimented my…whatever the opposite of innocence was. Corruption, maybe?

The smallest boy held my hand as I bent to his level. "I'm Clíona, but you can call me a nut if you want, pet. I've heard worse." Maybe I was better with kids than I ever cared to realise.

Flushed with embarrassment, he ran off with his friends while the oldest lingered. I swore he either had a twitch or was continually winking at me since his arrival. His blonde hair was braided back, much like Caolann's and the Fir na Solas. The young appeared to have shorter cuts. Then there was Rían; he could barely tuck his behind the ears. There was a wildness to it, to him, not even storms could tame.

"Secrets you wish to speak of, Lester?" Róisín asked with suspicious eyes.

He threw his apple to her. "Catch."

She did, snatching a zealous bite, apple bits barrelling over her tongue as she spoke. "You wish for her to witness your Bua."

He held up surrendering arms as if her accusation was preposterous, but her stern glare crumbled his facade into teethy laughter.

"Lester enjoys frightening others with his Bua." Róisín sighed, blatantly bored by his incessant acts. "He forgets it is not a toy."

"Well, now I have to see it." Curiosity always itched past my bone, right into the marrow.

Lester winked. "I do not believe a cracked nut could bear my Bua."

"Well, Róisín will vouch that I'm very good at handling things." She nodded in false solidarity. "So, I think I'll be okay." My nose scrunched as I said it, toying with him.

Taking two steps backwards, he unsheathed a battered knife from his belt. "What I hold within is a gift I have mastered."

"I cannot watch," Róisín huffed and twisted her head.

"You scream," he teased with his knife pointed my way, "and I lay my lips on yours."

I laughed—a real one, from the belly. "Oh, you're on."

He shook his free hand, cracked his neck twice and exhaled. Then, with a sudden swipe of the blade, two severed fingers fell to the ground.

I gasped, letting the appropriate—or perhaps inappropriate—words spill out in the exhale. "Holy shit! You lunatic!" I immediately felt the irony of my words. His fingers rested aimlessly by his feet. Bits of jutted bone above his knuckles spurted a red river that diverged down his forearm. "Why did you do that?" I shrieked, too high for even my own ears. People had turned to gawk, but he seemed to enjoy that part even more, dipping to bow for the crowd.

"Cast your eyes, cracked one." He extended his arm to show scabbed bumps had formed where his fingers once were.

A healing Bua.

"Your power is being a fool." That was the thing about curiosity—it always cheated me, and laid a false path to something that, in the end, I inevitably regretted.

He laughed, driven by my outrage. "The pain lasts but a moment. Your creased face will live in my mind until worms feast me."

I wiggled my marred hand at him. "I didn't get so lucky when I tried it."

"I am sure this land will find use for you even with your ailment, wild one."

Cheeky.

In less than a minute, two new fingers were back on his hand, minus the fingernails. "A kiss?"

I backed away into the non-kissing zone, wagging my finger. "Nu-uh. I didn't scream. I just shouted at you for being stupid. Besides, you're far too young for me, kid. And I'm curious to know, what would happen if someone cut your head off?"

He clicked his tongue. "Let us hope I will never see."

"Is it done?" Róisín asked.

I'd forgotten her. Softening to my rare side of nurturing, I turned to cup her cheeks. "Yes, the dismemberment is over."

"You are fun for a fiery-haired nut," Lester jested. "Perhaps I will keep you close."

I smiled to myself for how much he pushed boundaries. It was the perfect blend of confidence and hint of madness. He reminded me of Fionn in that way. It somehow made me feel close to Fionn, and so I guess, I wouldn't have minded if he kept me around.

An indignant girl whistled for him from the archery targets.

"My cousin. I best return before she cuts off my ears again." He bowed his head before leaving us.

Watching him blend into the commotion, it was easy to pick out the strong children. Some controlled the elements—a girl with unfortunate acne swirled a gust of leaves around her body as if it were a protective fortress, but she couldn't steady it for long. The elements were the most popular amongst them: earth, fire, water and air. But even then, no two appeared to be identical. One boy was oddly pinching his arms to incite tears. Then he shot them directly from his eyes into an iron shield. Each drop somehow dented the metal, near piercing it. An older boy, whose width hadn't caught up with his height, broke large rocks using nothing but his fingers to rip them apart. I enjoyed his the most—for his control.

When the evening chill rolled in, we regrouped with Caolann. The grass had cooled beneath our bottoms as we settled to rest under the encroaching shade of evening.

He discreetly passed Róisín two apples. "Rían will bring game when it finds him."

She squeezed his shoulder. "Thank you."

He bowed, slight enough most wouldn't notice. God, I wished he would express his feelings for the little things. He was going to implode someday if not. Which, if he was anything like me, wouldn't end well.

Caolann nudged Róisín and nodded to the setting sun. "It is time, little one." They paused, deeply inhaled, then stood in unison, her heading off with a wave while he called for the other children to fall into their clans.

"What about me?" I asked, feeling out of place now that everyone went about their business.

His eyes swept me over. "You travel with me. It is the only way I can ensure there is no repeat of last night's events."

"I do regret what I did to them." A half-truth again.

"No." I swore a smile pulled at the edge of his mouth. "You don't."

I embraced the thickness in my throat at seeing it.

"Come," he said, breaking the trance. "I must return you to Bébhinn. Other arrangements require my attention this nightfall." He extended his hand to help me up.

I stalled.

He sighed. "When it comes to the safety of my brother, I take no risks. You stay out of trouble, and Rathnor cannot seek him out. Now, come." A command not a request.

He gestured his hand again.

I begrudgingly accepted.

Effortlessly, he pulled to swoop me up, our bodies brushing close until there was more of me touching him than not. The encompassing warmth of his embrace provided immediate comfort, dissolving the chill settled into my skin, inviting me to linger a foolish moment longer.

Well, invitation declined. I stepped back, taking some of his scent with me. "I'm tired of being babysat. I'm fine on my own, Caolann. I always—"

The tiniest twitch in his brow.

"What?"

He surrendered his hands, the twitch migrating down into the corner of his lips.

God, why did that minuscule movement make me so annoyed. "*What*?" I said again.

"So, you *do recall* my name." This motherfuck— "Ahh...it sounds good stretching out of your mouth."

My eyes rolled, but not fast enough to see the twitch stretch into a healthy grin. "Oh, fuck off!" I snapped only to fuel his cheeky joy even more.

Calming and lapsing back into something more controlled, his head shook ever so slightly, teasing out that damn piece of hair again. It hung straight over his eye.

I grumbled a sigh and reached to tuck it in.

He snatched my hand, immobilising it in place as he tilted his head, brow raised with a silent warning.

"So, it's only fair when *you* tease?" I asked.

He hovered, his shamrock eyes unwavering like they needed something from me. Something only *I* had.

But I had nothing to give this man. I could barely stand him.

Who are you? Why do the Saoirsians adore you?

I succumbed to his continued, intense stare; my lips unlatched to O-shaped wonder. His thumb crept forward to droop my bottom lip like a spell had subdued him. Matching his gaze elicited a tingle in my navel so stark, I wanted to preserve it. Revisit it under sheets.

He dipped closer, but the movement pulled me from his seductive trance. It was me snatching *his* hand now, away from my lip, pushing back his wrist with my strongest grip.

He grunted before pulling himself free.

No. This was all surface. All on his grounds. I drew myself away. "Nice try. If my company is so boring that you're trying fuck me just to pass the time, might I suggest an alternative game of tag?" I sprinted away in what was probably the wrong direction.

"For once will you do as you're fucking told," he called as he chased me into the darkening forest. No sooner than passing the first trees, I slowed, smirking as he eased off and sighed at my silly game.

"This way," he said, veering right.

I followed, at least feeling like I'd won something, even if I was his open-air prisoner.

His hand naturally brushed over his hilt.

My smugness faded. This world was easy to get sucked into. But it was also easy to forget I was the weakest link here when I'd spent so long being the one to fear.

I needed to be more vigilant. This was a forced arrangement. I couldn't forget that. I couldn't get close to any man, let alone one undecided about my fate. Not when it would be easier for him to kill me on the spot than to put up with my bullshit any longer. And there was the little problem of my true identity and its fragile foundations.

One slip of the tongue and my brittle cover would crack, leaving space for a torrent of bad things to come. No. He was not worth a fickle moment of desire neither of us wanted anything more from tomorrow.

16

NO FUN, MANY GAMES

Caolann took the lead through the forest as I lagged, wishing *everything* about him was clearer. His interest in me—if that's what it was—was unexpected, but not in a self-deprecating way. There were other things about him: women seemed low on his agenda, and he appeared too scarred to enjoy, well, anything. So there had to be an ulterior motive. Maybe he was trying to fuck me into placation.

I sought a diversion from all the possibilities that didn't matter anyway, finally asking him, "So, why are you the one to help them? The children, I mean." People listened when he spoke, not because of the intimidation he flexed in his muscles or forced through his tone.

"I wish to guide them in the harvest of their Bua. If Ardagh made any good of me, it was how to train younglings," he called back.

I plucked a blue sloe and another, dropping the berries onto my tongue despite their sweetness twitching parts of my face. "That's awful kind of you. Hero by day. Advisor by night. Saviour at all times. What can't you do?"

His side profile, shadowed, edged over his shoulder to me. "Do not name me a saviour." It sounded more like a plea than a request. "I live in atonement." He paused. "Perhaps a prison you are familiar with?"

I gulped the berries with unnecessary malice. "What the hell makes you say that?" Presumptuous fool.

"You, my bound girl, hold sorrowful eyes."

I cast my gaze to the forest bed. "I do not." But I did live in atonement. I'd killed Fionn, and while it wasn't planned or even intentional, it was still my burden to bear.

As the clouded half-moon unveiled itself, it was Caolann who broke the stubborn silence. "In Bébhinn's home..." He paused. "My manners are rusty."

I knew what his mouth wouldn't let him say. What lingered in the air like damp, invisibly clinging to us. My fingers became sweaty, and I thanked their gods for the night's shield on my heated cheeks. "I was trying to comfort you. I'm not *all* stone." He was surely on to me. Could tell I was trying to take advantage.

He hesitated. "With a kiss?"

My chin recoiled into my neck, and my brows furrowed as I came to a standstill. "A *kiss*? I never! My God, you think rather highly of yourself, don't you?"

"It is of no harm." He glanced back again, a bold, unmistakable smirk on display this time. "I simply did not expect it."

The audacity. What did he see me as? I scoffed at him so hard I regurgitated berry skin and had to clench my eyes to get it back down. And yet, if that's what got him on my side, maybe I should have kissed him to survive another day. Although that just put me back into concubine territory.

Around and around in circles.

That's how it had been since the very first moment I landed here. A never-ending feeling of whiplash.

He surrendered his hands, his taut jaw fighting his side-lipped smirk. "I am mistaken."

"Very *bloody* mistaken." Just minutes ago, he was the one teasing the idea of us sharing a clandestine kiss. That was a lot of flip-flopping for one day. Unless he was playing me at my own game. Unless—

I threw my head back and sighed. That was exactly what he was doing. Riling me up again like it was foreplay.

Oh, you bastard.

Stopping in his tracks, he faced me, his burly presence touching my skin like a vibration. "Clíona, you...frustrate me," he stuttered, walking away again.

Always with the one-liners. Always switching from subtle flirtation to something needlessly serious. And I couldn't tell which version was the real him—if either.

His admission drew a long groaning sigh from my mouth as I followed, unsure of his motive or if that was all he planned to say. He didn't seem to know what he wanted. And it wasn't my job to pander.

I bit my lip to keep *my* frustration in—and the berry skin, too.

"You slaughtered those men, and paths changed."

Again with the paths!

"Hey!" I gripped his shoulder, tugging it for him to look at me. Lord, was there any part of him that wasn't muscle? My fingers slid over the cool touch of his armlet still wrapped around his upper arm and fighting the bulge of his bicep. Sprinting back to my train of thought, he interrupted before I could speak.

"It was a simple arrangement—you abide by my rules, and you got to live," he said. "And yet you broke them no sooner did you leave my cabin. Such foolishness. I want to shake you!" His jagged fingers shook the space around my head.

I swatted his hand away. "Those men were going to kill me." No question. It was self-defence. "I don't say that lightly, either. However grateful I am for you hiding those bodies, I never asked you to do it. I'm not in debt to you."

"Why am I protecting you?" he asked, anger and frustration chewing into each word.

I blinked at him so excessively I saw spots. "*You tell me.*"

His eyes glowed in the darkening light though the rest of his features had surrendered to the encroaching shadows. He remained silent—his tongue caught on whatever new secret he had but wouldn't share.

I paced back several steps to plonk onto a sappy tree stump. It pulled at the under hairs of my thighs. Dr. Hannas would say *stubbornness never leads to the desired outcome* and *seek rectification as opposed to aggregation*. But I was over his pesky platitudes. The time had come to start using my intuition. "You can go without me." I waved goodbye with fake grandeur. "Staying here with spiders in my knickers sounds *far* more appealing."

"You cannot stay here," he shouted, emerging from quietude to unsettle birds who squawked their grievances from above. "It is not safe to be out alone at nightfall."

"Well, thankfully, despite not always acting like it, I'm far older than the lost children of Saoirse." My nose scrunched with conviction. "So, I'll be just fine."

His eyes twitched and narrowed, and his stance became still—too still. "You understand nought of those younglings and plight of this land. I have tried to keep you alive though it grants me nothing. Nothing! And even now, you refuse to listen. You force my hand." He stomped toward me, his frame somehow twice in size now he decided to be a threat.

My power instantly surfaced. I threw my hands out to shield myself, unable to quantify how strong my defence would be. If there would be anything left of him but mush, dripping from bone. Pulsing fear forced my eyes closed. My hands pushed outwards, unloading. The pressure swelled, catching him in my...harvest. In its golden light of destruction.

Another person gone by my hands. And no matter the threat, I couldn't help feeling this wasn't even a little bit deserved.

"Clíona."

Alive.

My name never sounded so placating. So rewarding just to hear.

I peeked with a brave eye to find him frozen in a web of shimmers—caged by my subconscious command.

"The soil—holds my legs. My body—it is stuck," he strained. "I—cannot—breathe."

How?

Assessing him and how I could simply let him die, I couldn't ignore the twist in my gut—my intuition—telling me not to hurt him. The fallout of accidentally murdering the village's Robin Hood was a path I couldn't come back from. It was a logical choice to keep him alive.

Shit. Shit. Shit.

I bunched my hands, quenching all my unintended power.

He collapsed to his knees, clutching his chest to catch a breath.

His weakened hand blocked my offer of aid as he pushed my stomach.

I stumbled back, over the moss bank. Immediately finding my footing, I sought to help him a second time. "I'm sorry, Caolann. I didn't mean to." That was a lie. In fact, I *did* mean to. And my curse, no, *my Bua*, had obeyed. Not hurting him, but simply stopping him from hurting me.

He scraped himself to his feet, a wild look in his eye beyond its twitching anger. His teeth ground as he spoke. "No man in these lands, Bua or none, has the power to take command of my body." Caolann drew his knife, a sharp, black thing, squeezing it by his side as if he relished the excuse to use it. "Who are you?"

His words didn't make sense. He'd seen me use this very power only yesterday. What he'd seen last night was far worse than this and yet—

"Róisín said everyone here has power," I fumbled. My arms raised, puppeteered into the air by the commander of fear.

"Not. Like. This." He took a small step closer to me, cautiously. So cautiously, I couldn't decipher which of us he had decided was more deadly.

I searched his face for any indication of what was happening or what to say. "I don't understand."

He was edging onto my flank. I curved my step to match it. "Your Bua is beyond the hands of those I train. You were a spy all along."

A solidified accusation. Not a presumption.

I was screwed if I didn't give him a reasonable explanation. My tongue hovered in the centre, unable to decide which way to bend to form the right words. What does he know about me? I'm outspoken. Crazy. From the Tearminn. He doesn't know why you're from there...

"That's why they threw me in the Tearminn." I shouted the insinuation, hoping oppositional anger would throw him.

Another step closer. "On with it."

"It's hard to explain when you have that feckin' knife pointed at me." I gestured my arms to him, loosely, having him reflexively draw the knife to his ear's edge.

Ready to pounce, he leaned his knee forward. "Try harder," he said through gritted teeth. "Because I am willing to live with the burden of slaughtering you cold when this crime is enough to ease any guilt it may bring."

Lord, I should've kissed him. People were always loyal and stupidly forgiving when consumed with lust.

"You're from Ardagh, so you should understand. Imagine a child who was so—so messed up she couldn't control it. Couldn't even begin to understand it. Where would you put her?" I challenged him.

His brow furrowed deeper as he lunged.

"Tsk, tsk." I raised my empty hand to remind him it held a threat stronger than his. Steps faltering, he drew up short. Of course, it was a bluff since I couldn't actually conjure it on demand. Or knew what his power was to fight me off.

Why *aren't* you using it?

He froze without the use of my Bua this time, waiting to find a better angle of attack.

Ignoring my better judgement to challenge him on his own secrets, I chose self-preservation and doubled down. "You've never been to the Tearminn. You don't know the truth. The power, it allows me to—" What could I do? I tapped my temple with rattling fingers. "Things happen with my mind when I'm angry or scared."

He spat at the soil. "Then you would be a Dylis warrior. All Dagda craves is power, and you are a conclusive weapon."

I'd have to make a run for it, really do it this time, maybe even take up Rathnor's offer if it kept me alive. Or find Finegas and plead with him to find a way to send me home.

"People—people only love power when they can control it," I said, drawing words together with frail hope they might stick—or, at the very least, make sense. "Do you believe anyone could control me when I can barely do it? When you've seen yourself how much I rebel against authority to my own constant detriment?" Breathless from our battle, I almost convinced *myself*. "I'm done hiding, Caolann. It's exhausting. So please, believe me." At least there was truth in my final words.

Hooking me in his unwavering stare, I refused to bend to it despite the growing pressure. His eyes were relentless sentinels that ping-ponged between my own, searching and gathering.

Then he clipped his knife onto his belt, perhaps believing it would be of little use to him. "I cannot fathom my words. But I believe you speak the truth."

"You do?" I clutched my chest, unaccustomed to the relief it was pulsing out. There had to be trickery here.

"I have witnessed your rebellious nature by my own eyes. And Dagda, he is of the most powerful gods. Overpowering him, let alone rebelling, would commit him to a rage." Caolann raised his cautious, calloused hands and again I jolted back. He spoke despite it. "He is the reason I fled and brought Rían to Saoirse, before he could steal him to wield his power. What stirs me is why he did not slaughter you by his own hands."

I foolishly clung to the pounding feeling inside, telling me this wasn't a bluff. That there was something in him, in his eyes—trust. Not endless trust, but for this, I believed him. Popping a hand on my hip, I masked any hint of weakness with sass. "As you can guess, killing me isn't easy. I'm one of three to make it to this hillfort from Ardagh, and I survived a lifetime locked away. My strength protected me," I lied, and again, I'd started to sweat all over.

It was best, for both of us, if I stayed away. Like he wanted. There was only one solution. "Let me go to the fields despite your worry of infection. Let the rumours heal from the inside."

He stared off into the black distance, deliberating. With nails between teeth, I stopped myself from interrupting the silence over and over until he finally drew a sharp breath. "Then it is settled. I cannot keep up this task of watching over you, wildling, and I refuse to allow my brother to have any role in this. Come morning, you will travel to the fields with Bébhinn as originally planned. This is a final chance."

It was official, my sentence for all the lives I had taken would be carried out in servitude in the fields. What a mess I'd made for reusing this plan in the first place.

"Thank you," I said. And I think I meant it.

Under strict instruction to find Bébhinn, I entered the village alone. Caolann had hoped to deter any attention from Ardagh natives roaming the forest again at nightfall, and I was starting to realise he might be right about *some* things.

The pathways bustled, livelier than I'd ever seen it, trad music blaring and drifting into the night for dancers and feasting spectators. And yet, the aura was peaceful—not a neutral, passive feeling—how peacefulness is often described—but rather, it felt like a hum, as if soft lips were running over my skin. A whisper telling me this community might be my own one day, if only they gave me a chance. That perhaps I was always suited to this way of life when the precious objects of modern living were really no loss to me.

Roaming through the crowd, I people-watched; parents craned necks to keep their children in sight. Two men ferried rocks in and out of the square water pool built into the ground by the fire. This must have been the Fulacht Fiadh that Bébhinn had us contribute to—a pit to boil food. Surrounding it, stalls displayed meats, green vegetables and fruits. And though perhaps sparse, it was a potent display.

I spotted Róisín and Lester seated atop a log by fire, him sucking on an apple core as she chattered away in his ear. Midstride to ask where her mother was, a hand grabbed mine, twirling me to face the owner: a toothless old lady.

"Dance among us, cailín." She cackled, wafting a stench of old fish my way.

Absolutely stinking she was. "Oh no, I'd rather not," I politely protested, resisting her pull on my arm.

The woman tugged harder, her grip stronger than I'd expected. Unless the exhaustion of the past few days had finally caught up with me. With a sigh, I gave in.

Screw it. This might be my last chance to do something fun for a while, and what was five more minutes before finding Bébhinn?

Following the woman through the thick crowd toward the music, curved horns and yew pipes chimed loud in harmony with a single harp. It was beautiful. She dragged me centre of wooden flooring where people clapped to the melody, legs flailing about, and I prayed the fragments of my childhood Irish dancing routines would allow me to keep up, even sober.

Before long, my muscle memory kicked in, moving me through the crowd with wild abandon, weaving and ducking me under their arms. A man with crooked teeth took my hands and led me around the dance floor, dipping my body from side to side, sweeping us by the other dancers with barely brushed shoulders.

My jaw ached from grinning, and not even the ale in my hair could dampen my spirits. Around and around we spun. Until the stars above blurred and my heart mindlessly followed the percussion.

When the melodies gradually tapered off, the harp's ethereal notes drifted into silence. Applause erupted from the crowd, washing over me in waves until it, too, faded. The sudden quiet left me standing in the centre, trying to catch my breath. But as soon as the music was gone, guilt surged up like a bitter wave, pulling me under.

I staggered back into the grass, retreating to the darkness of a tree just past a closed stall where the noise of the crowd fell off. Piping, acidic pain forged a gully right into my chest. How *dare* I find a moment of joy after what I'd done. How dare I forget, even for a second. Forget that fencing punched through Fionn's gut as though he were nothing more than an afterthought in the fabric of our world.

Unable to mask the pain hunching me over, I pushed off the trunk and ran, not *to* anywhere, just...away. I needed to suffer alone, too ashamed to let anyone see.

Pockets of moonlight in the canopies guided me through a narrow trail of the southern forest. But for what most considered a beautiful sight, all it offered me was silvering illumination to spotlight my crimes. My mouth downturned, threatening to get stuck there for all the times it had stretched this way before. I couldn't quite believe how hard the pain struck. It was as if I had to suffer twice as much for those minutes of bliss. Still, that was only fair. Happiness was reserved for those worthy. I was a fool to forget that.

Twigs cracked, disturbing the calm that held night's hand.

With each slowing step, the long muscles on either side of my spine contracted. The rustle of leaves crept closer—a creature too big to be a badger or hare.

I held the rune beneath my dress for safekeeping. Maybe I *was* young enough to become another lost child of Saoirse. I froze at the thought of that until a tingle rubbed my spine.

In my peripheral vision, I saw a hand slithering around my neck.

"Well. Well. Well," the familiar voice said, pervading the cool air with mint.

Breathless, I spun to him—Rathnor. I'd hoped to get at least a few days before he came, not *hours*.

His lips creased into his trademark feline grin. "Do you not see what terrible creatures hunt in the night's forest?" He picked an invisible thread from his collar, indifferently brushing it away between two fingers.

I inched back, stifling any response. He'd just twist it to suit his narrative. Fear seeped out in shallow breaths anyway.

Closing the gap between us, he cocked his head as if I were some exotic creature barely worthy of his scrutiny. The gesture reeked of power, while I stank of fear, dreading all the scenarios that could so easily unfold in the coming seconds.

I stumbled, barely keeping my footing. "Leave me be, Rathnor. You got your token." My rattling voice betrayed me, giving him a final push of dominance. He pounced and clamped my cheeks, squeezing hard as he edged his mouth to my earlobe. I tensed my upturned jaw not to grant him the pleasure of my screams, but the parting of his sticky lips churned my stomach like he wanted to make butter of my insides. "I *yearn* to see your potential, Clíona. Solely second to that, do I long to take your final breath."

This time, fight back. The voice in my head was Caolann's.

My hands were already tingling and set alight with the shimmering current of my harvest. I didn't need to kill him. Just scare him.

My jaw shivered.

I was never the judge of that outcome. The power decided who lived or died by my hands.

Snatching myself from his grasp to create a gap between us, I readied my stance, palms straight. Stare narrowed. Rathnor let out a low, menacing chuckle and drew his sword, swinging it wide to ready himself. The blade split his grin in two.

Without hesitation, I screamed and shot my hands forward, letting the harvest bleed out in thick spurts of light.

Slicing through the night, he parried the attack, diverting all its light into the sky so tunnelled and high, creatures started dropping around him. Bats. Moths. Then the shimmers dissipated.

Scrunching my nose, I willed my Bua to surface again, near relishing the current running through me. Reminding me I was alive—and would like to stay that way. But a haze blurred my vision instead.

"I take my time, Clíona."

I tried to jerk away, but the command between mind and limbs was rapidly vanishing. "What does that mean?"

"The water, wild one. It is a slow acting toxin. You see, I wished to take you at night. That fool, Caolann...." He sighed. "He is tied to you by blood. It makes him fond of you. Like a pet. Which is an inconvenience for me."

The water. The water he'd given me in the field. "Did you...drug me?" I slurred. I swayed and hobbled backwards until collapsing just out of his approaching grasp onto the ground.

"Yes. Yes! Surrender yourself to me." His tongue slid over his lips while he untied the golden twine of his pants. The nausea ensnaring my tongue drew shivering gasps into my mouth.

This can't be happening.

But the longer I lay there, losing control of my body, the more options for escape slammed shut in my mind.

He gripped my ankle, dragging me closer.

I shrieked and bucked, my foot meeting nothing.

He pulled again. My dress rolled against the cold, uneven soil, pulling over my bottom. My mouth was too soft, too numb to make a noise. It forced all the panic to pool into my eyes, too frightened to even blink.

My stomach clenched. I knew what was about to happen and I was helpless.

Fight back! It was Fionn calling out to me this time. But I couldn't. There was nothing left in me. As if Rathnor had known the very hour, the very *minute*, my limbs would succumb to his depraved wishes.

Every inch of me sunk into a worse state of mush. Every part of my brain was winding down to only one outcome. One inescapable memory if I managed to make it out of this alive.

My nails dug through the hard soil as I pleaded with my body to stand—to fight. To not have to live the rest of my life suffering the echoes of this brutality.

Crawling barely inches, he flipped me onto my back. All the breath shot out of my lungs.

He seethed with what I feared was pleasure. Two burning tears escaped, sliding down and down until dripping into my ears. At least it muffled my growing cries. Tracing a finger over my lips still scabbed from our first meeting, he said, "It baffles me why you cry when all I intend to give you is pleasure."

"Please." The word was so strained and desperate I hated myself for even saying it. For failing to put the word 'no' at the end of it.

Rathnor gripped my inner thigh. "Mm-hmm. Say that again." He kneeled straddling me.

Please no. Please no. No! No. *No.*

Movement in the trees caught his attention. Something much larger than a badger. Something fast.

I barely managed to turn my head to the second threat of danger when Rathnor's wide eyes were met with a fist, the impact echoing like clashing boulders as it sent a spray of blood into the darkness.

Rathnor fell flat next to me, unmoving, his mouth carbonating red. I strained to focus on who had come to my rescue.

Green eyes.

A brother.

They stood above me, those eyes bulging, full of fury while gripped in their trembling hand was a knife.

Clamping its handle in their mouth, they bent to lift me as the drug took over.

"Oh," I slurred. "It's you."

17

IT WAS THE WORST OF TIMES

I woke with a stuttering gasp—the kind where you fear you'll never catch your breath again. I was living in some ancient form of Groundhog Day where death was endlessly on my tail. I wasn't sleeping. I was being knocked out, or drugged, or drained of my own power. My body constantly ached, dotted with so many bruises and cuts, the scabs were coming off only to be replaced by new ones.

My back lay stiff against the trunk of a heavy-rooted tree. I clasped my achy head to dull the throb in my temple as I tried to grasp a morsel of grounding to this damn world. The moments just before I passed out circled around my mind, replaying over and over.

I knocked my head against the coarse bark to stop it. How could I be so stupid to take water from him? Rathnor never did anything without an ulterior motive.

My gaze dropped to the rip running against the hem of my dress. To the spatter of blood dotting the material.

This was bad. He would come for me now, not just for his obsession, but with revenge. He was wicked in his bones, and without my saviour who knows what would've happened.

I did know, but I refused to let that thought come to the forefront of my mind. I wouldn't let the memory consume me. But Caolann...his green stare slit by a loose piece of hair weaved into my mind. The warrior. The babysitter. My forced keeper. He had protected me when it would have been so easy to look the other way. And be rid of me once and for all. He had hit Rathnor hard enough to make him colour-blind. And though the feminist in me wanted no man to fight my battles, for the tingling that flourished up the insides of my thighs...I wanted to see him do it all over again.

A pet, that's what Rathnor said I was to Caolann. Well, I'd take the title if it meant staying alive another day.

A gentle crack in the forest broke my frantic train of thought.

My legs pushed themselves into a feeble stance I'd half-remembered from Réimse Mór. I should have been on alert the moment I came to.

Hadn't I learnt anything since arriving here?

"You were meant to stay by Bébhinn's side," a voice said.

I spun in search of Rathnor, my breath jagged, but instead, *he* came with surrendered arms, softening my jittery fears.

"Caolann!"

Holding my hands up to plead my case before he barked a torrent of abuse my way, his gentle hands cupped my face, searching for something in my eyes. Stress maybe? Signs of trauma?

I opened my mouth to tumble into an apology. "I'm sorry. I—"

"No!"

I pulled from his touch, not getting far with the tree in my back. "No?"

A fury hardened his stare. "Do not apologise for his cowardice. It is beneath you. *He* is beneath you."

I found myself mute. Because this anger wasn't directed at me, it was *for* me. In my name.

But why?

He continued to check me for injury: my arms, my neck, my face. And I continued to let him.

He had a military focus—forcing him to be close to me until all *I* could focus on was his earthly odour that managed to be a comfort in itself.

I studied him in return: his coarse hair holding looser plaits...dark circles hugging his eyes, stubble shadowing his lower face. Had he stayed all night? The idea of that was flattering. Although this *pet* didn't think she was worth the gesture.

"What happened to Rathnor? How bad are we in it now?" My lip stung to speak. I dabbed it where a tiny wound had reopened.

Caolann's gaze lingered on the split skin, scrutinising it with something pulling on the edges of his eyes I couldn't quite understand. Opening my mouth to tell him I was fine, he doubled down, grasping my chin to inspect it closely.

He stroked the skin beneath the wound, flashing me the most fleeting, most impossible-to-read look, before letting his hand drop. "No infection."

I cleared my throat. "How did you know?" I asked. "How did you know where to find me?"

"You were not with Bébhinn when I returned. Then a light shot through the sky in this spot. A beacon calling on me. After you spoke of Rathnor's want for a token, I believed he would visit, but not with such haste. Many rulers tire easily, searching for excitement in the crevices of mortal torment. He slipped a concoction into your blood somehow."

I ran my fingers down my face, flushed and still ungrounded against the uneven soil. "But what's going to happen? That's the second time you've punched him this week. Surely there'll be consequences." I couldn't consider what those consequences would be. Not two minutes of the day had passed, and already I remembered how terrifying this world was.

His lips parted to speak, though they stalled. Then he nodded, slowly, confident in whatever unknown resolve had just found him.

Curious, I opened my mouth to ask when he slid his warm hand into mine. The simple touch raised the hairs along my arms. Because I realised he wasn't all that different from his brother after all. Which was perhaps why it was no surprise the same words left my lips again. "Are...are you trying to help me?"

Caolann's jaw clenched as he swooped his gaze across my body even though he'd already checked it twice over. I wanted to tell him I was fine, but something—something in that clench capturing his jaw and that steel look in his eyes, told me I wasn't the one who decided if I was fine anymore. That perhaps that wasn't even the reason he was looking.

"Come." His grip tightened as he led with too much force, drawing us deeper into the forest with no answers. No indication of anything, really.

Not long into our trek, my paranoia reached new heights, even in his company; I cursed my stupid feet for crunching loudly on fallen twigs in case Rathnor came back or sent his footmen. I wasn't invincible in Ériu. Not even close.

"Why not use your Bua?" he asked, still focused on wherever we were going this time.

A fair question after the scene he'd arrived at.

Unable to match his long-legged pace, my breath was loud. Struggling. "I did. I tried. But I thought it was better to hurt him…" I panted, trying to catch my breath. "…then accidentally kill him with my Bua and face worse consequences. Last night was different, though." I sucked in another breath. "Whatever concoction he'd given me had taken hold before I even had a proper chance to summon it. Besides, I can't control it." At least not when my emotions were deeply involved. And some part of me, even when it came to Rathnor, was just exhausted about the idea of taking another person's life. My death toll was at four. Redemption was surely lost when you went into serial killer numbers.

Gulping another mouthful of air, I yanked from Caolann's grasp to hunch, hands imitating teacup handles on my hips. "I've had it with you! I'm not moving another step until you at least tell me where you're taking me." His elusive nonsense was tiresome, and I didn't have space for anyone's bullshit but my own.

"I must leave."

No, don't leave.

The words nearly slipped out. I pinched my lips. The idea of being out in the open, being more vulnerable, seemed reckless when having a built-in bodyguard was clearly the better option. But there was something else in it. I didn't *want* him to go. "Why? Where are you going?" I managed, smoothing my expression.

"To sever loose ends."

"Nope."

He cocked his head. "Yes," he answered, unsure of the conviction.

"No. I'm not having it." I pointed my finger at him, stretched with malice and annoyance. I needed answers, and I was tired of not getting them. "I'm not your damsel, and I won't be left in the fucking dark. I've been spiked. I've been lied to, and I *know*, I know with my gut, there's more to this than you're telling me. Why do you get liberties? Why do you, an outsider, get treated with so much respect?" I was shouting now, too loud for someone who should be keeping their head down. "Tell me what in the name of Jesus is going on!"

He stared at me wide-eyed as if to say, *Who the hell is this Jesus lad she's talking about*? Then, after a long sigh, he said, "Moments after waking, Rathnor divinely moved to the mighty halls of Magh Mell." Caolann spoke slowly, as if my maimed mind couldn't take a normal pace. "I watched him from cover once dragging you far enough away that I believed you were safe for the night. I have an..." He searched the still trees before he came back to me with his clearly calculated wording. "...an accord with the Tuatha Dé Danann. This is not a village of warriors. It is a village of fishermen, blacksmiths and musicians. The ones who inherit great Bua, they fight well, but often they leave to enlist in the Fir na Solas or they perish in attempt to champion Lúnasa. Yet I have knowledge and skills from my days in Ardagh that protect the common folk from the likes of Rathnor. Now, enough! I waited to ensure your safe awakening. I must journey to Magh Mell before his twisted words meet our Banríon's ears. Mórrígan will forgive my actions if I can plead my case. I am sure of this. She is wise, yet I am a man who understands the need to place pride aside. I can fall to my knees to seek forgiveness and feel no shame."

Caolann's intention to speak to Mórrígan felt insane. Just an outright awful plan. Kneeling or not.

One second, he demanded me to stay by his side and the next he was off somewhere else doing God knows what. I was already shaking my head as I revved up to argue more when I forfeited. He was trying to help me, and I was being stubborn. I smoothed my face to stoicism, though I felt a flicker of lingering frustration still tugging my right brow. “What do you need me to do?”

His feet planted steady in the gap between us. “As you’re fucking told.” He cast a deliberate, piercing look at me. “For once.”

I swallowed. The subtle act seemed to mollify his stern glare into something barely softer.

“Visit an old land with me come nightfall?” he asked.

“What old land?” Was it a diversion from what was to come? I didn’t care—not of that or the blatant warmth flushing into my cheeks.

Fuck it. Let him see.

“Will you come?” His hopeful gaze tempered his sharp features.

I stuttered a laugh—not that I found what he said funny. “We’re alone now if you want to talk.” Everything in this world felt like trickery. What was to say Caolann was any better than Rathnor? He’d chosen not to kill me twice, and yes, he was helping me now, but that didn’t make him good. It simply made him decent.

Rooting his tongue in his teeth, he stifled a quiet laugh—or was it a huff? Then turning abruptly, he paced ahead before I could confirm his expression. “Caolann, wait.” I followed, my legs again struggling to match his pace as I chased this endlessly confusing man. Why couldn’t I have one second of trust? “Caolann, stop!” With a pulse of my hands, the flare of a subconscious command, he froze in his stride.

A golden rope, shimmering, stretched around his body, calcifying him into place.

I dare say it was beautiful.

Edging to get a better view, I realised my strength had grown. The harvest held him more controlled than last time, with no anger behind it, rather frustration. The lower level of emotion felt easier to manage. He could breathe this time. I circled him, keeping my hands steady. "Tell me what's wrong, and I'll release you."

He strained to escape, surfacing an estuary of veins. "I hope—you decide—for yourself."

I hocked my frustration for all the forest to suffer. "There you go again making no sense. Tell me why you want to visit an old land with me. Tell me what you want from me. It's not hard! You just open your mouth and say it!"

"Because death often seeks you out, Clíona!" he snapped. "And yet, when not planning it myself, it seems I am compelled to protect you from it!" He paused. "Why *am* I protecting you from it?" The lines between his brows dragged inwards as though he truly couldn't figure out the answer. Like he hadn't already asked me this question just yesterday. Asked me like it *tormented* him not to know.

"Why now?" I demanded slowly, forcing my need for answers to overshadow any inkling emotion.

"Not *now*. When you slaughtered those men. It was at that moment I decided to let you live despite it making every crevice of my cursed life harder. Only in seeing Rathnor try and take you last night did I accept this truth. Did I see my own lie in denying it." His nostrils flared. "He will never hurt you again, Clíona. Not a scratch. Not a single hair on your head will become a token of his again. Now, release me."

I dropped my hands, and the shimmers softened.

He staggered as my harvest trickled away.

I stood there, stunned, as shock surged through me, slamming into the walls of my chest with such force, I feared I might lose my footing. The tangible, pulsating sensation of being desired—if that's what this was—became difficult to ignore when it roamed through every part of me.

"What are you doing to me?" I asked with an upturned jaw. My power didn't seem to affect him the same way it would any other person. He was unnaturally strong. There was a temptation in that, a chance to not hold back.

So maybe this was temporary perfection.

He frowned at me as if I were the one who spoke in riddles.

"I still think you want me dead."

Caolann approached slowly, his arms slightly surrendered. "Having you dead would be easier, trust that. Trust that if this protective feeling had not overcome me in watching you take those men from their own bones..." He released a heavy breath. "...that night would have been your last. But I ask of you now, without thoughts of tomorrow..." He bowed his head to me. "Do you wish to be with me this nightfall?"

No. I refused to be so easily swayed. He was better to me as an ally. "If I let you fuck me—" I clicked my fingers. "Puff. All my leverage is gone. I know how the minds of men work. You want to taste it so bad, but once you're full, the treat is always forgotten."

Caolann cornered me against the tree, pressing his hands into the bark on either side of my head. The sense of confinement no longer felt threatening—only safe. "If I had you even once. One time..." His eyes roamed over me with hunger. His lips quaked. "I'd never eat another meal again. *You* are enough to satisfy me." He let his tongue slide across the inlay of his lips. "Can you not see, my bound girl? I want to rip that dress from your body and eat you in fucking mouthfuls."

I gripped the bark with my fingers. It crumbled beneath my touch, but better this than whatever I might do with them if the clenching stopped.

Mouthfuls?

It was me who was starving now.

"Caolann," I said, failing to force the rest of the rejection out.

He's better as an ally. He's better as an ally.

"Don't do that," he warned, his head dipping sternly.

"Do what?"

"Pant my name as though I am already in you." My lips parted; my heart pounded. He searched my face for a response then pushed even further. "I see it in you, Clíona. A badness. A seduction. A desire to lead your own way. Most women would have pleasured me in the cabin. I need not have asked, and they would have submerged their whole body into the tub to give me pleasure until all the air left their body and they withered beneath the water to their grave. Not you, though. I have no will over you." He traced a warm finger down the edge of my cheek. "The anger that holds the hand of seduction when you are near, gods, Clíona, I am weak for it."

Unfurling my grip from the tree, I lowered his touch from my cheek, willing away the residing heat. Tomorrow might not come if the obstacle of Rathnor wasn't rectified, and his intense, expectant gaze was impossible to ignore. His words were frighteningly seductive. And not needing to worry about hurting him in the process...bliss.

"Fine." I grinned devilishly wide as I squared closer to his mouth. "I'll come with you tonight, on one condition."

"Name your terms."

"I'm no longer bound to you."

"No." He pressed from the tree, turning as he cupped his mouth. Then he immediately returned to pin me, his hand, his enormous hand, planted heavy in the centre of my chest.

"I am to be your protector in place of that title."

"Can I roam freely?"

"Can you stay out of trouble from now on?"

I scowled, teasing. "Obviously."

"Then we are agreed."

I placed my hand over his, feeling the thrum of my heart pulsing through both of us.

That wouldn't do. I needed to maintain some semblance of control. "But you know now, I'm not so easy to kill. And I'm not so easy to please." I pushed closer, taking his exhale. "So, I hope you're better at holding your breath than those women in the tub."

"My breath?"

I rose to my tiptoes to meet his ear and whisper, "I tend to squeeze my thighs."

The corner of his eye cut to me. "I await it eagerly, wildling."

Slow footsteps approached.

I instinctively—pathetically—gripped Caolann's shirt to bring him closer. To cower from the threat.

Rían stepped out from behind a tree, his arrow nocked, its point oscillating between me and his brother.

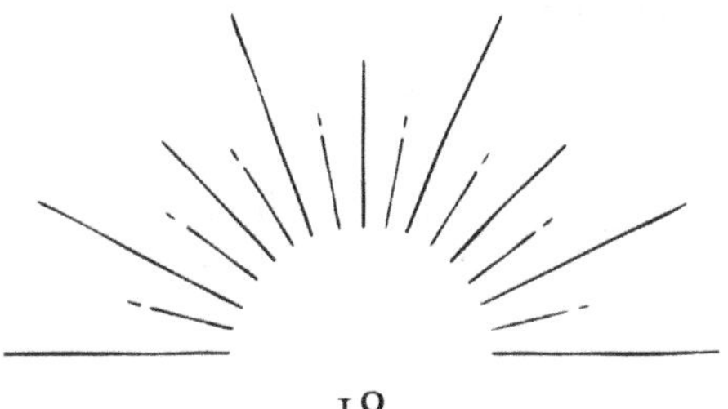

18
THE WARRIOR'S LINE

"Rían." His name trickled out. Fucking cascaded was more like it, releasing me of worry I hadn't realised I'd been carrying. I gently pressed two fingers to my lips. Why had simply seeing him lifted it so easily?

His cautious stare faltered when catching sight of us. When confirming we weren't a threat.

Dipping underneath Caolann's arm, I broke away from the moment.

I hadn't seen Rían since the Carraig, and now, here he was, unclouded from being forced into the back of my mind when all I was trying to do these past few days was stay alive.

I looked between their tense stare down, feeling tight in my core as the softness slipped from my lips. They were so alike, so wildly protective and strong, and yet I was drawn to both for different reasons. Caolann was heat. Dangerous. Whereas Rían appeared to be steered by righteousness. Willpower.

"I will take my leave, brother," Caolann said. "Bring her to Bébhinn at sun's descent. It will take no longer to settle this."

Rían ran his eyes over me, his jaw feathering. Then his stare shot to his brother. "Your duty was to protect her. What happened?"

Caolann inhaled deeply through his nose. "There is no time for this. I must travel at once."

Rían's hand gripped the bow tighter. "Make time."

My stare ferried between them, unable to figure out what was happening or why. Should I intervene? Was it even my place?

Still inhaling, Caolann pinched the bridge of his nose before dropping his hand and fixing his gaze back on Rían. "Rathnor has set his attention on her. We underestimated his interest."

"Underestimated?" Rían took a hasty step closer. "You assured me you had this handled." His voice surged. "It is the sole reason I agreed to stay away. To let you carry this burden alone while I hunted for traces of the young."

Caolann squared—warning him. "Respect the hierarchy, brother. My word is final. Recall, she is bound to—"

"Us!" Rían's free hand instinctively reached for his knife. "She is bound to *both* of us."

Caolann's face darkened, his expression shifting from surprise to a sharp irritation.

"I am bound to no one!" I spread my arms between them. This was ridiculous.

Settling his eyes over me—my stance—Caolann offered a slight surrender of his hands to Rían. I swore he enjoyed the confrontation. Enjoyed making out like he was someone who knew of things like restraint. "Well shall see, brother. Paths change. For now," he said, jingling still-surrendered hands, "if I may?"

Rían slackened his grip on the bow, fingers loosening.

Caolann nodded, seemingly more thankful as he dropped his arms. "If trouble comes, draw your sword, not words."

"I will keep the wildling safe, but be mindful," Rían warned him. "Make the wise choice."

Caolann and Rían exchanged a mirroring green glare, meeting halfway to lock their hands with a firm clash of comradery—a bond beyond the squabbles of a cracked nut with a great ass. Good. How it was meant to be. Then Caolann touched my hand, our fingers parting as fast as they met.

"Come back with a head, brother," Rían called in jest.

Without response, in seconds, he was out of sight. Even that felt too long when my mind wandered to what he was about to face in Magh Mell. I wiped sweat from my hairline. It was too hot for forest trekking and sexually fuelled interactions.

Rían's brows arched. "Be cautious. Not all with Caolann is truthful."

My own brows knitted. "Strange thing to say about your brother."

He huffed a smile. Or something that resembled a smile. It was as if tension bundled into his shoulders at the mere thought of interacting with another person. He didn't know how to be around others, like me when I was at home. Thankfully, I was beginning to creep away from my loneliness since he found me.

"Feels like the stars themselves have been keeping us apart these past few days," I said, my unexpected fondness for him persisting. This man who saved me. Because it might have been Caolann's command, but it was Rían who vouched for me. Nineteen years old and standing up to gods—it was impressive.

"Is it my brother who keeps us apart, not the stars."

"But why?"

"He is...protective."

I gestured both hands to our surroundings. "He just brought me to you."

"He needs you safe." A smirk tugged at his lips, teasing out his boisterous side. "I can keep you safe."

"Do you always do as your brother asks?" I teased.

His smirk faded to something more cryptic. "Perhaps he believes so."

"But not you?"

"No." He tracked my body, his jaw set rigid again as if some unspoken thing coiled inside him. "Not me."

I considered my next move. If it was too soon to pry. "And what if I asked something of you?"

"Asked what?" He sat on a nearby boulder, keeping a noticeable distance between us.

I leaned against a tree, legs casually crossed, relieved he dropped whatever tension he was building up no doubt to spite Caolann. "A question."

"Speak it freely, wildling."

"Why did you try to bring me to the Carraig when you captured me?" I asked. "You could have let me go for someone else to deal with. I am nothing to you."

He was sitting wide legged on the rock, his posture casual yet commanding, like he owned the ground beneath him. "If any other creature or Saoirsian came upon you, the soil would be feasting on your rotting body." He made it seem so obvious from his point of view. "Or perhaps you would have been presumed to be the wicked thing who takes Saoirse's younglings."

"But you didn't think it was me?"

He snorted a noise that unnaturally strained from his mouth. "You were too foolish and loud. They were stolen from beneath our nostrils."

"Huh. So why bring me to Rathnor?"

"In what other land could I have hidden you? Amongst the Giants of Blasket?" He shook his head, reinforcing the fact that the answer was obvious. I really was a cracked nut in his eyes. "I speak to Rathnor in a way others often cannot."

"What way can you speak to the unreasonable? He seems so—" I tried to find a word to sum up his horrid nature.

"Ungodly," he finished.

Close enough.

Rían slid his bow off his chest, checking its string for health. Much like Caolann, he didn't favour eye contact when uncomfortable. I found it endearing since everything else about them was so clear-cut and fortified from vulnerability. "My brother trusted me with your secret. You harvest a powerful Bua."

"I actually think with some practice, I might even be good at harvesting it. Maybe I should start training with the children in Réimse Mór."

He gestured to the forest floor for me to perform. "Show me."

My feet planted heavier into the soil, and my legs defiantly locked. I hated being told what to do.

That's because you can't handle authority. Always the rebellious one.

"What stops you?" Rían asked.

When I was with Caolann, my harvest had emerged from me in a fluid, frustrated movement; a connection between me and his body, but it was over as fast as it began. "I don't know what I can do. It's like my Bua only listens to the primal part of me. Although it's getting better, more loyal—holding people in place sometimes instead of hurting them."

"Stand strong, Clíona. Hold your body with pride, for it has great strength." He beckoned me from the tree.

I obeyed that much.

He drew his bow, his posture turning sideways as his chest widened with an inhale. He mirrored a bird with a tremendous wingspan that could take him anywhere he wished. "When I release this arrow, you will stop it before it pierces your chest." His assertive tone was absent of worry, but my body became locked and weak for his words.

"Rían—" I stretched his name, and my head cocked to warn. "I'm not doing this."

"In the face of death, we are our strongest self. Now recall your own words. It is a connection between your body and the object you wish to command. Do not think of me. Not my brother, or perils of the past. Focus on your Bua. Dominate it."

"I'm not doing this," I repeated sternly, my hands tingling with the reprise of power.

"Yes"—he winked—"you are." His finger unhooked.

My arms flailed with sudden heat and spurts of loose light.

The feathered arrow, millimetres from puncturing a vital organ, split down its middle and fell to my feet. My head dropped in disbelief. He'd actually done it. The harvest persisted, building in anticipation of a larger threat.

My head dropped in disbelief.

"You bastard!" Anger bubbled at the hands of my power, throbbing my head and stretching my fingers so fiercely, its tendons cried for mercy. Fixating on his bow, I *commanded* it to come to me.

Rían held it tight, understanding the source of the pull as the light leached from the air.

I strained further, releasing a burning grunt that ached all the way down my throat.

Then it was gone—the bow.

It didn't come—it disintegrated, becoming drifting ash, swirling into the ray of sunlight shining over him.

Rían reached for the floating pieces; they crumbled under his finger's weight.

Suddenly weak, my knees buckled to the ground. "I'm sorry. I lost control." I panted, clenching my eyes shut in accountability for my part. "The power takes hold of my emotions so fast."

His voice grew closer. "You destroyed my most valued bow."

I scoffed. "You shouldn't have tried to kill me with it, then." I stared up at him, unimpressed that was all he had to say, but we'd both gone too far.

He jutted his chin towards the ground.

Red droplets splattered the soil.

I dabbed my nose on my wrist's edge. Blood.

Rían offered his hand. "It will pass, love."

Ignoring his jibe, I accepted with my weaker hand, letting tension drift away in the breeze. Not a soul in these lands cared how many fingers I had. There was no disgust or stupid questions to keep the awkward conversation afloat. If anything, it annoyed me that this wasn't the way back home.

I tilted my head back to ease the flow of blood. "What just happened to me?"

He tilted my head *down* instead, holding a gentle fist of my hair. "Your mind will drown in blood if you worship Lugh. Worship the soil and Bíle will absorb the bleed."

I peeked at him through loose auburn strands. "I didn't take you for a worshipper."

"I believe in truth. I see that when one harvests great power, a debt is paid by the host," he said, rubbing my hair as the blood waned. "My Bua, too, holds great strength, beyond that of Saoirsians."

So, he saw us as powerful equals. That made me a little less annoyed. Made my throat feel balmier. I was stronger than an average Saoirsian. Or at least I could be. But was that what I wanted? It was a relief to understand this power, to already have found some semblance of control over it, but to unleash it to its full potential when the ramifications of it had already ruined my life once...that was a foolish route I had no intention of following.

Rían surveyed me with an unexpected glint in his eyes, drawing me out of the threatening guilt. "What fills your mind this moment?"

My mouth opened against my will. "I'm wondering what kind of filthy things your brother will do to me tonight." I clasped my traitorous lips.

The glint in his eyes migrated, bending into a smug grin so stretched, I swore he and Caolann could be twins. He looked good when happy. Healthy even.

Easing my hands from my mouth, I smacked his shoulder. "Have you done this"—I smacked him again—"to me before?"

He dipped from me with creasing eyes. "Recall our first meeting. You did all I asked of you, submitting to my will. Falling to your knees."

"I thought I did what you asked of me out of fear. The memory is hazy."

He folded his arms, a legion smaller than Caolann's, but still muscular and lean. Still stronger than any man I'd known back home. "That is its beauty. Unless revealed, you do not see the truth."

"Oh wow." I stretched the words. "This is how you got that guard to let you visit me in the Carraig." It was all too clear now. The way the soldier had turned so sinister so quickly after Rían had left. After he snapped out of the spell.

Rían nodded, his eyes drifting to the memory with satisfaction. "Your Bua is rare. Lúnasa's Trials would be a wondrous place for you."

"What is Lúnasa? I mean, I know it's the harvest, but what do trials have to do with that?" What I really wanted to tell him was that no wondrous place existed for me. That the state of grief and guilt I lived in was perpetual, and the fleeting moments of good, however common they were in this world, remained underserved no matter how selfishly I indulged in them.

"Lúnasa is a competition of Bua strength," he told me, syphoning me away from the darkness with his thumb gently placed on my chin. I edged away from it, and he didn't double down, letting his hand fall to his side. Yet something told me, once again, that he recognised that dark place—he feared it. "It is the sole route to power in these lands. The champion is invited to be a comrade of the Tuatha Dé Danann and granted any request—The Divine Gift, villagers name it."

I knew what my wish would be. "What do you get power over if you win?"

"Saoirse," he told me, his hands outstretched to the forest. "Rathnor championed, and for this, Mórrígan granted him the power to rule much of Saoirse's lands in her name. It is said he asked for his mother's return with his Divine Gift, but not even a god can return the dead unless the cauldron Treasure is wielded. Rathnor's failure made him bitter."

"What are they like? The Tuatha, I mean." I stared at the cloudless sky as if they might come down from the heavens here and now. They still felt like an unreachable concept, despite where I was and what I harvested. I was desperate to know if they lived up to Fionn's idolization. If he'd come here to find them. I wished I could ask, but I still felt too close to the edge of blowing my cover.

Rían crouched to grab a fist of loose dirt, letting it fall through the gaps between his fingers. "From all came two: Danu and Bíle. Some name them the True Gods. Most now worship their descendants, the Tuatha Dé Danann, for Danu and Bíle no longer walk this plane with a body. Many moons gone, they bore five younglings: three sons and two daughters. All other gods derive from them."

"The pure Tuatha," I repeated quietly. It was as Mollie had said in her story about Mórrígan. I flicked my gaze back to him. "Who are the other four?" I had my suspicions, but folklore had been twisted with so many inaccuracies or burned at the hands of the church, it was hard to know what was true.

"Their sons are Dian Cecht, God of Healing and Dagda, God of Death and War—my lineage. The other daughter is Brigit—Goddess of Fertility and Fire. I am told she still visits to deliver young during difficult births."

I found it ironic that both Ardagh and Saoirse's leaders both signified war. Two rivals at either end of these lands.

"Who's the fifth? You only named four."

"Nuada." Dusting his hands together, he rose from his crouch. "He no longer lives. Lugh rules in his place now."

"Well." I clapped my hands, pulling myself out of his Tuatha lesson to veer us back to the village. "I don't think I'll be entering anything that brings me attention. Living another day is enough."

"Your choice is wise, for you are not carved from the warrior's line."

"I'm not even going to ask what that means."

"The wisest cracked nut I have crossed paths with," he called after me. And I grinned, despite myself.

With evening tailing us home, I scraped the last of the crusted blood from my nose, rubbing it to dust. My Bua was the only reason I'd survived even a single day here. Still, the more I harvested, the stronger it became—a terrifying prospect.

No. I refused to worry about that tonight. Not when I had plans with Caolann—if Mórrígan doesn't kill him first.

19
WORTHY

Bébhinn's house held a sticky heat I'd become fond of despite the discomfort of my clinging clothes. She stirred sage above the fire while humming *sean-nós* in deep, melismatic medleys. The sound's beauty made me shiver.

Róisín nudged my arm. "Keep up."

My eyes settled on the pile of uncut carrots I'd been absently caressing while Róisín had already finished dicing her potatoes. I smiled at her how everyone did when caught daydreaming. How was it that humans are embarrassed by something we do naturally?

"Sorry. My mind is drifting."

Bébhinn and Róisín snickered in the tone of elderly men snoring.

"Hey! What's with all the laughing?" I protested with false offence and my knife swinging about. I knew exactly what stirred them.

"Perhaps your mind wanders to a face?" Bébhinn suggested as they grinned into one another, their noses scrunched.

"Whose face?" Okay, I'm a masochist. I wanted to hear his name.

"Caolann's," Róisín teased. "You wish to plant your lips on him."

"Yuck. I'd do better with these lips than lobbing them on a boy from Ardagh." I pursed them like a fish as she shrieked and swatted me.

"We do not live to entertain boys," Bébhinn said in a dry tone.

"She's dead right," I agreed as if I was the one instilling knowledge.

"I live in preparation to rule Saoirse's fields," Róisín declared with her head held high.

Bébhinn pressed loving lips to her head, looping fingers through her red ribbon. "My wise girl."

After supper, we chatted about the looming harvest thickening the fields and what Bébhinn called *strong crop fertiliser* when she really meant *animal shit*. She somehow made anything sound interesting, each word rolling off her tongue like it was that of legend. Róisín used the conversation as an opportunity to tiptoe away, barely making it to the door.

"Straight to Shayla's and no other land," Bébhinn warned, a tea towel thrown over her shoulder and a warming smile easing her firm tone.

"It is but a short distance. I am safe, Mother." She winked at me, and I returned it.

Silently taking over the washing, I said to Bébhinn, "It's fair to worry. Only right. I think I'd never stop worrying if I had a child."

"This is the curse of motherhood. There is no love without the endless fear of losing it."

I missed Mollie desperately. Even if I could just tell her I was okay that might be enough.

A knock rapped the door's arch.

I dropped the cup I'd been scrubbing then exhaled a breath I swore I'd been holding since he left.

Caolann.

He stood at the door frame, a dark-hooded cloak masking much of his face. His hands clasped the outside thatch of the house, eagling his arms out from the light material. Not even a mark cut his skin. *I'd* come home looking worse after being with Rían. Maybe Mórrígan could be convinced after all.

"Dia dhuit, Caolann." Bébhinn folded her arms. "Where do you wish to take my new youngling this eve?"

A blush creeped onto his cheek. He'd killed men, he'd fought rulers, and this—me—was what made him shy. "I intend to take her to a quiet land." He rigidly turned to address me, much too formal for the wild man I often considered him. "I will wait under moonlight." Then he left.

Bébhinn fixed the soft twine on my bust to give them a lift. "Enjoy his company, for he is a good man. A child with his blood would be a gift."

I laughed to stop from swallowing my own tongue. A child? The idea of a life as a mother, that this was something I'd might have one day...no. No child deserved that.

Outside swelled with darkness, barely lit by the distant orange moon. Caolann's eyes drew from the night sky, noticing me. I followed his watch to the distraction: thick stars amongst the darkness, endless, unpolluted by light or the flash of passing planes and satellites. I'd been so busy looking over my shoulder in Ériu, looking up was the last thing on my mind.

"Even darkness holds beauty." He offered me a smile—the one where it was gone before you'd time to savour it.

I wanted to ask if there were personal connotations to this darkness, but instead, we inhaled a breath of silence. He held my sights before I bashfully turned away. Lust really was a tricky feeling, coated with the sweet indulgence of *what if.*

I shook my head and sighed. This was one night. We were just getting the sexual tension out of our stupid primal systems. He was my only ally, I needed to keep it that way.

I toed a lump of loose dirt on the path. "I'm guessing all was forgiven in Magh Mell if you're standing here?"

He nodded, having nothing else to add, and I didn't want to push him on it. If he'd managed to escape the consequences of last night, this one was to be enjoyed, just as he said.

"Well, what's with all the waiting around then? Let's go." I shooed him.

He grinned and sighed all at once, unleashing a perfect smile with little fangs. All of a sudden, I wanted them in my skin. "Patience, Clíona." With a perfected whistle, his spotted horse ducked between two houses. She came to him, nickering for the encouraging words he whispered. "Meet Rhiannon."

From the satchel on her side, he pulled another cloak, smaller and soft green. "These nights can be cold. And if you plan on running into the forest at nightfall for the third night in a row, I can at least ensure your warmth this time." He swung it around my back, buckling the clasp with care at my neck.

His warmth coated my skin as I peered up at him through my lashes. But as I went to reach out and finally touch him, he dipped and turned, mounting the horse with a great leap so swift he stirred the breeze. "Let us journey." Tilting from her, he reached out his muscular arm, painted in silver scars that glistened against the moonlight.

Sighing at his teasing, I locked onto his grasp, allowing my body to be swung into position behind him.

Edging his head back, a foot above my own, he found my hand to place it on his hip. "We ride fast, Clíona." With the click of his tongue, Rhiannon sent us off through the forest so rapidly, I swore he only encouraged her to have me hold him tighter.

Little did he know, I would have done it anyway.

After travelling but a short distance, Caolann slowed her. His hand, rough to touch, caressed my fingertips as he lowered me with utmost care. Even that had a kindness to it I hadn't seen from him before. The chivalry was rugged, but it was there. And I took it. Kept it, just for me.

Once sturdy on my feet and adjusted to the dark, I tried to blink away the blue spots surrounding us. But these little fluorescent lights refused to fade; they seemed to be batting paper-thin wings to stay buoyant.

I reached out, stirring them like a school of fish.

"What are they?"

He dismounted as deftly as he'd gotten up and tied Rhiannon's halter to a roped tree where the bark had been worn from use. "Soilse. Nocturnal creatures of Sídhe descent." He stood next to me, gently stirring more. "The shade lives within them from feasting on sloes."

"They're really beautiful."

"Hmm...I prefer my sloes unspoiled by their bellies."

"Well, I hate to break it to ya', but if you're a fan of purity, you came with the wrong woman tonight."

His hand met my waist. "I will take my chances, wildling." He guided me beyond an overgrown hedge, his touch so soft I wanted to plead with him to give me more. Grip me stronger. I wanted him to tell me he couldn't be broken. I wanted to feel the strength of someone above me that wouldn't snap in half if I let loose for a while.

The Soilse followed, hovering their glow above a crackling fire he must have lit before my arrival. I chewed my lip to contain a smile I was sure would ache my cheeks. He played a good game. He somehow managed to dull the guilt. Made the present feel like the only place that existed.

A blanket rested on the log next to the fire, dusted in the aroma of charred wood. I shimmied beneath it to get comfortable.

Caolann sat close enough that our arms touched in that realm of fondness without reciprocated certainty. This happened to be another place I masochistically enjoyed.

I broke the barrier, kissing him with all my mouth while clumsily working on the twine of his pants.

He gripped my shoulders to push me back. "Clíona." There was a sigh in it, as if telling me to behave. I wondered if I would if he said that word out loud to me again.

I pressed against his hold, leaning with my chest. "I thought you brought me out here to fuck me. I thought that was the agreement. One night, you asked for."

His jaw was rigid. "That is what I said."

"Okay, then let's get to it." My hands were already back on the task of getting his pants off.

He slid his grip from my shoulders to my hands—stilling me. Stilling us both. "Don't you wish to know why I brought you to this place? Or do you see yourself as a whore carrying out a duty because I saved you? I want you here by your choice."

I scoffed and clucked my tongue before finding immediate composure—possibly a new trait of mine. "What I *see* is a woman who can have a one-night stand and not think twice about it tomorrow. You're hot, Caolann. Like really fucking beautiful now that I think about it. But we're not riding off into the sunset at dawn to marry beneath a willow tree in secret. I am not a good person, and neither are you. But I want to feel you on top of me, feel you inside me, feel weightless. I thought that's what you wanted, too? Someone you could fuck without worrying. Without loose ends."

"I do want that."

"Then what?"

He dipped his head to settle his gaze on mine, then scratched his tattooed brow like he needed a moment. "I want to tell you a story first. I trust you hold many questions of my journey to Magh Mell, but first, that is my intention—to tell you a story."

"So..." I twisted a loop of my hair. "Sex for dessert?"

"Yes." He kissed my neck, slowly, spreading the thickness of lips over the soft area. "For dessert."

As much as I wanted to know what had happened in Magh Mell, or get his pants off, we settled by the fire, me leaning on his shoulder, suddenly and unexpectedly excited to hear him speak more than a few words. "Then I'm listening."

He cleared his throat, leaning closer to the flame just enough that it teased the idea of hurting him. "My mother worshipped the True Gods, Danu and Bíle. She bestowed prophecies upon the Ardagh folk. Many claimed that the roots of Bíle's first tree grew in the depths of her eyes as a child, granting her divine vision. I trusted Mother to foresee what lay ahead for me.

"In my eighth year, she told me that when I took my first breath, the world changed. In my thirteenth year, she revealed that before the moon turned whole, my place in Dagda's army, the Dylis, was secure."

Caolann frowned at the fire, recalling his old life, every word causing his brow to knit deeper into his perfect, sharp nose.

"Upon recruiting me, the Dylis stripped me bare, throwing me inside a stone-walled cell with little water and grain to live. I spoke to my mind constantly, telling the voice they wished to test me, to see my strength grow. That I would prevail. Yet much time passed; doubt consumed me, letting the voice grow wicked. Had they confined me for I was not worthy? I saw myself pathetic. Weak. Without purpose."

He had been locked away like I had been in St. Brigid's. "How long did they keep you in there?" He didn't answer. Maybe he couldn't.

"Many endless moments passed until solitude ended with the unlocking of a door. I crawled into a hallway where a boy and girl, older than me, mirrored me in frailty; all of us covered in dirt and oozing cuts, craving the juice of dock leaves to assuage our pain. A Dylis warrior greeted us, speaking words never to leave me: '*You are three that remain of one hundred recruits. You are worthy.*'

"Moons passed under my assigned duty to train youngling recruits. I became an official Dylis warrior in my nineteenth summer. The initiation was to slaughter traitors guilty of treason. I simply heeded the command, conditioned by Dagda's rule. Travelling under nightfall, knife at the ready, I found the home. To my horror, the enemy was but two youngling girls, hidden beneath a bed. Now orphan twins who disappeared by the touch of one another. Their cold air breath forfeited their hiding."

"*Now* orphans," I gasped, recoiling from him. "You killed their parents."

"Yes."

"And the children?" I asked, not wanting that answer. Not wanting this night to be selfishly spoiled.

He shook his head profusely. "I ordered them to hide elsewhere. Told them Dagda hunted them. I know now he wished to destroy their uncontained power for their parents would not submit to him."

He poked the fire with a stick. "To take an undeserving life is something I take no pleasure in. But I force myself to remember." He traced the white knots that scarred his inner forearm. I counted three. Three lives he had taken with regret. But how many did he kill without any?

I took the opportunity to caress his stretched arm, running my fingers over the bumps. To let him know I understood. That I had my own notches to bear. That I supported his bravery to share his story and defy orders to not make it five.

"To leave Dagda's army is self-slaughter, and my end would soon come. I accepted my fate and so I paid my final visit home. But I returned to a terrible truth." The flames ravaged his eyes. "Often, younger kin inherit a weaker Bua, but Rían gleamed having me walk naked among the streets with a mere sentence of command. Such power to bend the mind so easily is unheard of. Dagda would wish to either slaughter or control him. This, Clíona"—his gaze darted to me, just for beat—"is why I trusted you when you spoke of harvesting great strength, for I have seen it in my own kin.

"Mother foresaw my slaughter and Rían's fate no better if we stayed. Her heart was broken, but she had Cáit, our sister, in her eighth year when we left. It hollowed me to abandon them, yet the journey would have..." He swallowed so hard his Adam's apple bobbed and trembled, but he pushed through the discomfort. "We seized our moment to cross Ardagh's border. A Dylis warrior, one I trained with since younglings, was loyal. His Bua shifted me and Rían beyond the stone wall.

"Having freed ourselves of Ardagh wishing to slaughter us, Glas—the long desert—swiped its claws for our demise. Securing a boat was impossible. Too many regions in the south were manned by his men. Too many Giants dwelling on coasts. Too many eyes forced us to go where only vultures could see us. We were stuck out there an entire cycle of the moon.

Our supplies were soon bare, and our legs collapsed, as did our hope. We believed our end had come, yet our withered eyes could not shed a sole tear." His voice cracked, and he covered his mouth in an attempt to disguise his vulnerability.

I slid my hand into his, squeezing tight, willing my heart to beat quietly so I could hear the rest.

"There is peace drifting into death, even as the vultures came and picked at our flesh, but amongst the delusions, I saw the night sky shone brighter in the distance, humming, pulsing with life. I spoke to my mind as I did in my cell, telling it I *was* worthy of being Rían's saviour. I dug into my core, searching for a final bone of strength. I dragged his body to the first sight of grass we had seen in days. And live, Rían did."

"You...you saved Rían when everything—every instinct—told you there was no hope."

He threw a log on the fire to keep it ablaze, its warmth reaching our fingers. "Do you always see value in people?"

Caolann's honesty allured me. He wasn't the man I presumed. This man was kind and heroically selfless—or at least part of him was. I envied him for doing what I could not. "Your life hardened you, but it hasn't made you cruel. Your value is easier to see than the sun."

His sullen eyes drifted to the sky, drenched in the guilt of his past. "If I shared all my cruelty with you..." No wonder he saw the sorrow in mine. But that begged the question: would he still want me if he knew my truth?

Pushing that away, I moved to rest my palm on his cheek, beckoning him to look at me, to pull him from his bad thoughts. He heeded my call, eyes soft and in awe as if they were still lost in the memories of starlight. Beaten by the nerves contouring my belly, I went to move my hand, but he clasped it, seemingly grateful for the touch. The warmth of his breath heated the tip of my tongue.

"I fear a sole touch of your lips will pull a forever unravelling ribbon, Clíona."

He was so right, but I inched forward into the lingering space of uncertainty. Waiting. Yearning. Pleading for him to touch me anywhere.

In a unified gasp, he filled the gap, meeting my lips with such passion and strength everything else became void.

His stubble prickled across my mouth's rim as his tongue curled into mine. I breathed in the fresh earth smell trapped in his hair. In his clothes. In his skin. Embracing our intensity so willingly, my eyes fluttered, too ravenous and greedy to focus on just one part of him. He wanted this, and I held his hair to show my want, too. My touch of his leg encouraged a groan from him, making his grasp heavier. Fervid, even.

It made me want to take all my clothes off and bare my soul to him, in that foolish way it always did when lowered inhibitions caught me by the throat.

The longing and kissing went on, lost to time and still, it would never be enough.

He edged away, breathless. The reassurance of seeing that was almost as nice as the kiss.

As he nibbled on my neck, and I stared at the sky I said, "I was wondering..."

"Hmm?" The noise was low and gravelly.

"You said you'd beg on your knees with no fear of losing pride if that's what it took."

"I did."

"Would you take a knee for me?"

He pulled away from my neck, his stare moving from my mouth to my eyes as he unravelled what my words meant. "Stand," he told me urgently.

I did, suddenly nervous now he'd taken the bait. I took my lip between teeth, hoping the night would mask the movement.

His expression had changed to something deeper and more serious. "Lift your dress."

I obeyed.

He kneeled, just as I asked, his heavy touch clasping the edges of my thighs.

"Now hold it there. Do not let go. Behave."

He wanted me to be a spectator of the pleasure he gave. Just the idea of that made me wet.

The first touch of his mouth to the sweet skin of my navel was loud and ravenous, startling the sleeping birds above us as my gasp echoed.

His journey lower was slow; my muscles contracted painfully so as not to force his head down with my hands. Thumbs found the tendons between my legs, firmly pressing on this as he clenched by bottom to pull me closer.

Clutching the bark of the tree, I hitched my leg, pressing myself onto my tiptoes so he could reach without having to go on all fours.

Then he sucked me in with his tongue until diluting it into the spot. *The* spot. Gentle brushes came over it slowly, tasting until it got faster and stronger like he was starved, and I was his only source of food.

I grasped his head with both hands, sliding my fingers over his wild hair, pulling him closer.

"Not half bad," I teased, panting.

He smirked, tickling delicate skin. Then he looked up at me, sucking and vacuuming the pleasure tighter and tighter, silently telling me this was just the beginning. The starter.

"Mmm." I sighed. "Better."

His fingers slowly slid to the interior of my thighs, a firm push spreading my legs further apart. A strained whimper seeped out of my mouth. The flames flickered over the edges of his body.

Twigs snapped—a strong reminder we were out in the open. Anyone could come upon us, but I didn't care when Caolann stole my attention all over again.

"I thought you just wanted sex in the way most do." I swallowed, forcing myself to speak through the gluttony of what he was giving me. "Driven by their own thoughts and desires. But you're thoughtful. Passionate." I fixed my hair behind my ears just to keep my hands from reaching out and squeezing his head harder.

He pulled back, coming up for air. "I cannot stop my will. You are a force."

My hand reached again anyway, curving into his neck so that my thumb rested on his lips.

He kissed it, then, ever so slowly, he slid his fingers in between my legs, pushing them gradually inside, touching that spot, hooking it for me to impossibly come closer. My eyelids fluttered and my leg hitched higher against the tree to show him I wanted more, and I wanted it harder.

And I wanted to see it.

And...

As I parted my lips to get lost again, a pitched scream echoed from deep within the forest.

Caolann drew back. My frame shifted and my leg slid down from the tree.

Another cry bellowed louder.

I pushed his fingers away.

"A child?" I asked.

He stood and threw a bucket of water on the smoking fire, stunned in indecision.

"Save me!" a child's voice pleaded.

I thought he would've run to the screams, would have rightly abandoned me here.

"Caolann!" I clicked my fingers so close they brushed his nose, finally snapping him out of it.

Coming back to himself, he grabbed my shoulders. "Use your Bua, Clíona. Show us where they are. Picture it in your mind. Hope for it! However the fuck your Bua works, use it now."

My hands rattled. "I—I can't control it! I don't understand. I don't know what you want from me."

With wild eyes, he searched for something to guide us. "The Soilse. They'll light the way. Come to us," he called out. Hundreds of them swarmed us in an instant, illuminating a blue pathway toward the screams. "We search for you, youngling," he shouted as we took off into the deepening forest with no care for the scratches and scrapes of the bushes designed to hinder us.

"Please!" the child cried out, blistering the air. Blistering the edges of my ears as I felt crucial seconds melt away.

We ground to a halt when coming upon a small shadow. The child's exhaling breaths of cold air were the only indication this little girl kneeling on muddied ground was still alive.

Then a sob strained from her mouth as she cried into fists. Something was clenched in them.

Caolann cradled her, letting her sobs wet his shoulder. "Are you of harm, little one?"

"A man took her," she wailed into the night sky. "His face I could not see."

"Who?" Caolann asked, shaking more than he should have. Such a little thing she was. More bone than child.

I think we both knew what had happened here. Another attempted abduction. But I couldn't focus on that when all my attention was still drawn to what she held in her hand.

"He told me to forgive him."

"He?" Caolann said.

A human. It's been a human all this time.

I peeled her fingers, one by one, to reveal something red and stringy. "Hair?" I told Caolann, looking for any sign of explanation on his face.

"You said travelling in twos would keep us safe. I tried to save her. His...his strength was beyond me."

All the air sucked out of me. "What's your name?" I asked her.

"What does that matter?" Caolann protested.

"Tell me your name, child!"

"Sh–Shayla. My mother named me Shayla."

"And who was it you travelled with?" I asked, knowing, just *knowing* the answer already. A gaping feeling shredded through me, excavating the tiny seed of relief I'd only just planted in my heart.

The girl wiped a string of mucus dripping onto her lips. "I travelled with Róisín. We came to pick the cold sloes. It takes the bitterness from them, but the boys already get them before we come in the morn. She said we should come at night to take them first. But he stole her into the night."

"There is no sense to this," Caolann fumed to the sky more than the child.

"We have to find her." I couldn't tell Bébhinn the alternative. I couldn't lose another person. I stood to leave...to call for her.

"Róisín—"

"You waste your breath. A taken youngling never returns. She is gone," he said, defeated, his frame widening as if he was rebelling against the hunch his body wanted to contort into.

Tears collected in my waterline, and the shaking in my hands intensified. "Are you fucking crazy? They were just here! You're meant to care for her. Now come on." Midstride he grabbed my arm.

I stared at the callous touch, and then at him. It echoed bad memories that made this exchange seconds from a bad fallout.

He stood from Shayla, his confrontational stare maddening the white of his eyes into something red and sinister. "I searched for moons for these younglings. She is gone. You running into darkness will divide us!" He yelled a harrowing roar before extending his fist into a tree so hard it stung my ears. "Fuck!" The tree groaned, its roots snapping as it took two more with it, falling to where they once came. Dust rose and simmered, until the forest returned to slumber.

Caolann raged into his palms, his knuckles bloodied and skinless to the bone.

I dared not ask him how he could punch a tree so hard it collapsed. He was more powerful than I ever thought.

Peeling free his hands, he scooped Shayla into his arms to lead us home, Soilse loyally following until the forest's end. Saoirsians emerged from their homes to watch, bowing as Caolann passed Shayla to her distraught mother. An older man, lip shrouded by an untamed beard, placed a meaningful hand on Caolann's shoulder. "We would be lost without your guide, boy."

The man's kind words made no impact. Caolann was but a shadow of himself. A shadow darkened even more for reaching Bébhinn's home. My muscles spasmed for the sight of it, bones beneath screaming at me to run. It was a selfish urge, but the duty of telling a mother that her child was gone wasn't a job I wanted.

I wiped my endless tears, checking them as if they might be different each time.

"Stay by my side," Caolann asked me. "I cannot hold this burden alone."

I held his hand to agree.

"Bébhinn," he croaked, his voice deceiving him.

She appeared from the house, uncaring of us as she rummaged through her apron. "Back so soon? Never mind. I am off to fetch Róisín."

Caolann stood to attention, returned to his warrior form. "It is Róisín." He paused, battling his jaw for composure. "It happened...in the forest."

Her attention drew from her apron, her smile fading at the sight of his bloodied hand. "What happened in the forest?"

"She's gone," I said. "They—*he* took her."

Her lip quivered. "No. She is with Shayla," she protested, an odd certainty in her response to prolong the illusion of normality.

"We brought Shayla home. We found her—" My voice broke into a sob. "—holding a clump of Róisín's hair." Bébhinn would never see her again. Róisín might as well be dead if she wasn't already.

Caolann wrapped his arms around Bébhinn's swaying frame before her legs gave out. "Forgive me, Bébhinn. She is gone."

"No, she—no. No. NO!" Bébhinn fought Caolann's hold. She kicked the air. Punched his arms. Her high pitch scream pierced the calm sky. "My baby," she wailed how only a mother could for their child before crumbling them both into the soil. "I carried her *inside* me. It was my purpose to protect her. All...all my children are gone." Saliva frothed along her gaping lips. Her eyes clenched into deep folds.

The loss of Fionn bubbled to the surface like boiling tar. I couldn't bear it. Losing the one you love most was worse than that of a thousand knives in skin.

It was nature's cruellest trick.

20

THE BIRD'S VIEW

How long had I been standing outside?

My bones ached, but with grief or the morning chill, I couldn't say. The hum of waking birds kindly dulled my sniffles which would be retching cries if I hadn't suffered so much heartache already. Still, I was no better for knowing life was inherently cruel because I should have done more. I should have scraped my hands through every thistle bush and prayed to all their fucking gods.

Poor Róisín. My sweet little friend. Who'd search for her if not Caolann? He seemed so defeated. They all did. Saoirse had accepted the fate of their children, and another innocent life had been snatched into oblivion, leaving nothing but a clump of hair. Nevermore would Róisín loop her precious locks in red ribbon. Never again would she laugh or rebel or harvest.

I flinched. No. I had to stop thinking she was dead. I was no better than anyone else with that mindset. I left then, pacing into the forest a little surer of my bearings that surprisingly, by instinct, brought me to Caolann's secret cabin.

Before going inside, I again checked for patches of blood on the forest bed. I'd murdered two men here not long ago, and the lack of true care or regret I had for that was starting to worry me. The rules were different in this world, but that didn't mean I had to be part of it. Did it?

In seconds, I drew a piping hot tub of water. Disrobing from Bébhinn's old dress and removing the bra I was happy to throw away, I dipped my toe in the water. The rest of myself quickly followed. I nearly salivated at how balmy it felt against my grimy skin. The freshness. The feeling of being clean and not having to think about anything else for a moment. It was blissful—a feeling I didn't know existed anymore.

"Clíona?"

Fucking seriously?

I shot up from the tub, then immediately crossed my arms over my chest when I realised I was completely naked and the layer of foam resting on the water's skin was not completely forgiving.

Caolann stepped inside, only to halt abruptly just past the threshold.

A loud dripping barely dulled the silence as his eyes, circled with redness, turned molten. Affixed to the suds melting and cascading down my curves.

I averted my gaze, as if hiding my eyes could somehow make me disappear. "Sorry. I should have asked first—"

"No." He took a hard step forward before clearing his throat to use his brassy tone. "I mean to say, continue. I understand the desire to wash the sadness from your skin."

A fleeting consideration of resuming what we started last night came to mind. His tongue on my body. My body curling around him. Melting our skin together.

Sex was the best way to forget everything—good sex.

Feeding off whatever I was giving out, his jaw turned stiff as his eyes ran over my body through the tiny gaps forming in the foam no longer hiding nipples or much else, for that matter. In the charged moment, the air felt crackled with a tension I feared might electrocute me where I stood. It was as if he was searching for answers beneath my surface, ones he knew I'd never dare to give him.

"Fuck, you are truly beautiful, Clíona." I seemed to spill out of him so fast I'd worried he'd lose his teeth if he said any more. "The taste of you in my mouth...it lingers. I have to refrain from licking my lips."

Quietly laughing at his brazen words, I loosely lowered to my knees to submerge myself back into the water's pleasant heat. My arm draped across the tub's ledge so he couldn't see anymore of me. The game of seduction between us was almost instinctual at this point. "You're quite handsome yourself, you know. I'd love every inch of someone like you in another life."

"Not this life, though?" He asked with little offence or care, adding a matter-of-fact nod.

I laid my head along my sudsy arm, looking up at him with a fond smile I wasn't expecting to come. "No. Not this one I'm afraid." Sex and love may be intertwined, but I could tell he was just as bruised from life as I was. That he knew love wasn't an option. Lust, attraction, even admiration, sure. But never love.

He moved briskly again, and in two steps he was crouching at the chest by the tub's foot. "Here," he said, taking a dress—maroon and white—from it. "Clean clothes."

I scooted to the tub's end, still kneeling. He was so close desire swelled in my belly, and above the call of logic. Gnawing the inside of my cheek, I forced myself to stare at the rotting wood. Now wasn't the time when a plan was forming in my head. One I started on my journey here. I needed it to stay at the forefront so as not to forget the finer details of my new delusion.

"An old lover?" I teased, keeping it light.

He smirked and came closer again, until we were nose to wet nose. "Yes."

I bit my lips and inclined my head, feeding into his silent beckon. "Maybe next time she'll join us."

Stay on track, Clíona.

His eyebrow arched. "Next time?"

"Oh, you thought I was done with you." I grabbed the dress from his hand and stood, letting all the water clinging to me crash back into the tub.

He flinched at the splash, drawing a soft laugh over my lips. Not even death and gore brought that out in him.

Solidifying my first thought that Caolann was a chivalrous man, he turned, jaw rigid all over again as I dried and dressed myself. The material was far softer on my skin than Bébhinn's tartan, and the white cushion holding in my breasts was, well, magnificent. A simple knotting of the string just swept the girls up and into place while the maroon fell in gentle folds, embroidered in gold swirls and catching at my knees and elbows. It was accompanied by a brown leather corset that I liked the look of more than the feeling.

"It's a really pretty dress," I said, signalling with a gentle tap that he could turn around.

Unexpectedly, his eyes swept over me more blatantly and longer than they ever did in the tub. Breaking the connection he clearly hated being controlled by so easily, he said, "It is the fabric of a god. Strong in texture, amorous, yet light."

"Where did your old lover get something this fancy?"

"She was a goddess."

"You fucked a god?" The outrage in my voice was unexpected. I might as well have forfeited our little game of seduction if I was going to be this dramatic over a past lover.

He folded his arms somehow making his muscles look snug when all nestled together. "I have been with many a god."

"Yeah, well..." I started for the door, briefly looking over my shoulder at him. "I bet it never reached the pleasure you had last night just from licking me." Not waiting to see his reaction, I walked out the door—because I was absolutely in the wrong. The porkie of all the porkies.

"Where are you going?" he called after me.

"Back to the village. I have business to attend to."

"Clíona." My name was a warning, telling me not to be foolish about whatever it was I was up to.

Maybe I was being foolish. No, I was *definitely* being foolish.

"Caolann," I turned around, mimicking his tone. "I know what you're thinking, but the bond is broken now, right? That was the deal. I'm no longer your *bound girl*. You can let me be alone for a couple of hours. I need to make my own choices."

"I still vowed to protect you in the place of that title."

Why did he have to say it with so much affection and protectiveness? And why did I so foolishly believe him when I didn't want this?

I smoothed my lips flat, not letting him sidetrack me. "Yeah, well, we'll see about that. Now come on. We need to get back to Bébhinn and Rían, and we need to go now."

He followed. "What plans do you have?"

"Just shut up and let me lead you for once."

Bébhinn, puffy-eyed, lumbered from her house as we approached, Rían by her side with a hand on her elbow to take the weight of grief from her. She must've been exhausted. Nobody ever tells you that: how tiring it is to lose a loved one. It's like your life source dries up as each tear leaves your body.

Reaching out, Bébhinn's arms wrapped tight around my shoulders, giving *me* something when it was meant to be the other way around. As the brothers disappeared inside, I wished I had useful words for her. Even now, when the world had taken everything from her, she was kind.

So why wasn't I? Why did Fionn's death only make me heartless?

Inside, Rían was tying new feathers to an arrow before placing it into the pile next to him on Bébhinn's kitchen table. Caolann was drinking something muddy and so eye-wateringly strong from the bottle I could smell it from the other side of the room.

"I searched for her until sunrise," Bébhinn started. "A trail formed, but footsteps ran dry, tainted by prints of wild elk." She paced as spoke—stern and serious. Revived since I'd seen her last. She hadn't lost hope completely, but even if she did, it was not for me to stand in the way of her earned grief.

If Róisín was alive, she would be terrified. A fate perhaps worse for a mother to be plagued with each night. My heart was heavy with helplessness. Which was why I had to use my power to find her. It had to have some light in its centre. There had to be a way to twist it into something better than the thing that ruined my life.

I could admit the plan I'd formed was surely the beginning of insanity, but I knew in my core it was how we could find Róisín. And if I could do that, if I could bring her home into her mother's arms, maybe I could be redeemed. Maybe hope was in store for both of us.

Rían huffed as he flexed his fingers along the groove of his new bow. "Our enemy is not elk. We must be wise. The trails were purposely tainted."

"Perhaps this predator—this *man,* did not hunt alone," Bébhinn suggested without conviction.

"That's a good sign," I said, making sure to smile at her. "It's easier to find two people because they'd have to speak aloud to plan their attacks. They're more likely to be overheard and caught. And if it's a man, they're more likely to brag." Róisín's abduction wasn't in vain. She'd given us a clue: the assailant didn't hurt her on the spot. They captured her. And Shayla said *he*, so they were human. And though we learned little more of him beyond that brief description, it was enough to fuel our hope that she might still be alive. "I see your mind." Caolann's arms folded so tight his biceps thickened atop his already large frame. "You plan a retaliation against this man."

"Like I said, it might be more than one. Either way, we have to take a stance." My words sounded hollow despite the truth of the plan revving inside me, only truly forming in real time.

Bébhinn wiped sudden, fresh tears on a ragged cloth. "This, too, has been said. We sent searches from Saoirse's clans since the first youngling vanished. Saoirsians pretend it does not happen until it is their youngling—when it is too late. I fear the sole route to finding them is if Mórrígan herself descends."

"Why doesn't Mórrígan descend?" I asked the room, fully aware I was heading into dark territory bringing up the insidious Banríon. But if there was ever a time to use my big, unfiltered mouth, this was it.

Bébhinn scoffed, mucous dribbling from her raw nose. "What truth lies beyond your words?"

This really was dark territory, so much so that my throat strained to stop me from speaking. "Why the fuck isn't Mórrígan doing anything to protect the children? Or any of these so-called gods. Why are they hiding in Magh Mell when they have a bird's-eye view of these lands? Huh?"

The room dashed hazel and green glares to one another as Caolann peaked through the door.

"Clíona, watch your words," Bébhinn warned me. Her finger, sharp as a nail, met the skin of my cheek. Could I blame her for not speaking out now when she'd risked her life for me upon the Carraig? The day I became indebted to her with my life.

"Let her speak. The gods have done nought for her." Rían spoke with enough venom to stain the grooves of his teeth black. I couldn't blame him either after hearing Dagda's wicked plans for him back in Ardagh.

"Yes. I've got a plan," I said, straining to keep my voice down. Not *wanting* to. "Bébhinn, I owe you my life. I'd probably be dead if you hadn't helped. It's time to repay you for that. The last few years of my life have been a blur of mistakes, and selfishness. Wallowing. And I'm sick to death of it. Sick of feeling sick and...guilty." I sucked in a deep breath as I prepared myself—and them—for my next words. "I'm going to give you that bird's-eye view. The one the gods refuse to. A view someone of the highest power would possess can only be sought one way."

Caolann banged the table, figuring out my punchline. "Clíona—"

I ignored him. "I'm entering Lúnasa. I'm going to compete even if it kills me. Because if I can't find a god to help, I'm going to have to become a comrade of the Tuatha Dé Dannan. Rían told me when you win, the gods grant you The Divine Gift. As long as the children are breathing, then the Tuatha are bound by their rules to find them. I know my Bua would be of value to them if I truly learnt to control it. I can be an asset to them." I inched my jaw upwards, channelling all my confidence into my next words. "I'm going to win Lúnasa—for Róisín."

The hush of my announcement was quickly blemished by the eruption of objections and flailing arms, clawing to reason with me.

"You cannot do this," Caolann fumed, the veins in his arms growing thicker. And yet he did not move even a fraction closer to me. "You lay your life in the hands of those who wish to slaughter you. You will not surpass the journey out to the first trial's terrain, let alone complete it unscathed. No. I fucking forbid it!"

I sucked my cheeks between my teeth to maintain composure while his temper got the better of him. His reaction was as expected and entertaining, but pointlessly humouring this side of him would be unwise.

Rían nudged past Caolann, to get out in front to voice his thoughts. "I warned you, Clíona, you are not carved from the warrior's line."

Damn. If even Rían wouldn't support me, my chance of success would be low.

"Are you truly gifted enough to wield a power beyond the warriors of these lands?" Bébhinn asked, striking some intrigue.

"If she were to begin her training as a youngling, certainly. But not even a god can truly bend time to such lengths. She is not strong enough," Caolann answered for me, heat crawling up his neck. "That is the truth of why Dagda sentenced her to the Tearminn—he could not wield her for his evil will." He threw me a stern glare, the kind where you just know someone is on the brink of explosion. "This path may reveal your strength, Clíona. Dagda is not the sole person who would fear or seek such gifts."

"Rathnor already has a fair idea of what I can do. I don't care! I don't care who I'm bound to or who's next in line to try their hand at taking me out. I'm doing this. So, it's either you all help me, or you don't. Like you said, Caolann, I'll probably be slaughtered before I ever start. You really want that on your conscience, *protector?*"

I was being cruel and unfair, but I didn't care.

"Amazing," Bébhinn muttered to herself, taking up a gnaw on her fingernails.

I took her hands in mine before she had fewer fingers than me, stealing her gaze from her own thoughts. "Bébhinn, listen to me. I'm doing it. I'm doing it for Róisín, and nobody can stop me. I owe you my life, yes, but I would have volunteered anyway."

"You are a woman of your own mind," she started. "I saw that the moment we met. I do not want you to compete, but the choice is yours. I love my daughter; you must know this. I would do anything for her. If my Bua permitted, I'd compete myself."

"I'm bringing her home, Bébhinn. You hear?" I pulled her into the hug I also owed her. We rocked as one as I repeated the words over and over. "I'm bringing her home. I'm bringing her home."

The plan was dangerous and far-fetched, if not impossible, but it was the only one I had, the only way. And for the first time in a long time, I had faith that I could achieve something beyond my scope. This was my path, and no Druid in a prison cell needed to foresee it for me to know it was the right one.

Caolann grumbled a thunderous sigh and rubbed his eyes with bunched fists. "You will never champion Lúnasa. Never. You walk the path to your death." The whites of his eyes had reddened, making them appear sinister and poisonous against the green. His anger rallied in his jaw as he stormed outside, the clatter of wood and gushing water signalling his anger beyond view.

Though I gently pulled from Bébhinn, I stayed put. There were bigger issues to tackle than comforting my beautiful, misunderstood warrior. Yet truthfully, I wanted to follow him, yearning for his touch. Craving the taste of his warm breath on every inch of my body.

I shook my head. Jesus Christ. Now isn't the time to be selfish.

"It is no youngling's game," Rían told me, perhaps coming around to the idea. Or maybe he just knew how stubborn I was by now.

Bébhinn pinched her lips, as if to keep herself from interrupting him.

He planted his hands firmly on my shoulders. "It is a battle, and the sacrifice of slaughter is always fulfilled before Lúnasa's end. The gods love no greater offering than life."

"Then help me," I pleaded, my hands breaking free to flail in every direction, annoyed it hadn't sunk in that my decision was final. "Tell me what I need to know, unless you have a better idea for how we're going to find Róisín. Find the other missing children."

"It is greater than any other plan I have suffered the detail of," Rían said.

Bébhinn rubbed his arm with maternal comfort. "Caolann is—"

I waved my hand to stop her. "I understand he's searched for them, but my plan means we won't need to. These children *can* be found." I couldn't sell this plan any better to get them on board. But with no guarantee, I also couldn't blame their hesitation.

Caolann stormed back into the room just as fiery and unsettled as when he'd left. "Leave us to speak," he said, locking eyes with mine.

I moved to leave.

"No *you*." He paused. "*Them*."

My gaze swept over each of them before the bite found my words. "This is Bébhinn's home. You can't demand her to—"

"I can and I have." His tone was suddenly calm. Almost chilling. "Bébhinn?"

His quiet demeanour only stoked my anger more. "Don't you dare—"

Bébhinn's fingers gripped my wrist as she said my name in a stern hush, like *I* was somehow the one in the wrong.

I opened my mouth to argue, but her head shake solidified the silent warning.

The seriousness of it finally hit me, and I managed a nod.

Alone, the unsettling silence stretched on as we stared at each other, unwavering, the needless standoff lasting far too long.

I wouldn't bend to Caolann. He must've known that.

"Rían will not help if I command him so," he finally said in a snooty, unfitting voice.

Now it was my turn to fold my arms tightly. "Rían is his own person. Therefore, you don't own him. You don't get to dictate his views. Or mine, for that matter. And I was never going to ask him to compete. I'm not that selfish." My hands untangled to land on my hips, and I left them there, staring, as the silence lingered for what felt like a lifetime.

"Ugh!" I flung them toward the straw ceiling with a groan that would hock up a soul. "Stop being so bloody stubborn and tell me *why*. Why do you think this idea is awful? My Bua has the potential to take me all the way. Rían said as much in the forest." Well, he insinuated it.

"The final battle is the place I worry of." He moved to fix his rigid body against my chest, caressing the baby hairs along my neck—a pleasurable reminder of my want for him. On my lips. Against my chest. Between my legs. I fought the foolish flutter of my lids.

"In the final trial, you battle a past champion," he spoke a little softer, sensing my anger loosening. "The gods, they choose your opponent—one who holds your weakness. Many battles still end in the previous victor's continued glory. You cannot beat him."

"Who?"

"Do you not see?" he shouted with a maniacal laugh cutting in and out with each quick breath he took. "Rathnor! Rathnor is a past champion. He will leap at the chance to lawfully slaughter you before all of Saoirse. Your life will be his final token. The grand ending of his game."

Though that prospect terrified me, I held my glare firm, swallowing the jitters clawing up my throat. "Or maybe I'll have the chance to fairly slaughter *him*." The threat came out empty. Caolann knew it, too. I may have killed my brother, killed the mayor, and killed those two creeps in the forest, but they were all accidents. And I'd suffered every second since taking Fionn's life.

I dipped my head from his touch, but his hand followed as if instinctively, sliding across my lips to pucker and misshape them. The guilt was reprising; everything was too close to home. If this mission did help me atone Fionn's death and dispel the guilt, would killing Rathnor just undo anything I did to make it right? There had to be a way to win without more blood on my hands.

"Listen," I stepped away, out of his touch. "I'll deal with him if the time comes. For now, all I'm worried about is how these trials work. So, can you help?" I tried to make my voice soft and pleasurable. "Maybe train me like you train others in Réimse Mór? Or better yet, come with me."

He squinted with internal anguish, wrestling himself for the answer. "No. And I will not guide you to death."

I clamped the bitterness on my tongue and turned to leave with heavy strides, grabbing a blunt kitchen knife from the worktop as I went.

"Where are you going?" He grasped my forearm, disarming me of my weapon in an instant.

I curved my shoulder and yanked from his touch. "I'm off to find someone who *will* guide me."

My words were met with silence as I marched forward with an extra kick in my step, the precipice of my madness in tow.

21
DIVINE BLOOD

Réimse Mór was still filled with the wonderful flowers Róisín had created. I bent to touch those on the field's cusp, but it only brought a pressuring well to cry. Before it happened, I stood with a deep inhale, dwelling on Caolann's worry and how it had been expressed through both his harsh and kind tones. His refusal had confirmed I was embarking on a journey so treacherous, he felt he couldn't be part of it. A journey I might not come back from...

"Lester," I called, finding him in the crowd for his blond ponytail and stretched frame. The boys with him shouted and joked.

"I bet she is an easy nut to crack," one heckled.

"Fear not, our Lester will tame those wild eyes," another teased.

All of ten seconds in my company would erase any of those presumptions from their minds. If Lúnasa accepted wildcards, immunity to subjugation would certainly be mine.

Still, I snickered as Lester shoved them like skittles to walk through their taunts, ignoring the echo of whistles and hoots chasing him across field.

"Dia dhuit, my fiery-haired friend. If you come to tell me of Róisín's disappearance, I assure you I searched through nightfall."

I failed to deter my gaze from his dark circles. God, he was brave for a boy so young. "That's why I'm here." Lester was always going to be my first choice outside the brothers. He really did remind of Fionn—the kind of lad who knew how to make an impression. Regrowing body parts was the definition of impressive. "Listen, I won't beat around the bush. I'm going to enter Lúnasa."

"And I wish for a hen who lays twenty a day." He slugged water from his skin-covered flask, exposing his armpit clung to by a mere six hairs.

I kept my expression resolute, ensuring he understood I meant every word I said.

As it dawned on him, he choked, spluttering water he tried to tame with heavy coughs. "A cracked nut. Cannot. Champion. Lúnasa!"

"Yeah, well, we'll see. Winning might help us find her."

"By the gods, you are cracked. What would my duty be in this?"

I shrugged. "Turn me into someone who could at least hold their own if it comes to it."

"I fear your mind is more maimed than whispered of. Yet"—Lester offered his hand, and I locked onto it, an unexpected smile mirroring our faces—"any cause in search of Róisín is one I surrender myself to. I am all yours, cracked one."

Appreciation swelled in me. I had him on board, an ally per se, and so, maybe a fighting chance of pulling this off.

Lester and I strayed beneath a large oak; its branches gaped as if to invite us to abide in its cooling shade. En route, Lester draped his arm on my shoulder, his breath tickling my ear: "No misdeed to you. You are a delicacy to be in company with, but our gods will not allow a nut to share their power."

Me being crazy was a consensus I'd chosen to no longer pay heed to—in both worlds. Maybe they were all right, maybe not. What was reality anymore but my own perception of it? I stepped through a portal to ancient Ireland for goodness' sake. Nothing was normal anymore.

"Cracked or not, I can harvest great power," I said sternly, to double down on the persona I need to embody from this point on. "I just need help accessing it without my emotions getting in the way." What great power constituted was actually a grey area to me. Isn't control part of the power itself? A poor wielder of a great sword was still going to get themselves killed.

Lester's arm fell from my shoulder, a grin on his lips puppeteered by his brazen core. He paced backwards, further into the tree's shade, arms stretching above his shoulders. "You know, I intend to compete myself, nut."

My belly constricted. He was a boy, not an adult. But surely nobody's winning was of greater importance than mine. Even selfishly thinking that constricted my insides harder.

"Second Lúnasa in a row. I barely evaded slaughter in Glas despite my quick healing."

"But you're so young!" The intentions of children who trained in Réimse Mór felt tainted now. Were they there to protect themselves or to murder others in competition? As I took stock of them, I couldn't help but think, who was I to judge? I was almost the same age as Lester when I killed Fionn.

"Trust, I am stronger than these full cheeks might have you believe." He playfully pinched them. "Now, let us begin. Harvest your Bua." His hand smoothed along the air like he was insinuating the field was a stage.

Nerves hit hard in my gut—which now felt more like Jell-O—compelling my hands to search for pockets my dress didn't have. I hadn't planned this far, and now that I had to prove myself to a child veteran, all that power I was sassing about felt unreachable.

Typical.

"Come on." His head playfully dipped sideways. "Reveal to the gods your strength. Make them believe they *must* grant you glory. Make them drop a boulder on your opponent because you are the one they want as their new comrade."

"Would they actually?"

"It is speculated. Who is to say they do not?"

Honestly, the possibility sounded like it would not go in my favour. "Who are these gods I'm trying to impress, anyway?"

He keeled in laughter at what was probably another ridiculous question. "Lugh, God of Light and wielder of a Treasure created these trials, for one."

The Four Treasures folklore was a pillar of learning in our household. We'd road-tripped to Meath annually to visit Lia Fáil—the last standing of the Treasures. So, if I knew anything, it was that Lugh wielded the spear that never misses.

"Come. Focus, cracked one. Harvest the strongest element of your Bua to your advantage."

Wax on wax off. I get it, Mr. Miyagi.

You think you're funny, Clío.

I wouldn't argue with that, but hearing Fionn strained my chest worse than any anxiety. Usually, I found comfort in him, but when I dwelled too long, it evoked anguish—a pain so great my head pulsed at the mere idea of never truly hearing his voice again.

Maybe that was the key: if I could syphon *some* of the emotion and abate it, it might be enough to help me harvest without hurting anyone.

"Go along with what I'm about to do," I said, shaking out my legs and hands.

Lester puffed out his chest, his grin never dulling. "You have seen my strength. I do not fear you, cracked one."

Smiling that much must hurt. "To think I was going to go easy on you."

The warm midday air filled my lungs as I extended my arms. It seemed to make the direction of my Bua clearer and concentrated, and while I'd never say it out loud, I also thought it made me look cooler. Superman flying with a fist forward was always more impressive than without.

My triceps immediately tightened with the familiar flex and warmth of power, harvesting strength from a single, fleeting image of Fionn's clown-like grin. Then I blocked the thought with a wooden door, returning to a place of safety but with enough assisted power. It flowed through my warming veins and into my tingling fingertips to envelop him with the golden sway of light in the shape of tendrils.

"Move." I smiled, confident he couldn't.

Blotches of red filled his face.

Satisfied, I released him as if telling my muscles to drop a heavy weight from my arms. It worked. The subconscious command had been obeyed.

It was working already.

He jumped on the spot, jiggling his arms. "A youngling's Bua."

His cocky attitude only made me more intent. Made my nose scrunch and snarl.

I stood wider, syphoning more power from worse memories: Fionn at his worst, not his best. Fionn sad. Fionn bloody. Fionn impaled. Fionn lifeless. My neck pulsed faster. My hands tensed so hard, I swore my palms lost their creases.

Lester's body slid along the ground, separating loose soil beneath his dragging feet.

"Easy, Clíona," he warned me.

I pinned his body against the shading tree, raising him higher into the air until black spots dotted my vision.

"Release him," Caolann commanded from behind me.

I jumped at the tone, my harvest failing instantly.

Oh no.

Lester flailed twenty feet through the air.

I froze, falling victim to my curse. A bystander to his fate.

Caolann bounded past to catch him.

"No. Please, no!" I clenched my eyes and balled my fists so tightly, my nails pierced the skin. "No. Not a child. Please."

"Release him. *Release him*," Caolann called several times before it registered.

Blinking away dense blotches, I found Lester's purpling face floated inches from the ground.

"But I'm not even using my hands," I whispered.

"Release him now, Clíona! He cannot breathe!"

A wisp of my thrumming fingers was enough to break the connection. He thudded on landing but seeing him safe wasn't enough to dissipate the feeling of dryness in my throat, blocking the apology I wanted to scream.

My vision became hazy as wet warmth dripped onto my lip; I'd overdone it, how I'd evaporated Rían's bow. God, that could have been Lester; ash floating in the soft wind.

Caolann grabbed the poor boy by the scruff. "She is a cracked nut, Lester. You wish to compete in Lúnasa?"

Lester nodded over and over, his tawny eyes much rounder than usual.

"Then do not play games with her! She could turn the blood of your body into a spray on that tree before the grin departed your amadán face."

His bunched grip on Lester's tunic unfurled. "Return to practice. I will take your burden."

Lester gave a weary bow to Caolann, then ran, tail between legs.

Overcome by weakness, I stumbled to a knee, planting my hand on the grass to assist me in staying upright.

It turned out, I didn't need to. Caolann scooped me up, tucking me close to his heated chest.

Fuck, he was strong.

I wanted to protest, tell him I'd walk, but my weakened state said otherwise. My head flopping on our journey barely held off the pull of my stream of unconsciousness.

Caolann lowered me onto a furred bed, his cheek fleetingly pressed to my forehead. Perhaps to check for fever. I rested on my side, watching as he rummaged through bowls and armour before disappearing outside. It was strange to see him scattered and absent of rigid composure.

Apace in his return, he tentatively wiped my nose with a damp cloth until it stained orange. My gaze on him as he cared for me wouldn't falter despite it being obvious. His touch was delicate, a far cry from the certain damage it had inflicted in his past. I reached for him, dissuading him from his dedication to mend me.

"Where are we?" I asked.

"Home."

"Home? I thought the cabin in the woods was home?"

"No. That was our home before the Saoirsians invited us into the community. We were outsiders for many a moon."

We're not so different, you beautiful man.

"Listen," he said, silencing my thoughts. Fingers caressed my cheek as he gathered more words. "I did not foresee your presence in my life, but since your arrival, my mind is filled with unyielding thoughts of you, and you alone. You have nested under my skin."

My want for him surfaced, undeniably, delivering heat to my core with a loud, aching knock.

"Caolann..." I wanted to tell him I craved him. That if things were easier, I'd pounce on him. But I had to think of Róisín. That was my focus now. I barely had time to prepare for Lúnasa without jumping into whatever we were.

He bowed his head as if understanding what I was thinking. "It is a near full moon this nightfall. Lúnasa dawns the next. If you survive, tell me of your true feelings then." He fixed a piece of hair behind my ear. "I will take the right path."

"What path?" I asked, stuffing down my feelings for a later day.

"A path to ensure your victory. Allow me to train you. It is your sole chance of survival."

I sat, too engaged by his change of heart to care about the heaviness still throbbing my head.

His form became postured, and his face rigid—the side of him I was growing to adore just as much as his gentle one. But there was something more to it: a restraint for whatever he wanted to say pressing out the vein on his neck. "Forgive me, for I have not been truthful."

"Lord above, this can't be good news." Secrets never were. At least, not mine.

He swallowed hard in hesitation. "I...claimed victory in Lúnasa two harvest's gone."

"You—hang on—*you* championed Lúnasa?" I blinked fervently. "And you thought that *vital* piece of information couldn't have been shared earlier? What the fuck, Caolann? I'm out here like a headless chicken when you could tell me every single detail about how to win?" I was shouting. When did I start shouting? My head throbbed, but I couldn't lie down when he'd landed this bomb on me.

"Clíona, hear me—"

"No, I will not. You listen to me. Why aren't you infiltrating the Tuatha Dé Danann for information? They might help without The Divine Gift."

"Lower your tone," he seethed. "If Saoirsians overhear, a sentence to the Carraig would be a kindness. And I told you, I severed ties with them on my visit to Magh Mell."

I huffed at him, more childlike than intended.

"To prove myself to Saoirse, I sought the hard route, for if I claimed victory in Lúnasa, perhaps Saoirsians would accept us as their own," he explained. "I do not care for immortality or worship."

My heart hammered, then surely stopped altogether. "Immortal?" It was a word that almost made no sense—a thing of fairy tales and myth. I inched closer to him as if to somehow check his eyes for signs of deceit. "I thought they let you become a comrade of theirs. Like Rathnor."

"When you champion the trials, you receive divine status. You become one of the Tuatha Dé Danann. The offering is solely stripped if chosen to fight in Lúnasa's final trial. In truth, I am part human, part god."

I clutched the frame above the bed to keep upright. "A demigod?" I breathed.

He nodded.

My breath caught in my throat, thick and suffocating. I ran my eyes over him. Immortal?

Caolann was immortal. He could never die. Never be lost like Fionn. It was an assurance nobody else could give me. I could never accidentally kill him.

I shook the temptations away.

"The Tuatha grant me travel to other lands to search for the younglings. They do not care for my words, for I choose to live among the humans, with Rían. I am all he holds in life. Without me close, he would not survive his demons. That was my Divine Gift: to keep a foot in both worlds." He leaned in close, his earthly smell, his steely warmth, enveloping me. "Hear me. Gods use the currency of power. What you harvest could tear down lands in a single command if permitted to reach its peak. Just as Rían would. Mórrígan will dive her talons into your skin if she learns of your strength."

His underlying threat wasn't enough to keep me away. The Tuatha Dé Dannan were the answer to finding Róisín. There was no path of resolution in the absence of power.

"I'm still going to fight."

Caolann pressed his lips together. "I know."

Then he stood and removed a crooked stone from the back wall of the house—one much smaller than Bébhinn's. Loose dirt fell as he reached in to retrieve a book bound in animal skin. A blow on its cover sent spirals of dust tumbling into a ray of sunlight barricading us from one another.

"Secret diary?" I smiled, acknowledging I was being awkward for the sake of it.

His lip twitched with the preface of a smile before it faltered, redirecting his gaze to the brown-washed parchment. He unfolded it onto the table; the parchment's corners perfectly touched the table's edges. "This is all you need know of Lúnasa. There is much to learn if we intend to keep you alive."

I joined him on wobbly legs with the blanket wrapped close, leaning on his shoulder to see a drawn mountain terrain. Sections of trees, boulders, livestock and fields were scratched into different areas of it, the peak covered in rumbling clouds.

"A mountain?" I hadn't pictured Lúnasa as anything other than fighting people in a big field like Réimse Mór.

"This is the *first* trial of Lúnasa. To champion, you journey the mountain to its peak where a coloured flame must be set alight and burned so bright the gods must see from Magh Mell."

"Oh, is that all? Here I was thinking some ancient dragon was waiting for me up there."

"There are no dragons upon the Comeragh," he said as a matter-of-fact.

That put me in my place.

Ogham delineated the corner, the script marked by long horizontal lines with angled dashes intersecting them. I'd taken a basic course in third-year history, clearly to little retention.

"Would you believe I can't read?" Another partial truth.

He placed his hand on the back of my neck to comfort my admittance, caressing my tiny hairs.

My eyes fluttered at his touch.

No.

I squirmed away.

If I gave in, he'd have me. He'd eclipse everything else, and any chance of winning this impossible trial would be futile.

He ignored my cumbersome manoeuvre. "Many cannot read Ogham. It says that we can compete in Lúnasa five times if death does not find us first. Trust, most *do* find death first. You will compete against Saoirsians who recall the mountain from peak to rump. Saoirsians who have trained since younglings. Saoirsians with a sole remaining Lúnasa to succeed. Then there will be you."

He drank me in. My wounds, my curves, my madness.

"I'm aware I'm literally a bloody mess right now, but I'll defend myself. I'm not naive to its difficulty, I'm just not aware of all its elements yet." I wished he had more faith in me, although I was genuinely surprised by how much I had in myself.

He clenched the table's edge. Pieces of it flaked away and crumbled despite his constraint. His strength made sense now. "You are not from these lands, Clíona. In my Lúnasa, all sought me out. Many Saoirsians leapt to slaughter Ardagh scum. Just two returned."

"Well, how many of these trials do I need to survive to win?"

"Four, included of that, the final battle. Let us focus on getting your life through the mountain first."

My spine spasmed and curved against my will. That settled it; I was in over my head. With weeks to prepare, I'd be cutting it close to train and control my Bua and learn about Lúnasa's trials. And if Caolann's words were anything to go by, I was going up against the best of Saoirse's competitors. But when I was the only one willing and with enough power, it was worth risking my life to have the slightest chance of saving Róisín's.

22

A LAWFUL SLAUGHTER

"Again."

My legs gave up twenty minutes ago, though I'd only just fallen to my knees. It was hotter than usual today in Réimse Mór, and with noon not far off, I anticipated it was only going to get worse when the children rolled in after lunch.

"I need a minute," I said between heavy breaths.

"*Again*," he repeated, stern as ever. The point of a blunt sword tipped my chin.

Wiping the sweat from my brow, I challenged the point's cool press if only to find a better angle to shoot him a warning glare. A glare that probably held little effect when every part of me was flushed in bright red. "One. Minute."

Rían eclipsed the sun as he towered over me. "I could always make you do it. One command. One word," he said rhythmically. "That is all it takes."

"You wouldn't dare."

He withdrew the sword and crouched next to me, hovering, as though caught between a decision. "Do not tempt me, love."

That word stirred a frustrated sigh in me. I swore he only said it when he knew I'd reached my limit and needed a final thing to send me over the edge.

Shimmers of golden light started to rise from my palms, tingling them and pulsing them as the power threatened to emerge.

His hand gripped my shoulder. "Good. Now control it. Seek the light. Be the host. Carve your line, and do not let it pass."

He was too close to me. He'd be sucked into the firing line. I wanted to scream and push him away, but the world was moving too fast.

"Why is it so tempting..." I panted, temporarily unable to finish my thought. "...to use it all."

He gripped me harder, touch firm but gentle, perhaps fearing I wasn't strong enough to fight my Bua this close to release. His hand trembled slightly, betraying the silent worry beneath his calm demeanour. "It feels good to hold this power, does it not?"

My eyes chewed into the swaying grass. "Yes."

"Because no fear lives there."

That sounded amazing.

The current in me thickened more.

Rían's grip slipped further into my neck, drawing me closer to him instead of temptation. "But Clíona, you are stronger than the harvest. You...you are," he drifted.

My stare snapped to him, finally.

What? I am *what?*

He bit the words, flaring his nose with—what? Worry? Something unreadable, but heavy, lingered between us.

A painful moan slipped from my mouth, muffled and desperate. The power was building inside me, relentless, and I could feel it slipping past my control. I couldn't hold it back any longer. My chest tightened, and panic twisted in my gut. I was going to hurt him, and there was nothing I could do to stop it.

I clenched my eyes when his voice came in a cool hush to the cusp of my ear. "Find good in your mind. Right this instant. Seek it out."

For a moment, I feared he'd used his Bua on me after all, but no, it was trust. Trust that I wouldn't hurt him.

Seeking out my usual route of a good memory, I found myself sucked into the present instead. Our eyes locked. God, they were so like his brother's, both an identical shade of the brightest green nature could offer, both carrying sadness. But for Caolann's gentle gradient, Rían's had a ring of black encircling his. I followed the circles as they pulsed, contracted, soothed me.

"Good girl," he murmured, his voice barely more than a breath. His hands moved closer, steady and reassuring, fingers sliding into the hollow beneath my jaw until they cupped both sides of my face. "Now come back to me."

I nodded, the weight of his words pulling me from the brink. I fought against the surge, pushing it away bit by bit, until I felt raw. Until I was no longer spinning in the vortex of power.

Blinking, I stared down at my hands, now empty of harvest. I gasped, a wave of disbelief washing over me. It worked.

Inciting the power was easy now when all it took was a bad thought—which I was in endless supply of. Keeping the pain from overflowing was the difficult part.

Though he was smiling, Rían's gaze darted back and forth between my eyes, perhaps checking me for darkness, or the seduction of it.

"I'm good," I reassured him.

A curt nod was offered. "Good." Unclasping his hand from my pulsing skin, Rían twisted to lay on his back in one swift move. With a single leg raised, he shielded the sunlight with his hand over his eyes. Then the world around us softened a fraction. "Let us both take a moment of rest. You exhaust me," he said with another, sudden, rare smile—a sight even rarer in the weeks building to Lúnasa. Weeks that had been a blur.

Every inch of me was black and blue. I ached inside and out. My hands had become calloused and my muscles more defined. And yet, the closer the days trickled down to Lúnasa, the more my confidence slipped away that I could actually win—even with Lester and the brothers helping me at every opportunity. They had told me of regular competitors, those who were about to hit their cap on the five-year rule. Those who had impenetrable skin. Shapeshifters. Even those with unsuspecting gifts like 'honey healers' who could secrete the sticky substance from their glands to mend wounds, and 'projectors' who had the gift of only letting you see what they wanted.

I drifted to Rían again. What had changed today to make him smile a record number of times, if two could be considered a record?

That first day in Réimse Mór after I decided to compete, it was Rían who arrived to train me, not Caolann like I'd expected. Like I'd hoped. But it seemed whatever words Caolann had instilled into his brother to keep me away from him, to keep him safe, no longer worked.

Rían *wanted* the burden of me. I think he hated his choice to save me falling on his brother. Another thing to create a wedge between their play of power.

So, no, I wouldn't ask what changed despite the temptation, because if I was being honest, the mornings with Rían—no matter how exhausting—were a joy. I felt accomplished after them. He focused solely on my Bua from its summoning and manipulation, to suffocating it out again. He taught me to fight the temptation of darkness. Afternoons, when the children came, was a stark contrast as I sparred with Lester in weaponry—a welcome change of both pace and humour. He also taught me combat skills, which I'd quickly learnt I had no skill in. Swords were heavy. Daggers got slick in the heat. Shields slowed me down to a snail's pace. Having a poor grip in one hand didn't help, either. But he also taught me physical moves, and the strength behind them.

"Your elbows and your knees are your friends," he'd tell me. *"Pressure marks are their enemy."*

I'd practise jolting my elbow or knees towards his quick blocks. Then he'd reverse the roles. Not a week into our sessions, I'd realised it was a dance and thankfully, I wasn't cursed with two left feet. It was the one thing I was actually kind of good at.

"Neck, chest and rear of the knee is a human's bane," he'd say as he pressed his fingers to the weak parts of my body. When I yelped for mercy, he'd press harder, forcing me to contain my harvest under duress.

It worked.

I'd spent longer on the ground than fighting until Lester let me incorporate some of my Bua into offence strategies with Rían's approval, but I was often too exhausted to even harvest by the time it came around.

And then there were my evenings—with Caolann.

We would convene at the strategizing table after he would cook dinner for all three of us, though sometimes he didn't have much left to tell me of the trials; instead, he just wanted my company—at least, that's what I thought. This first trial was straightforward. I knew its every crevice now. Every route. Every water source. We were expected to be divided into eight clans comprised of six or so competitors, depending on how many chose to compete.

Caolann said it never had more than fifty competitors. It was also random selection, just seconds before the trial would begin, so alliances were pointless. But still, I'd need to fight alongside my clan—if I found them—to summit in time to progress. I despised the idea of relying on others for that progression. And what made it worse was only half the clans qualified—if that. Fucking *half*! Those odds were downright awful. Especially when I'd learnt most didn't qualify because they'd be murdered on the mountain.

I curled onto my side, leaning my head on my hand to face Rían. My elbow dug into the cool soil beneath the grass. "Why are you going easy on me?" I asked him, suspiciously.

"You need rest to prepare for what is to come when Lúnasa falls two sunrises from now."

"And?"

"And." His attention was on the clouds. "I believe you are ready."

Oh.

He darted his gaze to me. "I would fight by your side if he allowed it. You know this, yes?"

"I know," I said quickly, wanting him to believe it. I believed it, too. I hated the power Caolann had over him despite knowing it was in his best interest.

They had done their best to keep me in the shadows of light. But eventually, I came upon Rían's darkness myself. Saw it with my own eyes how quickly the depression took him away. Took him to the edge of a literal cliff where the waves below had tempted him. One night, I had followed Caolann, and deep down, I wondered if he'd let me. His hunter skills were too attuned not to suspect I was there.

When Rían was soundly asleep inside, Caolann told me Rían needed the control of knowing he could take his life at any moment if the infestation of darkness—of subduing to his Bua and the power it held—became too much for him.

"If I was on that mountain...not a single graze of your skin would be marked. Not even a scratch." Rían paused, then said whatever was on his mind anyway. "I do not fear the hands of the gods, but my own. What I would do to those in my path if they subdue me to harvest for their treacherous will."

Rían was an atomic bomb of war. One word and he could tear down armies. Burn down villages with the torches of their own dwellers. Have men gut their own stomach and convince them it was a good thing. No. The kindness and solitude had to live on in Rían for the sake of everyone. However lonely and cruel a life he suffered on the inside.

He bit back something. Swallowing.

"Hey." I pressed onto my knees, my heart racing as I clutched his arm, fingers tightening around his warmth. "Hey. I know you'd come with me," I said again, softly. And I meant it. However much I couldn't understand why this boy had bouts of feeling protective of me, it still stood to be true.

He placed his hand over mine, lying there while my back was to all the clouds, and the hum of the early forest irrelevantly passing us by. And then, somehow, his fingers were on my cheek again. Brushing over my jaw. The skin hummed, and I realised it wasn't my harvest just minutes ago that had caused the feeling—it was him.

I blinked, stilling. Rían wet his bottom lip while I continued to do nothing. Not even breathe. I didn't see him as this fragile thing to be protected the way Caolann did. I saw him as...

Caolann.

My heart knocked.

Over and over I thought of his name. Rían looked so much like Caolann I was beginning to wonder if my mind was confusing them. But his brother must have told him why we went our separate ways. Why a platonic trio was the *only* way. I huffed a slight, manic laugh through my nose. This boy thought I was worth his foolish gaze, but if anyone was to shepherd him into the darkness he constantly resisted, it would be me.

Gently, I lowered his fingers. "I don't need your protection, Rían. Not yours or your brother's. These are my trials. Mine."

Rían pressed his lips together and nodded slightly. "Indeed. This is your fight. I do not wish to control your heart, nor your body. Those are yours, Clíona. Remember that most of all."

Us. Them. Two brothers willing to do anything, *be* anything, to keep me alive. Rían had a softness I couldn't find in Caolann. A control. For every way he wanted me free, Caolann wanted me bound. But Caolann, oh, every inch of me ached for him the longer I chose not to have him.

As if reading my thoughts—my sway—Rían rolled to one knee, grabbing my calf to slide me flat until I was under him.

My throat bobbed.

"Do not allow your emotions to lower your guard." His head bent towards the knife a mere inch from my neck. "It will be the death of you."

"The only thing that will be the death of me today is the weather. Now," I said, letting every lowered inhibition rattle out in a loud breath, "what's next?"

Finding my footing in the closest of the line of X's he'd drawn in the grass, I tried to divert the arrows he shot at me, directing them towards the bales of hay on our periphery.

Every time I diverted one, I grinned, and so did he, us pretending like I wasn't one arrow from death, and he wasn't attempting to casually kill me.

About to nock his final arrow, a torrent of screaming and cries from the village had us concurrently snapping our heads to the commotion. It felt all too reminiscent of that fateful night when we lost Róisín. We sprinted towards the disturbance before I even realised I'd made the decision, making it back to the village in minutes.

Saoirsians scurried between market stalls, laid bare or abandoned.

"Another child?" I asked, my words shaking. A messenger had come to the gates from a neighbouring village not five days ago. His note had read:

Two more.

Just since Róisín was taken. No matter how hard they were watched, whoever this nightcrawler was, he managed to get his claws on the poor innocents.

"It is Rathnor," came a deep voice I'd know anywhere now. Caolann marched towards us from the direction of their home, several paces behind and puffing his chest grander. "He comes to bring unrest before the harvest."

My belly churned—a recurrent sensation when Rathnor came to mind. I wanted to flee. Rathnor was a problem I had hoped to deal with at the end of Lúnasa, not before. In earlier lessons, it was decided that the trials had to be linear. Taken day by day. Dealing with Rathnor now wasn't the plan.

Caolann inched closer to me, his protective presence carrying the weight of everything I didn't want to hold right now. "No harm will find you."

"Agreed," Rían murmured.

I wouldn't hide behind him. Either of them. I had to look Rathnor in the eye and let him know I wasn't afraid of him.

A lie.

A huddle of women pointed toward the commotion, backs pressed against a stall. Caolann's name was all that came from their trembling mouths, a hope in merely saying it being enough to save them from Rathnor's destruction. Saoirsians reverently saw Caolann as a symbol of hope: the god who walked among men. Their admiration stirred hope in me.

A stall of stringed pig's feet lay overturned where just beyond onlookers gathered around an elderly woman, kneeling crooked in the dirt. Before her stood Rathnor, donned in his sapphire cloak and a sinister smile.

"I beg," the woman wailed. "Trust, I never stole from you. The tree brooch fell from your armour undercloth." The distraught woman reached out to Rathnor with withered fingers too aged to fight.

"And in returning my brooch, you thought perhaps my gratitude would feed your family for eternity?" He laughed and stroked his tattooed neck.

My hands tingled, drawing a soft, golden haze just above the surface.

"No—please—forgive me," she pleaded, her spotted hands toward him. "I wished its safe return to you."

"Lies!" Rathnor barked.

His boot struck her chest, thudding her body into a shroud of thick dust from the blow. A young girl fell to her side, tears trickling down her grubby face as she failed to cradle the woman's limp body.

I'd *never* witnessed someone be so cruel. The brutality stoked hot rage in me, boiling me over with power so fierce I had to clench my fists in a fight to contain it. "You slimy, good-for-nothin' bastard," I shouted, my legs impulsively pacing for him. I extended my arm, intending to fling his body—

"Hold your intent, Clíona," Rían called out.

My arm dropped against my will, light and power drifting away on the wind, yet the rage burned in my blood.

"Damn you, Rían," I cried, writhing. I'd succumbed to his Bua.

"Ahh, a new hero in our midst," Rathnor bellowed as he pranced towards me. "It has been many sunrises since our last meeting, maimed one."

Finite power burned on my skin so fiercely, I worried I might take flame. "Leave. Her. Alone."

He placed his hand on his heart. "I simply tried to redeem what is mine."

Everything about Rathnor was overdramatized. From his blasé tone to his exaggerated body movements. He revolted me.

"*I* am the victim here," he said as if perplexed.

"You just enjoy hurting people. I swear—"

"Clíona, do not," Caolann warned me.

"Ahh." Rathnor gleamed, wagging his finger. "Always the protector, Caolann. I cannot say I blame you with this wild beauty." He stared at me up and down, observing every part of my body. "Those majestic, child-bearing hips..." He ogled, licking his minty lips as if he savoured the thought of me.

My knees trembled, subdued to his twisted words—alphabetical acid being shoved down my throat.

Caolann growled and drew his serrated knife. "I pray to the True Gods your death will—"

"Hold your tongue, boy!" Rathnor swept his cape aside, revealing the gleam of a sword beneath. "No longer a god protects you in these lands. You barely held the divinity upon your leave."

Caolann fought with the rigidity of his jaw as Rathnor grinned at me. "Caolann cannot protect you where your path leads."

Was he talking about Lúnasa?

He chortled, reading whatever expression had contorted my face. "The gods are *always* listening. For me, being the kind underruler that I am, I volunteered to fight in the final battle."

Any intentions to express my eagerness to take him on dissipated from my body. All I wanted was to be alone and free of his toxic control.

"Little to say?"

Rían shielded me from Rathnor's view. "Rathnor, no Saoirsian wishes for hassle here. Return to the riches of Magh Mell." Rían was smart, harvesting under the guise of free will.

Rathnor opened his hand to display the golden tree brooch. Then he flung it at the elderly woman, still curled on the ground. His mouth parted into a final feline grin. In a blink he divinely moved, leaving the ground blacker than his twisted soul.

An elderly man helped the woman up, guiding her—crying child in tow—toward the house at the end of the path, which I had learned in Réimse Mór was occupied by the most affordable local healer.

I swiped the tear on the cusp of showing my weaknesses.

"Are you of harm?" Caolann asked me with a hugging embrace.

I pulled away, not wanting anyone's touch. My skin felt grimy being ogled so openly. I felt stained. "I hate him. I hate that he can do and say whatever he wants." I wished I'd stuck up for myself. I wished I could have ripped his heart from his chest, so he'd know what it felt like to hurt in a human's most precious place.

"You are the sole route to Rathnor's lawful slaughter," Rían seethed. "Are you prepared to take his life if you reach the final trial?"

I clenched my teeth, letting the insidious anger come forth. Contempt was a powerful sentiment to strike with, and Caolann always said to attack with your strongest self.

No matter what made him cruel, Rathnor was cruel all the same. And though it would taint my path of making up for all my mistakes, the conclusion of our exchange was a simple one: Rathnor's comeuppance was due.

His death would come by my hands.

23

No Guilt Came

A fur blanket dropped on my curled body, providing instant warmth. I must have fallen asleep at the table again, reading over my notes. They were really a scrambled mess of nonsensical conjectures, scattered over the maps, or lists concerning weaponry, and what plants or berries were poisonous and nonpoisonous on the mountain.

Hands planted on my shoulders from behind. "You sleep too long for a woman who rides into battle tomorrow," Caolann said, right on the rim of my ear.

Wriggling free, I stretched and let out a groan. "Oh, come on. You can at least be nice to me the day before I die."

He curved around my periphery to shoot me a warning glare, his narrow eyes near disappearing into their hoods. "Do not make light of this."

"There is no light when it comes to Lúnasa," I teased, repeating that line of discouragement he'd often given me at the start of this. When he still thought there was a chance I'd back out.

He sighed, battling that smirk on the edge of his mouth he refused to free almost every time it crept up. But when it did...

My stomach stirred like a cauldron full of spells that made me stupid—lustful.

In our lessons, now repetitive and tiresome, my mind easily drifted to the place I tried to avoid—the place where I imagined Caolann on top of me. Under. Sideways. Wrapped around my finger. We'd managed to keep our physical distance, but the more time spent in his company, the more I wanted to revisit our spark beneath the blue lights. The more I wanted to suspend myself into bliss, no matter how terrifying or undeserved it was. Because for the first time in a long time, guilt had stopped eclipsing moments of joy.

I fought his threatening smirk, grinning as I came nose to nose with him.

Come on—break.

He doubled down, a muscle twitching in his cheek. I could tell he was relishing how much he knew it teased me. Feeling rewarded was of the few weapons in his personal arsenal against me. Inhaling sharply, he retreated, turning right as the grin slipped out to sling a brown duffel bag over his shoulder.

"We must take our leave."

I stood. "For where?"

He swept a quick glance over me. "Your final lesson."

I paced a step behind Caolann through the forest as dawn broke the tree's quilt. The birds still slept, the twigs we trampled snapping louder in the absence of their singing. I'd lost my bearings almost immediately, but that never mattered when Caolann led the way. He was a human compass, always knowing where his path led him.

"Will you tell me now?" I asked, happy to let one mystery get solved today.

He was silent, focused on wherever he was leading me this time. I daringly reached out my hand to clasp his, but he turned, and I drew it back.

"It is now," he murmured, surrendering his knees to the soil.

"What is?"

With his brown duffel bag next to him, he unclasped it to remove a loaf of seeded bread. "This is your final lesson. It is now. Join me," he whispered with urgency.

I hitched my dress above my knees and knelt, observing his methodical movements. Unrushed. Thoughtful as he removed the contents of the bag: bread. He handed me the warm loaf as he dug a shallow hole.

Together, we squinted in harmony as the sunlight pierced our vision.

He held the bread to the sky. "I offer you the first of the crop, Danu and Bíle. Nature has brought me life. Your water runs in my blood. Your roots spread from my heart. Your morals unfurl my qualms. I worship you alone."

Tranquil to whatever spirit was permeating the calm forest, we inhaled the delicate essence of pine and fresh flora. Yet beneath the passing serenity, a silent understanding lingered between us; this calm would be gone tomorrow. We both knew that.

"Protection from conflict and battle," he lamented and clipped three dock leaves from a stem. Then he pricked both our fingers on a thorn to squeeze them into the hole before placing the leaves on top of the loaf I still held.

"What do I do?"

"Bury them," he said softly but with enough brass to make me swallow. I nestled them into the hole, his hands cupping mine as we buried the gifts, concealing them beneath the heap of soil.

Gently and unexpectedly, he eased me back into the crook of his legs, pulling me to rest all my weight on his chest. His arms came from behind to hold me tight as he spoke. "We are closest to the spirits of Danu and Bíle when the sun rises through the heart of their forest. They are the True Gods and the sole deserving of our harvest offerings."

We sat in continued quiet reverence, listening to the birds wake, watching the flowers unfold as the sun kissed them.

I tasted the warmth on my lips and felt the rays on my arms, chasing away my goose pimples, considering this was what the faithful imagined their heaven to be. It was strange; my quarrel with Mollie's holistic ways, and my belief that nature, in a sense, stole life, now felt wrong. Ériu had taught me time and time again how amazing nature was. Its plants fed and healed. Its animals clothed us and replenished the land. It brought not just existence, but life and legacies. It was a triskele: spiralling perpetual life and death, but also rebirth. And in renewal was the path to redemption.

Thank you, Danu and Bíle.

"All changes come tomorrow's light," Caolann said on the cusp of my ear, emerging out of the stillness. "In defeat or as champion, we will be different."

I curved my jaw towards his breath to get even the slightest glimpse of his face. "We?"

Answering my question, the backs of his fingers began to drift up my thighs. "I fear our time together is limited."

"I need to—" My breath hitched as his hands drifted beneath the hem of my dress. "Focus," I exhaled.

His thumbs dipped into the top of my underwear, stirring frustration as I dug my heels to inch my face higher, and see where his hands had gone.

"Have you lost the use of your arms, Clíona?" he teased, knowing full well I had every opportunity to resist him.

Rebelling, I gripped his forearms.

His mischievous growl vibrated my back as he brought my chin to match our lips until they brushed. "You see this is more than the desire to be intimate?"

"Yes," I said, only believing it the moment the answer left my lips.

"Then by your will, I wish to ask if you will open your bed to me. I long to sleep with you in my arms before perils threaten our bond."

His formality was undeniably charming. And for me, it brought such a strong rising sensation to my chest—a unique feeling— I knew my body wouldn't permit a refusal to his offer.

His throat bobbed as he waited.

I opened my mouth to tease him, eager to finally gain the upper hand when he stifled my words with a brash kiss, his tongue boldly dipping inside my mouth, curling into mine.

Matching his urgency, I kissed back harder, but still it wasn't enough to dull the feeling brewing in me. Each fleeting touch, each skim of his fingers over the back of my neck, only deepened this unsettling longing stoking inside of me.

His fingers slid up the outer, firm side of my thighs, hard enough to make the skin turn white.

I clamped down on his hands, shooting him a sharp look.

He looked up in earnest.

"Not here."

"As you wish, wildling," he replied with a playful smirk.

Hand in hand, Caolann tugged at me, urging me to hurry while contradicting that sentiment at every turn, planting kisses over my lips and neck at countless passing trees. The rough bark pressed against my back, caught in my hair, but I didn't care when each stop felt like a secret. A stolen moment just for us, where the world outside the forest didn't exist. The crisp scent of pine and damp earth filled the morning air, mingling with the aftertaste of each kiss.

When, finally, we made it back home, I couldn't say whether it was the journey or the pulsing that left me gasping so hard.

The soft pull of his hand guided me to the bed. My sensitive fingertips rested on its edge along the frame as he pinned against me from behind, tilting my neck to nibble it. "I have waited so fucking long for this," he said. His fingers ran over my breasts, gently squeezing them. A quiet gasp trickled from my mouth, only silenced by the sudden twist of my body as he pressed his warm lips to mine. His mouth was strong despite my willingness, tongue softly curling. I wondered each time I went for more if it was possible to get tired of this ravenous feeling. Each kiss pulled me deeper into the emotion I was certain I'd never felt before. Each suck and squeeze was a tantalising blend of pleasure and desperation.

Clutching the ends of the dress he'd gifted me, he lifted the fabric—slowly over my knees, my thighs, my bottom; his thumbs smoothed over my stomach, skimming into the divot between my ribs.

I raised my arms, inviting him to take it further, to pull the dress over my head. As it cascaded to the floor with a soft rustle, our gazes in unison followed to trace the contour of my naked silhouette. I wore nothing but the rune.

"Clíona," he said in a low hum.

I edged my chin higher to look at him.

"Hmm?"

"This is not as it was that night in the woods, is it?" Overshadowing the touch of concern in his voice, asking me if this was real, there it was in his eyes again: fiery heat, ready to burn me. I craved that melting heat on my body if its source was him.

"No. Not even a little bit."

He gripped onto my waist tight, leveraging me closer. "Good."

I gasped. How easily my body had offered itself to him. I could feel his eyes on me, like gentle caresses tracing my every curve.

"A body carved from the True Gods," he said, easing me onto the bed to sit.

I was used to being in control with other men, but he commanded this moment, and I wouldn't dare defy his orders. Didn't *want* to. Staring up at his stern glare as he undressed himself, I bunched my hands into the fur blanket not to touch myself or feed the pulse quite yet. I felt void, but it was no longer mine to touch tonight.

The act of removing his belt and clothes was intoxicating. Mouthwatering. And I didn't dare to revert my eyes for fear I'd never see something as beautiful again. He was chiselled to the form of his godlike status, each old scar knotting and whitening and twisting his skin only adding to his aura of provocativeness. This man had killed, and how easily he would do it again if I asked him to.

Staring up at him, I felt so small, so submissive. Embracing it and the anticipation of what was about to happen, I salivated on wet lips.

I clenched the blanket harder, failing to steady my breaths that raised my chest a fraction higher each time.

He barely had his leather pants off when I reached for him, gluttonous for how hard he was for me.

"You are mine now," he said.

I took him in both hands, clasping my teeth together not to thank him. A soft sigh slipped from his mouth; his eyes clenched as he released all his hardships to the night.

"Say it," he murmured.

"I am yours—"

His fingers pressed over my mouth to stop my words. They must have been the wrong ones. It took me all of a second to figure out the right ones.

I set my stare on his perfect green eyes. "I am bound to you."

"Hmm. Yes."

He grasped my hand, but I fought the clutch, *tsking*, forcing his hand to move in motion with mine as I pleasured him in perfect, fluid motion.

The muscles in his jaw rallied, over and over until a throaty growl drew from his mouth, frightfully animalistic. Then his weight was on me, restrained, heavy but not crushing. He was twice my width, cocooning me from the world. From the certain death of tomorrow, but for now we were tethered into each other's embrace.

I hitched my leg, drawing my hands up his thighs to pull him closer.

Fuck, he was beautiful. Everything and everyone unmatched to him. I'd never met a man who intoxicated me this way. I wanted to seal all the windows and doors just to bask in its lethal fumes.

Caolann cupped my nape to draw me to his mouth, quenching the brew of another gasp from my yearning mouth. His kisses were hard, eyes tight like it pained him to have restraint.

"I want you." The words flowed into his mouth. "I *need*—"

Reading my plea, he teased his fingers around the circumference of my opening. I needed him, desperately. Could he not see he was tormenting me?

"Caolann." His ragged name escaping from my collapsing body drove him to a standstill above me. Then he spread me and pushed himself inside with a hard thrust, watching as my chest rose and contorted my back's curve in response to a swell of pleasure.

He scooped his arm under my back to keep me suspended at the angle he enjoyed as he thrust again, softer than the last but just as eyerollingly pleasurable.

He slowed his rhythm, grinding, drawing his mouth closer to mine, but forcing me to fill that little extra gap just to barely brush his lips. His stubble. His jaw.

His hand roamed my bottom, rolling the thick flesh under his fingers.

"This feels so good," I said between kisses he finally let me have. My mouth hung, letting stifled breaths turn to moans as his rhythm grew faster, consistent, thicker.

"Gods." His head sprung back. "You tempt with those noises, Clíona."

"I'm right here. There is no need for temptation when you can have me whatever way you like."

Caolann's teeth softly burrowed into my neck. Each stroke was better than last, convincing me I could never get enough of being with this man.

That perfect spot of bliss was so close I thought the only thing keeping my physical form on earth was his weight, growing heavier, less thoughtful the closer he got to the climax I was seconds from myself.

I writhed under him. Sweat danced on my skin, warm beneath his touch.

"Come in me," I begged, foolishly. Blinded by how close I was, all I could imagine was the pleasure, if it might come to it, of leaving the world tomorrow with some of him still inside me.

He grabbed my hitched leg, pushing deeper. Harder. Stronger strokes, until his abs tensed. Until my fingers dug into his back. Until my moans ran through the village and—

Pleasure exploded inwards, locking my legs around his waist. My edges melted, forcing me to bite his collarbone as the waves of euphoria refused to wane.

My jolting and twitching sent him to a new level of intensity; he gripped the bed's wooden frame, snapping it beneath his fingers, leaving it to dust.

There was no return from this path that made me feel consumed in every crevice of my being.

I was a dying star, and he was the black hole I'd gladly be sucked into for eternity.

He writhed with soft grunts as everything left him, filling me with warmth as I clenched my legs harder, until I couldn't feel them or anything else but him. Then his lips pressed to me, tenderly before a quiet, breathless chuckle passed through them. "Perfect." His fingers brushed back my hair. "So very perfect."

The day went on this way; us resting in a tangled mess only leaving to eat or fuck elsewhere in the room long into nightfall, over and over, on the floor, against the table, until my voice was hoarse, caught in the lust of no guaranteed tomorrow. I rested my head on his scarred chest now, heavy of want for him. Not for more sex, but something else.

I toyed fingers over his golden armlet, gifted when given his divinity, to smudge iridescent colours along its circumference. This was a moment I'd fantasised about more than I should have.

I gazed at him with a longing, watching his hardened eyes beneath thick lashes mollify for me.

"I fear our lives will forever travel this circle. Fighting. Fucking. Avoiding death. Over and over again until one becomes permanent." He brushed the wave of hair covering my eye. "But you...you are worth the little time we do share."

"You're fond of me, aren't you?" I teased, feeling the pull of sleep finally come.

As his lips pressed to mine, I sensed the warmth of his gentle smile. "Yes, Clíona, I'm fond of you."

He cupped his fingers beneath my ear, the warmth of his thumb caressing my cheek to guide me to his cupid's bow.

Maybe this was happiness. Deserved or not, it seemed the True Gods wanted me to have it for a fleeting moment. Perhaps so I could know how it felt one last time before it was snatched away tomorrow. But I didn't care. Not on this euphoric day that would last in my memories forever.

PART 2

TRIALS

ALEX PARKER PUBLISHING

24
THE DAWN

I woke in Caolann's arms. He breathed heavily in his sleep, inoculated by the peace it brought. I sometimes worried it was the only time he was happy. That no matter what I might give him, it could never be enough. But it wasn't his fault. The conditioning of a young mind leaves marks on the soul.

I gently kissed his lips before slithering onto the smooth stone floor, letting him bask in what would surely be the short-lived feeling of peace. With that in mind, I left to catch a glimpse of the harvest morn's beauty—to see the comfort of my new normality before Lúnasa truly began.

Wandering the village, an aura of excitement and nerves crowded my belly. A bustle of men and women prepared carts for the field's first great harvest, their horses supping from a long wooden trough while swishing flies. Above them on shoddy ladders, owners hung bunting of four-headed seamróg across their stalls' arches. Other smiling faces, cleaner than usual, greeted me with subtle bows and salutes. Perhaps they knew I was to compete and considered it honourable, or maybe they'd warmed to me, and I'd been too busy training to notice.

Either way, it was nice to be considered something other than crazy or a spy. I was beginning to feel at home. Forget my old life. Rather, I hadn't forgotten it; I didn't miss it. Didn't miss the judgement. The endless work just to stay afloat when this world—the Otherworld—welcomed my differences and scars.

Being courteous to each gesture with nods and tight-lipped smiles, I ruminated on my ancestors. The ones whose harvests had been stolen by blight and quotas, just like here. The Great Famine—or, to those who knew, the *genocide*—a torture that left fathers' arms no thicker than the shovel they used to dig their children's graves.

Was that what was to come of Saoirse if their lives were to be left in the hands of a cruel ruler?

I found myself at the Carraig, changed drastically since Rathnor had tied me to it. Five stone figures of the Tuatha Dé Danann's mightiest extended its top. Each was grandiose and three times a normal person's size. I paced the steps two at a time, approaching Dian Cecht, the tallest of them, distinguished by bull horns. On his right, a sword by his waist, was the deceased Nuada. In the centre of all five, with a thick band of thorns resting on her forehead, was Mórrígan.

My mouth soured. Even in stone, I didn't want to be near her. Still, I knew our meeting would come, and I'd be forced to mirror the false smile on her face when all I wanted to do was gut her. It was a strange thing to hate someone you never met. But then again, I wasn't judging her cover, but rather the stories inside, written with the blood of her atrocities.

Lugh, who replaced Nuada in reign after he died, bore large antlers. Sharp and frightening. It made him mighty.

Was that my future?

I sat on his feet with a heavy thud to watch over Saoirsians who flocked, young and old, to lay offerings along the Carraig steps for these gods. A sticky heat pasted my arms as the sun rose, eating the shade of each step, one by one, engulfing the plentiful offerings, baskets of bread and crops of all colours, wooden trinkets, furred blankets, bundles of more seamróg, and anything else Saoirsians were willing to offer.

It rubbed me wrong, making my skin unexpectedly pimple despite the weather. The gods hadn't a want for anything in Magh Mell. And yet, there was Caolann. Even in his rebellion, he held the Tuatha status. Given his attempts to find Saoirse's children, to feed the poor with the spoils from his—and his brother's—hunts, and protect the village from Rathnor, didn't he deserve gratitude?

Even inadvertently thinking of Rathnor filled my saliva with a taste of wild mint, a flavour I now found putrid instead of refreshing. I tried not to think about him unless it was part of a lesson plan for the final battle. But sometimes the final battle was the *only* thing I thought about. Rathnor would be stripped of his godlike strength and immortality, making the playing ground somewhat even, but Caolann had warned there were whispers in Magh Mell that he carried a secret weapon.

I tilted my head to each side, feeling the satisfying crackle as I eased the tension in my neck, pressing my fingers against the resistant muscles.

Worse than any weapon was Rathnor's ability to twist words. This proved more powerful than his physical strength. It was how he championed his own trial: turning his clan against one another right at the end, so he could skip along for the taking.

Coward.

I hated him the most. I hated him so much, my eyes ached when imagining the exact moment I'd take his life. It wouldn't bring me pleasure, but it was my burden now. A burden I gladly accepted when that creep was probably sniffing my stolen hair before falling asleep every night.

I dusted the chalky layer of stone from my bottom and descended the Carraig, stepping over bundles of flowers in purple and pink tones. They reminded me of who I fought for. Who I was willing to lay down my life for, and maybe even kill for, if it meant getting *her* home.

Caolann crouched outside the house by the smoking fire, skinning a headless hare as I approached.

Rían sat by on a tuft of straw fletching arrows with spotted feathers. I'd told him once to trade some of his game for ones from the market, but he said he liked to keep busy.

"You departed early this dawn," Rían said. His expression was stoic, rarely unyielding, but I understood now that didn't mean he was eternally sad on the inside. There was contentment in him, too—at times. I saw it in him when we were alone. When time passed freely.

Caolann flushed beneath his growing stubble, now gutting the hare's innards.

Was he embarrassed we'd shared a bed? We both knew that meant more than any sexual game we'd played. It was real, even if it was the precipice of a future I couldn't guarantee—especially when I was mere hours from stepping into the belly of the beast.

My hand brushed across his tight, muscular back in passing. All our night brought me was the desire for more. To gasp fervent noises. I'd take no shame in that.

I joined Rían on the straw, taking up a spotted feather to stroke against its grain. "I went to see the offerings. Thought it might clear my mind before riding into battle."

Rían looped twine around another feather for fletching, a concentrated furrow squinting his eyes. "You have little to fear. Caolann cooked a breakfast fit for the gods."

Sizzling barbeque smoked onto the neighbour's land. "Mmm, I love a good bowl of burnt-to-a-crisp hare."

Caolann kept his rigid stare on the food as he dished it. Worry crept up my spine. Maybe he *had* regretted our night.

"It is fear. It holds his tongue," Rían whispered, not needing his Bua to know what bothered me.

My shoulders slumped to paltry relief. I didn't want Caolann to worry—no matter how warranted it was.

With hare grease barely wiped from my lips, the brothers had me stand and obediently shut my eyes. Anticipation tinged in my every nerve as they shuffled around ahead of me. My head followed the noise.

Caolann finally broke his worried silence. "Open your eyes, Clíona." Before I had a chance to react, he spilt into an explanation. "We intended for you to train in it, but the armourer's bones grow old."

Hung by his fingers' weight was a malleable bronze breastplate; tied its centre, a corset looped in a thin iron chain. My lips parted to give thanks, but nothing came out as I inspected every inch of it. The shouldered pelt hair was amazing; cut short, pine-like.

"Red elk," Caolann said with a fleeting smile.

The gesture made me cover my eyes all over again to hide their welling. Typical of them to make me emotional when keeping my shit together was paramount for this day. "Aw, boys...my heart...you're too good. There was no need to go through the trouble for me." I'd never even been bought flowers, let alone something like this.

Rían cracked a wide, dimpled grin and smacked Caolann's back to celebrate their gift's success. Finding I won the rare battle of making them happy in unison propelled my elation higher. Two soft souls, they secretly were.

"You see it now," Rían said. "We may not be with you on the mountain, but we will do anything, *be anything*, to keep you alive in these trials."

I placed my palm to his cheek, glancing between them both. "I know. I see it now."

"Allow me to fit it for you," Caolann offered, perhaps to make light of it.

Rían hitched a full quiver onto his shoulder and scooped leftover hare into his pocket. He paced for the forest. As he was just about to breach it, I called, "I thought I'd at least get a goodbye." There was an airiness to my voice even I didn't believe.

His shoulders rose as he dropped his head limp. He paused. Deciding. Perhaps considering the point of a goodbye when everything had already been said. Then he flung his bow to soil and jogged to me, reaching with his arm to scoop me in so tight my breath hitched.

"Goodbye."

"Goodbye, Rían."

His arm gripped me tighter. “Fight well...love.”

I curved my mouth at his words—at that *one* word embodying a sincerity I’d not heard anytime he’d used it previous. Before I had a chance to say or do anything else, his gaze retreated to its sombre, withdrawn state. Then he departed into the forest, bow in tow.

I watched the settling leaves long after he’d gone, hoping his demons left him be for a time.

Caolann came behind me to fix the new armour. “We must take our leave to the trial grounds.”

I ignored how much his words made me want to jump out of my skin and never get back in. Once I left, there was no turning back.

Caolann slid the armour on, reaching slowly around my waist to tighten the corset. His fingers were slow and mindful, but even this simple touch stirred heat in me. The urge to glance over my shoulder at him was tempting. To have one last look. I smiled and shook my head, refocusing on fastening my burgundy leather skirt, its slit running high along the thigh on both sides for easy movement during fights. The armour’s back, a crisscross of leather, was better than any bra support I had before. I looked...like a warrior.

I felt Irish, and proud, and as if I belonged. A descendant of Danu, ready for battle.

“It is time,” he said, sliding his hand into mine as his chin rested on my head.

I stroked his cheek, still staring out at those damn trees. “I know.”

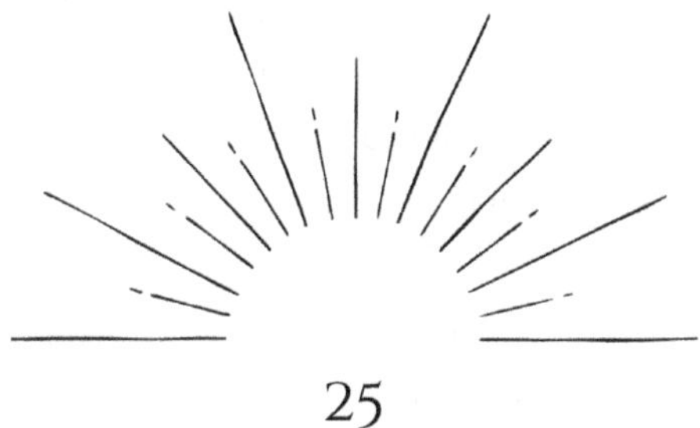

25

FRIEND OR FOE

Ériu's eastern sun burrowed through the forest's canopy, guiding us to the mountains. Caolann never stopped holding my hand, rubbing my thumb when words of comfort couldn't find us. The gesture meant so much when the whispers of spies and threats would never truly dull. But it was as if the threat didn't matter as much to him when there were bigger things to deal with. I was endlessly thankful that it was enough to keep my nerves from spilling out, but they still rumbled inside, just one misstep away from tapping into my Bua to set off an event of atomic proportions.

Competitors en route kept to themselves or with small familial groups. Others, from outside villages where inheritance of the Bua was rarer, spat at the soil when overtaking me. One woman, a head above my own, had the audacity to push by my shoulder when an elephant could have passed between us. Her black plaits swayed with feathers as she strutted ahead.

"You should hold your grudges for the trial, cracked one," Lester's unexpected voice called from behind.

I turned into a squeezing hug, full of warmth—a gesture miles beyond our parameters of friendship and a telling sign of what treachery was about to unfold. He withdrew with a smile that had me thinking *he* was the cracked nut. We could be dead in a few hours. Still, his enthusiasm was comforting. Made me idealise a world where we could respawn after each death.

Staring at the woman who had pushed by, I said intentionally loud and enunciated, "Let's hope she's not in my clan."

The woman's beaded eyes stared back at me, but I was relentless. Unblinking.

"Watch over her," Caolann told Lester, pulling me out of my stare down. "I was mistaken in my judgement of you. You taught her well."

They locked forearms, and Lester dropped a knee to bow his blonde-plaited head.

Caolann tugged at his arm to have him stand, his eyes dashing between the spectators who'd stopped to watch or bow themselves. "I am one of you, Lester. I possess no desire to be worshipped."

It was easy to forget Caolann's divinity when he remained humble. It was even easier to forget divinity was my potential future, too. But to live forever was a curse, not a gift. An eternity of torment. And still, it would be worth it if it meant getting Róisín home safely.

On the forest's far side, beyond the parameter of the hillfort, a spectacular valley greeted us, so perfectly oval I could envision the liquid hands of Danu carving it at sunrise. Mountains towered on either side of the valley pasture, barely anthills in comparison to the Comeragh. It consumed all land ahead, as if the peak was hidden in clouds to purposefully shroud what lay within.

How could my feeble legs get me to the top of that? I'd never climbed anything beyond Mollie's rusty stepladder.

Christ, I was an idiot. How the fuck did I ever think I could win this? No wonder Caolann was so against me entering. Look at me next to these warriors. Me, offering myself up on a golden plate for the gods to feast on.

I peered over my shoulders to the forest in the distance, feeling drawn by the temptation of surrender. Of abandoning this.

"Fall in, warriors!" Several tattooed and maroon-donned Fir na Solas had stationed themselves on the largest of the limestone rocks. The glistening stone tilted across wild grass like a god had thrown dice from the heavens; it was the only thing dividing us from the mountain's grounds. Two of the men held the large wooden boxes Caolann had spoken of many times. Fighting Saoirsians congregated by them, awaiting instruction or sharpening blades—the only weapon a competitor was permitted. What I'd discovered from Rían was that a Bua, no matter the power, wasn't an endless supply. It had a limit, and like anything requiring stamina, it had to be amassed, practised and utilised to last longer. Endurance was everything, and considering Lúnasa was a place where it would be used to its limit, a weapon could mean life or death.

Which was why I probably should have brought something beyond the pouch of pepper I snuck in my breast plate to rub in people's eyes. A gift from Bébhinn.

The atmosphere quietened, making my imposter syndrome scream louder and my hands shake. I flexed them by my sides. I don't know what I expected. A grand spectacle? Giant warriors? Well, there was one beast of a man sharpening his sword against his wrist gauntlet, but everyone else, on their surface, seemed...normal.

Lester nudged my arm. "We must join the others."

"I'll be with you in a minute, friend."

Lester travelled alone. His mother, Fay, was of the few in Saoirse who disapproved of their child competing young. He'd have said his goodbyes at dawn.

Caolann unsheathed his serrated knife, flipping it twice. "If you refuse to wield a sword, I wish for you to carry this. It is the sole item I hold of Ardagh, and heavy it lies in my heart. By the True Gods, I will it to protect you."

I caressed his hand as he parted with it, resisting the urge to kiss the Ardagh god in front of my enemies, but by the True Gods, I wanted to. Let them see. Let them all know.

Holding a lingering watch on him, I seared it with a quick turn toward the growing group of competitors.

"Recall what you fight for," he shouted after me.

I clipped his gift into my belt's sheath as Lester flanked left to rejoin me. "It brings me joy to compete with you this morn. Let us hope to cross in clan."

"Well, the alternative means I might have to slaughter you."

He chuckled. But we both knew blood would run down the mountain.

"Competitors, line up," a soldier shouted, his grip tightening on the sword by his waist.

I rolled my eyes at the passive threat.

A woman with grey hair flourishing down her armour coyly smiled at me. "Danu may have given men strength to swing a sword, but she gave us the knowledge to see size does not matter if the wielder is wise."

I snickered as we fell into line, but the humour quickly left me. My guts felt misshapen and unhappy, hungering for me to find safety.

Despite the selection of clans being random, I positioned myself behind Lester for comfort. Caolann had pointed out local competitors in the village, but disclosed with alliances being pointless, most kept to themselves. Even if now was the time to scope out my potential enemies, my eyesight was drawn to the red scar on the man in front. It sunk into his skin, jagged from spine to shoulder.

My heart thumped against my fitted armour as it hit me: very soon, I was fair game to these people. The voice in my head called louder to leave. This was my last chance to change my mind.

"Saoirsians. Welcome to Lúnasa," the large soldier on the slanted rock announced. His voice boomed into every crevice of the valley. "This tradition has grown greatly throughout the moons. Once simple funeral games to show strength and honour, now it is a chance to become a comrade of the Tuatha Dé Danann and receive The Divine Gift."

Competitors all around me cheered with raised weapons and hooted their pleasure, genuinely excited to compete—to face death.

And they call *me* cracked. These people were walking to their deaths with pride.

"The trial will commence when the sun licks its peak."

A second soldier tapped the arms of every alternate competitor, signalling for them to fall out of line.

Next was me.

Her touch was heavy-handed. "Follow my guide."

I sidestepped out, brushing my fingertips on Lester's as I passed. A simple goodbye and thanks for all he'd done in the weeks gone.

As the group split, they led us deep into the valley, the Comeragh growing on us like a towering shadow ready to consume.

We came to a singular collective halt, twenty or so of us, long out of sight of the other competitors doing the same. The commanding soldier gazed at the sun. In its zenith, it had conjured a stench of caustic sweat to suffocate the open air.

The next command was given with much less conviction than the previous one. "Step forward, choose from the box and create a wide circle."

I wished we could meet the gods beforehand, but Caolann had said they paid little attention to the first trials. This was to weed out the weak, and they held no time for such a thing. *This is the trial of savagery. Kill what you can.* He had said it like he believed it, too, but in a way that sounded like it was an indoctrinated habit rather than a current belief.

"Ardagh spy," the man behind me shrilled, punctuating his words with a nasty, guttural hock. Wetness splattered across my back, seeping into the crack of my bottom.

Sneering laughter erupted around me. "Fine shot, Ciarán."

My lip quivered in disgust, but I kept moving, forcing my steps forward. With every step, the revulsion added a new layer of thickness to my skin.

Would he have done the same if he knew I had the potential power to still his heart with a single thought and a mutilated hand? I suppose another question also stood: would I? Would I kill anyone on this mountain? A question I had been ignoring, really. Rathnor would have a warranted death, but villagers hoping for a wish?

Not a wish. Power.

Beckoned for clan selection, I approached with steady resolve. My head held high.

The soldier snuffled his nose as he opened a narrow compartment atop the box. "Remove one."

Prepared, my hand slid inside to retrieve a spotted egg so large the insides sloshed. It was a quick process, and once complete, I joined the circle—the spitting bastard to my right.

"Can you stroke a man with it?" he asked me.

"Excuse me?"

He nodded to my hand.

"Aw, is the wife not interested anymore?"

His mouth soured as mine spread with a monstrous grin.

One by one, the competitors followed, a silence of anticipation dragging endlessly. It somehow hushed even lower when a crystal-eyed soldier stepped into the centre of our circle, beckoning us to huddle closer, as if he held secrets he wished to share.

"The time has come, competitors. One of you will be crowned champion this Lúnasa. Fight well. Fight hard." His hands, tattooed and dark-skinned, rubbed together. "Take a deep breath, and I warn you, do not release it."

The simultaneous inhale frightened me, and I took two shorter ones to catch my breath.

A faint, blue light grew closer to us like the swarm of Soilse, pulsing, emanating from the soldier's body.

My view began to fade.

A ringing pulsed my ears.

Cold sweat crawled on my skin, the same unsettling chill that comes before fainting.

Something heavy pulled me. Not down. Not up. Just...away.

26

THE COMERAGH

Touch returned first: my knees scratching against rock, grating white flecks onto their grooves. In my damp hands, I hugged the egg. Cradling it to the point of gentle cracks branching out on its shell. Then came the numbness, pins and needles racing through me in electrified waves. Vision followed: the sun's heat striking my eyes. I recoiled from it like it was my enemy.

This triggered clarity. The sun was not my enemy as long as it was high in the sky.

Groaning, I stood to find any bearings. By the sun's guide, I'd travelled whole to the north side of the Comeragh. This was good by Caolann's teachings—easier terrains and coverage from enemies. Real enemies.

I cracked the egg's doming head on a jagged rock. Black slime spilt over the shell along with a half-formed foetus of some four-legged animal. If this were reality, I might've cried for the injustice, but this was Lúnasa; a place where the only life I needed to care for was my own.

I scooped out its liquid to paint the bridge of my nose, cheekbones and arms. It smelled raw and dried-in like a tight face mask, but I wore the colour as a badge of honour to symbolise my allegiance to my clan.

Lúnasa's first trial had begun. I was officially fair game.

Barely an hour in, sweat danced along my hairline, and each breath of crisp mountain air expanded my lungs to capacity. Still, it would be short-lived; once I reached higher altitude, the density would plummet, challenging my every inhale. I huffed to myself—*if* I reached a higher altitude. Paranoia had taken its toll from my first step, which was actually more of a stumble. I'd stopped a dozen times to check for other competitors—pausing for suspicious noises, abruptly crouching behind bushes in case someone's sights were on me.

Morning glory sprouted across the rocky terrain, its purple tones growing more plentiful the closer I journeyed to the trees above. Trees meant coverage, but I suspected it also meant popularity. Regardless, I had to keep straight towards them to avoid the sharp cliffs. Not because I was afraid someone would throw me off, but because I feared I might throw *myself* off. *L'appel du Vide* was the French term for it: the urge to jump off high places. Fionn had it, too, this urge. It was like our brains told us jumping was the fastest way to get to safety. Thinking of him surprisingly calmed me until a passing bird squawked, plunging me into fear again.

Damn birds.

Eventually, and with no bearing of how long had passed, the trees were close. I crouched to rest and sup from my pouch, letting its warm water cleanse the gritty taste off my tongue. My threshold for satisfaction had lowered to the point where even this had my eyes rolling.

"Halt," a deep voice called.

My body turned so stiff I thought I might shatter into a million pieces. I'd trained for this moment, but being here—knowing the person behind wanted to kill me—well, I was justifiably shitting myself.

"No sudden movements," he warned.

I kept my back to him, arms tucked close. If he couldn't see my markings, he mightn't risk hurting one of his clan.

"What markings do you hold?" the man asked.

I peered at him in my eye's corner, catching the glint of iron in his hand. "I'd rather tell you the colour of my knickers." Better not to tell him I wasn't wearing any.

"Face me, warrior."

I suppose we were wasting time not getting on with it, and though I didn't trust him, I twisted on the balls of my feet, power-drenched hands erect in false surrender.

A relieving breath escaped my lips. His cheeks and forehead were coated black—a contrast against his red hair, shaved on either side of his head to reveal fresh Celtic knots tattooed into the skin. This was a stroke of luck that wouldn't come twice. Unless the True Gods had heeded my prayers. Had feasted on my buried offerings.

He edged closer, squinting to observe my features beneath painted skin. A flicker of recognition. "The cracked nut!" His hands flung to the sky. "The gods have forsaken me."

"At least I'll compensate for the nuts you're lacking, you arsehole." I stood to point at his crotch.

He blocked it with crossed hands, still holding his knife but none of his dignity.

I laughed. How easily I'd stolen dominance. How quick men were to falter when their masculinity was challenged.

He retaliated, hocking spit by my feet. "Let us leave before another finds our position. We are bound to one another now. It has been decided by fate beyond our control. Come, nut."

I am bound to no one, I wanted to say. Instead, I resentfully followed his lead, managing to find a positive in the fact he was toned and muscled; the veins in his arms were pulsating, their blue currents meandering through freckled constellations. He was strong. He was useful.

And that was where the positives ended. He displayed his hatred for me like a passive-aggressive fool, letting each branch he pushed past flick into my face.

I huffed and slapped them away, biting back my desire to verbally tear shreds out of him and started with something simple to suss him out. "And what do they call you?"

He sipped from his pouch, wiping the excess dribble where a white scar blemished his chin. "Áed."

"Oh, that's a lovely name," I said for some unexpected reason, like an old woman might when affectionately squeezing your cheeks. "I'm Clíona."

"No. You are the nut who caused the double quota. My mother near snapped her back slaving in the cornfield."

Dammit, this was personal. "I didn't mean for the quota to happen. I'm atoning for my mistakes." All of them.

He faced me dead-on, so closely, the coiled hairs sprouting from the mole on his neck magnified. And was that a...*hickey* next to it?

"A harvest cannot feed the past." He scoffed. "You wish to be champion and give back to the village? Words as old as Danu. Trust *my* word, those who champion do it for glory."

The lack of trust was just one reason not to share why I truly competed.

He stared me up and down, squinting his disgust before turning on his heel to storm off, the clattering of his sword and shield echoing the air behind him.

I huffed back in a wasted retort, which was harder than it should have been. The air must have been thinning already.

Midday retreated over the mountain, perhaps afraid to see the inevitable death in the coming hours. We'd left the trees for an open field of yellow wildflowers. With little to hide us from attack, my paranoia returned with an ardent taunt. I dashed glares to the squawks above us. Even a rustle of grass in the soft breeze twitched my aching muscles.

Áed lagged to match my pace though still refusing to look at me. "Be truthful. Are you an Ardagh spy?"

I scowled. The cheek. Silly as it was to be offended, Saoirse indoctrination was an effective one. "You really need to start trusting me if you want to compete in tomorrow's trial. Chances are we'll be together for that one as well."

For this, he spared me the decency of eye contact, I suspected my words finding a hint of respect from him. "Time will tell. As long as you—" His gaze perked east.

I followed him. "What is it?"

"Shh." He dipped us below a thick bush, moving my chin above the bushes to see them: two men, a hundred yards ahead.

"Their markings kind of look blue," I said, hoping my blasé tone would mask my jitters.

"Trust they are our enemy until we see truth."

Oh, *that* you'll trust.

"The shorter man I know," he said, slowly retracting his sword from the scabbard. "He can sentence you to many hours of sleep with a sole touch. And though absent of eyes, he moves as any other would, wielding his weapon well."

I squeezed the handle of Caolann's knife for comfort that didn't find me. "And the tall one?"

"Not of our village or one I have crossed paths with. Let us hope he is among the weak."

I fluttered my fingers. "I've got something to scare them off."

"No." He grasped my arm to keep me grounded. "Follow my lead. We should force enemy clans *down* the mountain."

I put my pride aside—a personal feat. It was clear this wasn't his first rodeo, or he'd been well versed, and Caolann had recommended similar tactics.

Áed was cautious with each sneaking step; elegant, even. I mirrored his stealth, crouching by more bushes and rocks shimmering in snail mucous. An eerie quiet tailed us as we dashed from one to the next. My hands brushed over the triskeles carved into them, three branching spirals. A sign of a burial ground? It would be improper to enter, but exposure might leave me to the same fate as those beneath.

No, thank you.

Our enemy wasn't as cautious, both topless and absent of armour beyond their swords. They bickered and never scoped out their surroundings. That worried me. Worried me in those hidden places where at least Áed couldn't see. What if they harvested with such strength exposure didn't bother them?

In hindsight, it was better not to think of these things at all. Action was the better route.

I stayed by Áed's side, but as we ran out of bushes and boulders to hide behind, we found ourselves less than thirty feet apart, exposed and vulnerable. My heart throbbed my ears as if to send a quiet beacon to abort. But my brain knew I couldn't. There was no fast way to jump off this mountain. This was the way forward.

"Their markings are blue," he said, too loud for the proximity. "Prepare for attack."

The throbbing pressed harder, pulsing my heartbeat into my ears at a frightening pace. "What, right now?"

He winked. "Fight well!"

Shooting forward to make himself known, still, no sword was drawn. Instead, he beat his bronze chest plate. "Alas, men, let Lúnasa truly begin!"

My hands trembling, I stumbled from cover to join him.

Áed heaved with bullish nature. "Cast your eyes, cracked one." Hands rubbing together, a flame sparked within them, thickening and expanding, stretching in his hands as if pliable. With a smile that dragged the hook of his nose, he pushed his ignited hands towards them, surging an orange heat.

I staggered to avoid it, my mouth a cavern of amazement for his precision when I was so used to pissing in the wind.

His flames spiralled, a brute force igniting the line of berry bushes in front of them.

At first glance, the men cowered, protecting themselves from the ignited bushes. But in our dash to close in, I *swore* the tall one maniacally laughed in the flame's mirage.

Never a good sign.

Áed stopped with a stuttering gasp, his arm pressed against my chest to keep me at bay. "Forgive me."

His words hitched my breath.

As the eyeless man held back, his longsword drawn, the other stepped *into* the flames to unnaturally lap up the heat. It burned his clothes and quivered his mouth with creepy glee.

"How—he's—he's not burning," I murmured.

Áed's voice muffled his response. I was too captivated by the man in the flames—how it defied all logic while embodying a strange, haunting beauty. The man standing right next to me could summon fire, let it rest on his skin, and yet, seeing this man frightened him.

A scorching hand on my shoulder's armour pulled me from my trance. "Do you hear?" Áed shouted. "We are in grave peril." He started to head west. "Come. We cannot fight him once the transformation occurs."

Transformation? What in the name of all things holy was this man in flames going to turn into?

My calves cramped tighter with every bound to flank Áed as I raced away. But an instinctive trust was building in me that this was the only route to staying alive.

"Keep moving," he shouted.

An itch crept into my neck, enticing me to turn to our threat. I had to see what came for us. See if I considered myself strong enough to fight it.

Craning my neck so far it cracked, I found an impossible scene: a man-sized creature, scaled and four-legged. It whipped its tail as it slithered towards us, hissing its forked tongue.

"Áed! Why is there a fucking giant Komodo dragon chasing us?"

Its spiked head trailed us. The eyeless companion followed. And the gap between Áed and I widened.

"Wait for me, Áed!"

He didn't. I was losing him.

"Áed, please!"

One trial. I wasn't going to live past *one* trial.

"Don't leave me!"

He stopped in his tracks, letting out a frustrated roar, then turned and marched back toward me, so close his smoky scent seemed to seep into my skin. "A draconian feeds on heat. My Bua will make it stronger. *You* must harvest now." He drew his sword, battered and wider on its end. "I will battle the eyeless one."

This was the moment I'd spent weeks practising for, and though I'd expected it to be a human I fought off, I faced my thriving enemy, both hands ready and rattling with power from the mere thought of Fionn being dead.

"Alright, let's have it, you scaly bastard." Willing him to stop, I rippled my instant, golden force at him—a wave stronger than any current of the sea.

The creature stopped in place as Áed's sword clashed against his enemy's on my periphery. Each swing was parried, sending tremors through my body as I anticipated each one plunging into this stomach.

The dragon's neck unfurled a circular frill of thin skin.

Áed had fallen to his back. The eyeless enemy was poised as he harboured a final blow.

"Help me, wild one!"

My eyes skimmed back and forth, over and over. If I helped him, I was sacrificing myself. And I was never going to sacrifice myself for whatever was morally right in this situation.

Unless—

I split my harvest.

One hand funnelled my force to the eyeless one while the other remained to keep the creature in place. The eyeless man lifted from the earth, hurtling backwards ten yards until dust enshrouded his unmoving form.

My feet began to slide, forming deep lines in the gravel as the dragon edged forward using his claws for traction.

My palm throbbed to hold him off, yet he retaliated at my strength.

"Take cover," Áed shouted in his retreat, his longsword swinging with each bound.

"I can't. He'll—"

Áed tackled me to the ground behind another triskele tombstone, winding me.

"We must fight it until death finds a side," he told me, nose to nose.

"That's a terrible plan." I peered over the tombstone's edge, still pinned beneath his boiling weight. The dragon paced for us, hissing and grunting as its tail swept trails of dust.

If I couldn't stop it, maybe our playing field would.

With no time to second guess myself, I leveraged Áed off with a leg between his, swinging myself onto top to straddle him.

Thank you, Lester, for that trick.

Áed stared up at me wide-eyed, and—I think—a little impressed.

I scooted backwards off him, my palms planted on the ground, eyes closed to focus on the earth.

"What are you doing?" he asked, crouching now.

"*Shh.*" I had to focus. I didn't even know if I could do what I was about to attempt.

My harvest filtered out, fighting the burrow into thick soil and roots in line with an electrical synapse. Finding what I desired—*needed*—I called on my harvest, my beautiful golden shimmers, to contour around the water, willing it to rise. The bond to Danu seduced me. My teeth chattered with pure power as pockets of water sprung between the ground's cracks, merging to create a body of brown water.

"What is your plan?" Áed asked. "Draconians thrive in water."

"It's not the water I need. It's what it makes."

The ground thickened more and more into a muddy sludge.

It was working.

The dragon's clawed feet could find no place to secure its slipping legs. It collapsed onto its belly, lodged and screeching.

"It will not hold him long," Áed warned. "We must run. Fast. Can you do this for me, Clíona?"

He used my name.

I swiped the crusting blood from my nostrils. "Yes."

We left the hissing dragon to the fate of the trials, his companion nowhere to be seen.

But if I had killed him, I somehow didn't care.

⁂

Sweat dripped from every pore of my body from the climb, and my lungs burned as if Áed squeezed them with his ignited hands. We fell, together, into a quilt of moss by slanted stone to shelter our position.

"Water," he croaked.

I offered my pouch he took with a reddened hand. The sun had ironically taken its toll on his pale white skin, now a closer shade to a tomato.

To be fair, mine, as a fellow redhead, wasn't much better.

Áed relieved himself with a *gah*. "We shook them."

"Your Bua—is—incredible." I panted, grinning from the high of adrenaline pulsing through my veins.

"You also harvest great strength." He gestured to my crusted nose. "Perhaps too well."

I cupped my mouth and nose with water from the pouch to clear the worst of it. "When my emotions don't get in the way, I can do a lot."

"I burnt many a breakfast in my younger years."

I smiled, and so did he. It was bright and beautiful. Then we slumped onto our backs again, to catch more breath.

After too little rest to feel even close to recovered, we forced our legs to stand.

"We need to seek more of our clan if we wish to pass this trial," Áed said, taking the lead. "When those of an enemy clan come for us, *I* will force them to flee. You fight well, but this clan needs a wise leader."

The inflection of his 'I' was cocky. Filled with bravado. "Right. I do nothing while you take charge? Huh. I can't tell if you're a misogynist, egotistical or an idiot. Fat lot of good you've been so far. You'd be dead if I didn't split my harvest."

He looked me up and down, spitting at my feet before stomping ahead. "Filthy spy!"

I held my tongue, and for his sake, my harvest.

So much for getting along.

27

MORALITY IS A FUNNY THING

The sun flashed rays of orange in its descent, and the thinning air had turned cold. Yet it was the chaffing in my baby toes that stole most of my attention, surely bulbous with blisters by now.

Áed trekked ahead, and I was glad we didn't have to talk. It kept my breathing controlled. And, well, if we weren't talking, we weren't fighting. Not that I was against fighting, but I needed to at least have my clan on my side.

Rams with spiralled horns chomped on tufts of grass, keeping to themselves as we weaved around them and their fly-swarmed dung. In the peaceful moment I was sure wouldn't last, Lester came to mind. He could've been attacked and left bloody by now.

I shook the image away with a grumbling sigh, spurring a half-horned ram in my path to snort at me. "Listen, here," I said as I passed it with extra space, my hands in a surrender, "I didn't get this far to have '*murdered by a big sheep'* written on my headstone." Although that would certainly soften the morbidity of grave visitors.

Áed whistled for me, pointing to a figure further up who scaled through a thick mount of rocks.

A foolish, conspicuous route, Caolann would say. He'd be right.

The lone traveller must've caught a glimpse of us, his climb quickening though he fell many times on the slippery terrain.

I took the lead to capture him before Áed had the chance.

"Hold back!"

I flung my hands to the loner, my harvest spooling out across the terrain in mere seconds to snare him in my grasp. The distance sent a sharp ache up my hands, but I persisted, lassoing him to us. "I've got ahold of him."

Áed ran past me, kicking a pile of dung across the field. "You fool. He could be of our clan."

I smirked. "And you could be less dramatic."

Continuing, I summoned the loner's body through the rocks and across the field until he reached our feet, his face painted brown around thick lips and brows.

"Not ours," I said. "Unless that's ram shite on his face instead of paint."

"I beg of you." The man trembled with surrender heads by his chest. "No more."

His exposed legs were a mangled mess of blonde curled hairs and fresh, bloody wounds. His arms were no better.

I hadn't considered the damage of dragging him here.

Concealing the guilt spilling out of my hanging mouth, I drew my lips taut. The Comeragh was no place for weakness. Not mine nor his.

My fingers, free of the harvest but trembling, looped the rope attached to my belt. I hesitated to use it as the man's pleading for mercy only grew more wretched.

Get your shit together. This is no place for weakness.

Áed unexpectedly squeezed my shoulder, and though I couldn't bring myself to look at him, I appreciated it.

"Help me tie him up." Guilty or not, my plan remained.

The scrawny loner scooted back on his bottom. I crouched, staring at the somehow already yellowing scabs hugging the edges of his cuts.

A healer from Dian Cecht's line of immortal power?

Áed unhitched his own rope, nudging my back for me to stand aside. "We waste sunlight."

"I will not search for you. You cannot sit me here as a duck," the man pleaded with me—the easier target. "Too many came for blood this Lúnasa."

I didn't doubt the truth in his words, but someone's blood was running down the mountain, and it wasn't going to be mine.

Áed sighed and wrapped the loner's cut hands together to bind them, his knee on the man's neck. "Surrender your lies, Donnacha. I lay with you last nightfall in many hours of passion. You spoke proudly of accepting Lúnasa's stakes. Any other man would be slaughtered by my sword for his foolishness."

For his words, Donnacha's act of weariness faltered, sharpening into a flat, amused smile.

My head swung in a pendulum form between them, these...lovers. Well, I wasn't expecting *that.*

Áed finished his knot and released his knee from Donnacha's neck, both their faces suddenly softer. "If this day brings your end, mo ghrá, you will feast in the plain of pleasures, or the gods will make you reborn. This is not your end. Nor ours." Then Áed fisted his hair and kissed him. To my further surprise, Donnacha embraced it, their tongues twisting with raw passion.

Unable to tear my eyes from their heated embrace, I managed to keep my mouth shut for all the things I wanted to ask.

When they separated with a final fleeting kiss, Áed stood, and their rivalry returned with hardened stares.

Donnacha spat. "By the Tuatha, I condemn you." As he heaved to turn on his belly, Áed overpowered him, stomping on the man's oozing knee to summon a *yelp*.

"You condemn little. You are not fit for divine status." Áed's face softened. "Fear not, your binds are that which can be escaped in time."

Whatever game they were playing was one they both angrily seemed to enjoy.

I could relate.

We left him without even the courtesy of a goodbye as we entered the cluster of trees—the last coverage until we breached the fog I tried not to dwell on.

"We made the wise decision," Áed said, perhaps telling himself more than me.

While logic told me he was right, his stern facade faltered, exhorting my own guilt.

"What we did to him...Donnacha—it was awful, even if he can break free eventually."

"You are a kinder spy than I presumed." He joked with a helpless smile that stretched the scar on his chin. "Hold no guilt for him. He fathomed the stakes of battling for honour. He fucks well, yet he fights better. And trust, Donnacha would impale the skull of any turned head."

I returned his smile, unsure what sparked it.

A gurgling cry rang out, spoiling our exchange.

Áed's eyes mistakenly shot to where we'd left Donnacha.

My hand found my knife.

"No. Do not, Clíona," he warned, his head tilting. His eyes locked on mine.

In a breath, I twisted to the scream, my legs thunderously taking off. Donnacha was defenceless by *my* hands. I had to give him a fighting chance. There had to be a line to morality, even in a game like this.

Bounding through the thinning forest, I could make out the rams when a blast of fire scorched the tree in front. My legs came from underneath me, but before my hands hit the ground, Áed was on my back, wrestling my flailing arms.

"We cannot save him from slaughter," he struggled against my wriggle.

I wanted to challenge him for his cruelty and how easily he'd let someone die that he supposedly cared for. I wanted to fling him off of me. It'd be easy since I barely needed my hand's control anymore. But I didn't; instead, I chose to listen to his voice repeat the words, "We cannot save him."

The adrenaline simmered from my body, leaving me with nothing but a dry throat. "We caused this," I croaked as Donnacha's cry faded.

Áed ever so slowly released his hold, and my arms felt lighter not to have a weight on them. "Cast your eyes to him—the beast."

Where we'd left Donnacha was a man so wide in stature the blade he held resembled a dinner knife. He skimmed his hand along the weapon, flicking a spray of red onto a passing ram.

By the True Gods, he didn't even care.

"Con takes any soul who crosses his path. It is he who caused Donnacha's slaughter, not you or I. Has it not sunk in yet? They call these trials, but this *is* a game. A game must be played. A game must have a champion, and in turn, there are those who are defeated. Choose now, Clíona. Which is it you wish to be?"

A champion. I wish to be a champion.

"I will stand now, and I hope you rise with no intent to attack."

I lay on my stomach, watching the remnants of death on the man's spattered face, meshed with purple markings. We weren't safe so close to a monster. No one was.

"Don't you care?" I whispered.

"An aching heart beats in all Saoirsians. He was a lover, not my love, yet I will mourn him when the trials end." Áed swallowed whatever true pain wanted to escape him.

I stood heavy-hearted, unconvincingly telling myself Donnacha's death wasn't our fault. That it was his decision to compete, and only he could carry the weight of his life.

With the guidance of Áed's hand, still shocked, we fled the outskirts of the bloody scene.

In the depths of the forest, the high altitude had hit us with dull headaches, and my muscles hung heavier making each step harder than the last.

Áed had vomited onto a bed of daisies before casually resuming our trek, spitting whatever had clung from his stomach before speaking. "We draw closer to the summit."

"So, we need to find the other four people from our clan, or we're up shit creek?"

"No. Daylight departs. All we must focus on is evading attacks and igniting our black fire for the gods to see we fought well and grant us passage to the next trial."

I nodded in silent agreement and took his offered hand to match his pace. He knew so much about the trials. I should have trusted him more instead of trying to take control. Typical of me—gullible in thinking I'd glide through the trials without falling victim to its brutality.

"Have you competed much?" I asked. Áed physically looked to be in his mid-twenties, with his slight facial.

"I am in my twenty-fifth year. This is my third Lúnasa."

"I guess I should have listened to you more," I confessed, despite my stubbornness telling me not to.

Áed glanced over my shoulder, his smile fading as his golden eyes bulged. "Down!" His arms tackled my core, winding me so hard, breath abandoned me. A sharp pain surged across my upper arm as he dragged me by my armour's shoulder behind a large tree.

He seethed, his eyelids folding in on themselves. "I am wounded."

His thigh oozed in blood, meandering around a honeycomb of pebble stones meshed into his skin. My elbow to my outer shoulder had a similar sight, pulsating wedged stones.

My tongue rolled out of my mouth with a gag. The pain reverberated everywhere, and I didn't dare to seek out our enemy for fear of losing my eyes.

Voices called all around us like secrets of the forest. We were surrounded. It happened so fast. Control slipped from our hands in seconds, and the whispers grew louder.

Holding each other tight with heaving fear of the imminent death, I clenched my eyes.

Further attacks didn't come.

Áed peeked out from behind the tree. "We have foreign protection. A Saoirsian shields us."

Orange-marked enemies had distorted bodies as though we watched them through frosted glass.

"Up here," came a stern woman's voice. Above us, dangling from the highest branches, was a beckoning hand. Their features were delicate, feminine, and they wore a leather bracer that felt faintly familiar. "Move at once! The reflection will trick them for but a moment."

Time to question her allegiance didn't exist. Blood from Áed's leg dripped onto my face as we scaled the branches. He clenched his teeth on bark as he climbed, though his suffering seeped out in concealed screams and groans.

I pushed his weak leg to the next branch any chance I got, but my strength was turning to spaghetti.

The woman's dark hair and black markings became visible through the greenery as she perched on a branch thick enough to hold all three of us out of view.

Her shield collapsed into shards on the forest bed.

Orange Clan searched beneath where Áed's blood dripped and dotted the fallen leaves. We waited in breath-holding silence, praying they wouldn't look up. But the primitive part of me that grew stronger each hour we spent on the mountain wanted to jump down and attack them, signalling the time when I'd come to embrace these urges was close.

I was even beginning to consider it just.

Áed grabbed my arm and shook his head, reading my foolish, narrow-eyed intent.

The clan of gruff men moved on. A body bearing the same-coloured markings on a makeshift stretcher pulling behind them.

"Thank you for helping us," I said to the woman when it was safe to speak.

"It is *you*," she seethed, her voice so snaky it rattled the feathers in her hair. She drew her knife from her bandolier front as her familiar, beady eyes bore into mine.

The woman who'd pushed me earlier on our trek to the mountain.

My nostrils flared with the echo of disdain.

She edged forward, her knife pointed.

"Fucking try me," I sneered.

Áed spread his bloody hands between us on the groaning branch. "Contain yourself, Muireann."

"I offered my Bua to protect an Ardagh spy. The gods will curse me." She spat at me, though I couldn't tell if she was more disgusted by me or herself.

Great. Here we go again with this. I unsheathed Caolann's knife, unfitting and heavy in my hand. I was hoping for luck rather than brutality.

"She is not a spy," Áed defended me. "What do you plan to do? Slaughter her? Then none of us will claim victory."

Muireann shoved her knife out anyway, edging towards me as she held the branch beside her to spring.

I'd had enough. I was tired of being called a spy and being underestimated. "Take a step closer, and I'll put that knife through your beady fuckin' eye!"

She hesitated for the crazed look in *my* eye, then smirked as she jolted.

I shoved her chest with a swift, thrumming harvest, forcing her to lose her grip.

She grabbed a branch to save herself but missed, dipping into leaves, bouncing from branch to branch with grunts and moans.

Inches from the ground, I reverted my harvest to dangle her body so close to the roots I was sure her nose had grazed them.

Áed grabbed my wrist. "Her shield is of value. Lower her safely."

"Let go of me, or I'll drop you, too," I threatened him. "Not another word about being a spy out of either of you. When I'm angry, when I'm even annoyed, all I have to do is *think*, and you'd be nothing but entrails on the forest bed." I hoped they bought the empty threat. I hoped, even more, it *was* empty. "Now, are you gonna' play nice?"

"Yes," she gasped. "Release me, and we will secure our place in tomorrow's trial."

Her body dropped with a heavy thud.

I snickered, and Áed mirrored me. Although, I think more so out of fear of the cracked nut.

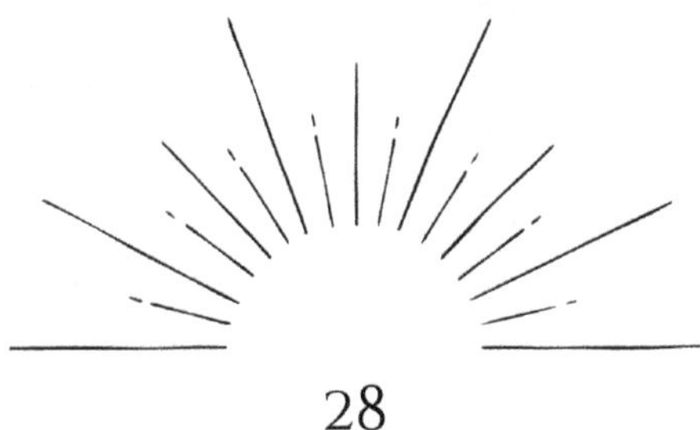

28
CREATURES OF THE MIST

In side-eyed hostility, the three of us approached the mountain's final stretch. Without the moon and stars, we would be blind once inside the mist—the insidious part of the trial, but at least I wasn't going in alone.

Muireann had barely spoken since our fight, too busy sucking on imaginary sour fruit. She needed to get her head out of her arse because with only three of us, we were surely among the weak.

Áed's leg was strapped with cloth, worryingly red in stark comparison to the grey tone leaching into his skin. My arm wound stung after picking out the stones, but I'd be fine. A surface wound, at worst.

"Two enemies come for blood this harvest, wishing to slice our backs in the mist," Áed said with a grunt as he clenched his hip for support.

"Con always comes for blood," Muireann stated, toying with her feathers like these threats meant little to her.

"He is close. He sacrificed Donnacha," Áed warned her. "Lindy will hold no prisoners, either."

"What can she do?" I asked though I was sure I didn't want to know.

Áed had begun to lean weight on me, and I quietly took it. "Lindy stiffens the body. Not in your manner, hers"—he squeezed his eyes in pained folds—"hers resembles the bite of a yellow spider. Yet it is her sole strength. She weakens fast."

"It is also Con's final Lúnasa," Muireann interrupted. "He will slaughter whoever crosses his path. He is our greatest threat for he has nought to lose."

The threshold of mist crept up on us, the air suddenly thick and grey. Áed drew his jaw tight and clenched his leg like any man of war would. But behind his strength and the chilling weather, he sweated too much. We had to get to the top before he passed out. We had to progress. Or this would all be for nothing.

Muireann unsheathed a dagger from the fleet on her bandolier. This dagger was carved with notches. I could easily guess what they signified: victims. "Stay close and silent. Our rivals surely walk among us."

The ghostly quiet brought my heart forward to throb against my plated chest.

Movement came from ahead: a patter of footsteps.

My breath rattled—even that too loud. "Did you hear that?" I whispered.

"*Shh*," Muireann shot back, steadying her hands to harvest her shield. It stemmed out in an oval mirage, clear. The fog bounced off it, curling to our sides to create a short pathway.

I drew Caolann's knife with my free hand, still doubting I'd use it.

Áed slowed, mumbling something beneath his scattered breath. I couldn't crutch him much longer, each breath of mine growing too loud under his weight.

He was a liability. If I could leave him behind, it would be the better choice.

Even thinking it had me biting my lip so hard something popped beneath the soft flesh.

Footsteps skittered closer, freezing me still.

"No," someone cried in the distance. "I beg. No, Con."

The gurgling of what I pictured was someone choking on a river of their own blood quickly drowned out.

"Can you move this fog as you moved me?" Muireann whispered to me.

"Why?" I asked.

"We are the underdog in the darkness. Too many hold the strength to thrive in such conditions."

Exposing ourselves to our enemies seemed insane, but she might've been right.

A closer yelp and gurgle sliced the air.

My nails dug into my skin as I clenched the knife tighter.

"Listen to her, Clíona. Use your Bua, or we will be next," Áed's strained voice seeped through clenched teeth.

"No. I can't hold you and move the fog."

"Leave him," Muireann seethed as she rescinded her shield to drag him down.

I sheathed my knife to fight for him with both hands. "No. I won't do that!"

"Better our lives!" she said in a hushed voice.

We tugged over his ragdoll state, yanking him back and forth more forcefully each time.

She couldn't have him. "Get off him, Muireann!" I shouted.

Muireann stopped mid pull, her eyes sickly bulging. I knew as soon as I'd done it. Knew it in how my blood ran cold despite the heat of Áed still pressing on me.

I'd given away our position.

Then, all at once, the screams of many played in the bleak melody of death. I'd dropped the stone to cause the ripple, stirring the fear out of everyone desperately trying to hold it in, and now we'd all suffer.

A figure skittered past, whipping my hair around my face. I stood completely still—not even blinking. Were they hiding or hunting?

I gasped. "Áed?" I no longer bore his weight. "Áed," I called out louder than I should have. "Muireann, help me." I spun in circles, not knowing which way to look. "Muireann?"

Please. Please don't leave me.

Her close voice called, "Clíona, where are—"

A clatter of swords twanged.

The ground grew steeper with each aimless step forward.

"Forgive me, Lindy," another cried.

I stumbled onto my knees, crawling over rocks, reaching my hands out until I grabbed something supple. With a tug, it came to me, its weight softening. A plump, hairless arm flopped in my hands, dripping with blood and ripped tendons. I flung it and stumbled back onto my bottom, panicked whimpers toppling out of me. My stomach churned, wanting to make butter of my insides.

People were dying. *No.* They were being murdered. Brutally. Right before my aching eyes. My naivety caught up with me too late. I was in the middle of a bloody massacre. I could die at any second. Worse, I might have to *kill* at any second. The necessity of that...the temptation...

Heat poured into my fingers. Tendons rolled over my knuckles. I raised my trembling hands to the sky as if to expel the fear from my body, harvesting my Bua. It radiated through me. It burrowed warmth into my palms until I was steady. Power spilt out, a bright light, shimmering golds in a heavy, wide stream.

The fog rose like rumbling clouds. Even nature feared the girl with the uncontrollable power.

The mist evaporated to reveal the entire summit's plain, and then the rain came, bucketing down.

"What have you caused?" Muireann gasped, mere feet from me, blood spattered across her. It ran down her cheeks and arms into diluted oranges as the droplets smacked against her skin.

An orange flame simmered into the open night sky, now illuminated by the full moon. It must have been Druid magic keeping it alight with such heavy weather.

We were closer to the top than I'd expected, as were all our rivals we'd blindly brushed past. Competitors stared at each other like deer caught in headlights about to meet their death.

Then the inevitable happened.

"Run!" a man shouted.

"Get to the fire ring," a young girl screamed.

Clans disbanded as self-survival kicked in. Áed lay perched on a triskele-carved rock, unmoving in the distance.

"Protect us," I pleaded to Muireann.

"He is of little use in rainfall," she sassed, suddenly grappling the eyeless man I'd attacked earlier.

"Do it now, or we won't fight tomorrow," I shouted over the man's shoulder like he was an inconvenience to more pressing issues.

She rolled her eyes and stabbed his heart, twisting the knife like a key to lock him into inevitable death. How quickly she'd done it. How uncaring and skilled her strike was.

Acidic bile rose into my throat as she pulled my arm away from the massacre. Her shield masked our race to Áed's placid body through knife jabs and acidic slime, all impervious to her shield.

I crouched to his side. "Áed, are you with me, friend?" I shook him.

"He is stiffened by Lindy's touch." Muireann crouched next to me, breathless and her nose bloody from overexertion—a worrying sign her shield wouldn't last much longer.

"Wake up." I smacked his cheek. "We have to go."

Áed opened his groggy eyes and sat with my hand's support. "Where—"

"Don't talk." I blotted his wound with loose moss like I knew what I was doing. Infection was tomorrow's worry.

"There's no time to find the rest of our clan. We must hope they summit alone," Muireann said.

A yellow flame tumbled high into the night a hundred yards above us.

Blood trailed from Muireann's nose for outside attacks on her shield. "I cannot hold it," she cried as a sword struck it.

I stretched Áed's arm around my shoulder, hitching him up. His leg still dragged, leaving a path of blood so thick even the worst tracker would find him.

A beastly man with hair from navel to head charged Muireann's shield, headfirst, leaving it in shards.

My stomach levitated into my throat. Con had come for us.

Áed collapsed to one knee, and I went with him, tumbling onto my stomach.

Con beat his gorilla chest as if toying with his food. “I will relish this slaughter.”

His wet mouth snarling, Con clenched Muireann’s throat. “I will take you first. You slipped through my grasp in Lúnasa of last.”

Her tongue lolled from her mouth as she scratched his hands, yet they made no dent on his impenetrable skin.

“Release her!” a young, red-haired boy roared. He leapt onto Con’s back, wrapping his black-painted arm tightly around the beast’s broad neck. Flimsy in stature, the boy persisted, jabbing his rickety blade into Con’s jugular.

I winced at the impact as I staggered upright, but the blade bent.

Con bellowed loud laughter, revelling the fight.

“Ruadh,” Áed cried as he harvested his rain-sizzled flames in spurts towards Con.

Con pinched the boy off his back to raise him high—a mere insect standing in his way to merciless glory.

I had to do something. This was my clan. There was no way forward without them.

I stumbled, falling twice until I found my footing, and harvested. Golden ropes of thick mirage snatched the boy from his grasp, jolting him left, away from the beast like a prize in a claw machine.

Con merely laughed. We were all here for his entertainment until he got his divine status.

“Foolish,” he snorted at me. Then with one swift move, he leapt towards me, plunging something cold and terribly sharp into the centre of my chest.

I cupped the knife’s tattered handle, unsure what to do with it.

Áed hobbled towards me, but as I opened my mouth to reassure him I was fine, it filled with the taste of rusted iron.

My vision blurred, making the rainbow of fires on the mountaintop beautifully mesh together. My legs buckled to the ground as a horde of painted faces mounted Con. His body disappeared beneath a pile of competitors until all to be seen were his thick, twitching fingers.

"We cannot break the skin, so we will steal your breath," a man with cleft lip and yellow markings cried. "In honour of the younglings slaughtered by your hands in past trials."

Competitors suffocated him, more and more in surprising unity piling their weight until Con's deep gurgles drowned out in my ringing ears.

The fighting around me faded into selfish dashes to the peak, but in the midst of it all, Lester skidded next to me, his eyes circled in green paint.

I coughed through splatters of blood. "Get me to the summit."

Only my sense of pain spoke as I writhed in my dewy flesh, wishing death or home might grant me mercy.

"Open your eyes," a familiar voice called out.

"Mam," I croaked, longing for her comfort. A warmth caressed my forehead as I lay in a familiar bed.

"It is I, Caolann."

My eyes, crusted and strained, half-opened.

"Am I dying?" The words didn't sound real.

He swallowed hard, repressing the blatant pain that crumpled his sullen eyes. "No. You will find strength to survive," he reassured me—and himself. "I pray to the True Gods, you must find strength."

The sharp pain in my chest pulsated, and a shiver climbed my body like a ghost.

"Did I pass the trial?"

He placed a cup of water at my mouth. "Do not worry of trials."

I weakly rejected it. "Tell me." This journey had to be for something. Otherwise, I'd yet again be reduced to nothing but the girl who killed her brother.

Lester stepped into view, bloodied and covered in dirt. "We dragged your body to the summit. Me, Muireann and the boy. You passed the trial."

"Did you pass?" That question seemed just as important.

"Yes."

A flourish of relief lifted my spirits until I swore I could see them hovering over my bed.

"You showed the strength of a warrior on the Comeragh," he told me as he grasped my limp hands. "I will claim victory for you."

"I *will* be competing tomorrow." I coughed through my words. "I can't leave Róisín. I can't abandon her!"

Caolann and Lester dashed a wary glance to one another.

There goes the cracked nut talking about fighting while on her deathbed. "Find me a healer." The bite I hoped would leech onto my words was lost to weakness.

A whimper escaped Lester's mouth.

I hadn't realised I'd meant that much to him.

I swallowed the taste of iron. "Listen to me." My hand shook as I pulled him closer, "I can survive this." I hoped saying it aloud would make it true.

"But I need..." I winced. "*Gah.* I need you to help me." He held my gaze, but could he understand what I was asking for? I didn't have the strength to spell it out.

Lester looked to Caolann; he immediately nodded.

Collapsing back into the bed, my voice and will to say any more gone. I would be a bystander to the last moments of my life if Lester didn't agree.

Through the darkness pulling me under I heard him whisper to Caolann, "The cost is ten years of my life."

No.

My tongue pressed to the roof of my mouth, but the once simple word wouldn't come out.

An unwavering response came. "She is worth it." But not Caolann's voice.

No, that voice belonged to—a muddy figure had stepped into the room beyond the proximity of my blurring vision—Rían.

"Ten years, brother," Caolann contested, calling on Rían to understand the gravity of that sacrifice. "Let *him* make the choice. Fight the pull of your harvest."

After a tense silence that could have been a moment or minutes in my disillusioned state, Rían gripped Lester's shoulder.

Caolann stepped between them to interject, "Brother, no!" The slice of his blade came down on Rían's arm, nicking the skin as he dodged, taking Lester aside with him.

"Lester, you want to help her," Rían's spoke in quick, soft tones. It was too late. Caolann muttered indistinguishable anger. "You will turn to Clíona now, and you will heal her with your Bua. When you are finished, return home and speak of this to no one."

Lester turned and placed his hands to my chest.

I shifted uncomfortably, my sweat-slicked from writhing in an attempt to fend off the slow, relentless sting that had taken root deep in my core. The sensation grew, intensifying with each passing second, until I could no longer contain the scream that tore from my throat. My body arched involuntarily, muscles tensing against the onslaught of pain as I gasped for breath that offered no relief from the searing heat of his foreign harvest coursing through me, overwhelming every sense.

He withdrew his hands, and my head lolled.

"She is too far gone," I heard a voice as the world's edges were lost. Until even the darkness abandoned me.

Please, Danu and Bíle, save me.

29

GLAS

My fingers trawled greasy hair. It stuck to my forehead so firmly, I nearly had to peel it off. Every inch of me ached with stiffness. When I tried to call out, my voice caught in its dryness, refusing to cooperate until I quenched it with the bedside cup of water.

Looking around the room—Caolann and Rían's home—my solitude distracted me, making me sit in the reality of what had happened: I nearly died last night.

Not like the crash, or by Rathnor's wretched mercy, or any other attempt on my life these past few weeks. Last night, I stood so close to the gate of death I could smell the rust on its hinges. I could feel the peace of it that, for a moment, made living feel like a burden.

Gasping, I sat up to kick the fur covers to a bunch at the bed's end.

Cloth encircled my chest and stomach in tight, constricting loops. I unwound it slowly, giving care with each bend of my elbows, to aid me even if involuntary winches seeped out beneath clenched teeth.

I froze.

"What?" I whispered to myself.

Smoothing my fingers over the silver scar across my abdomen, I could have sworn the mark was ten years old, not ten hours. *Ten years.* He'd done it—Lester had healed me. Sure my hunch had paid off—that perhaps his ability to rapidly heal was one he might share. But still, if I had known the toll...

What if he had said five years? Or even *one*? Would that have hit the threshold of my tenuous morality?

An echo of last night swirled into my thoughts: his hushed whispers with Caolann as the darkness was pulling me to death in those final moments. Lester outright said it would cost ten years of his life and...

Rían. Didn't. Care.

I flinched from the thought.

Perhaps Caolann would have eventually forced the deal, too. But I was certain now I wouldn't have accepted if my voice worked. No. Never. Not when it went against the very thing I fought for. Rían must have known that.

I exhaled my annoyance through my nostrils feeling no better. The logical route would be to forfeit the trials. To finally seek Finegas out and get my answers. But then who would find the children if not me? And what about the ones not yet taken? What about Róisín?

My jaw tensed. That was all the convincing I needed.

Swinging my legs over the bed's edge, I washed and dressed quickly; wearing tightened armour still stained in blood, I meticulously crossed its corset chain into a knot, forcing everything that happened in the trial not to seep into my brain like a flesh-eating virus to consume me. I was pulling at the seam of death when I'd barely managed to sew it in the first place. There wasn't space to worry about what could unfold when another trial awaited.

So, I tucked that part of me away, sheathed a new knife from Caolann's collection into my thigh holster, and left to find him.

Rían stood in the frame of the door, blocking my path.

I drew back into the shadows of the room.

Even that brought a flash of pain over the edges of his mouth, pain he couldn't hide fast enough.

Good.

I straightened, letting him see my reluctance to be close to him. Let him know I'm appalled. That whatever trust I had for him was irrefutably tainted. "How *dare* you do that to Lester. And in my name!"

Rían stepped into the room, drifting his hand over the curved skeleton of the house. If he was attempting indifference, it was frighteningly believable. "Thank the gods I taught you to contain your Bua well. Perhaps I would be spatter on the wall already if not." Was he—my chin jerked back—intentionally riling me up?

His stare dashed to my hand. I followed it.

A soft light was already forming its centre, hovering like a tiny, endless galaxy just above the surface.

Rían performatively cracked his neck side-to-side.

Oh, he wanted a fight. He wanted me to know this side of him now that it had slipped out. He wanted me to condemn him.

No, I won't be the outlet of your guilt.

"Leave," I said, suddenly at a loss for any other words.

He sparsely surrendered his hands into a shrug. "Recall, this was my home first. You do not get to decide who visits."

"Just the same way you didn't get to decide if Lester should have healed me."

He clicked his tongue, keeping it rooted in his teeth as he looked out to the village for a time. Then he said with absolute conviction, "I would do it again."

"Don't."

He stepped closer. "I would do it"—his gazed flick to me—"a thousand times over with no regret. I would slaughter every person who competes in Lúnasa to keep you safe."

"You're exhausting."

"And you wish for me to be the easy brother."

I fisted my hands, not trusting myself. "I wish nothing"—my jaw tightened—"of the sort. This isn't a game to me! And I don't know why you're starting to treat it as one."

He softened a fraction, just in shoulders—his tell. "Clíona, to be bound to someone goes beyond the clause of force. Protecting you is my *duty*. Keeping you alive is my duty. This is no game, nor is it a case of feelings."

"Then what is it a case of?" I asked, my head perched forward and low.

"It is an oath."

"Oath?" I repeated, confused, retracting that perch. "You don't even care about the gods. You hate them. Why should it matter what they say?"

"The rules of Ériu are governed by the True gods, Danu and Bíle. There is a higher power of magic involved in these lands beyond the hollow words of Rathnor that day upon the Carrig."

"But Caolann told me the bond was broken."

He smirked. "You fear the brother who speaks the truth so much you forget the other lies."

"I'm still mad at you." To put it lightly.

"So be it."

There wasn't time for whatever this was. There was a trial to get to. I rushed to brush past him.

He gripped my arm, tightening as I tried to shake the touch. "Clíona."

Settling, I looked at him. "What?" I spat.

"Come back alive today." He dropped his hand, and though I stalled for a fraction of a second in his personal space, I quickly steeled myself and left without another word.

At Bébhinn's, Caolann, a shadow of the warrior I'd known, came in and out of view though the linen caught in the breeze. He leaned with a single arm and his head pressed against the house, his stance meeting the roof for his height. His eyes were red and depleted, and a fragility had overcome him.

"Caolann." I spoke softly not to startle him.

"Clíona!" He staggered and clenched his heart wide-eyed as though it beat for the first time. "I thank the True Gods." He raced through the linen, his arms embracing me whole.

I muffled beneath his hold, "I'm fine."

"I believed..." He held my gaze firmly, forcing me to see the pain behind his glassy eyes. "Lester could make no guarantee."

"I really am fine," I said less monotonously while pushing back from his hold. It wasn't fair to disregard his pain in this situation even if I felt I wasn't worth it. "Caolann, we need to—"

He pulled me in to share a firm, warm kiss. No matter how much his lie about the bind annoyed me, I still matched each press of his lips with fervid pleasure. Because I could feel it now, the separation from lust. The foundations of whatever we were melting away for better ones. One that made me think having him in my heart might be nicer than in my bed. Or, well, *his* bed.

I was weak for how he showed his want of me: each press of his lips passionate and stronger than the last. Each touch of his fingers in my hair meaningful. Each look through his shamrock eyes heated.

Conceding entirely, I curled my fingers around his large frame, letting him arch my back and grab my bum to keep me close. Breathless from giving in to nature, I pried myself away, wiping a thumb across my lips to savour the taste of him.

"We waste time," I teased.

"No moment with you is wasted, Clíona. Now come, you must rest more."

I jerked from his gentle lead back home. "Rest?" I laughed, obnoxiously. "I don't have time to rest. We need to leave, or I'll be forced to forfeit my spot in the next trial. I'm healed. I'm ready to fight."

He gave me a familiar frown, the kind that always appeared when he thought—or more often *said*—I was a cracked nut. "You wish to risk your life after nightfall's turmoil? I forbid it."

I scoffed. "Forbid?" My annoyance morphed into something crueller. I jabbed my finger at his chest between the bumps of his abs. Harder than I should have. "It's not your decision what I do. It's mine and mine alone. Us being together—or whatever this is—doesn't give you ownership, no matter how good your intentions are." Educating an ancient demigod about autonomy posed to be a difficult task. "And you lied to me about our bind being broken."

"Forgive me?"

I smoothed my face. "No."

"Then perhaps, my bound girl, you will allow me to make amends."

The muscles around my mouth twitched as I fought to keep them still. But the only thing I wanted now was the swell of my lips and the chance to snuff out the quiet urgency rattling inside me to unbuckle him and take him in aching mouthfuls.

Reading me, he hitched an arm beneath my bottom as though I weighed nothing, taking me between two houses where no one might wander.

His jaw was so rigid I feared it might shatter as he kept my body suspended, pressing me against the wall. "What would be worthy of your forfeit?" he asked, two fingers running across my cheek until pressing them against my bottom teeth to forcefully droop my mouth. "Me speaking to the Tuatha? Would that make you happy?"

I shivered, perching to kiss him.

His hand covered my mouth to stop me.

"Or will I regain their trust by living in Magh Mell? So perhaps they might offer resources in my search for the young. Would that convince you?" His seduction has an undertone of manipulation I was well familiar with. The offer was so tempting, I bit down on my lip behind his palm.

What he offered meant leaving Rían alone. Rían couldn't be alone. If not before, then certainly not now. His mind wouldn't survive it.

I sighed, shrugging from his hold to untie my stained armour. To show him where I'd been stabbed. All that remained was the silver scar. Stretchmarks had given me a worse day than this. "I can take care of myself." It was a simple counter to his offer, but I hoped it was enough.

He smoothed his coarse thumb over it, eliciting another shiver in me. Fighting the temptation of him was painfully difficult, having me clench my thighs to stay on point.

He smirked. "What happened on the Comeragh would have me assume otherwise."

I pressed my toes against the dirt track to reach his face, so close I arduously resisted kissing him when everything inside me was calling for it. "I'm going to compete, and not a soul will stop me until I take my last breath," I whispered with a finishing smile.

His eyes hazed. "Allow me to journey with you to the trial grounds to remind you of what lies ahead."

I took his olive branch; in return he took my hand.

Travelling through the empty southern forest in silence, late to the grounds, it was apparent that we were wasting valuable strategizing time. But emotions made everything difficult. Especially when I was stubborn, too. Yet, how could I be mad at Caolann for caring? He thought I was on death's door, and I was shipping myself off to cause him further anguish.

I rubbed my hand across the small of his back as he often did with me. "Remind me. Only three competitors are in a clan this time," I egged to dilute the lingering tension.

"Indeed. Clans are chosen from the previous if there are enough survivors."

"I hope Áed is healed enough to compete. I'd like him on my side." Our rocky relationship was outweighed by our need to survive, and better the devil you know.

"Heed my warning," Caolann said. "With Áed by your side or not, recall but three clans move forward to tomorrow's trial."

I let that reality sink in as the ground below our feet changed from pines and soil to a sludgy grey muck until we broke past the shade. Before us was a spread of endless desert, scattered with competing Saoirsians and mirages of, well, more desert.

"Hang on." I grabbed Caolann's tricep. "Am I losing it, or is the sand...green?" I knelt, scooping it simply to let it fall through the cracks of my fingers. On closer inspection, it was more of a muddy brown, though in the distance it became emerald toned and sparkled.

Caolann crouched next to me. "It is Ciaróga." He grit sand between his thumb and finger. "The beetles shell turns the sand green upon death. Much like the Soilse."

"Huh."

"Come." He helped me up. "It is too warm to stay idle." Losing the forest cover had exposed us to a sweltering heat my vexed, freckled skin didn't take to kindly.

We closed in on more slanted limestone where competitors gathered, sharpening swords or leaning on them to pray in hushed whispers.

Caolann started into a lecture, "Each trial strains greater than the last. You may have fewer an enemy, but the battleground is limited, and the Cluster is dangerous."

Foolishly ignoring his words, I savoured him as he squinted to fight the blinding light; savoured his Celtic tattoos and wild plaited hair, savoured his kindness habitually concealed by his endlessly feathering jaw. Yet, he was beautiful and strong, and every time I was forced to part with such things, the harder it was to say goodbye. But here we were again, death eager to stand between our tormented souls.

"Clíona," a voice called out.

The familiar voice peeled my lips into a smile. "Lester, my friend."

He embraced me far tighter than my lungs considered comfortable and beyond what had been the norm for our relationship. Now I was in debt to him.

"I will never be able to repay you for this," I whispered in his ear as we pulled from one another. I didn't think there would ever be more space inside for new guilt, but there it was, getting cosy.

He cocked a squinted eye at me, a humorous front as always. "Just offer me a pass if the moment comes this day."

I nodded.

Caolann clenched Lester's shoulder, perhaps thanking him in the way men silently do. "Rían will bring game to your family every morn of Samhain. Your family will not know hunger. Now fight well."

Lester bowed before rejoining the other competitors.

"Use it this trial," Caolann said. The cold metal slid into my hand. My fingers curled around his serrated knife, and a sigh of quiet laughter escaped me to masquerade the jitters creeping in minutes from being back in the face of death.

He kissed my forehead, and this time, he left without another word.

I joined the competitors, many battered and bruised. A dozen or so Fir na Solas armoured with spears appeared from the forest, marching in maroon rows towards us—a sure sign the time of risking our lives was upon us again.

I gripped the hilt, feeling twice on edge when a hand smacked my back.

I spun to the inflictor.

"I believed you would not survive." Áed smiled, his hand taking to scratch his scarred chin.

Unfurling my hand, I reached to pat his shoulder. "Oh, hun. I'm not so easy to get rid of." I definitely wasn't lying about that. "And your leg?"

He smacked it as if to prove sturdiness. I found men to do that a lot. "There is little spit and dock cannot not heal."

"Keep moving," a disgruntled soldier shouted as they closed in. "Rejoin your clans."

Like schoolchildren, we shuffled along to fill out the lines hauntingly smaller than the previous day.

Several Fir na Solas scaled rock while others stood in succession, colourful sacks in their grasp. Last in the row was a black sack for us.

Ahead in my line of six was Áed, and behind me, Muireann, new spotted feathers hanging from her hair. The young boy I'd saved from Con also fell in.

Áed was called forward first to dip his unwavering hand inside the sack. He turned to us, a red pebble between two fingers. Another soldier swiped red marks across Áed's arms and cheeks.

My turn.

True Gods, please let things go my way for once in my unfortunate life.

I dove my fingers inside, running them over the stones until brushing off one softer than the rest—like that meant anything.

Please be red. Please be red.

I clenched my eyes upon freeing my hand.

"Red," the soldier announced, marking my skin.

Áed clasped my hand in a united handshake that echoed a relationship miles beyond what had been a day of knowing him. Facing death together was an unreplicated tool of bonding.

Muireann removed a black stone, waving it at me in particular.

Then, for all her vileness, she spat at my feet.

Not allies anymore, then.

I retaliated with my middle finger. I wouldn't rise to this bitch, but I also couldn't help finding a minor personal win.

The soldier pushed her to his right, though she seemed uncaring of his touch, her beady eyes fixed on me.

"Any competitor who fights before the trial begins will be deemed too dishonourable to compete," he warned her as the red-haired boy I'd saved from Con received a red stone.

"Hear, hear," Áed celebrated. "The gods have blessed us."

Áed embraced him with a headlock, knuckling his short locks.

Their odd affection struck my curiosity. "You know each other?"

"My brother, Ruadh." Áed released the boy to puff his chest like he couldn't be prouder.

"Of course, the spitting image of each other." Both had the pale and freckled gene, complimenting their hooked noses. More distinctly, both had a Celtic knot tattoo on their forearms, shaped in a tangled flame.

Áed nudged his brother forward giving him little choice in the matter.

"You saved me from slaughter upon the Comeragh," Ruadh said as he bowed. "I am beholden."

"Refrain from attacking the strongest this trial, and perhaps you will fight another day," Áed jested, rustling his brother's hair.

Ruadh knocked his hand away. "Stop treating me as a youngling. I am of my fourteenth year."

"Yet you are too unskilled to bear Fás Fada." Áed's hand ran down his own locks, confirming its length was a symbol of honour—the long grow.

"Clans," the bearded soldier boomed upon the rock slope. "Contenders will enter the Cave of Glas to retrieve three Nimh Álainn. This alone will secure a clan's passage. When Lugh's sun descends from its peak, time will not long be an ally. The cave will lower, whether you dwell inside or not."

Too consumed by the implications of his final words, all I could do was watch as the soldier stretched his hands open, pointing them towards the sun while chanting quietly to call on something beyond the mortal eye. Beneath me, the ground rumbled, vibrating the sand like broken shards of glass. The rupture of earth quickly rose into a mound, stretching to the sun until forming into a sand-splitting arch. After a moment of quiet awe, the opaque cave's entrance revealed an engraving across its arc in rigid Ogham.

Escorted by Fir na Solas to the cave's gaping mouth, nearly twenty of us lined up in our clans at a starting line of tiny triskele rocks. Yellow Clan stood next to us, led by a girl who had exceptionally white hair I might have been jealous of in my teen years. The competitors all stared at the cave's mouth with a concentration I wished to lovingly adopt.

Focus, Clíona. Focus now.

Two soldiers, adjacent to the cave's opening, extended bronze swords above their heads to tease out the suspense. I would've heckled them to get a move on if it wasn't for the sudden hush of anticipation. That was enough for me to second guess my ability to protect myself...second guess I could protect my clan if they needed me.

The Fir na Solas plunged their swords into the ground, charming up a cloud of sand that rose around us, but I didn't move. My legs planted firm, struck by the weight of fear that once I entered, I might not see the light of day again.

A forceful hand grabbed my pelted shoulder, dragging me forward. I coughed and spluttered in a blinded abyss, but I mindlessly obeyed its pull.

The coolness of the shade shivered my skin as we crossed the cave's threshold.

Then darkness engulfed us until daylight was nowhere to be seen.

30
VINE SNAKE

Áed's hand had guided me into the tunnel at the end of row.

My eyes adjusted to the poor light granted from the jagged dome ceiling, and my fingers had instinctively found my knife. Softening my grasp on it, I found, to my anxious relief, nobody had followed or even attempted to fight. This trial's enemy was amongst clans, but only secondary to that of the true threat. The terrifying one: *time.*

Time until they sealed the cave.

Bastards.

The steepening descent through the tunnel forced my ears to pop, and our chorus of pants felt kind of eerie now all my sense of sight was dulled. Coarse rubbing of Áed's hands echoed until sparks of orange ignited from them. Its heat on my cheeks brought comfort, though not enough to dull my chaotically beating heart. I couldn't grow used to the sound despite the recurrence these last few weeks.

The tunnel illuminated, exposing the high-rising ceiling beyond the reach of any man, and I scraped my fingers along the damp wall, too close to run freely without nicking myself. The condensation stank, its stale stench clinging to my wet-dog nose.

"Where are we?" The echo of my voice sounded like someone else's. Someone braver.

"A maze tunnel," Áed answered with a sniffle. "These passages lead to the Cluster."

Even in single form, our pace was surprisingly slow, and I'd already lost count of how many times I'd scratched my arms. In a way, I was masochistically grateful for the scratches; the pain pulled me away from the thoughts of all the things that could go wrong in here.

I needed to remind myself this was life or death, and for all my reckless behaviour, I didn't want to die. I'd never truly wanted that.

"Forgive me for my manner on the Comeragh," Áed called back.

Was...that an apology? I bit down my urge to gloat. Though he needn't have felt bad. I understood his sour feelings from his mother's hardship after the crop quota, and to be fair, I'd fallen from the sky and bombarded Lúnasa. Expecting trust was naive.

Ruadh edged ahead, his shadow scurrying on the light's edge. Áed paced faster, keeping him in sight.

I was glad for the slight gap between us because I was boiling, and boob sweat gathered beneath my armour so badly, its resulting rash might be the actual thing to kill me off.

His voice, edged with worry, said, "I visited at nightfall to see if you lived." He stalled, shooting me a glance. "The woman—Bébhinn, told me why you compete."

I wiped my brow and tutted. Exposure to the plan was dangerous when those who could be trusted were of limited supply. But it was Bébhinn's daughter who had been taken. Her beautiful, fierce Róisín—so I supposed it was her right to share our goal.

Áed lagged, close. It seemed sensual though I was sure that wasn't the case. "Our youngest brother—Fintan—he was taken. We searched the forest for moons to no end."

"I'm sorry. It's awful." My ribcage shrunk in on me. "I lost a brother, too."

The echo of our heavy footsteps filled the silent recall of our siblings.

Don't you know I'm here with you, Clío? Always am, always will be.

I wiped the tear that snuck up on me, but Áed must've seen. In what appeared to be his single act of comfort, he clenched my shoulder, and I glanced at his shadowed face with a tight-lipped smile—the one that always made me look far more innocent than I ever could be.

"Clíona, I pledge on my flame to deliver you, if not myself, to the final battle. I have witnessed your strength. It would carry you far within the Tuatha's rule. You saved Ruadh, and in the shadows, you fight for the truth of Fintan's disappearance. I am indebted to you. If not for the promise to my family to fight for food, I would fight for them, too."

I had asked Caolann once in our lessons why no one else had declared competing for the lost children. The answer was surprisingly quite simple: people were hungry or wanted power. Those were the priorities of this world, not children they presumed dead.

Áed's offer swelled my heart to hear he thought me worthy, but it sounded too formal for the man I thought him to be. Then again, I didn't know him at all.

"You don't want to be here at all, do you?"

A laugh escaped his nose. "No. My true love is art. I work with burnt charcoal, sketching images of life. My father died young. I foolishly competed for his honour as a youngling. When Ruadh announced his desire to compete, I had to protect him, clan or not, I would fight for him alone. The gods gifted me with the talent and Bua for war, but that is not me."

"A light," Ruadh called back to us.

Áed's hand found the hilt of his sword. "What do you see?"

"Our blessed day," Ruadh laughed more like a boy than a man. "By the will of the gods, Nimh Álainn hangs."

I'd somehow almost forgotten. Cursing the sting of jagged rocks snapping at us, I ran into an opening thankfully big enough to fit us all. The Nimh Álainn above couldn't be mistaken, hanging from a long, delicate vine, and shining a bright green as though it were a ripened apple.

I wanted to hold it, its beauty casting me under a spell how all beauty did. I guessed that was why things like gender weren't a determining factor in what Fionn and I considered beautiful. Mollie had truly gifted us with being open to all love.

Ruadh conspicuously gawped down the passage. "Could it be a trap?"

"No other clan travelled this pocket," Áed's reply echoed. "Let us worry of danger when it is imminent."

Ruadh nodded his agreement as they conferred the best tactic to retrieve it. "I say we burn the vine."

Áed shook his head. "I harvest too much power to hold my flame alight."

"I will shoot it down," Ruadh offered, though it sounded more like he was seeking Áed's approval. "My aim improves."

Áed's face twisted, crow's feet hugging his eyes where they absolutely shouldn't for someone so young. Was Ruadh's growing independence worrying him or just the general risk of Lúnasa?

Either way, I cleared my throat *twice* to draw their attention. "Lads, I harvest a Bua, too—a good one at that. Pledging yourself doesn't mean I've become redundant to the cause."

"What pledge?" Ruadh protested.

"If you believe you can secure it, I give you my trust," Áed agreed, likely to silence the question.

"Okay," I started, feeling satisfied. "Here's what we'll do: Ruadh burns the vine. When it breaks, I'll harvest. It'll come to me safely. Áed, you make those flames brighter for us to get it done right." Was I always this authoritative? Of course I was. I probably came out of the womb demanding milk.

Áed's focus turned to his flames, doubling in size with little more than a frown. Ruadh cleared his throat until sparks of fire rolled off his tongue like flint. With ease, flames shot from his mouth in continuous spurts, burning the blackening vine until our Nimh Álainn snapped free; I stopped it, mid-fall, my hand's vibration steady and controlled. It lowered under the caress of my hold until I held its glass exterior: light to touch, though its core swirled smoke like a potion rested within it.

Áed's flames dimmed, pulling me from the adoration. "Careful, Clíona. It is poison to open wounds."

Another obstacle in this death trap.

He opened a pocket in his belt filled with straw for me to place it inside, nice and snug.

I winked at Ruadh to encourage him. "Impressive Bua."

He smiled wryly. "It is why they name me Dragon."

Áed playfully wrapped his thick arm around his brother's neck, hands alight though bringing no burn to Ruadh's skin. "Not a soul names you Dragon," he teased. "Now come. We must quicken our pace."

The echo of our breaths and footsteps dominated the tunnel. Then shouts began to pierce the air from afar. Intensifying into shrieks and screams, they rippled off the stone walls, carved through the darkness as each one reverberated into my ears harder.

Caolann had told me of the place we approached many times: the Cluster. A place where all clans must travel for the magnitude of Nimh Álainn it holds.

Áed drew his sword in anticipation. "We must be quick if we wish to escape unscathed."

"I will lead." Ruadh puffed out his chest despite it making no difference to his slender physique.

Our pace quickened to a sprint towards ever-building bellows. My hands trembled as I recalled the mountaintop and how quickly the silence turned to chaos, yet I couldn't draw the knife.

"Prepare yourselves," Ruadh shouted.

"Fight well, little brother."

Unstable sand walls crumbled as we ran into the huge, stirring cavern. Slits of light shone past Nimh Álainn—hundreds of them glistening and clustered from a thick vine like a grand, upside-down apple tree. Stalagmites and pillars dominated the cave, forcing clans to weave as they entered from endless tunnels.

If I nervous-puked on my enemies, maybe they'd leave me alone.

Most clans were already fighting or retrieving when we reached a steep mound to scale down. And it was bloody loud. Each scream or cry was heightened by the cave's echo, like the moments of despair after a plane crash in a movie.

The fight would find us any second. I clutched my armour, finding it difficult to breathe. The only cover left was from low hanging stalactites.

Orange Clan emerged from the tunnel opposite, knives and snarls at the ready. Recalling they'd injured Áed with honeycomb stones, I stretched out my thrumming hand, but they descended into the cave without entertaining us a second look.

A petite woman sporting grey locks and similar armour to mine intangibly passed through pillars, throwing uppercuts at anyone en route. It was the woman who had told me size didn't matter.

It appeared she was right.

My leg slipped on the slant from the distraction, and I grunted while digging my heels into the mound to shimmy without slipping. "We need to get into this fight."

"Let them pick one another off," Áed said. "This is why I took a slower pace."

His words didn't lessen my apprehension. Being in the thick of it was almost better than this. My chest pumped stronger against my ribs, and I would've clenched it if I wasn't clinging to the mounds' jagged edges to stop myself from tumbling.

"Incoming!" Ruadh shouted over my shoulder. A stream of sand hurdled head-on, enough to bury us all and our mothers.

Ruadh leaned over me, his knee resting on my back as he held a protruding ledge. A stream of fire shot from his mouth, solidifying the sand mid-air. It instantly matured into clouded lumps, shattering on landing.

"I might have to start calling him Dragon," I called to Áed as we slid onto the cave floor.

Áed beat his chest with his sword as laughter bellowed from him. "You hear that, brother? Dragon, it is!"

Exterior pillars, twice my width, distorted our oncoming view, but they also protected us from clans who could be mere metres away, waiting to use whatever power got them this far. The clustered vines on the cave's high ceiling spiralled to the ground from missed targets and retrievals. We hung back behind a pillar, peeking at the commotion of harvests and clanging swords.

"Do not run as the crow flies," Áed warned, dashing to the next pillar as we flanked to cover every angle. On the run, Nimh Álainn smashed into shards by my feet.

Áed skidded to a stop, grabbing my hair to yank me.

I spun to him, the stench of burnt hair filling my nostrils and a heap of swear words on my tongue.

Gulping to catch his breath, he pointed at the smoke, curling green in a ray of light. "The poison."

"Right. Thanks." I meant it. Definitely still the rookie. "Let's take the longer route to the Cluster, and attack when needed." It sounded easier than it would ever be.

Áed bravely led, meandering us around glassy brown pillars, his flames ready in one hand, his sword in the other.

Shots of fine-pointed stalagmites hurtled toward us head-on, like needles. I latched onto their force to deflect them, whipping them away to dart into a wall, but they'd barely crashed when faster ones came from our right.

The brothers melted the ones I missed, but the charred remains scalded our arms and necks, singeing them black. Yet somehow, there wasn't even time to cry out for the pain they'd inflicted.

"Take cover." Áed led us to a smooth divot in one of the pillars. Forced to huddle, sweat stung my eyes relentlessly, my attempts to swipe it away, pointless.

“We do not hold...” Ruadh tried to catch his breath. “...the communal power to defend ourselves.” He panted again, then added, “From these attacks.”

Áed threw him a wild-eyed glare and clenched his scrawny arm. “In defeat, you will soon find death, brother. Are you not carved from the warrior’s line?”

“I am,” Ruadh shouted, sizzling spit flying into his brother’s glare.

“Jesus Christ, shut up! Now’s not the time for a brother’s spat! We’re strong as one.”

“My power dwindles,” Áed admitted, staring at the rescinding flames on his hands. A drop of blood dripped from his nose. “I must conserve it for our safe passage out.”

More pointed needles skimmed past the pillar, making us huddle tighter.

“Daylight will not be seen if the enemy is not threatened,” Ruadh shouted. “I *am* carved from the warrior’s line.” He turned, facing the threat head-on, flames flying, spurting from his mouth until we dragged him back to cover.

Ruadh’s tricep was torn and jagged in blood, and my hand returned bubbling and blistered from touching him mid-harvest. Áed chided him as he knotted his wound with cloth while I used what was left of our water supply to soothe my blistered palm. The burning persisted, but adrenaline dulled the worst of it.

Áed peaked from cover. “They surround us.”

I stared at my mess of a hand, bubbling. I worried it might start making popping noises. But it didn’t bring me queasiness; it brought me an idea. “Follow my lead. On my say. Áed, shoot your flame to the left of the pillar they’re hiding behind.”

I turned to run when he clenched my shoulder. "I will not let harm come to my brother. Be wise."

I broke from his grasp and ran. No one else's brother was getting hurt by my hands. Never again.

Needles attacked us, bigger in size now, like javelins—dozens of them.

"Shoot, Áed." I propelled my arms through a gust of miraged light to divert the javelin.

"I waste my harvest shooting at nothing," he protested.

"Do it now!"

He sucked in a resigned breath and heaved his thick flame. It spiralled towards the pillar, but just as the flame hit it, I changed my harvest's focus to help contort his Bua. Within a thrumming hold, my power surrounded the flames to harvest it left, *around* the pillar.

For this, my power was given colour, so fierce from our combined power, the fire turned gold. Amber. Beautiful.

Oncoming attacks ceased as wretched screams came from fleeing clans, flames ravaging their behinds.

I was thankful it looked more comical than painful just to steer off the guilt.

Áed's flame dried upon reaching the pillar where we slumped onto bottoms to rest and, for some reason, laugh. We laughed how one at the pub might, too loud and merry for our circumstances. It felt good; wholesome, even. With another dash, we might even be under the Cluster.

"You—harvested—my—Bua," Áed said as he poured water from his pouch over his face and hair to shake it off like a dog.

The idea had come after Lester healed me. Why not bend those rules in a different way? Amalgamate our strength.

The brothers communicated a whole conversation in blinks. "No other has commanded our flames," Ruadh told me. "You are remarkable."

I stood, patting my knees. "I've had less said to try to get me into bed." Didn't they know complimenting wasn't the Irish way? That self-depreciation was embedded into the culture.

With new determination, side by side, we headed for the final dash and into the Cluster. Only upon reaching it did I realise how huge it was. Thousands of green glass balls hung above, their lethality equated to an atomic bomb if they fell as one.

We'd need to be fast.

"Create a wall of fire," I told Áed. "We can stop the clans from getting access when we secure ours."

He ignited the last of his flame. "I trust in you."

Once I latched onto his harvest, it worked through my veins like a tug of war I had the upper hand in. The flame encircled the perimeter, us inside for the taking.

"It's up to you to shoot them free, Ruadh," I told him. "And please, for the love of the True Gods, don't drop them!" All of us had fatal injuries if the smoke crawled inside us.

Contorting the flame needed absolute concentration, and between us, our energy was at critical. Clans had come just outside the flames, desperate to retrieve Nimh Álainn before time ran out.

The girl with white hair from the yellow clan attacked our fire circle with an icy blast in stark opposition of Áed's fire. Its force knocked me back a step, and another, her ice gnawing my fingertips and stumps, burrowing further into my purpling skin.

"Clíona, I cannot hold it."

Our upper hand was dwindling.

Áed's bad leg collapsed, and with it, our perimeter flame froze, shattering into icy shards so loudly, the echo mimicked that of a thousand smashing chandeliers.

Scorned clans stormed the Cluster, hollering battle cries. In my dash to regroup, the brothers were overrun, barely unsheathing their swords to keep the fight at bay.

A competitor with a scabbing gash on their forearm blocked my path to their aid. As he drew his machete to hack me into pieces, I raised my thrumming hands; suddenly, we stopped, mouths agape in a strange moment of caution and realisation.

"Lester?"

For the first time, we were enemies. Both stuttering and voiceless.

He asked for a pass in exchange for time he'd given me to heal, and I'd silently agreed.

But neither of us moved.

Deep down, we knew this might come—the moment where we remembered Lúnasa had one champion.

One god.

31
WALKING SUN

In my periphery, a man with claws for fingers bounced off Muireann's shield. He stumbled, falling back into the smoke. She'd take no prisoners.

I looked to the brothers for help. Maybe I selfishly wanted them to do my dirty work. Ruadh's mouth was gagged with an unnatural layer of skin he clawed at to no mercy. He had curled in a ball between Áed's legs, who fought off the ice of our enemy with bursts of dwindling flame and half a jagged sword.

This was barbaric. Every fucking bit of it.

I could hardly breathe. Hardly think, let alone decide what I should do.

"We foresaw this moment, though neither of us spoke it aloud," Lester called with a facade of boredom to his tone.

Though I couldn't quite believe he'd hurt me, I played the game anyway. "You know I can take that machete from you," I warned. We slowly side-stepped in a circle.

With a cocky tilt of his brow, his stance remained poised. Ready. Every muscle flexed and primed for action. "Clíona, I have seen you wield a weapon. Taking mine will only cause injury to yourself."

What was this? Him hoping I wouldn't force his hand?

I shook my head, sweat flying off me. I didn't want to hurt him. I couldn't. Not when I'd taken so much from his life already.

Our tension hummed, vibrating me with alertness. This game had to end right now before paranoia and dark voices convinced us this was the right path. As I raised my hands to gesture my surrender, he reflexively drew his machete. The glint of iron mirrored my disfigured reflection back at me. I looked feral; loose strands of hair sticking to my face. Dirt and cuts clinging to me.

"Lester, no," I pleaded, despite my exterior still holding a fighting stance. Softs flurries of lights danced on my hands.

He shuffled another step closer, gripping his weapon tighter, but I could see the uncertainty making his eyes rounder and coating them with a sheen.

"You don't have to do this," I warned. "You don't need to make *me* do this."

"There can be a sole champion, Clíona."

He charged, his scream stirring a single Nimh Álainn to smash to pieces upon impact within our no man's land. I staggered back as its repulsively sweet smoke billowed out, chewing up my inner nostrils. The gravity of what was about to happen dawned on me too slowly to do anything to stop it. I watched as it swirled around us, unphased as he pointlessly swiped his machete through it.

"Clíona," he called, watching it eat me up, too. He sheathed his machete, reaching me in seconds. His hands cruelly pushed onto my blisters. In return, a green tint ran through the veins in his hand, dividing like an estuary up his forearm where a scab hadn't fully formed.

"Lester—no—the poison is in your blood."

He squeezed my hand harder, two tears spilling over his focused stare to admit the magnitude of our situation. "The darkness of the harvest brought me too close to the edge. Forgive me. One of us should live."

Yes, one should. But not me.

The once green poison meandering through his fingers now bubbled black.

I couldn't let another death happen on my watch. I owed this boy so much.

Resolute, I snatched his machete clean from his sheath—a dirty move under any other circumstances.

"You'll thank me tomorrow, friend." I sucked in a shaky breath and yanked his arm straight.

He fought my tug. "No. Clíona. No!"

Drawing the machete behind my head, I swung.

The blade hacked into his elbow crease. His mouth shook and his tongue curled before unleashing a gut-wrenching cry that brought the commotion of the trial to its knees. Warm blood spattered my face as I sliced him again. His humerus crunched with a brutality so vile, I swallowed my own watery vomit.

Lester squealed in breaths, tears sliding into his ears as he writhed. "Please. Please stop!"

His forearm dangled as I took a final swipe, tearing muscle how toffee in the sun might do. It squirted like a roughly chopped loin, but thankfully a scab already crusted the rim. Was it enough? He could regrow body parts, but reproducing blood was never mentioned. Ripping the hem of his tunic with a clean pull, I wrapped it above the severed limb to make a shoddy tourniquet.

His bloodshot eyes rolled upon collapsing.

"You'll be fine." I smiled, maniacally, reassuring *both* of us. "I would've done the same if it didn't grow back." The humour didn't find him, which in hindsight, I should have known considering his state. I was clearly being funny for my own sanity.

In the violent crowd, Áed and Ruadh had finally gotten the upper hand on their opponents.

As I moved to call out to them, the ground beneath me rumbled ominously, causing my thighs to tremble with the force of it. A sense of dread, of the inevitable, tightened my chest.

The cave groaned like an old man leaving his chair.

My feet sank into sand, slender pillars snapped, and my stomach landed in my arse.

The first of the Nimh Álainn crashed to the ground as the sand rose faster than I ever anticipated.

I grasped at Lester's sweating head to ferry it above the rising sand, watching on as clans left for the tunnels, crashing into one another with no desire to secure more Nimh Álainn. Those bludgeoned by whatever harvest or sword that found them were already swallowed, stolen from traditional burial. Snapping back to the urgency I screamed, "Help me, Áed!"

He loyally ran to us, an unwavering resolve in eyes I mistook for help. Instead, he gripped my hips, dragging me from Lester's body with stifled grunts. He was so strong and unyielding. No. I wouldn't leave. Elbowing him just under his chest, right into the solar plexus, I swore I heard the gush of air fly out of him. "Leave him, Clíona. We will not..." He coughed, spluttering to fight his breath. "...survive the burial if we carry the extra load."

"Extra load?" Anger reverberated inside me. "Are *you* a cracked nut? No. I'm not fucking leaving him here. Help me carry him or lose me and any chance of winning, too!"

Áed dropped his hands from my waist to hitch a grey-faced Lester off the ground without a second thought.

That pledge had its perks.

Ruadh grabbed the other side of him—the side with an arm. Then we moved out as fast as our legs could take us through the dark tunnel. I thanked the True Gods this path was wider than the last.

Sand shrouded our eyes as we sprinted, banging from wall to wall as they caved in around us.

"Leave me," Lester begged as he came to, his legs still dangling behind him under their hold.

Clumps of sand crashed onto us, harder and harder, quenching what little was left of Áėd's flame.

We were drowning.

"Leave me," he slurred again.

The cave's mouth shone safety's light, no taller than my height.

"Clíona, we must abandon him for our survival," Áed pleaded. "I beg. For Ruadh."

No.

No more than a foot of light was left.

Even if we dived to roll under, we wouldn't make it.

No. I wouldn't let them die. Not these wonderful, kind boys.

As the mouth sealed in thundering finality, I threw my hand out with my final gasp of air, harvesting from the endless river of pain I drowned in.

Forcing the image of Fionn's impaled body into mind, reeling it over and over and over.

The cave's wall shuddered as I screamed through the overexertion clawing my veins so fiercely, I feared they'd rip clean out of me. With one final push, the wall detonated outwards, sending us tumbling. The unbreathable heat of the desert was immediate.

Warm blood ran into my mouth—I spat it onto the sand. Nosebleeds were irrelevant. Because I was alive, and so were they.

That's all that mattered.

Hobbling to where we'd gathered earlier in the day, we rejoined what was left of the other clans. The Fir na Solas would demand to count our Nimh Álainn.

I didn't even know how many we had.

Many along the row, bloody and bruised, shared what was left of their water. Others locked fists to congratulate another day of survival. It seemed we weren't enemies, after all. We were people. Saoirsians with a common goal to receive honour and maybe, for some of us—hope.

Áed helped Lester on the ground at the rear of his clan: a group I was tempted to scold for leaving him. A bright pink stump was forming from his wrist, though his face still held a grey complexion. But I cherished the sight of it. At least, I did over what I thought his fate would be: buried. Mouth full of sand as he tried to draw his last breaths.

“The first three clans who offer Nimh Álainn will proceed,” a bearded soldier announced.

My thoughts turned the odds. As the last clan out, they were positively against us.

“Disqualified,” the soldier’s voice bellowed as he made his way through clans who’d come up empty.

The first clan left, then the next, their heads low and bodies bloody.

Áed held our Nimh Álainn. “Brother, did you retrieve well from the cluster?”

Ruadh cowered at the sand as he unclasped his bag and handed him one. “Forgive me, brother, for I have failed us.”

One short. It was over. I pulled my hair by its roots. I’d failed. Failed Róisín, and all the other children. Failed the fire brothers, betraying them and their sacrifices for Lester.

It was better when I didn’t feel much at all.

“You are mistaken,” Lester croaked. “You hold three.” With his intact arm, he presented to us a perfect, green ball, its glass glinting against the sunlight. “All I ask in return is to spend a night with the red head.” He winked at Áed, whose cheeks flushed as he scratched along his Celtic knots.

“Saving you was the wise choice,” Áed managed to jest. “But perhaps when you are older.”

The soldier appeared before Green Clan. The tallest of the three, a noodle-haired boy, stood forward to offer theirs.

It was spare. Their offering was spare!

I grabbed Lester’s offering.

“Red Clan. Present to me your Nimh Álainn.”

As Áed handed them off, I counted the remaining clans. Black and green. Two. Just two.

“Red Clan, you will proceed to the third trial.”

For the second time this day, we burst into a wild, roaring laugh. And God, did it feel good no matter how much it hurt my ribs to do so. We'd defied the odds and lived to fight another day.

Lapping up the comfort of the forest's shade, we hobbled for home, all of us competitors in such exhausting silence a passerby might mistake us as walking *to* our deaths rather than from it.

Áed lagged to my side. “A moment?”

I stopped short. “What?”

Without hesitation, he pulled me close to—of all things—hug me.

Shock rippled through me like an electric current, rendering me momentarily paralyzed. I wrapped my fingers around his warm back to offer him something—anything to show I cared when words refused to come. My unlikely ally—who would have thought not yesterday we would be here. I guessed the trials intensify every emotion when bonded by walking on the precipice of death with one another.

“Forgive me for refusing to help. I feared it would be our end.” He released his hold, a personal disgust swelled in his sullen eyes, trusting he meant it.

I nudged his arm to squash the awkwardness, but his smile didn't return. He was too consumed by Ruadh travelling ahead with the disqualified ice girl. “Worried about him?”

He spat at the spoil. “Competing should not be for the young.”

“Then why let him?”

He frowned at me how everyone here seemed to when I'd asked a *rational* question. “It is his birthright. Our father encouraged him as he did with me. But he is a youngling, too weak for the strength of his rivals. We almost met our end, and I fear tomorrow will bring greater threats.”

"At least you're here to protect him." The words sounded weak against my positive tone.

"I consume my mind with worry of him. I solely thank the gods that destiny paired us. To lose him would be my end." He shook the bad thoughts from his head. "I could not bear the pain of losing a second brother."

"What was he like—Fintan?" If someone were to ask me the same question about my brother, I don't think I could summarise it, but maybe it could be cathartic for Áed.

"He was a youngling of many gifts. Taller than all of his year. And the strength of his flame...it was magnificent. The morn his Bua gifted his body, I challenged him to a fire battle in Réimse Mór. I planned to give him a chance to raise his confidence." He laughed to himself. "I conjured flames from my palms, where it naturally harvests. He would learn where his strength is sourced." Áed outstretched his hand, igniting a tiny flame on it. "Fintan closed his eyes, unhappy in his struggle to choose a sole body part. Still, I surged my fire towards him, knowing he would protect himself. I did not anticipate what happened next. It was magnificent, Clíona. His whole form ignited. *The Walking Sun,* we name them. It had been seven generations since the last."

"Like a god among men." My eyes widened as sparks flew from the lightbulb illuminating in my head. There it was. The missing link I'd been searching for. It had been staring at me.

I yanked Áed's arm to follow me away from any who might be listening. "Maybe that's why he's missing. Why he was taken."

"You cannot believe he lives." His squint told me he was sceptical, perhaps annoyed I'd even suggest it when it would only uproot the pain.

If I said yes and reinforced how much I believed it to be true, was it false hope? Either way, it wasn't my right to hide this from him. "Think about it. No bodies found. And you mentioned he was strong. Exceptional for his age?"

His eyes lit up brighter than his flame as he fantasised about his little brother's return. "He was taken for his Bua? Did Róisín harvest strength, too?"

"In a way, yes." I paused. "But what if..."

"Speak your mind, friend."

If I did. I was speaking more false promises. "The younglings—what if the children were taken for a reason?"

"Could that be a possibility? Did any of the other younglings show strength in Réimse Mór?"

His eyes flickered back and forth as if running through his memories for the answer. Then his gaze stilled and set on me. "Yes. The ones who were taken were strong."

I sucked in a shaky breath. Everything became clear; maybe it wasn't an act of opportunity for some sicko, but a calculated decision.

The only missing link was now *who* stole them.

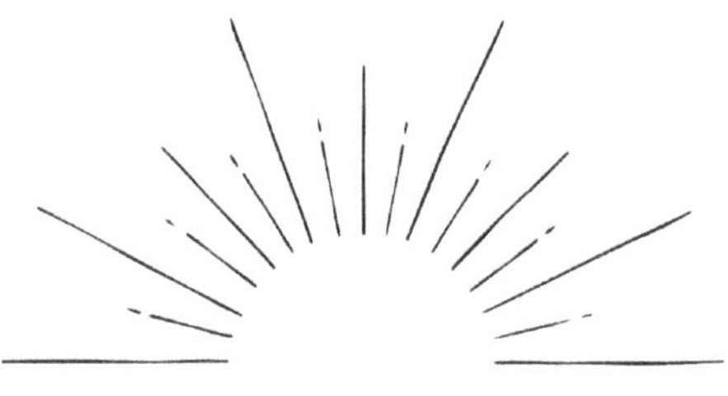

32

YOU CALL YOURSELF A DRUID

I sat at the foot of the Carraig, waiting to greet dawn, just as I'd done several days previous. Whatever I anticipated the trials to be then had been naive. Hope masked danger just as much as it helped one face it.

I absentmindedly picked at the fraying petals of someone's wilted offering: a basket of flowers and foliage once vibrant. It was no different from the ones on any other step behind me. Staling breads. Blankets already fading from sun exposure. Trinkets picked apart by scavengers—or the few who perhaps didn't believe.

"Is it yourself you're offering?" came a voice, low and in tune with the hush of morning.

I snapped my head to him. "They fucking wish." But wasn't that the end goal of trials?

Rían smiled a little to himself as he kicked at a loose stone, scratched the back of his head. "You asked me to come?"

I stood and dusted my bottom. "I did."

"And what of Caolann?" He stepped closer, that slight smile deepening to a smirk. "Can he not help his 'bound girl' this morn?"

I held my tongue though my insides, my gut, clenched to the brink of retaliating.

Thankfully, he conceded. Glancing at the rising sun behind him, he said, "You will not have much time." His tone was more reminder than warning, as if he already knew this plan would fall short of what I wanted.

"I know." It was an intentionally stiff response, but it was also the truth.

Rían sighed through his nose, lifting his head slightly. "Clíona." My name was a stern thing on his tongue. A subtle indication of what I already knew: I was being difficult. And even though I was still mad at him for what he did to Lester—more than mad—I also knew he was reminding me that I'd asked *him* here. I needed *his* help. And for better or worse in our friendship—he came.

"It's hard not to stay mad," I muttered, pressing my lips together. This felt harder than the actual trials—trying to find a way to forgive him. Because I missed what we had before.

He turned on his heel, heading straight into the heart of the Carraig. Over his shoulder he called, "Then remain angry. It changes little in this plan."

"Wait up!" I followed him right into the blind darkness. At least I still had some semblance of trust.

A torch sprung, flaring inches from my face, its flame clenched in his hand. "Thirty paces ahead, then a sharp left. Last cell on the right."

"You're not coming?" God, why did my voice sound so weak? Like I was disappointed.

He offered the torch, uncomfortably warming my cheeks. "We must all have our secrets. Now go, without haste. The next guard rotation is soon, and two compelled by my Bua will draw suspicion I cannot risk falling on the ears of Rathnor."

I gave him a curt nod and accepted the torch. He lingered a moment.

"What?"

He held my gaze, his eyes flicking with flames. Maybe he would say we were even now. That he'd gone out of his way to help me again, and instead of questioning his morality when I was hardly any better, I should stop punishing him.

"Be careful."

Following his guide, I surprisingly made it to the cells promptly. It was easy when all I had to do was follow the rancid smell of piss I thought I'd been rid of forever. Blocking my nose and mouth with my hand, I checked each cell. *Empty. Empty. Empty.*

I reached the final one.

"Finegas," I whispered. "It's me, Clíona. The girl you spoke to several weeks back." I placed the torch in its holder on the end wall.

Silence.

"Finegas?" I spoke a little louder, gripping a single damp bar of his cell.

The familiar aroma of herbs caught in the stale, fetid air. His faint green light flickered to life, illuminating our conversation. "We meet again, child."

"You knew," I blurted, knowing I was going in too strong. Too emotional.

"I understand not."

"Ha! You call yourself a Druid. A man of prophecy. You know why I've come. You lied to me." Had I been this angry five minutes ago? I couldn't even recall where it had come from. I needed this man's help. Still, the feeling wouldn't simmer.

He studied me, unflinching. "You are braver now, I see."

"It's kind of a requirement of being exiled in a world that tries to kill you! If you had told me the truth that first day I met you, it might have helped. Told me about the rune! Told me if you knew my brother. If there was any way to leave this place."

"Hmm..." Finegas arched to hang up his hexagonal crystal on a hook that partially gave way, spilling debris from the wall. "Why have you not returned sooner, if you seek a way home?"

I crossed my arms, feeling a flicker of irritation. He was right—I would have come sooner if that really mattered. "And my brother? Did you know him? How else would you have recognized my rune and told me it would bring me a journey of anguish?"

"I fear we have little time to speak. The guard will come soon."

I peered down the black corridor before reverting my attention to him. "Then tell me what I need to know."

"The three secrets are still kept."

"That's not what—"

"Need, not want," he interrupted. "This is what you *need* to know."

There was something in his tone that made me less sceptical than I'd been during my last run in with him. I was more cautious; it seemed he was warning me. Protecting me from something.

"Why not just tell me what they are instead of being elusive?"

"That is not the way of Druids," he said, and I swore he shrugged. "We can warn and aid, but the words of the divinity, offered to us by our gods, are not ours to freely share."

"Well give me something—anything," I pressed. I gripped the bars, feeling my time slipping away.

Finegas glanced down the corridor as though he truly could read my thoughts. "One answer, I *can* give. One that is mine to share."

Footsteps echoed nearby. My grip tightened as I pressed my face against the bars, desperate.

"Yes. Tell me? Tell me please!"

"You're brother, Fionn..." My breath caught. I hadn't heard his name on someone's lips for so long. "He walked this land thrice. Though not in the way you had hoped."

"Fionn," I choked on his name.

The footsteps grew closer. Too close.

"How? I mean...*when*?"

"There is no time, child. You must run now." He unhooked his light, commanding it to fade with a quick rub. "Go. *Shoo*."

Searching the room for another exit, I realised how easy it would be to get lost beneath the Carraig. The passageways could be endless. With no time to spare, I grabbed the torch and plunged it into the trough beside me, snuffing out the flame. Darkness swallowed the room whole. My breaths were too loud in the echoes.

Feeling my way along the cells I reached the door taking a sharp right.

A burning torch, held in the hands of a lone soldier, illuminated me—caught me.

Fuck.

His surprise quickly twisted into a snarling delight. "I was just contemplating how I crave something truly...delicious. The gods favour me this morn."

I flicked my gaze to this hand, hovering on the hilt of his sword. Then to either side of him. The passage was too narrow to go around him. I summoned my harvest—ready to strike. He only had one hand to fight with after all.

"Concede, soldier!"

The soldier released his grip on his weapon as his eyes filled with a steely gaze into the darkness beyond me.

Oh, I'd know that voice anywhere.

Rían walked into the light, calm, without fear. He shot me a stern look. "I told you to be quick."

"No. You told me to be careful."

He slid past the docile warrior to meet me. Check me.

I exhaled sharply. "I'm sorry." I'm sorry I'm so mad at you. I hate it, I wanted to say.

"I will fix this."

"You're making a habit of doing that."

He dipped to meet my gaze, and my throat annoyingly bobbed. "It is how I said before, all I do is to protect you, in light or darkness."

"Rían..." How could I tell him I appreciated it without forsaking Lester?

He smiled: the one where his eyes fought the squeeze of their lids and the lines of his mouth creased a fraction, and, God help me, I couldn't stop myself from smiling back.

"Go, love."

And I did.

33
LOVE HATH NO FURY

Caolann had blindfolded me with silk cloth, guiding me into the forest but a few feet before I lost my bearings entirely. My eyelashes fluttered against scratching fabric, but despite removal of an entire sense when I'd been trained to use them all, I kept it on. Even enjoyed it a little.

I also didn't want to kill the suspense that accompanied Caolann leading me through the tickle of what felt like high grass. He didn't need to know about this morning. My visit to Finegas wasn't something I had to share.

My maroon and white dress hugged me—as ever—in a complimenting way. The kind of way where even blind I could still sense him savouring the shape of me in it. It was too warm for armour, and given my company, the only thing I expected to be fighting off was the urge to devour him.

I chewed my lip to keep my smile at a level that didn't give too much away. But I needed this escape. With the threat of another trial looming—and learning Fionn had actually been to Ériu, too—something to lift my spirits was overdue.

I followed Caolann's wild scent more than his touch. I'd know it anywhere now, chasing it to the ends of this world and mine if it meant keeping him forever—a prospect that might be possible now the divine status was closer to my grasp.

Because he was frighteningly addictive. All I've ever been addicted to was misery. The constant brought me comfort. How it fit me so perfectly I didn't have to think about it anymore. How without it, I might cease to exist. Now, Caolann grounded me to this world. He was gravity, anchoring me when the weight of my guilt and uncertainty threatened to pull me away.

"Are we nearly there? I actually have a date with death after this one."

The huff of breath through his nose might have been a silenced laugh, but I couldn't be sure. Even now, when I wanted to say I knew him better than most, I still couldn't say who he truly was. But I wouldn't hold it against him. I had layers, too, the core of which were things he might not forgive for how much he loved his own brother.

"Your patience has not balanced," he called back.

I mimicked his quiet laugh. "I don't suppose it has. But I'm not going to be late for the trial to fill your nefarious intentions."

As much as I wanted this, I also couldn't keep thoughts of Róisín—and what I'd figured out—at bay. The answers were close. I was sure of it.

"What if it's Rathnor? What if he's the one behind the children?"

Caolann's coarse hand slid from mine. My head followed the soft rustle of grass closely encircling me until I lost track of him.

"If Rathnor wanted the younglings he would make it known to all." The words were but a whisper on my nape. "He would revel in the pain of their loved ones. Ease your mind but for one morn, wildling."

He unravelled the blindfold with fingers that barely had to touch my skin to make me breathless.

"No way!" I gasped. "The poppy field." We stood near its edge, the waterfall far enough away to not consume all sound. I arched my back to smile up at him.

He kissed my forehead though I wished he'd considered how sweaty I would taste on his lips. "You spoke of this place once with a fondness."

"Perceptive." Not even biting could contain my grin now. His romantic edge always surprised me because he was subtle in his emotions.

I paced through poppies, left speechless as I searched the coats of black and red like they held the words my mouth couldn't unearth.

He followed my carved pathway, his spreading a little wider.

I twisted to him, and in two quickened steps he reached me, playfully catching my knee to throw me off balance. Just to catch my fall. Holding me so close our breath mixed, he lowered me into the flattening poppies.

I curved onto my side, elbow propped and hand on hair while he sprawled next to me in earnest wait for my reaction.

In return, I told him exactly what was on my mind. "I love it." I truly did. With my heart and soul. "You're getting soft." It sounded like an accusation.

His hands pillowed his head. My eyes drew to his face, now pasted with an easy, lingering smile. He was no longer battling the urge to keep it locked away. I traced my finger on his bulging tricep, running a line from each freckle to the next until I reached his armlet. His strength filled an unexpected, primitive desire in me—one I constantly fought.

"So, Caolann, man of the people, what do you plan on doing with me here?" I asked in playful suspicion as my fingers toyed with the twine of his pants.

He raised his brow, pressing a crease into his Celtic knot. "Oh, all I please. I could take your life. No soul would suspect."

I tapped his knife on my belt. "You might be a demigod and twice my size, but I've got your lucky charm."

He leapt forward to grab my arms, pulling me on top of him.

A witch-like cackle erupted from me as I resisted his playful hold, grabbing his wrists to even the fight. "These are some—cheap—fighting moves, Caolann."

He stretched his arms wide, tricking me onto his chest, then wrapped his arms around me to cuddle close. "This is what I dream of when you leave for your battles."

I inhaled his scent as our fingers entwined. "So much for staying away from each other until Lúnasa ends." That conversation the day he'd revealed he was a god seemed so far from where we were now, and I never wanted to go back.

He didn't reply. Perhaps out of guilt for sidetracking me.

He shifted under me. "Clíona. I believed I lost you upon the Comeragh, and I fear these threats will never cease, for wickedness always looms in this world." He pressed loose hair behind my ear, and I wished it fell again just to have him reenact it. "So let me hold you while I can. Let me plant my lips on yours so I might never forget such beauty."

I shimmied up his body until our noses touched.

He sat, moving me with him, cupping his hand under my thigh to hitch me closer. Already breathless, I straddled him tightly. His fingers clenched my bum, watching me closely to ensure it was what I wanted.

I whispered, "Please" through the linger, our breath intensified in desperation, waiting for our lips to touch like they needed permission from the True Gods themselves.

Then we kissed. *Hard*. His stubble scratched my chin while heavy hands ran down my curling back to contort it.

"Surrender to temptation," he whispered, kissing my neck.

My body pushed into him harder as my thoughts willed me to give myself to him. "I could stay in this field forever," I breathed, struggling to keep control. Not wanting to.

He rolled me onto my back, and I perched forward, kissing his neck, relishing his fluttering pulse on my lips.

Every touch only had my soul crying out for more.

Caolann drew me back to him, his breath tickling as he kissed my neck where a raised freckle had rested since birth. "I wish to imagine this is our life," he said. "Calm and simple. Without knives and battles." Soft lips brushed my jaw before he sat away from me. "Yet I must share my truth, Clíona."

All my intense feelings deflated with a sigh. Of all the moments to come clean about whatever this was.

I sat up, arms folded. "I thought you'd laid everything on the table when you told me you were a demigod."

"I will never hurt you with intention."

"Intention?"

"Yes." His eyes settled on the waterfall. "You cannot ask yourself the question I hide from all."

I tutted. "Stop being elusive."

He tore his gaze from the water to look at me in his admittance. "My Bua, it is hidden."

I'd presumed it was a form of great strength since he knocked down a tree using his fist. Now he had me thinking that was a god trait.

"I wish for you to understand our moments are palpable," he said like he was about to break the heart he'd just taken.

"Jesus Christ, Caolann. What did you do?" I preemptively shouted.

"My Bua is attraction based. Akin to Rían's, yet its power sways another way."

"Sways how?" The words came out slow and gritted on my tongue.

"People are drawn to me. Emotionally, physically, intimately..."

Oh no. Please, no. "Did you use your Bua on me?"

"No, never. I promise you that! But it was my intention the night I brought you to my cabin. I planned to try and seduce you first, but you were stubborn. You did pander to me how most do."

I stood to elevate my voice but all that came out was a simple, "Why?"

"By Mórrígan's command. She suspected you to be a spy. Her awareness of Saoirse extends far beyond what the villagers suspect."

"Except I'm not a spy. In fact, you were the one spying on me!"

He stood to reach for me, but I recoiled, not trusting what my hands would do if I used them.

"When I discovered you were different. A rarity..." he stammered. "The night in the cabin, when you spoke, I became frustrated...lost for words. And when you slaughtered those men. I galloped with the little left of them to conceal what you had done. Confused why you, a Tearminn girl, ignited such fire in me. Or why I ached for your return."

Why wasn't I angry? And my chest heavy? I ran my hands through my hair, clenching its ends. "You arsehole."

"Forgive me. My actions were treacherous. They were carried out by a man I no longer consider myself to be. Clíona, I beg," he breathed in a final attempt to preserve us.

Persistence rarely endeared me, but he'd broken my resilient barriers long before this. I growled from the pit of my stomach, wishing we could return to the bliss of five minutes ago. "Neither of us realized how much we'd care for one another, but finally admitting it after weeks of pushing it away shouldn't be followed by such a fucking downturn of emotions." I huffed, letting some of my frustration simmer.

"You are the reason I parted with the Tuatha. I will do all in my power to regain your trust."

He placed his forehead to mine, and I let him. I had to believe he wouldn't have spied if he knew what would come of us. I also knew he hadn't betrayed what we'd become, rather he was just stupid not to speak his truth sooner.

He kissed my hairline, pulling me to his chest. "It lies in your palms to trust me."

The funny thing about trust is it works both ways. If he knew what I had done or where I was really from, wouldn't I hope for forgiveness? The truth lay heavy on my lips. It would be so easy to tell him. To let him decide if he wanted me, bad parts and all.

I shrugged from him to stare at the unsettling sky. "Woah. How long have we been here?"

He followed my gaze, his jaw sharpening. "Not enough to justify the light departing. Come, Clíona, the trial is upon you."

I jogged into the darkening forest, anxiety rising in my stomach.

"You forgive me?" he called after me.

"Ask me again if I survive the day."

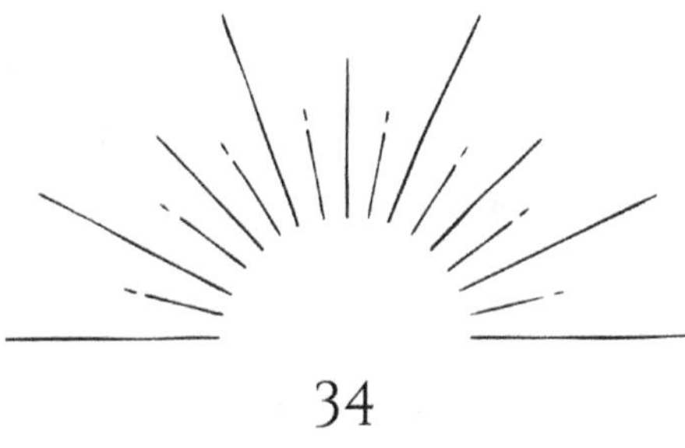

34

BLACK SKIES

We merged into a crowd heading north towards the Carraig, many holding torches despite the orange-crested moon being enough to light the way. Within the dim lights, a chatter of confusion hummed, making me feel at one with Saoirsians for the first time; I shared their worries for what would unfold under darkness.

Lining the Carraig's steps and rising to the Tuatha Dé Danann sculptures, bronze bowls of chopped wood burned. Fir na Solas exited the Carraig's opening in twos, dividing to scale the steps. Each halted adjacent to a fire bowl to illuminate their stern face. Still, I didn't fear them anymore. The version of me they'd attacked my first day here was long gone. I held my own now.

A bronze chest carved in triskeles looked displaced on top of the Carraig. Bolted with a heavy lock, it was large enough to conceal a man. My imagination burned with the possibilities of what it held.

The crowd pulled closer as we fell into the area like cattle, ironically some to our slaughter. Caolann grasped my fingers to keep me close in the tide, but I lost him to the herd. Besides, if this chest was about the trials, that was my battle.

Against the movement, I pushed and weaved until coming out front to mount the Carraig's first steps. Muireann's clan had already gathered, as had Lester. He mirrored my wide eyes. When did I become so anxious? Or him, for that matter.

"Are you well?" I asked.

His new hand patted my back. "I am healed, friend. Thanks to you."

"Well, I'm glad you're not angry with me. I couldn't let you die." The thought made me feel sick on the back of my tongue. But his tawny eyes folded into their lids for his trademark grin, softening it a little.

"I believe we are now equal in the act of saving one another from slaughter," he jested.

Our short-lived smiles drifted to the statues as a figure materialised next to the chest. The crowd erupted into croons and wild, vibrating chants as the figure revealed himself. A bronze helmet adorned with antlers jutted from atop his head, its edges seamlessly blending into his chiselled jawline. His armour matched his helm; dark Celtic tattoos, a mere shade lighter, branched out from beneath it to twist around his arms.

"It can't be." It was laughable how slowly it hit me. The Treasure confirmed it: the spear that never missed its aim. He banged it twice to draw silence, though his presence alone sufficed, for this was Lugh, God of Light.

I was in awe of him. Lugh emanated authority and youthful ferocity that created a sudden urge in me to cry. This was Fionn's idol, and I was seeing him in the flesh.

His sultry brown eyes almost glowed, boring into the quiet crowd. "This Lúnasa, Mórrígan brings to thee a new trial," his deep but clear voice boomed. "This chest"—he tapped with his spear—"will become agape. Inside lies a darkness: a being known as Taibhse, captured from the Underworld. Taibhse will be released to reap among you. It smells terror. It feeds on your power. Many Bua will be lost forever, yet warriors will be carved."

The crowd gasped, and their fear permeated the clearing like an apparition.

I locked my jaw to hold my own fear inside. The idea of losing my Bua, just when I was learning it was a gift and not a curse...my jaw locked harder.

"Hush, and fear not," Lugh commanded. His expression was firm, yet something about him felt inviting. Be it the curve on his lips to hint at happiness or the way he nodded to the Fir na Solas with not just authority but appreciation; he appeared somewhat permissive and absent of the tyranny Rathnor relished. "This creature will only cease when a sole Bua remains. But recall my warning: until this trial ends, darkness will remain. I am the God of Light. I can take as easily as I provide!" A flash of light battered the sky in golden branches before plunging us back to night again.

I seethed, repelling the light with my hands.

"Where is it to be unleashed?" Lester called to him, a warranted shake in his voice despite him standing tall and brazen.

Lugh kept his sights on Lester. "Wise question. The Fir na Solas tell me you battle well. So, I will tell you where it intends to reap. Competitors must fight inside the perimeter of the northern forest, barricaded for no escape."

Lugh banged the chest with his spear again. It rattled violently, and the adjacent soldier stumbled backwards, knocking a bowl of fire. In the commotion, Rathnor had appeared behind Lugh, like a dirty nettle branching out from a beautiful flower. Our eyes locked. He licked his lips and blew me a kiss I swore I could smell.

I'm ready for you, you slimy bastard.

As the crowd scattered to their homes, the Fir na Solas directed us towards the Carraig's stone entrance.

"Clíona," a voice called through the thinning crowd of bobbing flames.

"Bébhinn?"

My armour rattled in her arms as she came to me. "When I saw the skies descent into darkness I worried for your protection."

We hugged tightly, only for a moment. Then I fitted my pleated skirt as she knotted the corset with a mother's touch.

"Go on home," I told her. The darkness told me no Saoirsian would be safe anywhere until this was over.

Whether it was instinct or madness, something ominous lurked in the absence of light. Darkness was creeping in, leaving the door open for worse things to seep through—something bad was inbound.

She hesitated, then pulled my hands to her chest. "You have no debt to repay. I was foolish to let you compete. Please, Clíona, the creature will reap your Bua. We must accept Róisín is lost to the forest."

I pulled her close to make it look like we were whispering our goodbyes to the lingering soldier. "All is not lost, Bébhinn. I promise you I'm getting close. I think—" I held my tongue, afraid to give more hope. But if she had none, then what was there to lose? "Róisín might be alive. Taken for a reason."

She caught a spluttering cry of happiness with her hand as a smile I'd forgotten she could bear crossed her lips.

"Now, go." I shooed her with newfound hope. "And stay inside!"

Down the bleak hallway of the Carraig, a soldier guided me to a room poorly decorated by a long-planked table and chairs no competitors had chosen to use. Torches lit the far wall, offering us a dim light as we waited for the stragglers.

The girl from Lester's clan who wore her hair like those who had Fás Fada, came next. Áed and Ruadh were the last to join, followed by a soldier who lingered by the door, puffing his plated chest. Disciplined to his core, he surely thought of himself. Really, he was no more than a compliant sheep under Mórrígan's rule.

"Two have already forfeited. You seven must decide," he told us. "We will return to escort those honourable enough to fight."

Dashing glares rippled out amongst the room. To be fair, it was called for when it was every man for themselves. Still, the brothers stood by my side. But our clan was gone, and I had to decide if my winning was worth not just their loss of the gift of divine status, but their Bua.

"Why would they force us to suffer a life without the gift of our harvest?" Lester asked the room, not actually appearing to want an answer. He, too, stood by his clan at the table's far end where Muireann now sat alone, crossed feet sprawled, toying with her knife's point.

Nobody spoke.

"I fear this creature. As should you all," Lester admitted with passion. "There is no shame in being unwilling to sacrifice your Bua."

Mollie would say bravery meant embracing fears, not battling for triumphs. Lester lived up to that ideology in every way.

The older boy—the one with noodle hair—shook Lester's shoulders too dramatically for my liking. Half the room groaned with me.

"Be wise, Lester," he said. "We are carved from the warrior's line."

My nose involuntarily scrunched at him. The idea of someone declaring themselves carved from the warrior's line seemed self-glorifying. Caolann said it was an honour bestowed, for those who fought so well they had to be a descendant of Nuada, the Tuatha Dé Danann's first king.

"Competing in this trial is self-slaughter, Fead," said the girl from Lester's clan.

Muireann scoffed at her as she sharpened her knife. "Words of deceit, Aoife. You wish for your enemy to forfeit and take the glory."

Aoife unsheathed her longsword from the back of her baldric, swinging it full circle before aiming it at Muireann's face.

Muireann snorted another laugh and edged the tip of Aoife's sword to the wall with her own blade.

Aoife started for the door. "I will not sacrifice my Bua."

Though it was against my odds to intervene, the inner voice I could never subdue spoke out. "What was the point of any trial if you forfeit, Aoife? Hmm? You could've been slaughtered on the Comeragh. The cave could've trapped you in the desert. A god might kill you in the final battle with a sole swing of their sword. How's this any different?"

"For one to live without their Bua is a worse fate than death for a warrior," Áed said, breaking his silence. I could sense the turmoil raging in him, heating him—literally. A quiet battle had been playing out behind his stoic facade knowing the inevitable: either him or Ruadh would finish Bualess.

The very thought ached me. Siblings, bound by blood and kinship, forced into enemies. It wasn't right. A cruel twist of fate. Or maybe fate didn't have a hand in this at all. It was the gods, after all, who chose the trials. It was the rule of this land who savoured this cruel game. I bet they hardly cared about inviting in a new comrade.

"I believe the nut's words are fair," Aoife agreed. "We desolate our time in argument when a strategy could be formed."

"Recall we are all enemies," Fead said, crossing his arms. Somehow even just speaking five words had his hair swaying. It kind of looked like flavourless noodles.

"We're fighting Taibhse—not each other. At least I'm not, anyway," I spoke up. "It'll be hard enough to beat this thing without getting battered along the way by all of you."

Muireann shot me a daggering glare as she toyed with her fresh white feathers. "Are we truly hanging on the words of an Ardagh nut? She wishes to take all the glory."

"And you don't?" Hand on knife, I squared to her.

"Woah. Woah!" came voices as bodies edged between us from all around the room before a strike could meet skin.

Lester had gripped my hand behind my back as something similar played out with Muireann and her teammates. My teeth still bared at her, I fought his hold to little result. "Fucking try me. I dare you!"

Growling in another attempt to break free, I found myself deterred when a loud horn rang out from the village. The room held a united breath. Time was up, but we were none the wiser of anything except knowing of the seven of us, only one was seeing sunlight with our Bua intact.

A handful of Fir na Solas marched with us, carrying torches and grim stares. Flanking either side, they suffered most of the cold weather rolling in. Still, the air bit my skin past comfortable, pulling at the hairs on my arms to stand.

Each step closer to the trial was filled with thoughts that wouldn't prepare me. It was all just speculation spiralling me into a state of fear I didn't need right now. My Bua, no longer a curse but a gift, was being threatened. Only months ago, I would've gladly given it away. And my friends...they were now my enemies. However much I cared for them, deep down I knew I had to be the only one to leave this trial with power. I had to win.

We hadn't walked far into the forest when the Fir na Solas stopped in sync.

"Is this it?" I asked. "Are we here?"

Silence.

I wasn't brave enough to ask again for fear they'd say yes, and I really couldn't change my mind.

A soldier marched ahead, briskly turning on his foot to face us with a final stomp. "The trial will commence when Taibhse cries out. Where you will travel and how you protect your Bua is of no other's burden but your own."

"Where is the perimeter?" Muireann asked.

He pointed into the distance. "Along the trees."

The illusion of the perimeter became clear, appearing from nowhere as illusions do. The trees looped, each stuck tightly to the succeeding one: an impenetrable wall of bark fading into darkness.

"They have been bound by a red Druid's touch. There is no escape."

The Fir na Solas converged around the soldier who'd transported us onto the Comeragh. With a deep breath, blue light emulated from his body, his eyes shining ice blue. Then they were gone in a blink like a video that skipped.

"We should seek its weakness," Ruadh courageously spoke up. "Lay a trap for it."

"I suggest we split paths," Aoife called as she started to move north into the thick of the forest. "Plan your protection, or you will be Bualess by sunrise."

Muireann started west after her, leaving just the five of us to face this thing together.

As the rustle of her departure faded, an eeriness penetrated the cool night air, leaching into my skin. It was sickly silent, each of us dashing looks at one another and the sky, waiting.

Ruadh eyed the black sky then his brother. Lester looked at me, his hand grasping the hilt of his blade.

My breath stopped short.

In its absence, the heightening, skin-crawling screech of Taibhse rang out.

35
IT COMES

My body planted itself in the soil like I'd somehow become a denser object. For a moment, I couldn't feel my legs at all.

Fead drew his knife, clutching the bent blade so hard his tendons rolled over his knuckles.

Áed cocked his head. I knew all too well what he was thinking: it was a little early for semi-finalists to be freaking out. He was right—for Fead *and* me. But I was stronger than the fear consuming my bones and telling them to rattle.

"Are you alright, Fead?" I asked. "You're making me nervous." He wasn't.

Jabbing his blade at the air like the flies were out to get him, his hollow glare turned on me.

I clicked my tongue, both hands raised—a warning, not a surrender. "You better sheath that knife immediately! Or you won't be happy with the next place it's going." I was past the recurring theme of being underestimated.

Fead edged back, beads of sweat dripping from his noodle hair onto bitter-lined lips. He'd become deranged in a matter of seconds. It made no sense, even if he was cautious to compete.

"Can you not feel it straining your skin?" He pulled at his neck like it was a layer of clothing he no longer wanted to wear. Red marks persisted where his fingers clawed. "It runs through my head. It comes for me."

"It comes for all of us, amadán," Lester whispered loudly, approaching from his left.

If Fead was any louder, he'd out our position, and my patience had worn thin. "You need to be quiet if—" Áed clasped his hand over my mouth from behind.

I peered back at him from my eye's corner, not fighting his hold. He stared into the calm night sky, skimming his eyes across the clouds and stars.

"It will find me," Fead shouted as he darted off into the darkness, his arms flailing. "It comes. It comes!"

Áed's hand dropped as he staggered back from the sudden screeching in the sky. It grew closer, like an impaled crow, calling for us—for me.

Fuck. Was it me it wanted first? I was the perfect target. Too powerful for my own good. Too tempting for such a creature.

Pushing my foot into the soft soil, I took off running, into the direction I considered away from Taibhse.

"Clíona, wait," Áed called, but I didn't stop. He was safer away from me.

Seeing little ahead of me but the shadows of trees, I scratched past thorn bushes and overhanging thistles until my arms were cuts and blood and nothing more. My breathing heaved too loud for the muted forest, too loud for my usual stamina. "And people thought I could be a spy," I huffed to comfort myself in my lonely travels.

I came to a skidding stop in front of the rippling hump of a tree. A weary realisation came to me: I'd been running for at least an hour. The tightening pain in my thighs was the tell—always a good indicator of how far I'd gone.

Why did I run? Where was I going? I'd left my friends behind. But the moment I'd decided to do that was a blur.

I sat on the hump, running my fingers through fluffy moss as I took deep breaths to smooth its pace.

Okay, Clíona. You're going to rest here while you come up with a plan...

Or you could run more.

I squinted to take in my surroundings as if doing so could overcome the darkness, but my bearings were distorted, and the peripheral trees were wavy.

Focus. Think rationally. You can't hide from it. You can't run forever...

You should kill your competition.

I smacked the side of my head. The trials had leathered my skin to the point where even a blade might not penetrate it, and I didn't like it.

I'd never hurt the brothers or Lester...

Yes, you would. It's how you will receive the divine status.

I leapt onto unsteady legs, holding my fists as I darted stares to every cracking branch or hoot, ready to fight.

"Stop stealing my thoughts!" It was as if the creature was projecting a darker version of me into my mind.

I took off running again, into the bleak darkness, praying the thoughts wouldn't follow.

I stood by a river, Caolann's knife in my clenched fist. When did I unsheathe it? My spine contorted, and my skin crawled, plagued with invisible bugs.

Then, I was running again, faster than my legs should have for such uneven ground, but paranoia had lodged into my head like the rusty tool of a lobotomy. Taibhse had chosen me, stamping me with a black spot. I was its food, and it was toying with me to prolong the satisfaction of its feast.

I never looked back. Not once. Too afraid it lurked in the corner of my eye, prowling in the shadows.

I stood by blackberry bushes, oddly caressing their soft, bumpy skin. The crackling of snapping branches broke my daze.

I wanted to call out, to be comforted by a familiar face, but it was too risky.

The noise grew closer.

I apprehensively squeezed a handful of berries. They popped and squirted, the acidic juice bringing me clarity upon impact. "My fucking eye!" I clenched it shut to soften the sting to little avail.

Goddamn, that hurt.

"Clíona?"

"Who's there?" I whispered despite just bleating my woes for the whole forest to hear.

Lester walked into dimmed view with surrendered hands and stinking of sweat.

I lunged forward to hug him despite the smell, but he edged back, darting his gaze to my knife and bloody arms.

"Are you of harm, Clíona?"

I caressed my cuts, smearing the blood in soothing circles.

So satisfying.

Lester shook me ragged. "Hear me, you are not yourself. We scattered when the screech of Taibhse came. I have searched for you since."

His voice gradually grounded me, flushing out some of the paranoia that crawled and whispered in my ear.

Tie him up.

"Why search for me?" I sheathed my knife to protect him. "You should fight for yourself. For your family."

"I do not wish to fight," he admitted with a rare shyness pinking his cheeks. "Sacrificing my Bua for the opportunity to receive the divine status was foolish. If I spoke sooner..." He spat at the ground. "I would rather be buried in the soil than live without it."

Hardly hearing his words, I erratically danced my fingers along my forehead, feeling *Taibhse's* pull leech back in. "That creature," I seethed. "It's in my head."

"As it is with Fead. I believe it is how it chooses us. It tells you. The fear of waiting for an outcome has driven many a warrior to madness." Lester kneeled, tracing his hand over a footprint. "The perimeter is too confined. We cannot run for eternity."

Clíona...it seeks you.

"Stop it. Stop it. Stop it!" I thrashed and dug my fingers into my hair, dragging them out bloodstained. Skin curled under my nails like parmesan cheese shavings.

Lester shook my flopping shoulders harder, rattling sense into me. "I will protect you, but we must defend ourselves, or six will leave this forest Bualess. Six who will never be whole come morning's light."

My senses teetered on the brink of paranoia, my breathing erratic, rising against my armour too much for even a moment's comfort. "We need to find them, Lester. And fast. I'm almost lost to it." My legs moved before the words came out. "If we run the perimeter, we'll cover more ground."

We travelled side by side in search of the rest, but Dark Clíona hit in waves, each thought closer to the next, clawing for me to listen to her.

DON'T TRUST HIM. STAB HIM IN THE HEART.

I scratched my hand on a thorn to block the bad thoughts. It was enough to think of Áed and Ruadh. Young Ruadh. He was just a child hoping to honour his family. A child I needed to protect. For now, he came before the vanished children.

Lester skidded to a stop, pulling me to match him.

"What's wrong?"

He pointed to a figure lying on a bed of browning moss. Shrugging off his hand, I edged towards the sobbing.

Aoife cried, "It came for me."

"And your Bua?" I asked, crouching my her. Smoothing her hair.

She upturned her quivering palms. "I have tried to summon it. My Bua grants me eternal energy. This feeling in my body, it is as though I am drained of strength."

I pitied Aoife, truly. But we had to find the rest before they met the same fate. "We need to keep moving, Lester," I reminded him as I stood without a second thought.

"What of me?" Aoife cried.

I couldn't face her as I said it, "We can't carry the dead weight. I'm sorry, but our only choice is to find the others."

When did I become so brutal? I guess the Tuatha Dé Danann designed the trials this way for that reason. There's no room for weakness in ruling.

She wailed as we left, howling into the night sky.

SHE DESERVED IT. SHE WAS WEAK.

Continuing our search in a haze of lost time, footsteps suddenly pelted towards us, their pace intensifying with each second until a figure emerged from between the tree silhouettes, charging for us.

I harvested him still with nothing but a thought, embodying him with my golden light I wanted to run my hands through. Fead froze, eyes bulging, dilated, bloodshot. I'd recognise that noodle hair anywhere.

"It comes for me." Fead seethed through the strain of my hold. "I feel it, whispering in my ears."

"The light will draw attention, Clíona," Lester warned.

He was right. I retracted my Bua, and Fead slumped to his knees, crying. "It lurks in the trees. It seeks me."

"We have a plan," Lester reassured him, helping him up with a tight clasp of hands.

"The moment of plans has left us." Fead fumbled to a stand and dashed past us. "It is upon us."

Lester chased him. "Come, Clíona. We must protect him."

As I went to follow, a putrid, slurry stench caught in my nose. I froze, something catching the corner of my eye; something swift, with an eerie rattle.

It's found you.

"Run," I shouted to Lester. "Run!"

"It comes!" Fead called.

"Keep running, Lester!" If he got away, at least one of us would be safe.

Submit your power to it.

Taibhse screeched through the flanking trees.

I spun to the movement, tumbling face-first onto the forest bed with a *humph.*

Something prickled my back, like a ghost you convinced yourself couldn't be real. I twisted slowly onto my bottom to find it floating above me, and I swore my heart stopped instantly.

A glimmer of moonlight shone onto its humanoid face. With black, leathery skin, slit in weepy gashes, it hovered closer. So close, its teeth rattled, dripping with sticky venom, inches from me. Extending its long-fingered hand, I willingly surrendered, allowing it to claim me.

With its touch, all I craved was its appeasement.

A bright light rippled from its fingers like electric silk to consume me in a warm cocoon.

Yes, I submit my Bua to you.

36

RED ASH

The pain was gone.

The sorrow.

The guilt.

All of it.

I was free—subdued to everlasting serenity. There was nothing but the white expanse. I floated within, letting the dense air cocoon me.

Maybe dying wasn't so bad after all.

"Clíona," a voice called.

Dark rays shot into the cocoon, leaving gaps for the pain to seep in and disgruntle me. Why would anyone want to disturb me from this peace? Didn't they know how happy I was?

I clawed to keep the light around me.

No. Please. I want to stay.

The darkness grew thicker until a heavy thud hit, sending a stiffening shock up my spine.

"Wake, Clíona."

The chill of the night soil stirred me back to life. I struggled to open my heavy eyes as forceful hands shook me.

"What happened?" I slurred on my numb tongue that felt double in size.

No one answered.

I winced as Lester pulled me by my armpits and hoisted me to my feet, though it took considerable effort on his part to keep me upright.

Dragging me for some time, I gradually began to carry my weight.

"What did it do to me?" I asked when the sensation returned to my tongue.

"It attacked you. A white light surrounded you whole," Lester explained, too vague for my liking. His only concern was moving forward.

Fead moved ahead of us, holding branches for us to pass. Had he been with us the whole time? Had they calmed him down? Somehow snuffed out the voice?

"Then what?" I asked, hoping he wouldn't tell me that it reaped me. That I was Bualess just when I had come to embrace it.

"Please, Lester—"

"*Psst.* We dwell here," Áed's familiar voice interrupted in the poorest attempt I'd ever seen someone whisper. The brothers emerged from behind a grand tree.

I smiled—the last thing I thought I'd be able to do in this trial. But seeing them safe was enough relief to pry it out of me.

Áed's returning smirk subsided as he came to cup my cheeks, his eyes searching my face too wide with worry for my liking. "Has it taken from you?"

I must've looked terrible.

I groaned and dipped my face from his touch without an answer.

"It attacked her," Fead interrupted.

I scowled his way, but as much as I wanted to uppercut him for his continued annoying presence, it wasn't the time for bickering. It was time to find out what was left of me.

"Mind if I check my Bua on you, Ruadh?"

He held his chin high. "It would be my honour."

Sidestepping from the last of Áed's hold, I stood of my own accord to harvest. My fingertips and stubs were sensitive and tingling, but I persisted, willing the power deep within to resurface. A sudden warmth in my core flowed into my hands with ease as the thrumming grew stronger. Gentle flurries rippled toward him, shaking him first, then effortlessly rose him off the ground. I sighed so hard with relief I almost deflated. The brothers and Lester echoed me.

Thank Danu and Bíle.

Surprisingly, I felt stronger than ever.

"Better lower me before Taibhse sees," Ruadh called in a hush. I did, albeit the landing wobbled, but it was enough to know, by some miracle, my Bua was intact.

"Soley gods have the power to stop such a creature," Fead shrilled as he spat at my feet. "How does a dirty Ardagh spy possess the power of a god?"

"Ardagh spy?" Nostrils flaring, I turned my thrumming hands on him, but Lester lurched forward, tackling Fead to the forest bed.

"I will leave you to the worms if you speak another word against her." Lester's furrowed stare fell on Áed and Ruadh. "Do you agree?"

"Agreed," they said in unison, arms folded to puff what muscles they had.

Fead scooted away from Lester, a guilty wallow smeared on his rotten face. "I am in fear. I feel it clawing."

We ignored his useless reply. I was too busy being flattered they'd stood up for me. Feeling like I had...friends.

Friends that I wanted to wake up tomorrow feeling whole.

"Look lads, I don't know about any of you, but I'm not running around this fucking forest like a headless chicken anymore." My exhausted, aching legs wouldn't carry me much further anyway. "We are resigning ourselves to loss if we wait for it to pick everyone off. Lugh himself said it could be defeated, just that it wouldn't be easy. If we face it together, we might have a chance of surviving."

Lester rose to his feet. "Clíona, I ask of *you* to lead the fight."

I spat a laugh. I was no leader. Besides, how was I going to defeat Taibhse when it had taken me out once already?

"Listen to yourselves," I fought back. "If I battled it and won, you're all sacrificing your chance to receive the divine status."

Áed placed his comforting hands on my shoulders how he always did. "You will claim victory to rightfully battle Rathnor, for you are the worthy one. *You* are carved from the warrior's line."

Ruadh followed his brother's lead, placing his hand on my shoulder.

Then Lester, with his healed arm, said, "Never a doubt in my mind." He half bowed his head.

"Not even in the caves?" I teased, gripping his touch for a moment.

"Perhaps for a mere moment," he winked.

Finally, Fead joined us, his reluctance set in a locked jaw, but still, begrudgingly, he placed a hand atop my shoulder.

"We trust in you alone," Lester declared, his eyes sparkling with unwavering resolve.

Their weight on me was stark and undeniable. The choice had been made. And who was I not to respect these men who were undoubtedly carved from the warrior's line?

I smiled at each of them, biting back a feeling that swelled in my chest. Though I couldn't quite articulate the emotion, it was heartwarming, even if they were all mad for putting their trust in me. Cracked nuts the lot of them.

"Perhaps I saw you through too wicked an eye, Ardagh nut," Muireann called as she emerged from the trees. By her saunter, and the way she played with her knife's point, I knew her power was safe.

"Here to join the party?" Using the direction of my eye, I flung her knife into the nearest tree.

Harvesting my Bua was so simple now. The source was always burning when it was a job of flint and stick to spark even the tiniest source of my power.

Muireann's gaze followed into the forest's abyss, though she didn't pander to my passive-aggressive move. Smirking, she said, "A shadow creature comes for us, lurking in the black of night to pluck us of our rightful power. I will not lose my shield. For no man nor god."

"Not for Mórrígan nor the Tuatha will we sacrifice our birthright," Áed confirmed.

Muireann hesitantly placed her hand on my shoulder. A sharp-eyed exchange between us solidifying a temporary truce. It was settled. Acknowledging I was their hope was an uncomfortable pressure, like the kind you got in your ears when you touched the bottom of a deep pool; still, I had to be brave now. Show no waver. No fear.

Stepping out of their touch, I stood straighter. "If you choose me to be your leader this nightfall—" I looked at each of them as my voice rose. "I will stand to the mark." It's what Fionn would do. It's what would help me find Róisín. "I can't promise victory, but I'll fight it to the death if need be. No one else has to lose the honour of their Bua. With the guide of the True Gods, we have a chance!"

"We are with you," they echoed.

"Then let's slaughter this beast."

Lester hooted as Áed and Ruadh locked hands, wildly grinning.

We set out to Réimse Mór to execute our plan—a terrible plan, but we had no choice when Taibhse held the advantage. We needed a level playing field. All I had in opposition was that it didn't want me. Or at least, it couldn't reap from me for some reason.

It wasn't long before Ruadh's eyes dilated and scattered. He itched with fear and suspicion the closer we got to the field. We recognised the symptoms by now. He'd offered himself as bait, much to the dismay of Áed, but being chosen by Taibhse made him a perfect target. I'd have gladly volunteered Fead, but he was too unpredictable to be trusted with any task.

We planned to use Taibhse's only weakness to our advantage—it literally told you it was coming by inducing fear. I just prayed it wasn't smart enough to realise we were luring it to a trap.

A distant clatter of thunder rolled in by the time we reached the field, and Danu's rain fell in drones, sloshing into puddles of muck so heavy the grass thinned with tiny streams.

Lester and I took the eastern post of the field perimeter, our teeth chattering like those silly Halloween skeletons.

I whispered, "If it's pneumonia that kills me, I'll be so annoyed."

He licked the rain pouring onto his lips and shook his dripping ponytail, knowing better than to entertain my modern riddles.

I nudged him. "Thanks for having my back tonight."

His eyes shifted to the side to glance at me. "I thank the gods you came to this very place in search of my guidance. It is my honour to fight by your side."

Ruadh whistled—his signal he felt Taibhse was close.

Blinking raindrops off my lashes, I barely made out his small frame in true warrior form, centred in Réimse Mór with a sword drawn near matching his size.

A haunting screech bellowed from the south, scaring the birds from their slumber. It moved fast, and the trees rustled as it skimmed by them.

My hands thrummed with anticipation I couldn't control, growing stronger as Taibhse appeared in the opening. Slowing on approach, it glided into the field, tatters of cloth dragging behind.

"Attack," Lester whispered as it closed in on Ruadh.

"Wait," I whispered back, not wanting to scare it off.

I didn't actually think it was afraid, but this would be our only chance to defeat it. There was no plan B.

"It gains on me," Ruadh nervously called as he edged backwards, swinging his sword wildly. "Brother, help!"

Shit. "He's blown our cover."

We leapt from the bushes, Lester by my side. Here we bloody go.

"Attack!" I bounded to Ruadh, Áed and Fead flanking us from the north. Taibhse was closer to Ruadh than we were.

I'd left it too late. Oh God, why did I leave it too late?

"Ruadh, run to us," Áed shouted, his voice strained in desperation as his harvest failed over and over, flames sizzling in the rain.

I slipped in a puddle, foolishly dragging Lester with me to catch my fall.

Muireann came from the far side on the run, throwing her shield above the clearing to blanket the weather.

"Harvest your fire, Ruadh," she ordered him. "Protect yourself."

He threw down his sword and ran for his brother, slipping in the mud with each step. Áed's flames spiralled forward, an orange vortex, past Ruadh to pierce Taibhse's chest. The creature screeched fiercely, its mouth stretching beyond a bear, but the flames inside him condensed to white light.

It somehow absorbed them.

Lester helped me to my feet, but Taibhse's silk light had already begun to branch out of its withered fingertips like an encapsulating fog. It took Ruadh's ankle first, slamming him into the mud, metres from reaching Áed.

Ruadh stretched his hand. "Brother," he screamed. "Protect me!"

The pitch of his scream jittered my teeth as the cocoon of light enshrouded him, instantly cutting off his screeching pleas.

"Clíona, help him," Áed begged as he shot wasted balls of fire towards the string of light dragging his baby brother away.

Watching our plan go horribly wrong, I scolded myself as I ran, Caolann's knife drawn to attack while the other thrummed with steady power.

Fead, living up to his name, blew a sonic wave towards the creature, so forcefully the pitch ached my inner ears. But Taibhse's focus remained on consuming Ruadh, its lips rattling as it savoured its feast.

Áed focused on thrusting more wasted flames. He called for me. "Clíona! You vowed to save him!"

Taibhse's other arm latched onto Muireann, spoiling her power, and the heavens opened again. Lightning shocked the sky, illuminating its haunting features. Features scarred onto a creature no bigger than an average human. No bigger than any other threat I'd managed to take on.

I sheathed my knife as an unexpected calm rested on my bones. The confidence I'd adopted from Queen Medb as a child rallied. "You didn't take anything from me," I called to it, my voice clear, smooth as I stood beneath it. "That was your first mistake."

Muireann screamed as she drew a second knife from her ankle to swipe at the light enshrouding her arm. Hacking it over and over.

I blocked her out. I blocked them all out.

Taibhse's hollow eye sockets dipped to me. The time for parlour tricks had ended. The days of living without fear were overdue. All I needed was a final push.

Taibhse hovered close enough now that I didn't need to shout.

"I know what I'm capable of, and what runs through my blood, always lurking, always *SCREAMING* at me to free it."

I held my dripping hands to it, heaving and harvesting. I thought of Fionn and his death...of St. Brigid's. Of Róisín and Bébhinn. Of this world's useless fucking gods.

Taibhse's leathery skin began to pull from the bone as he droned an unsettling screech. Slits on its skin unfolded, peeling from its charred skeleton and flapping against the wind.

My chest pulsated.

My veins thickened.

My feet pushed deeper into the soil as its power fought back, light against light, but we were no such thing. We were two dark forces. I saw that now.

Its hands curled into themselves, cracking and distorting.

Blood seeped down my smile lines, collecting on my chin.

Then, as the thunder clapped and a flash of lightning terrified the sky, I harvested its bright, electric pulse. It descended, piercing Taibhse's smoking skull in a blink. The creature's sadistic form dissipated, crumbling to the wet soil until all that remained were ashes of red, the rain sizzling it into a pile of nothing.

The light recoiled from Muireann and Ruadh, leaving his curled body limp on the grass. Áed hugged his motionless brother, his sobs barely muted by the torrential weather.

"Clíona," Lester said. I watched him from my trance. "Return to us. Redeem your power from darkness."

His riddled words extinguished the black cloud in my mind. I'd become someone else. Beyond even the sinister voice Taibhse put into my head.

"You vanquished Taibhse." Lester shook me.

"I did," I confirmed with a smile, feeling more myself just to hear his voice.

Áed joined us, cradling Ruadh in arms.

"Is he okay?"

He kissed his forehead. "We will see when he wakes."

"We defeated it," Muireann said in disbelief as worse for wear she hobbled to us, her leg lagging.

"*We* did not defeat it," Lester interrupted her. "It was Clíona who saved us." He locked his dripping hand into mine and leaned into my chattering wet lips. "You championed the trial. And now you will compete in the final battle of Lúnasa."

37

ROT

I woke in Róisín's bed, fingers running through linen that smelled of her: roses. Somehow my exhausted bones landed there after my battle with Taibhse. I'd hardly remembered the journey home.

Bébhinn had wrapped herself in a red plaid blanket, asleep though escaped tears dampened her gaunt face. My words of hope obviously couldn't subside a mother's worry. If Róisín was alive, she could be in pain. Be afraid. Be treated poorly. That torment was enough to drive any mother crazy.

Her fresh pain was enough to reignite my fire, despite my exhaustion, that my debt to bring her daughter home stood until my last breath.

I left for the village, taking their narrower pathways, where they offered you tea even if you were too poor to barter. Mórrígan had 'kindly' granted a traditional day of rest preceding the final battle. Kindness wasn't a word I associated with her—she didn't care about her people. Nor did Rathnor—the only person standing between me and victory. If I could just sew his mouth shut, I might have a chance of winning—a concept which felt more unreachable now than it did upon the Comeragh.

Trudging past a stall barely clung to by withering seamróg, thoughts of Fionn flowed freely in place of the bad ones as I weaved around the morning crowd. Finegas's words about him had turned over in my mind at least a hundred times since our last meeting. But still, I couldn't grasp the importance of mentioning it had been three times that Fionn had visited this world. Or what those damn secrets were—if they were connected. I swore the mystery of them had subconsciously plagued me all this time, wondering who it was that kept them. My mouth downturned in frustration, fearing I'd never get to the bottom of it.

I looped my fingers around his rune, squeezing it tightly, finding endless comfort in carrying this piece of him with me. Then I took a long, deep breath. It was time to say goodbye, because if I wasn't dying tomorrow, I was becoming something else—a demigod. And with that, change was certain. Going to Magh Mell was my best chance of bringing Róisín home to her mother's loving arms.

Approaching the fire brothers' home, a gust of wind crept up on me as if beckoning me to run the other way. I squared my shoulders. I wouldn't take the coward's path.

By the door, a room of red-haired Saoirsians silently greeted me. Eyes running over my freckles now bruised and cut through in so many places I'd lost count. Or had never bothered to count in the first place. I didn't care about the scars or how unapproachable I was, and yet in this moment, with all the eyes eventually meeting my stare, I'd never felt more aware of how others perceived me.

I'd brought nothing but pain to this family. Good intentions didn't matter when it was the good people who got hurt.

Ruadh slept while loved ones tended to him, bathing his limp body with cloths, wafting sage over his wounds. The grey had left his complexion, but it was hard to say if his Bua burned inside. Either way, I was adamant that he never cut his hair again. He'd earned Fás Fada ten times over.

As I reached to knock on the door's arch, Áed stood in my path, his unwavering stomps backing me out to the blinding sun. The subtle rise in warmth around him hinted at the anger quietly simmering beneath his calm exterior.

I cautiously raised my arms to calm him. "This answers the question I came to get."

He flexed his hands before hiding them behind his back. "What question?"

Was he hiding flames from me? I stood straight, wanting to keep a distance, but if Caolann taught me anything, it was to not let your enemies see your fear. Áed wasn't my enemy, was he? The worry brimming my belly told me he no longer shared the sentiment that we were friends.

"I wanted to know if he had it...if it had taken from him."

He scoffed with deep, unexpected laughter. "Taibhse reaped his flames and reduced him to smoke. Eternally he will be but half a man, absent of honour."

"At least you don't need to worry about him competing." The reassurance sounded weak on my tongue. I don't know what I expected to come of this visit. His brother had taken the fall for my victory. There was no other way to spin it.

Áed's shoulders shrunk, and harrowing creases persisted around his kind eyes. "It is not your burden to carry alone. We all offered him as bait."

"I'm sorry, Áed. I never wanted Ruadh to be the one to suffer. I wanted everyone to be safe." That was the truth. That's all I ever wanted.

His hands dropped to his sides, and I breathed a sigh of relief at the absence of flames. "Do not waste your breath worrying about us fire folk when your battle approaches."

"Now who sounds like the cracked nut?" I joked, edging closer to nudge him. "You're my friend, Áed. And I can't say I have many of them." I meant that. "Time with you is never wasted."

He nodded over and over, his head dropping lower as his eyes shut, emotions overtaking him.

"Hey. Hey! It's okay. It's okay to be sad."

Arms wrapped around me, warmth soothing my ever-aching body, while his friendship eased the ache in my heart.

On my tiptoes, I rested my chin on his shoulder. "You pledged yourself to my cause when you barely knew me. I'll never forget that. And when I find these children, neither will they."

"Let us hope it truly is the path to finding the younglings. To finding Fintan."

"There he is." The words came out without conviction or even sincerity.

Lester sat before a low-lit fire, resting his elbows on widespread legs. It felt like a lifetime since I saw him cut off his fingers in Réimse Mór—a shadow of the place we stood in the night previous.

I kneeled next to him, my bones clicking from the demands of Lúnasa. "How are you?" A stiff question.

The answer was in his puffy eyes. The loss had struck him harder than I anticipated. After hours of training, near losing his life in Glas...his sadness was justified. I wondered then, if he felt the loss of those ten years without realising, too. Or if I'd ever find the guts to tell him.

He sipped from a cup of strong-smelling poitín. "Have you visited Ruadh?"

I nodded, and he slugged his drink despite the distaste in his clenched eyes. Even the smell of it burned my nostrils.

"We did what we thought was best," I told him, sternly. Told myself. "Five of us harvest a Bua because of his bravery."

Lester's cheeks flushed, and his lips trembled as he stared into the flames.

I'd never seen him so vulnerable.

I squeezed his knee, knowing from my conversation with Áed that words weren't needed right now. The trauma, the things adrenaline masked throughout the trials, were finally catching up. My friends had been watered down to just their fragile parts.

Lester slammed the bottle against the floor, clear liquid splashing out, sending blue flashes into the fire. Before I could react, he was suddenly in my face, nearly nose to nose. My breath caught, startled by the closeness. How unlike him this was. "You must claim victory, Clíona. My stomach sits on its side. You feel it, too. The Tuatha Dé Danann are no saviours. We need not look up to them because they are above us. Yet you"—he traced a line down my forehead—"I have praised you since our meeting. For you are carved from the warrior's line." He turned back for the bottle, his lips wavering against the cup's rim. "Whispers spread that Rathnor plans to enact a new quota until Samhain descends its chill upon the land. You must slaughter him, Clíona! Even if he surrenders, you must fight until Dagda's lost cauldron could not revive him. For the sake of my people...*our* people."

A tear hung from his nostril. He sniffled before swiping it away.

I hated seeing him like this. I'd take all his pain if I could. This boy who gave ten years of his life for me. The last thing I wanted was Lester and others starving because I didn't get the job done.

Rathnor had to die.

I just hoped I had the strength—the will—to get it done. It was the righteous thing for Saoirse—if murder could be considered the right thing.

The evening heat pressed on my neck as I approached Caolann and Rían's house. What if someone else had found me in the forest my first day in Ériu? I owed Rían for my life and Caolann for protecting me at any chance. They were the ones who dragged me out of the pit I'd buried myself in these past five years. Although maybe it wouldn't hurt to give myself some credit after all I'd been through.

Caolann rested on a bed of straw by the outside fire, propping himself at the sight of me. I loved seeing him—a literal god—in such simple, *human* environments. I loved—

"I wondered when you would return." His mouth pressed to hold his smile. I knew it all too well. Adored it.

Rían emerged from the house, throwing me a casual nod. Not enemies, but not quite friends yet.

"I had people to visit. You two were last on my list." I twisted to face Rían, my movements rigid and awkward, the nerves of my vulnerability making me feel exposed. "Rían, I wanted to thank you for helping me the day we met. You could have slaughtered me, but instead, you risked yourself for my freedom." If there was one thing I couldn't deny, it was that he had meant well for me. "So, thank you, endlessly."

Unable to pull his watch from his bow, he left me with some final words. "Give Rathnor all you harvest at the battle. He will wield his sword well and spit venom from his lips, but you will harvest the power of the god you are destined to be."

He wrapped his arms around my back so tightly, the gesture was impossible to return. Then he headed for the woods, his sanctuary, a bow looped over his chest and a quiver full for game.

Caolann stood to brush the clinging straw from his clothes, deliberately avoiding my gaze. "I have plans for us."

My nostrils flared, fully prepared to fight him. "If this plan is to get me to forfeit the final—"

"I have learnt my lesson. Your intentions are your own." He shook his head with a timid smile—the one that creased his eyes more than his lips. "Will you travel to the cabin with me this nightfall? Allow me to right my wrongdoings. I seek you in my thoughts when without you, Clíona, and I believe you seek me, too. We are bound to one another—without an oath enforcing it." He said the words with such suave and confidence any hope of resistance was futile.

I pursed my lips. "Oh, I seek you out, do I?"

Running his tickling finger across my jaw, he touched his lips to mine, just for a second. But it was enough to send a quickened flutter all the way down my navel.

"I wish for us to spend a final night together...away from the madness of this village." His bow lips curled, and I succumbed to the green glisten of his eyes. A night alone with Caolann twisted my stomach, but for the right reasons.

"Say yes?" he asked.

"Yes." There was nothing I wanted—*needed*—more in this moment.

He led the way, our familiar fingers entwined.

We walked past the threshold, hand in hand, the rotting mildew walls reminding me of how unromantic it was. Only cobwebs and weathered furniture decorated the room.

"Why don't you get wood for the fire, and I'll make the place homier," I suggested, hanging an old tunic from my finger before dramatically letting it drop with exaggerated flair.

"As you wish." He kissed my cheek and headed into the darkening forest.

Looping my hair in a loose bun, I rearranged the sparse furniture and rotted debris to one side of the room to make space for a makeshift bed. We wouldn't get to sleep, but still, I expected things would get...heated.

I dragged the rotted table, barely supported by the wall. It was light, and the first layer of wood crumbled in my fingers.

If I win this damn trial tomorrow, I'm renovating this shithole. Although—I peered over my shoulder—I'll keep the tub.

Just then, something stole my attention where the front leg of the table had been. Where the ground was tarnished with a patch of rotting floor.

My stare ferried between it and the door Caolann had just left from until finally settling on this thing, too bright and out of place, for the longest time. Like it was a riddle I couldn't solve. My mouth opened and closed a dozen times, giving nothing to the world, taking nothing in.

Kneeling to my discovery, I took it in my hand. My mind raced to that place where I didn't want it to go: the darker version of Ériu. A place where not even Lugh could restore the light.

The riddle unravelled—and I feared my heart, too.

"Oh my God." The words hollowed me out.

I held out my hand in open-mouthed disbelief. Saliva gathered in the hollow between teeth and quivering lips.

On my palm lay a small red ribbon, slightly frayed at the end.

Róisín's red ribbon. The ribbon she'd been wearing the day she disappeared. Wrapped in hair I'd found bloody in the grasp of her friend.

And it led me to ask myself a dangerous question. The question I feared I already knew the answer to. A question of irreversible consequences.

Why is this in Caolann's cabin?

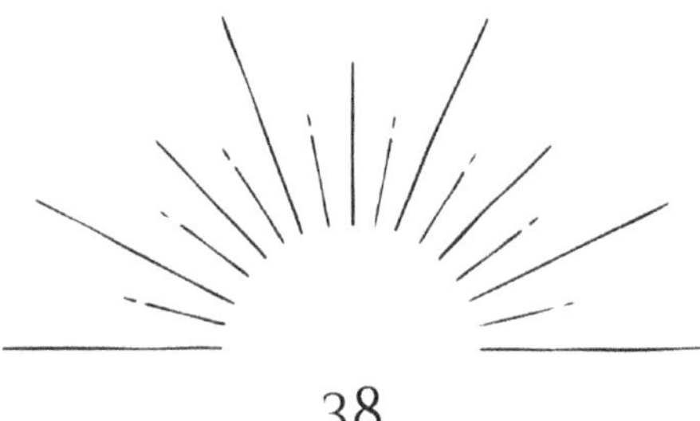

38

THINGS THAT GO BUMP

The door creaked.

I stuffed the ribbon into my pocket. The time to privately react had escaped me.

Caolann cocked an intrigued glimpse at my betraying cheeks. "What flushes your face?"

I smiled with fake overexertion. "I'm just...hot from moving stuff around." My tacky mouth made all the words sticky as they left my lips, causing beads of sweat to collect on the small of my back.

He dismissively kneeled by the fireplace at the cabin's far end, unbundling the foraged kindling into the hole.

With his back to me now, my smile collapsed, allowing my true state to surface: dry mouth, and eyes that frantically searched the room for an explanation. And why couldn't I catch my breath? I grabbed my stomach, unnaturally hunching to ease its discomfort. This was madness. Outrageous to even consider. Caolann couldn't have been the one to take Róisín.

He wouldn't do that—*couldn't* even. He was with me that night—kissing me…bearing himself to me. It didn't make any sense. Unless…

None of it was real.

He was using me. His pet. His plaything. His cover story.

The ribbon's soft material rubbed against my palm as I scanned the room for a way out of the horror taking shape. She never took the bloody thing off. This…it was no coincidence. There was no escaping it. No logical route out of the pit of poisonous fog that funnelled into my lungs.

I cleared my burning throat with a heavy cough and stood tall, taller than all the pain crawling up my skin with nails, because if it was true, I was going up against a demigod. A god not stripped of divinity. Not motivated by competition, but by the *necessity* of keeping their life intact. And chances were, I wasn't winning that fight.

"Caolann." His name felt foreign on my tongue. Already an echo of what once was.

"It is almost alight," he said, still turned from me.

I scraped the ribbon from my pocket using fingers I couldn't stop from trembling. Such a delicate thing to decide one's fate. And yet, somehow, Caolann might have decided a little girl's fate. "Caolann. Look at me."

Arching, he stared up in wonder from his crouched position, that perfect loose strand of hair cutting through his eye. Those perfect bowed lips I'd kissed under moonlight, under sheets, under the illusion he *cared* for me.

Who was this man staring at me if not the one I was falling for?

The answer was in my hand.

Trembling, I held out my fist. The ribbon slipped to dangle between my stumps.

Nothing. A sheet of indifference cloaked his face as if he hadn't yet reached the point of accusation.

It was his brow that broke first, dragging downwards. Then his jaw, slightly inclining.

Then, his eyes knowingly widened to my silent accusation, and his mouth stuttered too long for a man of innocence.

My feet felt like they were sinking. Getting dragged to hell. I tensed my legs not to have them crumble.

"Clíona." He surrendered his hands and yet, my name was a cool warning. "Your mind's conclusion is false."

He stood from his crouch, his fist still locked on the fire poker he'd been using.

I recoiled backwards into a curtain of cobwebs. It was foolish to let panic take hold instead of the anger I desperately needed to get the job done.

"Do not fear me," he pleaded, but there was anger in it, furrowing his brows deeper.

My eyes dashed to the poker, forcing it out of his grasp and into the wall like a dart wobbling at its tail.

He stared at it, a slight nod to his head as the accusation fully dawned on him. That a simple game of seduction wouldn't work anymore. "Clíona, I am no creature of wickedness."

Though every inch of me wanted to trust him, I raised my hand to warn him away. God, why did it have to shake so badly?

He heeded, arms raised again. But there was no mistaking the act; he didn't fear me, not truly. He was simply looking for a way not to hurt *me*—not physically at least.

But why? If it was all a lie, why not just take me out? Perhaps he thought I had been better as an ally. Or at least easier as one.

"Tell me I'm wrong," I pleaded slowly. Each word felt like grit, barrelling over my teeth as I latched on to some final prayer that a logical explanation was on the tip of his tongue. A tongue not moments ago I was planning to wrap my own around.

Though his mouth opened to speak, nothing came out. Not so much as a breath.

Fight me. Show me that this is all a lie, I wanted to say. That you weren't keeping me sweet all this time to blind me from the truth.

The words were jammed in my throat where a well had begun to form. I harshly swallowed. "Weak," I spewed, holding back the brew of oncoming tears. "You are weak."

How blind was I? Ogling heart eyes over this bastard when I knew from the moment I stepped foot in this very cabin that his seduction, his *games*, were all a ruse to get me on side. And what did I do? I fucked him anyway. I bought into the fantasy of finally meeting my match. Finally allowing someone to breach past my vicious barriers.

My Bua began to harvest, drawing back his feet.

"After," he shouted in transit, sternly, as though I was the one being unreasonable.

I fisted my hand to release him as I bit a churn of nausea. "After what?"

His jaw flickered, fighting against him. "She—Róisín—came here *after* she was taken."

The admittance sent a literal pain into my heart—one that lodged and settled itself in me, getting comfortable and taking up permanent residency. But I had to keep pressing him for answers on the off chance I made it out of this alive. "How...how did you take her if you were with me? What—did—you—do with her, you fucking monster?" I shouted, spit flying as my control dissipated. I didn't want the logical path anymore. I wanted justice. Whatever way *I* saw fit. "It was *you* who took those children from their mothers?" My voice grew louder and harsher and more rasped with each syllable. "Took their lives from them. Let everyone believe they were probably dead. You led the fucking search for them! Where are they now? Buried beneath our feet?" My thoughts were shards of glass, each slicing my heart deeper. My heart, which was a broken thing before I met him, now felt disgusting and used.

He worked his palms into his eyes for a moment. "To know purpose and to know you, Clíona...it has torn my heart in equal halves." Desperation clung to his tear-filled eyes, where I had expected something colder. "They were never slaughtered, Clíona—quite the opposite. I know it is difficult for you to see. But please, hear me. All I do is to protect Rían and these lands."

"Does he know you're doing this?" It stung to ask. But I had to know.

He scoffed, the act enough for two tears to slide down his usually stone face.

I flinched from seeing him this way. Wished it didn't foolishly hurt me to see his character crumble before my feet.

Of course, Rían didn't know. I should've listened when he warned me from Caolann that day in the forest. When he told me lies. I should have begged, kicked, screamed until Caolann granted him the sole burden of being the one I was to be bound to.

I watched this man in front of me, trying to understand his logic. If he knows yet that letting me walk out of the cabin means his life is over.

His corpse will be hanged from the Carraig by dawn. Bébhinn alone would happily slit his throat. Clean the blood on her apron and move on to getting her daughter back.

"You have to tell me why, because the Caolann I know—knew—wouldn't do this. When Róisín was taken, you were so upset you punched a tree onto the forest bed. Or was that part of the act, too? Huh?" The rev of anger chaffed my words before they ever came out. "And the ribbon?" I flung it at him, bunched. "How is it here?"

His head dropped to it, hanging heavy for what I hoped was the suffering of shame. I was starting to think it would be easier if he dropped the facade from the get-go. Just fought me outright.

"Answer me," I demanded through gritted teeth. The heat inside was pouring in thick and fast now.

He gripped the wooden beam above, like he needed the extra support to keep him upright. It was a move of opposition in itself; him telling me he didn't want to fight. That he was at my mercy. "The soldier who took her was foolish, ignoring the rule of taking a youngling who travels alone. He brought her here for she was in despair. My Bua simply guided her, Clíona. So she did not fear what lay ahead. In the end, she *wished* to go—to fight for Saoirse."

"She didn't *want* to go, you fucking psychopath!" The audacity. The brainwash. The selfish belief that this was a righteous act. The fire in my chest burned brighter, until everything inside felt blistered and bubbling. Until the urge to hurt him finally surfaced and seared my useless fucking feelings for him.

Our relationship had ended the second I saw Róisín's ribbon.

Anger battled through my veins so thickly, I worried they might collapse. The relentless darkness called on me to release the harvest, to revert it to my basic form with no reserve or control. Consequences. Logic. Emotion. All irrelevant. "You could have rescued her! You could have been truthful."

All this time he hunted under my nose, snatching children from the forest. All this time, *he* was my enemy.

Was he laughing at me? At Bébhinn? Rubbing his hands together with glee as he snatched another child away under our noses?

My fingers unfurled.

Unlatching from the beam, his weary hands pleadingly reached for me as I flung him backwards using little more than a flick of my head. His body crashed into the wall, collapsing him onto the unlit fireplace where debris sprung into dust around him.

Cracks formed in the rotted walls, spreading across the room like the dainty branches of a tree. My chest rose more with each rattling breath as I gave in to the primal beckon. The pulsing power of the harvest flowed deeper through my veins, pulling currents to the surface of my skin. Until my hair floated into wild, red tendrils and my skin shimmered with an electric blue pulse.

I couldn't control it.

I didn't *want* to.

A golden mirage encapsulated my hands whole, vibrating them.

None of it was real. He used me. Subdued me and fucked me and made me scream his name. Made me think I wanted it. Made me think I craved it against my very sanity telling me to stay away!

I screamed so hard my tonsils burned. My hands rose and parted, and a flash of brightness blinded the room as my body catapulted backwards into the cobwebbed wall.

Pain. Everywhere. Everything.

My body went limp.

Then there was nothing.

39

WEAK

My throbbing spine brought me to, though I could tell from the warm wetness running from my nose only minutes had passed. I stretched my mouth to stave off a ringing that provided only paltry relief. In the dust-filled aftermath obscuring my sight, I could barely see past the crumpled debris. Moments ago, this had been the wall and roof. Moments ago, I hadn't known betrayal like this.

My eyes skittered over rubble and the chalky layer of dirt on my skin.

What have I done?

Róisín's marred ribbon poked out of the rubble, like the sprout of one of her very own creations.

I grabbed it and scraped myself to my feet, hand cradling my lower back. Through a chesty cough, I instinctively called out, "Caolann? Caolann?"

His name was a ragged cry on cracked lips.

I waited for a reply, but the night was quiet, as if it knew the darkness within me was far greater than its own, because for a moment I'd swallowed its stars and the sound of rest.

I'd killed him. My lips quaked. The version of him I selfishly wanted was gone. He'd never even existed. So why did I feel regret? Feel so empty in a world where he was not?

A cough bellowed from the dust, growing louder. Caolann stumbled into view. A thick gash had split through his eyebrow, cratering it open. Not invulnerable after all.

I wanted to reach out, to comfort him. No. I locked my arm. It was just relief I hadn't killed him. It had to be...

Now that the initial anger and adrenaline simmered, all I wanted was to run. To be free of this hurt. But I couldn't. He was my chance to hear the truth. I owed it to Róisín to stay, and to Fintan, and to every other child he'd stolen.

"Tell me everything," I demanded through gritted teeth. "Now."

His reddened eyes settled on mine, feeling all too familiar to my heart.

The True Gods were his only witness. I saw that now. I couldn't be his persecutor. I didn't have the strength nor the right.

He took a hesitant step closer, his hand reaching out. "Your leg."

I recoiled, avoiding the sight of whatever had alarmed him.

"Tell me the truth, Caolann. Give me the fucking truth."

"Mórrígan."

Mórrígan. Shock hit me like a blow, freezing my body in place.

"She sought Róisín's audience," he said, and the words came with such fluid ease it was clear—clearer than all the stars illuminating his sharp features—this was a release he'd been holding for the longest time. More words tumbled quickly from his mouth. "She was entrusted to grow a private crop. The rising quota was not enough. You saw with your own eyes; Róisín holds the gift of growing things with no water or soil. The Fir na Solas could march right through the desert undetected to our enemy."

"Travel where?" I pressed. "What fight does Saoirse have?"

"Do you not see? The younglings were recruited for war. A war laid dormant for a thousand years. But hear me now, my bound girl, the threat rises. No matter your feelings for me, you must listen when I tell you it spreads throughout Ériu, growing closer to Saoirse each sunrise. Dagda seeks possession of all, and the Tuatha do not hold the strength to defeat him. It is said he trains a new warrior. One with godly strength. That we may be but dust by Lúnasa of next."

My head was shaking, but at his words or my susceptibility to believe him, I couldn't say.

"Dagda *will* invade, make no mistake. They will ride in on mighty red elk with antlers sharpened to slice our young. Our crop will burn. Our homes. Families. We must be on the living side when they come—and trust, they *will* come, Clíona. This, I promise you. Our youngling warriors will be the clan to save us. They are the new age of the Tuatha Dé Danann, trained in secret to stop word travelling to Ardagh on the lips of spies. They will be an unstoppable force when gifted the divine status."

Barmy laughter poured out of me. The crying would come later, in solitude, if I didn't bury it first. "Let me guess, 'Man of the People,' you planned to train them? And what happens when a child is made immortal? Are they to be trapped eternally inside a youthful body while time spoils their mind. Their *soul*. Do you compensate their families for the torture of thinking their children are dead?"

His head hung low, letting the blood trickle faster from his wound. "I intended to train them in Réimse Mór. Mórrígan would not allow it. The rest...the rest I hold no answer for."

"You must've known I'd find out if I won Lúnasa." My hands found my hips, and I scoffed painfully hard when another realisation came to me.

"Now I understand why you refused to help me train—in the beginning. It wasn't the threat on my life you feared, it was the threat of me uncovering your dirty little secret. That you are no man or fucking god, but a coward." How could I be having this conversation with the person I'd been searching for all along? Did he really believe he was doing the right thing? Christ, maybe he was in some twisted way. I hadn't considered that.

The utilitarian viewpoint: the greatest good for the greatest amount of people.

But no.

That couldn't be right. I had to judge him on his actions, no matter the outcome. No matter how many people he thought he was saving. The lives of those children were not his to decide.

A sheen cloyed his gaze. "I feared this day since the moment you told me of your plans to compete. I prayed to the True Gods once you received the divine status you would understand why they were taken. You would get to witness the joys of them living in Magh Mell."

I huffed at him, too exhausted to do anything else. He could probably get the upper hand on me now and easily win.

His brow dipped. "Forget not. You hold secrets, too, Clíona. Each happy moment between us slightly tainted by reprising guilt in your eyes. One that spurs only from great wrongdoings. From bloody hands."

"This is too much." My face sunk into my hands, bloodied from my nose.

Caolann shuffled closer. I shot him a piercing glare. "Don't you dare."

He dared anyway, reaching for me with outstretched hands.

Maybe showing false forgiveness would get him on my side. I let him take my hands. To squeeze comfort into them I wished I'd hated more.

"I am no longer with the Tuatha, not since our night beneath the blue lights. I told you, I went to Magh Mell to sever loose ends. Too many young were being taken for the cause. Too much pain had plighted Saoirse. I feared little would be left to fight for." He shook his head, fighting tears that sparkled like silver under the moonlight. "Yet she sent another to take the younglings, replacing me." It was so easy to see the boy in Caolann now. The innocence the Tuatha had stripped of him too young, so they could put him back together how they saw fit. He never stood a chance.

His guilt is irrelevant. Your feelings are irrelevant. Keep pushing.

"At least help me return them to their families."

"I cannot." He shook all his frustration into my hands, holding my gaze. "The choice was never mine."

I fought from his gentle touch. "Yes, you can! Tomorrow I will fight Rathnor. I'll become Tuatha, and we'll do it together." Saying it aloud sounded like a pipe dream. A nightmare of my own making. But I needed something to hold onto. Keep my failing legs upright.

"If you reveal my truth, it is self-slaughter!"

I mired in my anguish and shrugged at that prospect. A lie. A lie to suggest such indifference when I knew, *I knew*, I wanted anything but.

He swiped the blood crusting his eyelid, nodding slowly for whatever occurred to him. "I hurt the people I care for, and worse those I do not. I see now there is but a sole path to your forgiveness. I will visit Magh Mell this nightfall and harvest my Bua to change Mórrígan's will. Perhaps she will return them—"

I gripped his face despite my better judgement. "You're gonna get yourself killed trying to manipulate her!"

"What is the alternative?"

Only our stifled breaths filled the forest. His question had no answer, and we both knew it.

He was dead either way, every moment simply a countdown to the inevitable.

A fleeting smile of resolve settled over him. "Atonement is upon me." He kissed my forehead, inhaling my hair. My eyes closed, succumbing. Too exhausted to fight.

Weak. I am the one who is weak.

"Keep your guard tomorrow," he muffled against my head, breath heavy. "Follow the plan and you will have the chance to strike him down." He pulled back despite his fingers lingering through the ends of my hair.

My eyes flung open in horror. This was a goodbye.

The end.

He turned on the run, sprinting away.

"No—wait, Caolann!" I reached to harvest him in place, shimmering tendrils shooting into the nothingness of night as his divinity beat me to it, leaving behind the acrid scent of scorched earth and a patch of charred debris.

I was sprinting—bounding. Beelining through the forest blind. Praying to the True Gods I found my way back to the only place I could go before it was too late.

I erratically stumbled into the house, two feet forward instead of one. My hip slammed against the strategizing table as I barreled past it, sending both of us momentarily off balance.

A small candle within a waxy dish lit the room by Rían's bed, teasing close to his mouth with each breath.

I dropped to my knees, dipping into the soft flame's light as I rustled him from his sleep.

A hand gripped my forearm.

His eyes were suddenly open. Alert.

"It is unwise to sneak up on a man who lives by the instinct of the hunt." Rían shifted, slipping his arm from beneath the pillow, a newly whittled blade clenched in his hand.

I pulled from his grip still locked around the circumference of my arm. "There isn't time for games this nightfall."

He didn't forfeit.

I tugged again. "Rían. Enough."

He blinked multiple times, shifting to complete clarity as he noted my wounds. In a wide-eyed gasp, he was upright though barely clothed. "Who did this to you?"

"I..."

"Tell me who harmed you. He will not live to see dawn."

I'd never felt so disjointed. Never wanted someone else to put me back together so badly. Yes, I'm harmed, I wanted to say. I'm falling apart, and I need someone—or just *one* person, to keep me in *one* piece so I can get through the next twenty-four hours of my life.

"Caolann has gone to the Tuatha," I said. The truth. I had to give him that at least. "He's in trouble. It was him all this time. He—" Nausea curled around my tongue. I spoke despite the feeling. "It was him who took the children. Rían, your brother is a monster." Every time I replayed the truth of those words, my mind still pathetically searched for all the ways it couldn't be true.

Rían pulled away from my grip on his elbow—a hold I must have taken unconsciously. He stepped into his trousers before gathering his bow and weapons belt in the dim light.

"Do you hear me?" I said in stern, hushed tones, following him about his tasks. "This whole time it was Caolann. They're being recruited by Mórrígan. He said Dagda is coming."

He counted his arrows in the quiver, two fingers running over them as he mouthed the numbers.

"Rían."

He tied his belt methodically, fastening it in the larger notch next to the worn hole. I hadn't noticed how much he had filled out until this very moment.

"Look at me!" I snapped.

He stilled.

Why wouldn't he look at me?

It was his fist that broke composure, *slamming* into the dry mud wall.

I recoiled with a sharp gasp.

Bits crumpled onto the floor as he gently drew his hand back out to flex it. "Brother, you fool."

My hand found my hilt as I edged back. "You don't sound surprised." I couldn't take another betrayal. Is that why he wouldn't look at me?

Please look at me.

Rían stood closer to match whatever unease I couldn't stifle, let alone stop. He watched my grip tightening around my weapon as his face turned noticeably stoic. He watched the bob of my throat. The shake on my bottom lip. The ends of my hair curling in blood and sweat that hadn't yet dried, before he finally, *finally* looked at me with those entrancing green eyes.

Relief bellowed out of me.

It was clear now: the sheen. He was just as betrayed as I was. There was no denying the coating of it irritating his eyes.

"Recall, Clíona, the Dylis raised him," he said, his voice thick. "His kindness lives in his core, always wanting to escape, yet he is trained to obey those of great power. All he understands is accepting orders. To be a fucking pawn...to be a prophecy of our mother."

Rían's gaze dipped, but just as I geared up to tell him not to wander off in anger again, I realised his eyes had simply fallen to trace my body in the soft light. The parts of me that weren't afraid. The parts that weren't injured.

A flicker in his jaw. A tightening in it as he tugged a small wedge of debris from my thigh. I seethed and hunched a fraction before recalling I'd suffered worse. Until his gaze met my awaiting one again. There was something new about it—wild. Hard where it had once been soft—even in the days when I was a prisoner. It was a look I envisioned might become permanent if his path didn't bend a better way. A kinder way.

I curved my head to get a clearer understanding of him. The answer came immediately.

Oh. He knew. He knew my wounds were the result of fighting his brother. It wasn't me who angered him.

It was Caolann.

His protectiveness gave me permission to falter against my better judgement. "How could he do this to us?" The question was so quiet I wondered if he heard the sadness in it. Or heard it at all.

Whatever tiny gap was still lingering between us, Rían managed to fill it further until there was no space for paranoia or distrust. His arms wrapped around me, holding the weight of my pain until I lost sense of everything. Threads of indecision melted away into the floor's crevices. The shadows of flame danced lazily on the wall ahead. Rían's warmth spread into my skin, soothing me. My breaths steadied, finally allowing me to catch a grip of the turmoil wanting to pour out.

As I pulled from him, he traced the gash on my forearm. I'd hardly noticed. My eyes lazily ran over it, and I still couldn't care. Couldn't tell if it was even meant to hurt.

I sniffled into resolve. "I'm a mess. There is no time for this." I moved to find something to bandage me up.

"Clíona, wait." Rían's rigid hand pressed to the dead centre of my chest.

My chin scrunched as I took in his touch that immediately replaced my sadness with a rising grievance. "What are you doing?"

Rebelling, he pressed closer again, his head inclined a near foot above my own. "I would never do that to you, Clíona. I would never cause you hurt the way he did. Even recalling shooting that arrow into your skin...it aches me." His hand slid up into the groove of my neck so that his fingers rested softly over the old scar where he had hit me.

This poor boy and his demons. I wasn't worth the ache. I didn't even care about what he had done anymore. I'd do it every day for the rest of my life if it kept him away from the edge of dark clouds and cliffs.

My eyes closed as I turned from his gentle touch and beckon, surely fuelled by how heightened everything had become in an instant. This wasn't the time to pit brothers against one another. For Rían to use me as his beginning point of revenge against Caolann. There was nothing between us beyond friendship, which I needed now more than—

"I knew you were never from the Tearminn." My head jerked. He began to move his hand in small circles over the scar, keeping me in place. "You fell out of the sky. A beautiful, broken star. A thing of jagged light. And when you called into my darkness with such a loud knock, such brightness, it gave me passage back to the surface."

I swallowed, immobilised by the shock.

He knows.

My cover was finally blown.

Rían took my shock, my silence, to explain—or perhaps condemn. "What Caolann thrives on in strength, I hold in quiet observation. I do not always need to force the words from one's mouth to know what is true. I have wanted to tell you for so long. That these words have endlessly ached and tumbled over the inside of my mouth, calling on me to say it. To say I knew you were from another world. A blanket upon our own. My mother prophesied that long ago. Told me as a boy that when I grew up, I would meet a woman with red hair in a forest. That an eyeless man would count the fingers on her hand faster than a seeing one. It was said she would fall to her knees for me, and it would be my duty to protect her. Not Caolann's—*mine*. I denied it when first laying eyes on you..." His stare is a mesh of intensity and openness. His thumb slotted into the curve where my ear and jaw met. "But leaving you to the suffering of the Fir na Solas, that nightfall, imagining you all alone in the crypts of the Carraig..." A grunt stirred from his locked mouth. A noise too firm and inward for me to think he was angered by anyone but himself that night. "I knew I had to protect you. I kept the truth, even from my own brother, to keep you safe."

"You knew," came those two words looping in my mind.

"I knew." Rían's voice was deep, quiet, reassuring. Telling me it was okay. His thumb slipped to hook my chin and bring me back to him.

The movement was so sharp, so swift, a bolt shot through me heading south.

Getting ahead of his thoughts, ones I pretended not to have, I warned, "Don't."

God, how long have I been shunning this...whatever this was?

My lips parted. It would be so fucking easy to kiss him right now. To satisfy him. To delight in the pain it would bring Caolann. Let that bastard know betrayal, so he could have a taste of this feeling channelling through us, drawing us together.

But was that all this was? Hurting Caolann?

Because why did every thought I ever had about Rían up to this point suddenly feel so chaotically buried? Ignored. Pushed aside from the moment he brought me to my knees on the forest bed.

Why does my heart beat this hungry way whenever he is near? Or my lips feel so plush in constant anticipation for when I might dig all those hidden moments up with hands, and teeth, and not a single shred of patience?

Rían's finger ran along the inlay of my lips.

It really would be no great effort if I were to tilt up and kiss him right now. No great effort to pretend I didn't in the aftermath.

Perhaps reading my thoughts, Rían's free hand slid down the slope of my chest to my stomach. My eyes followed and my breath stopped as his fingers crept around my waist. I lost sight of them to their tight clasp of the skin barely above my bottom. It felt out of place for him, the gesture too sensual. Too sure when I'd never given him a reason to think as much. It was Caolann I wanted. Always Caolann.

My eyes reverted to Rían.

Then why am I not walking away?

He moved a loose piece of hair behind my ear. I fed into it the tenderness of it, pressing my lips against his palm.

"Rían." God, why did the name I'd uttered to stop this madness suddenly feel like an exaltation? Like it was a word given to my lips for guilty worship alone.

He inched closer to me, if possible, his hand drifting lower onto my bottom where flesh met grip that only intensified the seduction of his words, slow against my ear. "*My love.*"

My love.

There was no ask in return with those inevitable words. No demand for love back. Not even ownership. It was messianic. An exhale of devotion. It was...intoxicating.

I took in a sharp inhale and clasped the skin of my lip between teeth. Those two words hooked me. They sent me into a state of suspension I didn't want to come back from. I suddenly felt so weak, I wanted to fall to my knees for him without any Bua enacting it this time.

I flinched, a fraction at how quickly I'd fallen into lustful madness.

It drew a lazy grin from his mouth I wasn't expecting.

I grit my teeth, barely fighting. "You shouldn't call me that," I warned, head inclining.

Grabbing my bottom firmer, his thumb pressed into my hip where the skin was supple. "Simply tell me no, and I will stop."

My head dropped to his ever-tightening grip. No. All I had to say was no and this feeling that shouldn't be there could drift away. We were friends. Or maybe not friends, but definitely not this.

His close-lipped smile persisted.

Why did every part of me have the urge to jump into his molten eyes and let their heat turn me into an irrelevant vapour?

Oh, how wrong I was. There was heat in him, too. Not the fiery blaze his brother emanated, but rather a simmering magma. I imagined it as a slow and thick thing, waiting to erupt from within. Waiting to burst out and wreck me.

Returning to his stoic expression, he lifted his free hand to my hair until all his fingers ran through it, tugging for me to stare up at him. "Tell me no."

"I—"

"Tell me."

No. No. No. NO.

"I—I can't." I flicked my eyes to him.

If there was a Chronos of this world, orchestrating all time, he had chosen *this* exact moment to stop turning the cogs. We were in immutable status, just staring, swallowing each other's eyes within this plane where endings didn't seem to exist.

And if this strike in the timeline wrecked the expanse of every moment and design and law of physics, the before and after and beyond, just to have this feeling that shouldn't exist last even a fraction longer than I ever deserved—so fucking be it.

Then, as if needing to catch up, everything forwarded in an instant; something ravenous narrowed Rían's stare, heaving him. Grabbing my chin without a moment to waste he pressed his lips to mine, staggering me back several paces, and yet his mouth only pushed harder.

I needed air, but he'd silently told me it wasn't mine to have anymore. I needed to be rational, but his tongue twisted into mine with fervid intent I matched over and over.

Dipping both his forearms under my thighs with a quiet grunt—my body shaking at the sound—I followed his lips, only breaking free to gasp and moan as he hitched me up against the wooden beam with all his weight against me. His fingers rolled and stretched the skin of my bottom as his tongue slid over my neck, warm and wet.

He unbuckled himself.

This was too much. Too delicious. Every buried trace of my tucked away yearning was undeniable now. I'd always seen him as too young and distant. And yet here he was understanding every inch of my body.

The insides. The outsides. The sides so wet it was becoming impossible not to drop mere inches down this wooden beam and take him in me.

My hips rolled.

I slid lower, feeling him rub against me.

His fingers ran harshly down the inlay of my thigh. So close. So close I—

"Rían," I said, unable to stop the plea in its stretch.

He froze, catching me with his beautiful green glare that meshed together with too many moments I'd shared with his own brother. This was wrong. Twisted. Greedy.

"We need—"

"I know," he said, deflating. His grip loosening. "I know."

Still pulsing, he pressed his lips to mine twice more, then lowered me gently, pulling away to fix himself and fit a knife into the baldric strapped to his chest.

"He's gone to talk to Mórrígan," I said while fixing my skirt. Straight back to business despite the hum still coating my body and—I stared at his groin—the blatant bulge still in his pants. I cleared my throat. "He plans to ask her to let them go. He thinks she'll listen to him if he uses his Bua on her."

"She will slaughter him for questioning her."

"Come," I said, finally snapping to and fixing my own armour. "We need to find Lester and Áed. Just don't tell them all the truth. It'll do us no good for them to know."

Rían slung his quiver over his shoulder as I finished knotting my breastplate. "Our sole hope is she casts him to the Carraig until deciding his fate."

"Then do what you do best and talk him out of this mess."

"We must divide. Find your recruits. Under darkness I will scout the Carraig, subdue the Fir na Solas and hide among the trees to await his and your arrival."

"Please help him, Rían. We need him to rescue the children. For Róisín."

Rían grabbed the back of my head to lock me into his forehead. "No, Clíona. You need him, for he lives in your heart."

40
HUNGRY HOG ROAST

"He should be here by now," Lester said.

"Five more minutes," I answered.

"You said that five minutes ago."

"Yeah, well, I fucking lied then, didn't I." I clasped my thigh, hard, failing to syphon some of the painful worry away from my thoughts or the bite from my words. I wanted to believe so badly that Caolann was safe. That maybe Mórrígan could show forgiveness. That he could find penance without finding death. But my coiling gut told me otherwise.

This was never going to be his story.

Our story.

I had run the long route to the Carraig through tree cover with Lester by my side. Áed had rushed ahead to scout with little need of convincing. I hated lying to them. Áed's own brother, Fintan, had been taken by Caolann's hand and I was asking him to offer protection. In some ways I was becoming no better than Caolann himself. Or maybe I'd never been any better no matter what I'd tried to convince myself since signing up for the trials.

Taking stock and staking the grounds from my hidden position a hundred metres out behind a line of bushes, I counted a wall of Fir na Solas barricading the entrance.

Outnumbered.

Another formation marched into the area.

Very outnumbered.

Despite my worry, I somehow smiled—a real one. This could only be a good sign. Nobody guards a dead man. But thirty odd Fir na Solas—that was for a god.

"He lives," I called over my shoulder to Lester.

"For now."

I could hear the undertone in his voice telling me not to be naive when we needed to focus.

This was true: Áed had to be kept in our sights. He was in a heated exchange with two soldiers who refused to entertain his dirt-kicking antics, maintaining steadfast loyalty to their command.

He really was a good friend to have my back like this when I'd led him blind.

But will he be tomorrow?

"He should be here by now," Lester said again, his tone impressively neutral when I was undoubtedly on his last nerve. "Do you hear me, Clíona? Rían should be here by now. I sense a disturbance. The wind pulls a foreign way."

I peered over my shoulder to him, to the worry he was holding in his eyes. He blinked, shutting me out, but it was too late. The smell of death festered in the air worse than anything the trials had offered us.

I sighed and dipped my head. No more hiding. Time had run out.

"Let me scout the northern side for Rían," he said. I shot him a firm stare, slotting back into the role of leader. "Wait for my return."

We clasped hands and then he was gone. A sword on his back, and without his trademark smile. I worried his youthful days were over. He was sixteen, but this world had carved him into manhood with blunt tools that would inevitably leave scars.

Alone, thoughts of the awful things happening to Caolann flooded into my mind in black, sticky waves. They could have been pulling his fingernails as he begged for mercy. What if they'd captured Rían and were torturing him to get to Caolann? I flinched from the thought. I couldn't lose them. I couldn't bear the thought of being without either of them.

I *had* to know.

I ran into the opening, betting on the poor odds that my new status might provide me answers.

"Áed," I called. My grip was steadfastly locked around the knife on my thigh holster.

He paused, squinting against the rising sun behind me. His words were indistinguishable as he suddenly waved to me in wide arches.

"What?" I hesitantly stepped closer, and that grip tightened on my weapon even more.

The repeated words finally unravelled in my ears. "Run back."

Run?

"*Run!* They wish to capture you. They intend to make—" A soldier walloped the butt of her spear into his stomach. He clutched his midsection as the pain drew him to his knees.

I skidded to a stop, dragging grass from the soil. My heart became a thing to choke on. It was frighteningly loud. So loud, it echoed in my ears and sent waves of pulsing energy through my entire body.

Fir na Solas stomped in unison.

An indistinguishable command brought their spears to a horizontal line, all aimed in my direction.

Another command.

They charged, their voices loud, their legs trampling dirt.

Instinctively turning, I made it a mere foot before a warm, tar-like substance wrapped my legs. With a jolting tug, it flipped me. My face hit the grass before my body so hard, I swore two knitting needles had been rammed up my nose, blinding me with pain until my vision wobbled. Blood trailed as they dragged me, belly down and backwards. I grasped high patches of grass with my good hand, desperate to break free of the numbing suction as my dress rose above my knees, my thighs, my bottom.

Think, Clíona. Think.

The soil saved me once upon the Comeragh. It could do it again.

I focused, latching onto the roots as an anchor. Pleading with the True Gods to help me. To see me as worthy. My dragging core began to vibrate against the rattling soil. My harvest thickened, pulling deeper and deeper underground; my teeth chattered for the pleasure of tasting this raw power. How easy the seduction drew me in.

A switch clicked, soothingly, making me feel distant from the surrounding chaos.

A single word came to mind: destruction.

I unleashed my harvest into the vast spread of the area. I imagined all the roots beneath turning golden.

A breath.

Another.

Mounds of earth shot to the sky around like detonated landmines spraying dirt in every direction. The noise mimicked explosives as soil rained down around me.

The stringy warmth on my legs loosened enough for me to roll onto my backside.

Soldiers all around me contorted in awful shapes, though those left standing furiously continued.

Áed was subdued beneath the foot of a soldier who must have harvested a great bruiser power to keep him down.

My patience snapped into two colluding pieces, egging each other on to wreak havoc.

And who was I to stop them?

Breathless, I stood from the settling ground to address the soldiers. "Don't you realise who I am? I am to battle in Lúnasa. Where is your respect for the tradition of trial? For your gods!"

Even when one fight away from being a god, *their* god, I was treated like nothing. Like I was less than nothing—Ardagh scum.

A murderous urge revived in me, once again tainting my path to absolution. My harvest rumbled, growing hotter and thicker, stretching my veins and muscles. "You thought I wouldn't retaliate?" I addressed them. Addressed them all. And they were listening now—finally. With faces that had me think a far worse creature stood behind me. "You thought you could attack me, and I'd take it? No. That's not me. If you lead with threat, expect me to follow without mercy! I'll kill every last one of you if I fucking have to. I'll do it with pleasure," I said, my tongue sliding out of my mouth as my teeth grated over it.

They hesitated, siding unsure stares at one another. I enjoyed that—relished it, even. They were enduring the same fear I was forced to suffer my first day in Saoirse. When they attacked me. When they shoved my face into dirt and hog roasted me.

Now was my chance for warranted revenge.

An eye for an eye doesn't make the world blind, it makes it easier to ignore the bloodshed of necessary vengeance.

With the guide of my harvesting hand, nail beds *aching* from wedged mud, fingers and stumps glowing in golden shimmers I could finally see for its beauty, I rose the Fir na Solas. The spurts of light stemming out of me spread like tentacles, grabbing one, and another, until I'd locked onto so many I'd lost count. What did it matter? They weighed *nothing.* Insignificant beings dangled midair for my pleasure alone.

With a burst of motion, one still on foot hurled his spear at me, its force crackling through the air with static harvest.

A mere thought diverted his weapon into a tree.

And a second cracked his bones into a submitting kneel, I only gave a glance because he wept so loud.

Pathetic.

The soldiers above twitched, recklessly battling with what little power they had over their limbs.

The whites in their eyes turned red. Their faces purpled as oxygen depleted. But no remorse came. I was so powerful. So beautiful in this savage glory.

Áed shook my lax shoulders. I hadn't noticed his approach. "They cannot breathe! This is not who you are, my friend."

Let them suffer. Let me have my revenge. It's good they couldn't breathe.

Áed repeated, "This is not who are, Clíona. Fight the darkness."

His words pressed down on me, but the darkness whispered sweetly, promising power and vengeance. I was tempted to give in, to let go of the light that had guided me through all my mistakes. My body trembled, caught between the seductive pull of damnation and the faint glimmer of hope that Áed's voice ignited within me.

Didn't he know I wasn't strong enough to resist the allure of darkness when everything inside me screamed to embrace it? Revenge burned through my veins. Yet beneath that, a sliver of who I used to be called out.

Áed's soothing words entered slowly, distilling the anger in me. "Fight it. Fight the harvest." I growled from my core, pulled the dagger from my waist, and jabbed the tip into my thigh, cutting the line of power. I shot him a weary glance and tugged the knife. A grunt followed.

My hands fisted, and the soldiers concurrently dropped. A rippling of snapped bones and groans reverberated the clearing. But again, a lucky few were on their feet.

"Capture her!"

I wasn't strong enough to harvest a second attack so soon. Not when the guilt was ripening again. My dripping nose throbbed so hard I feared it might explode.

Áed grabbed my hand, leading me into the forest.

We'd need to regroup with others. We'd need—

Áed fell first; the crack of his head against the ground was a sound so visceral, my stomach lurched.

I staggered, each step another against the rising tide of dread.

And yet, I couldn't look back despite my harvest lassoing onto his limp body to drag him with me. I couldn't even turn to see if he was okay. If *I* was making his injuries worse! The forest loomed ahead, our sanctuary we had to reach, but the distance seemed to stretch with every faltering stride.

Thick droplets from my nose began to dot the soil. My arms were entirely numb. "C'mon Áed, you heavy bastard, don't give up—"

Sharp impact exploded across my head, searing through my senses.

The ground rose to meet me.

My cheek hit the cold grass.

The trees muddied as a bind wrapped around me, squeezing, until I closed my eyes.

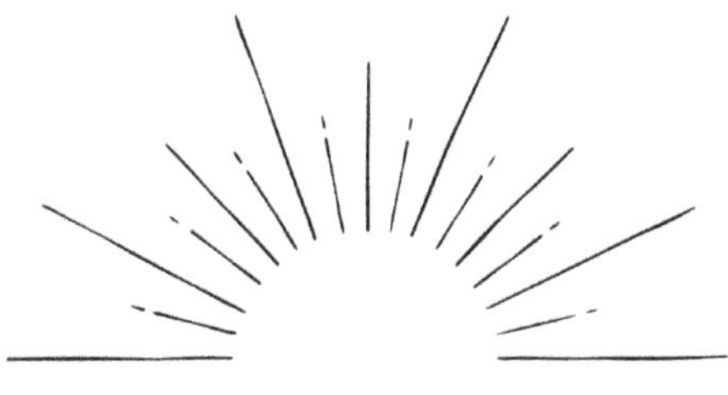

41
NOT MY VANGUARD

Still blinded, my hands were bound, chafed against my tailbone. My arm—*oh fuck*—the searing pain forced me to draw a deep, cavernous gulp—as if pain were a thing I could swallow and be rid of. It must have been injured in my fall.

Rolling a little sideways, I continued to take stock of my awful condition—okay, not just the fingers, but the whole arm was a write-off against whatever I was about to go up against. But what else? I was bleeding from my thigh. Yes, self-inflicted, but still hurt like a bitch. My nose was likely broken, and my strength was also pretty much drained after the run-in with the Fir na Solas. It was like I had to fight as a human. A *weak* human with no Bua—and no clan.

A crowd rumbled around me. As I stirred myself onto bruised knees, their chatter hushed. My spine chilled. I didn't need my sight to know all eyes were locked on me.

"And they say we marched in twos. From the womb of our mother into the crook of an old tree. There we learnt the power of the root..." The crowd mumbled along the words in hefty unison with that of a woman's lead voice, a lilting, melodic one that spoke the words with complete clarity.

"...what is the day in the life of the eternal. The immortal. The blessed. Then to devote oneself to the virtue of good people. Of Saoirsians. The chosen mortals."

The crowd silenced.

"And so, I bid thee welcome. Come forth, all who dare, to the final trial of Lúnasa."

A pause.

Just my own breath on the wind.

A hand ripped the bind free from my eyes.

I squinted against the sun's peak light.

The crowd erupted, their cheering, their roars, shaking the ground. I never guessed so many would want to witness the misery I'd fallen into.

The final trial. I couldn't tell if it was relief or blinding fear cutting through my body in shaking waves.

"We unite past glory with present in this deciding battle," she continued passionately, her voice rising over the noise of the crowd. "A battle where our final competitor faces a previous successor." This gentle but fierce voice was unfamiliar, and yet I knew wholeheartedly who *she* was now. It was as though some tether between worlds had been thickening, and shortening, until reaching this moment.

Encircled by rows of Saoirsians and a makeshift wooden platform rising off the ground, I bitterly concluded where I was in a broken heartbeat: Réimse Mór. The place where Róisín introduced me to the world of harvesting Bua was no longer welcoming. The crowd made the field appear minuscule, eclipsing its true form, filling each corner; even the trees were mounted with younglings looking in. I kneeled on the cusp of an inlaid circle, another mirroring my actions on the farther side.

My tongue—why does it feel so big in my mouth? Why can't I suddenly breathe? What if I swallow it? At least that would trap the sheer hysteria crawling to escape as the reality of what was happening caught up with me.

My bones trembled; a torrent of tears hovered on the edge of falling. Turmoil would be an improvement over both.

"Caolann," I whispered in a wheezing breath.

This battle was no longer about the Tuatha finding a new comrade. It was a game of revenge neither wanted to play.

My head swivelled to Mórrígan.

She smiled malevolently from the platform's centre with not so much as a wrinkle creasing her skin. She stretched her thin arms flared with green silk, consuming and relishing the crowd's mumbling adoration. She was how I imagined her: exuding grace and beauty. Hair rippling down her back in waves, a glistening shade of onyx in the sun. A bronze crown, hammered into the shape of flowers and thorns, rested on her head.

"This Lúnasa, our competitors are Clíona of Ardagh descent, and Caolann, previous champion, *former* comrade of the Tuatha Dé Danann," she declared in elegant tones from her position amongst the opulence decorating the wooden platform. Golden cushions. Meek servants dressed in sheer gowns. Goblets and decanters of wine in sparkling whites and ruby reds.

Offerings from the villagers also spotted the edges of the platform. Hundreds, just like on the Carraig. Discarded and haphazardly tossed aside with no care for the sacrifice the Saoirsians had made. Food that could have fed their family. Fabrics that could have clothed their children. Reckless symbols of adoration, imbued with hope. A crude reminder of the intentional divide between human longing and divine disregard.

Reading my disdain, Mórrígan's eyes gleamed with a malevolent spark, dark and glittering like sharp, unrelenting shards of obsidian. They were eyes that could charm tides and seduce winds, yet cunning was wrapped in their depths.

I bristled. Malicious sow. Didn't she know I'd never harm Caolann for divinity, despite the betrayal I felt?

Rathnor, behind, mimicked her joy, hands clasped behind his back, no doubt taking pleasure in my suffering.

"With great heartache," she continued, "I have discovered these warriors are loyal solely to my brother, Dagda. They are Ardagh spies, sent here to wreak havoc on our lands." Her smile collapsed to deathly stone, so sharp, her cheekbones resembled blades. "As tradition goes, I have stripped Caolann of his immortality and so for their crimes"—her smile settled on me—"this battle will be to the slaughter. The sole living will perish in the bleak cells of the Carraig."

The crowd burst into whispers and gasps. Others heckled, condemning us.

A ringing pooled in my ears, taking me so far away from her words I thought I might be able to pretend I hadn't heard them. It was my body that took the blunt force instead; I slumped into the grass. Each breath brought me closer to green blades that curled around my limp fingers—my stubs.

I wouldn't kill Caolann. I *couldn't*.

The forced hand of death often invoked the truth. A confession to a lie. A declaration to a past lover. A forgiveness to bring selfish peace at the end.

Still, I knew with my guts and the bits in between, regardless of the awful things he'd committed, he wouldn't kill me either.

My eyes sought his, but distance veiled his reaction. He hadn't moved even an inch from his kneeling position.

Mórrígan drew cloth from a large wooden sundial. "You have until the sun licks its peak." The light approached noon.

I looked at his frozen state, the warrior, *my* warrior, then back to the creeping light touching the grain: ten minutes at most.

Nothing happened. Nobody moved or made a noise. Not the wind nor the birds nor Saoirsians. Afraid of their gods, they didn't dare speak up to protect the outsiders.

"I won't kill him!" I shouted, my voice trembling and cracking with the strain of my weakening resolve. "You can shove your status up yer' hole. I'm no lackey to your bidding."

"Well." She smirked, throwing a high-browed glance at Rathnor.

"Bring in the others," Rathnor ordered, his tone rash like his patience and enjoyment had finally run thin. Unless he was sour it wasn't him who got to take my life.

Get in line.

A platoon of Fir na Solas divided the crowd by force, rippling them outwards. I edged forward to get a better view of what else they could possibly throw at us when the answer became all too obvious.

"One, two, three." I inhaled with each count. "Four."

Four people—bagged and bound. With little care, the soldiers thrust them to their knees beneath the platform. Harboured muffles came from beneath their bags, drawing similar from my mouth.

I searched Caolann for a reaction, but still—nothing.

He must have known. Just how I did. We had entered that place, that dark version of Ériu, where there was no return.

At the sight of their freed faces, bruised and bloody, pain rippled through me, making my very being turn buttery beneath the sun.

Before me kneeled battered versions of Bébhinn, Áed, Lester, and Rían. Rían—gagged and suffering an eye so swollen and black he could hardly see from it. And Lester. My stomach twisted. All but two fingers remained on his hands, fresh blood painting his knuckles. How many times had they cut them off to make him look so pale?

My lips quivered.

"They're not healing," I whispered to myself.

"Enough," Mórrígan shrilled, her fingers splayed to quiet the growing commotion of the suddenly riling crowd. "If you do not participate in this trial, your most loved will be sacrificed for Saoirse."

A soldier cut the binds on my wrist.

I instinctively stood, staring at each of them—or what was left of them.

Blood dripped across Bébhinn's forehead, her feathers now clumped and crimson. Her eyes met mine, and her lips tightened into a firm line. She shook her head ominously, a silent refusal. She would not pit her life against mine.

I stared back at her relentlessly, teeth gritting. I had to at least try.

There had to be an angle. To save them all.

I couldn't save Caolann and myself—that much was certain. But them...maybe? My thoughts fought themselves into a circle. Or maybe I was just moving in a circle.

Caolann finally stood from his stupor. I cradled my arm. Saving them meant killing him, or myself.

In some twisted way, that last option felt like the best one.

I turned to Mórrígan and huffed a laugh. What else could I do at this point? She thought she could threaten me when only *I* knew her biggest secret. "You wouldn't be this brave if I told these people what *you* did to their children. To their young."

Her nostrils flared. The slightest movement cracking her pristine exterior, but oh, I saw.

A flurry of chatter broke out in the crowd.

Rathnor divinely moved to Bébhinn's side, yanking her blood-stained hair. "We will start by slaughtering this creped woman."

Bébhinn remained ever brave, breaking her tight-lipped disgust to spit at Rathnor's feet.

The crowd murmured, rising into unhappy heckles. "The innocent cannot be punished."

"Lester is but a youngling," another cried in dismay.

We were outsiders, but Lester, Bébhinn and Áed...that was a step too far for Saoirsians.

Commotion rippled through the riled-up crowd, the squeal of disgruntled babies pitching highest.

"*Silence,*" Mórrígan roared. "I am your god, Banríon of the Tuatha Dé Danann. None will question my rule. None will dare to even *think* such treasonous things. I did not simply descend this day to entertain trivial battles. I came to deliver a wicked truth. A truth my loyal Saoirsians deserve to hear. Yes, we keep your young in Magh Mell."

The crowd collectively gasped, and the moment of bravery I'd found to challenge her crumpled with my shoulders. She'd sacrificed my one piece of leverage—my one chance to get us all out of this without harm.

A curl crept onto her lip as she revelled within her glory. "Those said to be lost to the forest. The younglings of Saoirse. They serve a great purpose in these lands, and you will deem them honourable. Do not dare to question my rule, for they came to us *willingly*. You see, war threatens the lands of Saoirse by the hands of Dagda's army. A war that intends to perish you all and take all that remains. Take your chopped limbs for supper. Take your home's wood to set alight the fires they wish to spread across all Ériu. It is the most gifted young who will save you. Those who bravely train in Magh Mell are to become the new age of Tuatha Dé Danann."

Control dwindled from my body as she pressed me further and further into a corner. Suffocating me.

Caolann hadn't said a word. Not when told of a battle to the death, not when Rían was revealed. What was he thinking? Would he try to influence my decisions? Would he stand down?

"Now on with it, Rathnor," Mórrígan directed. "Kill the woman."

Rathnor pulled Bébhinn's head back, his dagger inclined to swipe her throbbing jugular.

"No!" I begged, staggering forward. "Not her."

Rathnor released her head and sucked his white-rimmed lips.

A bout of nausea licked the back of my tongue. I knew exactly what I'd done—started a new game.

"No, you say?" He cracked his rolling neck. "*Ugh*. Very well." He walked behind each of them, back and forth, brushing his hand along their backs to toy with me. To squeeze me to see if I might burst. "You choose, wild one."

He pressed. "Perhaps Lester?"

Lester whimpered as he brought the knife to his neck.

"Or Rían?"

"No!" Caolann shouted—finally.

No, not Rían. I couldn't live in a world without Rían.

"It seems that leaves us with..."

I looked at Áed, and he looked at me, terrified, shaking, utterly resigned.

"No," I pleaded to Rathnor, hands conjoined as I bore my most vulnerable self to him. "I'll do it. I'll fight Caolann." Icy dread washed over me, each heartbeat pounding, pounding, *pounding* with the weight of this impossible choice. My throat felt barbed. I choked on the agony of knowing my decision, my *words,* were tearing apart what remained of my shattered world.

"Yes, you will fight Caolann. Alas, for your hesitation and ill speaking of your Banríon, Áed will be the brunt." Rathnor grinned, hand clenched around Áed's Fás Fada. "Never forget, Clíona. It was you who caused this."

I reached my weak, harvesting hand in a futile attempt to intervene, but it was too late. With one deep, slow slice, Rathnor dragged his knife across Áed's neck with tortuous precision.

Torrid fire hollowed my organs, turning my insides to ash. The backdrop of the world was tearing apart.

A waterfall of red cascaded from the gaping wound in Áed's throat, staining the grass, his clothes, his arms. His eyes, once filled with hope and determination, achingly widened, *pleading* for my help. A way out of the unfolding of his life.

My breath came in ragged wheezes. I wanted to tell him he'd be okay, but we both knew, staring at one another with tear-filled eyes and stricken with fear, nothing would ever be okay in this dark world again.

"I'm sorry," I choked, my voice breaking into ragged sobs. My hands trembled as I clasped them together, wringing them raw. "I'm so—" My breath faltered. "—sorry!"

"Oh, leave some of the theatrics to the rest of us," Rathnor sneered with grizzly amusement. Then, with an air of cold finality, he raised his sword once more and chopped it down on the back of Áed's neck.

I jolted back, my sticky mouth agape.

Áed's head, severed from his lifeless body, fell haphazardly, rolling to its disturbing rest. The blood-soaked body slumped forward, eerily still as the macabre pool of crimson spread across green grass beneath.

He was gone. *Murdered.* Taken from me. From Ruadh. From reuniting with his lost brother. And for what? A sick game?

Rathnor's chortling bravado sucked me from my anguish, contorting it into wrath. My hands and chin trembled as I heaved like a bull had possessed me, and though my head was lowered, my eyes flicked to him.

He grinned and drew his longsword from beneath his sapphire cloak—always one step ahead of my own plans.

Running a finger along its sharp edge, he allowed it to slice his flesh, leaving a trail of blood across the blade. "You see, Clíona. This is no ordinary sword. A simple blood sacrifice, and it is much, *much* more."

A soft glow began to take shape around the weapon.

"Mórrígan gifted me this. Her late brother's sword."

My organs revived, filling with knots for his words. This was Nuada's sword. The fourth and final Treasure. A weapon no mortal being could defeat.

My determination to kill him didn't falter despite the crippling odds. Win or lose, I had to try. I had to avenge Áed, lifeless on the ground. Two pieces. Never to be whole again.

Caolann rushed to me across the clearing. "Do not fight him, Clíona!"

Reaching me, red-eyed and depleted—he clutched my arm. I trailed his touch with my gaze, wondering if this was the last time I'd ever feel his skin on mine. If I hadn't driven him to march to his own death, might there have been a chance to find forgiveness?

"He still holds his divinity. And no mortal is a match for Nuada's sword."

"Help the others," I whispered. "Get Rían's gag off. Free them and run. Run anywhere. Hide."

His fingers curled tighter around my forearm. "I beg, Clíona. I will not let you sacrifice yourself for us. I will fight him in your place."

I shrugged from his touch. "You don't get a say. You never did."

"Clí—"

"Go! Help the others. Get Rían out of here." Swallowing whatever his next words were, he used his lips instead to fleetingly kiss me. I savoured it, sure it would be our last. Then he was gone, dashing to Rían's aid, respecting my wishes to carry out what had always been *my* fight. And it made me wonder: was this always the way it was meant to be? Had I been brought to this land by the True Gods themselves to eradicate the blight rooted in their legacy?

With clarity and confidence, I began to harvest; heat poured into my cupped hands, brewing a powerful storm, miraged and bright, flurrying around me, stretching wider and beyond anything I'd ever controlled. I didn't need my primal side anymore. I was the powerful one. *Me*. I'd never felt more in control within the chaos.

Rathnor rounded his glowing sword, readying himself with hands gripped on its hilt for what was to come.

Fit to burst and heated whole, I harvested toward him with a lengthy roar. The bystanders staggered while Mórrígan stood taller, still with that cunning look in her sparkling eyes that ingested torture for pleasure.

Flexing his sword with a controlled swing, he parried me single-handedly, his thickening light dissipating my golden flecks to nothing against the clash of *twanging* metal. Judging by the widening of Rathnor's feline grin, his offence was something that brought him pure delight.

All it did for me was enhance fury.

Resolute, I harvested again, surging it out with both hands as I edged closer to him.

Again, he fought off the attack.

Again. And again. Draining me.

Blood dripped from my nose as I reached him, Caolann's knife drawn.

He swung to strike me vertically.

I dodged it diagonally with grace I'd never owned before.

A rotten noise shrilled from his mouth as he punched me clean in the eye.

I staggered back onto my knee. "You wouldn't—stand a chance—without that sword," I said between heavy breaths.

He barely raised a brow.

I'd need to press harder—more personal. I needed to play him at his own game of twisted words.

My shoulders pressed back as I rose to him as best I could. "You disgrace your beloved mother. To have a son like you"—I spat at his feet—"I bet she turns in her grave from morning to dusk."

Rigidity overcame him, and his lips thinned until they disappeared at the hands of his fury.

"What a disappointment you are, Rathnor."

"Slaughter her," Mórrígan ordered.

Boasting, he sheathed his sword and bowed to me so close we were nose to nose. His minty breath was inescapable. His muddy gaze, wild with power.

Every muscle in my body screamed to turn, to be rid of the sickly smell, but I stared into his evil eyes for nothing else than to prove I was brave—even in the face of death.

Rathnor brushed the crusting blood from my nose and falsely frowned. "It would be so very simple...to take your life and end your suffering. But no," he sang, wagging his finger. "I have a better plan before I take my final token."

He brushed his cape aside, with the deft slick of his hand, withdrawing a blade from its hilt.

I seized his wrist to stop him.

He unclenched the weapon, allowing it to fall securely into the hand he'd positioned beneath. Then he let it fly, right toward my loved ones.

My eyes frantically flickered between them to find his chosen victim.

Each of them mimicked me for the answer until collectively, we found it as one.

Caolann.

Subdued by two soldiers in his attempt to free Bébhinn, he slumped to his knees by their side. Blood pooled around the knife's rim in his chest, soaking his tunic.

"Caolann!" I cried through a gut-wrenching inhale.

Rían roared, tearing free of his gag as his arm reached wildly from beneath the Fir na Solas pinning him.

Rathnor's grin curled wider until he burst into maniacal laughter.

Our agony was his amusement. I raised my good hand to him, stretching it so far, I thought it might come from my socket. Rage harvested the thing he never used directly into my hand. The thing that served him no purpose.

My palm pulsed with a foreign beat.

In it, Rathnor's heart rhythmically slowed, his blood pooling and soaking my skin.

His smile sank to a cough-splattered pause, his hand covering the hole in his chest as he collapsed.

A glimmer of satisfaction overcame me as his sapphire cloak covered him. Good riddance. I'd never have to see the fucking sight of him again.

Horrified Saoirsians screamed. Fir na Solas shrouded Mórrígan with their bodies, and I rolled Rathnor's heart onto the grass with an inaudible thump. For all my hesitation, I'd murdered him without even a fraction of remorse.

"Clíona," Bébhinn called. "Help him!"

Caolann. I ran to him, disarming the soldiers restraining him with mere thoughts before sliding to catch his body as it tilted backwards.

"Look at me."

His eyes met mine, not perfect shamrock green, but muddy and clouded.

I pressed my trembling hand around the knife to stop the flow of blood, but it quickly seeped through the gaps of my fingers.

He reached toward my face, forcing his rigid smile, lips pressed and barely risen. "Do you forgive me?"

I nodded repeatedly as if saying yes might heal him.

He lamented through blood-stained teeth. "What little time we shared will live past this life and into the next."

"Don't go getting sentimental on me now," I said, sniffling. He was clearly speaking in the tongues of a dead man. A species that had nothing left to lose.

Rían commanded the Fir na Solas with a sinister tone. "Break the bind of wrists." After fulfilling the command in unison, Rían flexed his hands. "Now. Turn around and walk until your hearts no longer beat." He found his footing to fight the soldiers amongst the fleeing audience, commanding more to surrender or fight each other as more droned into the area. Béb-hinn flanked him, wrapping roots around their feet and spears.

"Clíona, go!" Rían shouted amid a grapple. "Go and never return."

A deep, unsettling pain rooted in my chest at the idea of never seeing him again. Never seeing any of them. But the Tuatha would come for me any second to condemn me for my crimes.

"No. I...I can't."

Rían plunged his blade into the apex of the soldier's chest, pushing his limp body aside to give me all his attention amidst the chaos. "My love," he spoke sternly and quickly, and yet I could still feel the adoration in his words. "Do not force my hand."

"Then don't force me to leave you. Leave *him*."

The rims of his eyes hugged Caolann a little closer, and I could see the battle within him draw to a conclusion. "I command you to—"

Muireann ran from the crowd to protect me with her shield—from both the enemy and Rían—providing vital seconds. "I am always with you in battle now."

I offer her the slight bow of my head as thanks.

Caolann's coughs drew me to him.

"Rían is right. You must leave."

"Stop saying that. Everyone needs to stop saying that." I jutted my jaw. "I won't leave you here to die. I won't do that."

I took in our situation: Áed lay, lifeless. Bébhinn and Rían fought to what could be their last breath.

My options were stretched to one choice. One selfish decision that wouldn't reward anyone but me.

I had to save *someone.* Just one. One person had to make it out alive.

Caolann reached for me, his hand smoothing my cheek before finding Fionn's rune, dangling outside my armour. He caressed it, as though savouring the memories it conjured. The moments of intimacy when it was all I wore.

His thumb swirled across the metal, retracting it to the inside layer.

"Beautiful," he murmured.

I gasped, immediately noticing the liquid—the purple liquid beneath its glass—full to the brim. Just as it was the night I used it in the cabin.

Caolann's eyes lulled.

He was still. Too still.

Even when sleeping, I swore there was a part of him always switched-on. Ready for an enemy in the night.

But now...

I gripped his jaw. Shook his face. "Caolann," I said, as if I was trying to gently awaken him.

Nothing.

My breath hitched, toying with the temptation of never exhaling just so I could follow him to the place I was certain he had gone.

"No. Not like this." I sobbed, running my hands down his cold cheeks, over and over. "I forgive you. Do you hear me?" I shook him. "I forgive you!"

With no time to consider or think of the repercussions of wasting precious moments, I yanked the rune from my neck to loop it around our hands, screaming in pain from bending the broken bone I'd so easily forgotten.

Pressing my thumb, I let it bite me. Let the needle jab into my nail bed with a fleeting sting.

The instant dizziness I so desperately longed for—the one that would finally take me home—spun the world around me at a hundred miles an hour. Colours, shapes and blurred outlines of Réimse Mór meshed into a chaotic whirl as my vision darkened; my body weakened, surrendering. With each spinning moment, the distant beckon came closer. I was becoming a ghost, unlatching from earth.

I must save him.

I weakly pressed his thumb to the rune with my final ounce of strength, letting the overwhelming scent of sweet berry fill my nostrils.

My head lightened as I fell onto the grass, hand no longer in Caolann's.

Body no longer in this plane.

Please, True Gods, bring him with me.

Save him.

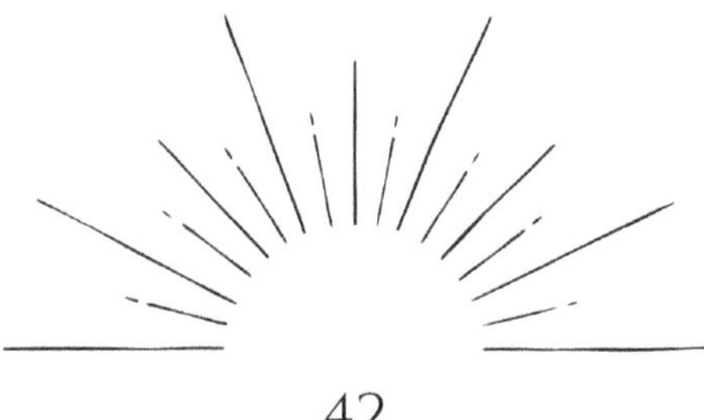

42

IT PERCHES IN THE SOUL

4 weeks later

The kettle came to a rolling boil, its condensation licking the cupboards above.

I dropped a tea bag into the mug, then edged closer to the kitchen window, pressing my pelvis against the counter to get a better look at what I'd just glimpsed. With the arrival of autumn had come hints of red, spotting the splay of dogwood in our back garden.

The new season had also brought the ripening of blackberries—now drying on a paper towel next to me from Mollie's morning forage. *Any later,* she had said, *and the devil would have pissed on them.*

Even the stretch of evening was getting shorter. At a quarter to eight, the sun already kissed the sky with oranges struck through by clouds.

Any other person would have called these things lovely. But all they brought me was a premature rise of loneliness. Because it was easier to keep myself occupied in the day, but at night...at night, the grief visited. New grief, to sit in the place of the old. And there wasn't a soul to share my secrets with. Of why I felt this way. Of whom I mourned.

Still, I had to keep moving forward.

And so, I took a deep, perturbed breath. Then, I carried my cup of tea to the kitchen table, my arm, in a makeshift cast, balancing its heated bottom. Mollie hid behind her newspaper, a pen between two fingers and a mug of chamomile next to her.

"I heard the Garda knocking this morning." This was a recurring visit, and so I had said the words needlessly. Casually. *Casual* was the closest I could come to neutral right now, and despite my grip of my harvest being stronger than ever, I still needed to remain somewhat level-headed to float above the darkness.

"I sent them away. They think you're long gone," she said through a grim headline. How quickly I'd forgotten this world kept turning. How the pain and suffering didn't end without me in it.

"You're not worried they'd want to search the place again?" I pressed. Was it so irrational for a wanted fugitive to look for a bit of reassurance from her own mother that things would be okay, even though they weren't? Sure, she promised to never give me up to the authorities—or St. Brigid's—but I didn't care for expected gratitude or the rules of righteousness right now. I wanted the warped, rose-tinted version that everything could be grand for a moment. Let the evening stretch a little longer before I head up to bed and replay all the horrible things I'd done. All the things I'd lost to bloodshed.

Mollie *hummed* her acknowledgement and turned the page with such a ruckus I swore my company wasn't wanted. To be fair, both of us were lingering in the realm of hostility since I'd returned to the treehouse—or what was left of it.

I flinched at the memory, immediately recovering by pretending to swat an invisible fly. To be exiled in a world you once called home. Knowing all the people you couldn't save had been left behind in your new one.

I recalled the battle in Réimse Mór. We were outnumbered tenfold.

Even one survivor, I'd take.

I could find solace within the improbability that one managed to escape.

I didn't *want* to forget, either. However much that undoubtedly would help. Because remembering made me grateful for what I *do* have—the crumbs of simply having *known* those courageous souls for a time.

My gaze returned to Mollie as I snuck a stale custard biscuit from the rusty tin.

She lowered her newspaper slowly. "You ready to talk?"

"At this point"—I shrugged—"I've got nothing to hide."

I had thought the many truths gone unsaid these past weeks was a good thing—and that the disappearance of the rune in the aftermath was also a good thing. But there had to be some truth between us. So, however painful this conversation would be, I deemed it *good*.

She folded the newspaper—poorly might I add—and with a glaring watch on me, her fingers dug into her cardigan pocket.

If she was angry or nervous, I couldn't tell, but my patience had worn thin from all her dillydallying.

I hocked my frustration. "Mollie, what's in the bloody pocket?"

She tutted and pulled *it* out with an exaggerated ruckus.

The rune.

Shit. Shit. Shit.

I sat straighter, lips flat. This means nothing, I repeated in my head, convincing myself that was true. "How do you have my..." I cleared my throat. "...necklace?"

She laid it on the table to caress the tree's risen bumps how I had done a hundred times before.

"I think, Clío"—her mirroring eyes met mine—"you've stolen *my* question."

The crackle of a silent current filled the dense space between us. It raised the hair on my arms, my neck, my head.

"Wha—hang on, *your* question?" I blinked profusely. My mouth hung as the pieces slotted into place with an odd satisfaction beneath the dizzying shock. I gripped the table's edges to keep myself upright. "*The rune is yours.*" My frame slumped into the chair as my gaze followed the propelling ceiling fan. Round and round and round. "Fionn got the rune from you."

"Fionn must have *stolen* the rune from me." She huffed a laugh, much like my own, where the context isn't even funny. Maybe laughing softened the blow for her. "Must have found it hidden in the attic. No surprise there when he was always getting into things."

I shot her a glance, my heart beating double time, and asked the most important question I ever would. "So, you know where I've been?"

She continued to caress the rune, her face not giving anything away. "Yes, I know. I realised when I found this"—she tapped the rune—"the morning after you returned to the ruins of the treehouse. As soon as it dawned on me, I wanted to *strangle* you." Her fingers turned clawed before unfurling. "And kiss you. And never let you go! It all made sense then."

I set aside the swell in my heart that urged me to say kind words to her when it had been so long, forcing the conversation to continue. "What did?"

"Oh God, Clío. Where do I start?" A well formed in her eyes, a sight I'd never grow used to—or try to prevent.

"Start with how you got the rune," I said, my tone stronger than hers. The roles had unnaturally switched: me being the maternal listener while the onus and explaining were on her. Derailing this conversation with emotions wouldn't get me answers.

She huffed another laugh. It was enough to prompt two tears over the edge as she held my good hand despite it being covered in crumbs.

"You've probably been wondering why I left. Why I never actually tried to come back," I pushed on to allow her the space to recover. "I didn't mean for it to happen. Killing Mayor Gallagher...opening a portal...*any* of it."

"I've been trying to find the right words." Her voice scratched against her woes. "Why do you think I've held everything in the past few weeks? How could I tell you the truth—or the lies, I should say." Wiping fresh tears aways on the cusp of her cardigan, she inhaled her expression into that of something more stoic. "Do you remember the story I told you the night you went missing? *Banríon*. You remember, don't you?"

Bile crawled up my throat at the mere mention of her name, a physical match to the intense loathing I felt. Mórrígan was unreachable, a phantom, haunting my thoughts. Sparing her any thought sent me into a frustrated frenzy so fierce, my jaw ached from clenching it. The very idea of her presence was enough to make my blood boil, leaving me teetering on the edge of control.

"Wasn't it about her killing babies?" I said with forced smoothness.

"What if I told you..." She hesitated, pulling her bottom lip. "What if I told you Fionn was one of those babies prophesied by the red-robed Druid to overthrow her reign."

My head swivelled so unsteadily, I clasped both sides to keep it from falling entirely off my suddenly cold body. "Hang on. Wait. That would mean—" The words came out in stifled breaths.

"You are not of this world, child." Mollie switched to the deep tone of the mother tongue. "You and your brother." She tapped the table with her fist before naming our titles. "Clíona—Nuala. Fionn—Nuada—Óg. Children of King Nuada—a *pure* Tuatha Dé Danann and before his wretched death, my husband."

"Then my dad..." For all the things she told me, him being from Cork. Acting like he was just two hours down the road not giving a fuck about his kids. Not showing up for his own son's funeral.

"I know this is hard to hear, but you Clíona, my beautiful, savage daughter"—she gripped me in her hold—"*you* are a goddess. A demigod, once destined for great things."

Her hazel eyes glazed. "I had no English. Nothing but the clothes on my back. Granny Murphy was real. I'm sure you remember her, after all—but she was no blood relative. She found us in a field when out picking potatoes not two miles from here. A child to each breast with nothing left to suckle for. You were a mere three days old, Clío. There's few and far between that would steer you as right as that woman. She saved our lives."

Jesus Christ. A field? The unbalance of shock hit me in a second wave. "*I'm* Saoirsian. Tuatha Dé Danann." It made sense how I had the strength to kill Rathnor now, without him being stripped of his divinity. But what did things like that matter now? "How did you get here? To Wexford of all places," I said. "I mean, you could have picked better. Somewhere with more facilities than the rocks behind Tesco to day drink on." I was glad of being able to form words though my curiosity for answers outweighed the distortion making the room sway like a sickly fun ride.

"A Druid offered me a path to refuge where Mórrígan couldn't harm Fionn. Using divine magic. The Druid—Finegas—created a rune for us."

That name—the man I'd met in the Carraig my first day in Saoirse. *Imprisoned nearly twenty years*, he'd said. The dates matched well enough. He'd known of the rune all along. Known it all right from the beginning. My nostrils flared, barrelling the steam out of my mug.

"But you could go back if you really wanted?" I'd been wondering for other reasons, too.

"The berries of a Tree of Life possess power beyond any science of this land. Powerful enough to open a portal to another world. The rune, I believed, was designed for a sole journey. It seems now that wasn't the case. It's more of a slow charging device. The Druid couldn't measure such a magic of this power to be exact. I never even considered your Bua coming to you in a world without magic. I should have known your *path*—your destiny—would lead you home."

The door in the mudroom banged.

I jumped to my feet, sending the chair clattering to the tiles. Mollie gripped my arm to get in front of me. They'd finally come to arrest me. They'd caught us off guard. We hadn't been careful enough.

My hands started to thrum.

Our assailant turned to the corner to linger by the door's frame, drying his hands with a tatty tea towel like this was *his* home. He was wearing a woolly hat and busting out of his navy zip fleece.

He glanced at the fallen chair, and then to me.

My cheeks flushed; my harvest receded with a simple thought. "I thought—" I stammered, unable to fight each quickened beat in my chest despite there being no need.

"I should have taken greater care." Caolann bowed a slow nod, after which he stole me a glance I swore had a smile to it. Or rather, not the silent anger and self-hatred I'd lived alongside for almost a month.

And that feeling of loneliness I swore had been festering these past few weeks suddenly didn't feel all that true.

"Throw them in the pot on the hob." Mollie pointed to the two skinned hare hanging over his shoulder. "*Déanfaidh mé cócaireacht orthu don dinnéar.*"

My saviour, I'd told her. The secret man who had given me refuge from the manhunt on a remote island off the coast of Galway. No wonder she didn't question it. That or why we'd appeared in the middle of the night, him with a gruesome knife wound. She knew. She goddamn *knew* he wasn't of this world. But I suppose, in a way, amongst all the lies, he *had* been the one to protect me. Him and Rían.

I clenched my eyes at the thought of Rían, then opened them to the reflection of him I saw far too often: Caolann.

He slid the woolly hat from his head and ruffled his short locks, ones I'd never grow used to seeing. He deemed himself too dishonourable to bear Fás Fada anymore, and had cut them the day Mollie had taken him home from the hospital—her alleged new 'toy boy' for nosey neighbours who found the whole thing equally disturbing and believable.

Though I wouldn't dare say it, I kept some of the hair hidden beneath my floorboard. I wanted a piece of him, to prove he existed if the day came when he left. When he'd become the Tír na nÓg tale I told to my grandchildren with a weathered voice. I stole a glance to the rune, painfully realising once he saw it, that day would be soon.

After lobbing the hare on the draining board, he poured himself a tea from the stove, his stature twice as rigid as it ever was in Saoirse. God love him. Caolann had struggled to adjust to this world. The doctors. The technology. Not to mention the language barriers. Apart from a few hospital staff and Ms. Hegarty, the Gaeilgeoir down the road who passed for daily walks, he hadn't spoken to anyone apart from myself and Mollie. I empathized from my own travels, but with my embrace for the Otherworld came his reservations. He had been trapped in this modern world. A prisoner of my life, and despite saving him, I couldn't blame his chosen solitude. And not to forget, I carried anger of my own since his truth came to light. That was enough to divide any form of romance we'd had. To have us skirt around each other like opposite ends of a magnet.

The rune caught his eye, freezing him in place as if I'd harvested my Bua on him. He stole me a second glance, and everything I feared materialised in his emerald eyes. He was leaving, prepared to return to a world where both sides of the war wanted him dead. But Rían's fate would be no better if he didn't find him.

Caolann snatched for the rune, spilling his tea onto the tiles.

Mollie smacked his hand as if he were a bold child, not a warrior. I gulped my tea to hide the unexpected smirk creeping onto my lips as he cowered his hand away. It seemed in this house, being a former demigod was low-end status now.

"Listen, I'm no amadán. I can tell what you're both thinking." Mollie picked up the chair I'd knocked over, needlessly cradling her back. "But I won't allow—"

I slammed the sloshing cup onto the table. Oh no you don't. "I'm not thinking about it, Mam. I'm doing it!" The words came out before I'd realised the decision was made. I didn't want to be a grandmother telling tales of the man and world I'd not fought for. No matter who reigned it, it was our home, and I'd defend it from Dagda to the death.

There was nothing left for me in this world anymore.

Caolann nodded his agreement, knowing once my mind was made up, there was no changing it. He reached his hand again, but this time to hold mine. I'd forgotten the feeling that accompanied his warm touch: safe in every form.

Maybe I'd never noticed that feeling until right now.

Mollie slugged the last of her tea as she stood from the table. "I know you're doing it, pet. It's part of us to fight. And that sow, Mórrígan, has reigned too long." Stuffing the rune in her pocket, she rattled a glorious sigh. "So, I'm coming with you."

I drove the nearest butter knife into the table, sending a crack all the way to her mug. "No way in hell are you coming. You're mortal. You'll be slaughtered in a heartbeat!"

She shook her head, smiling at me. "My darling, I'm far more than anything I've ever led you to believe. You have no route of returning to the Otherworld without me. A savage daughter is forged in the womb of a powerful woman. Every inch of you is me, Clíona." She lowered to match my hardy gaze. "*Every. Inch.*"

We battled a minute long stare before I drew a breath and pulled the knife from the table. "Well, then—" I flipped the weapon and for the first time in ages, I smiled. "I guess that makes three of us against the entire army of Ardagh. May the True Gods help them."

43
EPILOGUE

The future, the past—or the adjacent, depending on who you were talking to—was a place where treacherous things were inbound. I longed to stand on its frontlines the way any other Irish person would when their land was being threatened.

Now I knew the truth, and amongst all these revelations any normal person might crumble upon hearing, I found myself experiencing something clear. Like a wish in the form of a dandelion, it held a form, too.

It was white and light, and feathered.

It birthed in my chest, providing a rising sensation so strong, I thought I might float.

It was a feeling for the future—hope. Hope of seeing Róisín. Hope of returning to Ériu and winning the war. Hope that better days were to come.

And with that, the happiness I'd once considered only for those worthy wouldn't be too far behind.

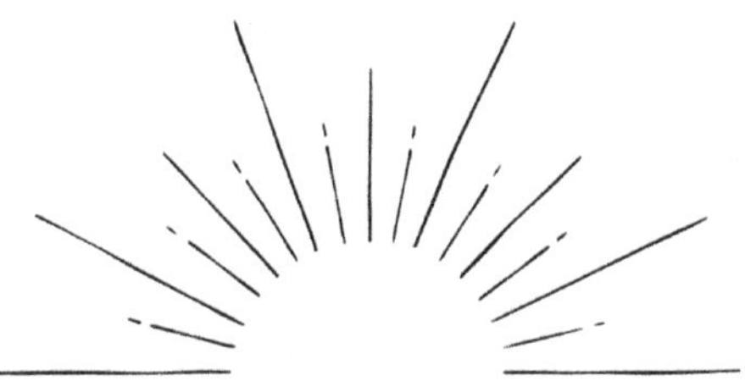

PRONUNCIATION/TRANSLATION GUIDE AND GLOSSARY

(Note: Ireland has many dialects and pronunciation of Irish words may vary. This is based on my own interpretation and learning from living in the South East of Ireland all my life).

Character Names/Pronunciation	**Meaning/Translation**
Clíona — Clee-na	Shapely/Queen of Banshees
Fionn — F-yon	The Fair One
Rían — Ree-ann	King/Controller
Caolann — Kee-lan	Fair/White/Slender
Finegas — Fini-gas	Blessed Poet
Bébhinn — Bay-veen	Fair Lady
Rathnor — Rath-noor	*No true translation
Roísín — Row-sheen	Little Rose
Áed — Aid	Fire
Ruadh — Roo-ah	Red-haired
Fintan — Fin-tan	White Fire
Muireann —Mwur-in	Sea White/Sea fair
Donnacha — Dun-ah-kah	Brown-haired Warrior
Rhiannon — Re-ann-non	Night Queen/Moon Goddess
Fead — Fad	Whistle
Aoife — E-fa	Beauty/Radiance
Cáit — Caw-t	Pure
Ciarán — C-ear-awn	Little Dark One

Gods:

The Tuatha Dé Danann — Two-ha De Dan-anne — Tribe of Danu

Mórrígan — Mor-ih-gan	Phantom Queen
Lugh — Loo	God of Light
Brigit — Bridge-it	Goddess of Fertility and FIre
Nuada — New-ah-dah	First King
Dagda — Dag-dah	God of Death and War
Dian Cecht — Dean-kekt	God of Healing
Danu — Dan-ew	The Mother
Bíle — Bee-leh	The Father

Places:

Wexford — Wex-ford	County in South East of Ireland
Ériu — Air-uh	Old spelling of Eire/Irish Goddess
Tír na N'óg — Tear-na-no-gue	Land of Youth
Saoirse — Seer-sha	Freedom
Ardagh — Argh-dah	High Field
Magh Mell — Mag-Mell	Celtic Mythical Realm
Réimse Mór — Rev-sha More	Big Field

Four Festivals of Ancient Ireland

Imbolc — Im-bul-uc	Bealtaine — Byow-lt-ana
Lúnasa (Lughnasadh) — Loo-nah-sa	Samhain — Sow-in

Treasures (Important to note there are different versions of this lore)

Lia Fáil	The Stone of Destiny
Dagda's Cauldron	Provides abundances and rejuvenation
The Spear of Lugh	A weapon said never to miss its target
The Sword of Nuada	Ensures victory in warfare/An embodiment of fate

Words:

Gaeltacht — Gale-tock-t	Regions where vernacular language is Irish
Carraig — Car-ig	Rock
Fir na Solas — Fir Na Sul-as	Men of Light
Tearminn — T-char-man	Asylum
Bua — Boo-ahh	Victory
Banríon — Ban-re-an	Queen
Amadán — Oma-dawn	Fool
Cailín — Col-een	Girl
Sean-nós — Shan-no-s	Old style
Sídhe — She/she-d	Fairy/Fae Folk
Soilse — Sul-sha	Lights
Bean sí — Ban-shee	Banshee
Ciaróga — Kear-oh-gah	Beetles
Glas — G-loss	Green
Sémroc — Sem-rock	Shamrock
Sliotar — Slit-er	A small ball used in traditional sport
Mo ghrá — muh-graw	My love
Fulacht Fiadh — Foo-locked Fee-ya	Way of cooking using hots stones to boil
Fás Fada — Faws Fod-ah	The long grow
Dia Dhaoibh — De-ya Yeev	Hello (Multiple/group)
Dia Dhuit — De-ya Gwit	Hello (singular)
Taibhse —Tie-v-sha	Ghost
Ogham — Oh-am	Ancient Irish script
Fomorians — Fom-or-ians	Supernatural race in Irish Myth
Comeragh — Come-er-ah	Named after a mountain range
Garda (Siochána) — Guard-a	Irish peacekeepers i.e. police force

CONTENT WARNINGS

Please be aware that this series contains the following:

Blood, Car Accident, Death, Death of a child, Grief and Loss Depiction, Dismemberment, Mental Health Hospitalization, Murder, Kidnapping, Misogyny, Profanity, PTSD, Sexual Assault, Sexually Explicit Scenes, Brief Suicidal Ideation, Violence

ABOUT THE AUTHOR

(She/Sí/Her)

Flourish by the Night
RARE: An Anthology of Secrets (late 2024)
The Shadow of Samhain:
The Light of Lúnasa Book 2 (late 2025)

www.laurafoleyauthor.com

Laura Foley is an Irish author hailing from the Kilkenny Countryside where she grew up on a small dairy farm. She now lives on the coast of Wexford with her husband and three children.

With a BA (hons) in Applied Social Studies, she graduated top of her class in 2016. Although writing for four years at this point, after completing her thesis she finally found the confidence to consider writing as a career.

Laura likes to write in every age category from picture book to adult. But specifically, she only writes stories centralized around Irish characters and places. She also loves writing with lyrical tones and enjoys stories that take place within time or place constraints to amplify the emotions of both the characters and readers.

Fans of the female Irish literary scene will be drawn to her romance work.

ACKNOWLEDGEMENTS

To Lee, my love. You will always be the first person I thank. Thank you for having ears, so you can listen to all my writerly woes. Thank you for getting into weird positions so I can reenact scenes to get them right. Thank you for having lips, so I can kiss you. Thank you for never having doubt in me, even when I do. And thank you for supporting me at every step of this ambitious journey. You are the blueprint for the perfect love interest, and I'm not even talking about the fact that you're tall, dark, and handsome.

Layla, Lúca, and Lúnasa—my little ones. I love you so much. Thank you for giving me these lines on my face because you are all just hilarious. You are the centre of my gravity.

(For those wondering, the book came before the baby, but the baby was not named after the book)

My cousins; Gemma and Kathy. I will never ever get tired of rating you two as just the best people in the world. I'm constantly inspired by you. Thank you.

Leona and Liz (Isa), my beautiful book friends, you are endlessly supportive and that will never go unnoticed. To never meet someone in person and still feel the value of them in your life is proof you are both wonderful people.

Christine, my critique partner for life. Look at us, having books in the world! You have given me so much through the years; advice, confidence, feedback, and endless support.

Thank you. Thank you. Thank you.

My editor, Julia. You've moulded this book into something beautiful. Thank you for having a keen eye and the patience for my inability to stop tweaking a manuscript.

To Stephanie, thank you for placing such a strong faith in me to be the one who puts the first stamp on this publishing house. The parameters of what you can achieve are endless. Also, I think in an alternative universe we are soulmates.

www.ingramcontent.com/pod-product-compliance
Lightning Source LLC
Chambersburg PA
CBHW030933170125
20531CB00039B/288

* 9 7 8 1 9 6 3 0 2 9 0 8 6 *